W9-BOM-959

MURDER AS A
SECOND LANGUAGE

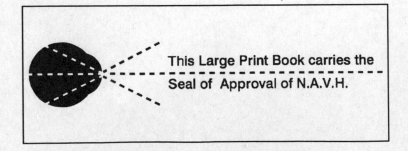

This Large Print Book carries the
Seal of Approval of N.A.V.H.

A CLAIRE MALLOY MYSTERY

Murder as a Second Language

Joan Hess

WHEELER PUBLISHING
A part of Gale, Cengage Learning

GALE
CENGAGE Learning·

Farmington Hills, Mich • San Francisco • New York • Waterville, Maine
Meriden, Conn • Mason, Ohio • Chicago

GALE
CENGAGE Learning®

Copyright © 2013 by Joan Hess.
A Claire Malloy Mystery.
Wheeler Publishing, a part of Gale, Cengage Learning.

ALL RIGHTS RESERVED
This is a work of fiction. All of the characters, organizations, and events portrayed in this novel are either products of the author's imagination or are used fictitiously.
Wheeler Publishing Large Print Hardcover.
The text of this Large Print edition is unabridged.
Other aspects of the book may vary from the original edition.
Set in 16 pt. Plantin.

LIBRARY OF CONGRESS CATALOGING-IN-PUBLICATION DATA

Hess, Joan.
    Murder as a second language / by Joan Hess. — Large print edition.
       pages ; cm. — (A Claire Malloy mystery)
    ISBN 978-1-4104-6623-5 (hardcover) — ISBN 1-4104-6623-X (hardcover)
    1. Malloy, Claire (Fictitious character)—Fiction. 2. Booksellers and bookselling—Fiction. 3. Women detectives—Fiction. 4. Life change events—Fiction. 5. Murder—Investigation—Fiction. 6. Arkansas—Fiction. 7. Large type books. I. Title.
PS3558.E79785M86 2014
813'.54—dc23   2013042936

Published in 2014 by arrangement with St. Martin's Press, LLC.

Printed in the United States of America
1 2 3 4 5 6 7 18 17 16 15 14

For my beloved grandchildren,
Annabelle Hadley and Jack Benton
Born July 8, 2010

1

"Why's your shirt covered in blood?" Caron asked as she sat down at the kitchen island and held up her cell phone to capture the moment.

"It's mostly tomato sauce," I said, peering at the recipe. There were twenty-two ingredients, and I was facing number sixteen: "easy aioli." Apparently, it was too easy to suggest directions. I did not have Julia Child on speed dial. Number seventeen in the recipe was one cup of dry white wine. An excellent idea. I poured myself a cup and leaned against the counter, temporarily stymied but not yet defeated.

"Mostly?"

I waggled my index finger, which sported an adhesive strip. "I'm working on my knife skills. Cooking is not for sissies."

My darling daughter wrinkled her nose. "It smells fishy in here. What on earth are you making?"

"*Bouillabaisse.* It's a classic French fish stew. I intend to serve it tonight with" — I glanced at the cookbook — "crusty bread and a salad with homemade vinaigrette. For dessert, Riesling-poached pears."

"Are we eating at midnight?"

I refused to look back at the horrendous mess that encompassed all the counters, the sink filled with bowls and utensils, the vegetable debris, open jars and bottles, and a splatter of tomato sauce, sweat, and tears. "I'm making progress," I said loftily.

"Whatever." She took a few more photos, then put down her cell. "You will be relieved to know that I may be able to go to college in a year, despite your lack of guidance. Otherwise, I'm doomed to survive on an annual income of less than twenty-five thousand. I won't be able to go to the dentist, so all my teeth will fall out. No matter how badly I'm bleeding, I'll have to tie a dirty rag around the wound and limp into work. My last manicure will be for graduation. Do you know how expensive fingernail polish is — even at discount stores?"

"I have no idea." I went into the library and looked up "aioli" in a dictionary. "Garlic, egg yolk, lemon juice, olive oil," I chanted as I returned to the kitchen and opened the refrigerator. Once I'd found eggs and lemons, I set them on the counter. "What specific lack of maternal guidance has imperiled your future education?"

"Community service — and I don't mean the kind that some judge orders you to do. It has to be voluntary. You didn't tell me that you have to show the college admissions boards that you're committed to helping the less fortunate."

"I applied to college in the Mesozoic era. I did so by filling out a form and submitting my transcript and ACT scores." I paused to replay what she'd said. "Shall I assume you're planning to fill that gap in your résumé? Did you volunteer at the homeless shelter or a soup kitchen? I can't quite see you adopting a mile of highway and picking up litter in an orange vest."

"Inez found this really cool place where we can volunteer to teach English as a second language to foreigners. It's like four hours a week, and we arrange our own schedules. I figure that if we're there from eleven to noon, we'll have plenty of time to go to the lake and the mall." Having rescued herself from a lifetime of cosmetology or auto mechanics, she moved on to a more crucial topic. "Can I have a pool party this Saturday afternoon? I want everybody to see our new house. I may even invite

Rhonda Maguire and her band of clueless cheerleaders."

"Our new house" was also known as my perfect house — a hundred-and-fifty-year-old Victorian gem, spacious yet cozy, with bits of ginger-bread trim, hardwood floors that gleamed with sunshine, and twenty-first century indulgences. It was located at the far edge of Farberville, with a stream, a meadow dotted with wildflowers, and an apple orchard. There had been a few problems with the resident Hollow Valley family members involving malfeasance and murder, but I'd solved the case for the Farberville Police Department (and vacated the valley of the majority of its occupants). We'd moved in two weeks earlier. Now Peter, my divinely handsome husband who had been blessed with molasses-colored eyes and an aristocratic nose, had his own tie rack, his own wine cellar, and his own chaise longue on the terrace overlooking the pool. I'd claimed the library as my haven and spent a lot of time playing on the rolling ladder that allowed access to the highest shelves of books. I'd also arranged the contents of the walk-in closets, added artwork, located most of the light switches, and mastered the washing machine and the dryer. I'd barely seen my beloved bookstore, the Book Depot, since Peter hired a grad student to be the clerk. My presence was tolerated as long as I approved orders and invoices and signed checks. Lingering was not encouraged.

After a few days of reading poetry in the meadow, I felt the need to do something of importance. It was too early to make cider, and the idea of knitting made me queasy. Thus I had decided to master the art of French cooking. My *boeuf bourguignon* had been a success, as had the *coq au vin;* the *terrine de filets de sole* had been less so. My *soufflé au chocolat* had sunk. My *petites crêpes aux deux fromages* had been met with derision. *C'est la vie.*

"Yes, you may have a party," I said as I attempted to separate an egg. "You handle the food — unless you want to serve *tapenade noire* and *mousse de saumon.*"

"How do you say 'yuck' in French?" Caron was too busy texting to wait for a response. "Do you care how many people I invite?"

I picked up another egg. "I suppose not, as long as you clean up afterward. I don't see what's so easy about aioli. Is there a utensil to crush the garlic? What's wrong with garlic powder?"

"Oh, no!" she shrieked so loudly that my

hand clutched the egg with excessive force. "I can't believe this! I've already sent thirty e-vites. Everybody's going to think I'm an idiot!"

I held my hand under the tap and let the gloppy mess dribble down the drain. "What's wrong? Did Rhonda decline?"

"I got a text from Inez. We have to attend a training session at the Literacy Council on Saturday from ten in the morning until six. Eight hours of training to point at a picture and say, 'Apple.' It's not like I'm going to explain the difference between the pluperfect and the imperfect. I don't care, so why should they?"

"You can always be an aromatherapist."

Caron gave me a contemptuous look over her cell phone. "You are so Not Funny."

During the week, I attempted to conquer, with varying results, *gratin de coquilles St.-Jacques, quiche Lorraine,* and *vichyssoise.* My second *soufflé* went into the garbage disposal. Peter was so impressed by my relentless enthusiasm that he insisted on taking me out to dinner on Saturday. As we lingered over *bifteck et pommes de terre* (aka steaks and baked potatoes), he suggested that I might want to spend more time at the Book Depot, learn to play bridge, take a

12

class at the college, or volunteer for a worthy cause. It was very dear of him to worry that I was expending too much time on housewife duties and would enjoy a respite. I gazed into his eyes and assured him that I was having a lovely time in the kitchen, although cooking and cleaning up could be wearisome. My eyes almost welled with tears as he spoke of the wealth of knowledge and experience I could share with the community, were I to sacrifice my nascent culinary goal.

I was thinking about our conversation the next day when Caron and Inez slunk in and collapsed on the sofa. Caron was fuming. Inez, her best friend, looked pale and distressed, and she was blinking rapidly behind the thick lenses of her glasses. I wiped my damp hands on a dish towel and joined them. "Problems at the Literacy Council yesterday?" I asked.

"Yeah," Caron muttered. "The training session was interminable. The teacher basically read aloud from the manual while we followed along, like *we* were illiterate. We broke for pizza and then listened to her drone on for another four hours. After that, the executive director, some pompous guy named Gregory Whistler, came in and thanked us for volunteering. I was so thrilled that I almost woke up."

"Then it got worse," Inez said. "The program director, who's Japanese and looks like she's a teenager, told us that because of the shortage of volunteers in the summer we would each get four students — and meet with them twice a week for an hour."

"For a total of Eight Hours." Caron's sigh evolved into an agonized moan. "We have to call them and find a time that's mutually convenient. It could be six in the morning or four in the afternoon. We may never make it to the lake."

I noticed that her lower lip was trembling. It was oddly comforting to realize that she was still susceptible to postpubescent angst at the *très* sophisticated age of seventeen. Caron and Inez had provided me with much amusement in recent years, along with more than a few gray hairs and headaches. Their antics had been inventive, to put it mildly, and always under the guise of righteous indignation. Or so they claimed, anyway. In the last month alone, they'd figured out a way to bypass a security system to get inside a residence. They'd abetted a runaway, hacked into a computer, and perfected the art of lying by omission. There may have been a genetic predisposition for that last one.

14

"Do you know who your students will be?" I asked.

Inez consulted a piece of paper. "We have their names and telephone numbers. We're supposed to call them and schedule our sessions. I have a woman from Colombia, a woman from Egypt, and a man and woman from Mexico. I wish I'd taken Spanish instead of Latin."

"And I," Caron said, rolling her eyes, "have to tutor an old lady from Poland, a Chinese man, an Iranian woman, and a woman from Russia. How am I supposed to call them on the phone? They don't speak English. Like I speak Polish, Chinese, Russian, and whatever they speak in Iran. This is a nightmare, and I think we ought to just quit now. I say we set up a lemonade stand and donate the proceeds to some charity."

I looked at her. "That'll impress the admissions boards at Bryn Mawr and Vanderbilt. Of course, you can always stay here and attend Farber College."

She looked right back at me. "Yes, and I can live here the entire four years. Imagine the size of the pool parties when I meet all the freshmen. They can come out here to do their laundry and graze on *bouillabaisse*. You'll be like a sorority and fraternity housemother. Won't that be great?"

15

I went into the kitchen and leaned against the counter. I do not sweat, but there may have been the faintest perspiration glinting on my flawless brow. I'd created some lovely fantasies to explore after I recovered from the empty nest syndrome — which would be measured in hours, if not minutes. In the foreseeable future, scissors and tape would be in their designated drawer, my clothes would remain in my closet unless I was washing or wearing them, my makeup would lie serenely on the bathroom counter, and I could cease putting aside cash for bail money. I'd resigned myself to one more year — not five more years.

"All right, girls," I said as I returned to the living room, "here's my best offer. I will volunteer at the Literacy Council and take one student from each of you. You can decide which ones after you've worked out your schedules."

Caron pondered this. "That means you only have to be there for four hours a week, while we have to be there for —" She stopped as Inez elbowed her in the ribs. "Ow, why'd you do that?"

"I think that's a fine idea," Inez said to me. "You have to do the training, though, and I don't know how often it's offered."

I shrugged. "I have a graduate degree in

English, and I was a substitute teacher at the high school. My grammar is impeccable, and my vocabulary is extensive. I'm likely to be better qualified than this teacher you had yesterday. This will not be a problem. Trust me."

The adolescent Japanese girl purported to be the program director gave me a dimply smile. Her deep brown eyes twinkled as she said, "I am so sorry, Ms. Marroy, but the next training session will not be held until the third week in August. I hope to see you then. Now if you will be so kind to excuse me, I must return some phone calls."

"If you want me to read a manual and discuss the material, I will do so, although it's a waste of time for both of us." I kept my voice modulated and free of frustration, although I was damned if I was going to twinkle at her. "I speak English. Your students want to learn to speak English. I fail to see the need for eight hours of training to grasp the concept."

"It's our policy."

This was the third round of the same dialogue. Keiko Sakamoto, as her nameplate claimed, had feinted and dodged my well-presented arguments with "our policy." I felt as if I were at the White House, trying to persuade the secretary of state to abandon the prevailing foreign policy. My chances in either situation fell between wretched and nil.

Keiko picked up the telephone receiver and with yet another twinkle said, "We always need volunteers for our fund-raisers. Please take this brochure with information about our program. Have a nice day, Ms. Marroy."

I left her office with as much dignity as I could rally. The Farberville Literacy Council occupied a redbrick building in the vicinity of the college campus and had been designed well. The central area had clusters of cubicles equipped with computers, and a lounging area with chairs, tables, and freestanding bookshelves. On one side of the front door was a reception desk, unoccupied. On the other, the interior of Keiko's office was visible behind a large plate-glass window. Rooms with closed doors lined the periphery. The passageways had black metal file cabinets under piles of boxes, books, and unfiled files. Everything was well lit and clean. As I hesitated, a classroom door opened and a dozen students emerged, talking to each other in several different languages. I recognized Spanish, German, and Arabic. Three young Asian women stared at me and giggled.

A tall, lean, fortyish woman shooed them out of the doorway, then hesitated when she spotted me. Her white blouse and khaki trousers would have suited her perfectly on safari, although Farberville had a dearth of exotic animals. I suspected she was trying to determine my native tongue as she walked across the main room. I was interested to find out how she would address me, so it was a letdown when she merely said, "May I help you?"

"My daughter and her friend are new tutors. They're still trying to get in touch with their students. I was hoping that I could help out, but the next training session isn't until the end of the summer."

"You must be Caron's mother. I'm Leslie Barnes, and I was the trainer on Saturday. It was a very, very long day for all of us."

I had no trouble interpreting her look, but I wasn't about to apologize. "The girls are excited about meeting their students, but leery of calling them on the phone because of the language barrier."

"All of their students speak some English, as I told them. However, if they want to come here this afternoon, Keiko can help them make the calls and set up their schedules. I have another class in a few minutes.

19

Nice to meet you, Ms. Malloy." She went into a corner office and closed the door. I hoped her residual scars from the training session had not driven her to drink in the middle of the morning.

Two people emerged from an office beyond the reception desk. The man wore a dark suit, a red tie, and an annoyed expression. His hairline was beginning to recede, and his features seemed small on his tanned face. The woman had short blond hair, blue eyes, and deft makeup. She was wearing a tailored skirt and jacket and high heels, and she carried a briefcase. "Gregory," she said as though speaking to a wayward child, "we're still waiting for the receipts from your trip to D.C. two months ago. Are you going to claim your dog ate them? If so, you'd better have that dog at the next meeting."

"They're in my office somewhere," he said. "Why don't you ask Rick where they are? He's been coming by after work to paw through the files. It's a friggin' miracle I can find my desk, much less the manila envelope with the receipts. You've got the credit card statement. I don't see why you want a bunch of bits of paper."

"Willie wants them, not me," she said.

The man now identified as Gregory took

her elbow and tried to steer her toward the front door. "You can't have a meeting until you have enough board members present to make a quorum. That won't be until August, will it? I'll find the receipts before then — okay?" There was a hint of mockery in his voice.

The woman stopped and pulled herself free. "I suppose so. I need to have a word with Keiko before I leave." She swept past me and into the office, muttering under her breath.

Gregory glanced at me before he returned to what I presumed was his office. I stood there for a moment, feeling as inconsequential as I did at the Book Depot. It might be the time for the third stab at a *soufflé,* I finally decided and headed for the door. Purportedly, it was the charm.

Before I could get into my car, the blond woman came outside and said, "Claire Malloy?" When I nodded, she held out her hand and said, "I'm delighted to meet you. I've read all about your involvement with the local police. Tell me, what's it like to confront a murderer?"

"Unpleasant," I replied. "And you are . . . ?"

"Sonya Emerson. I'm on the board of the FLC — the Farberville Literacy Council. In

21

my spare time, I work for Sell-Mart in the corporate office in the Human Resources Department. What's more fun than a sixty-hour workweek?"

I wondered if Mattel had released MBA Barbie in the last few years. "It's nice to meet you, Sonya. I came by to apply to be a tutor. It appears that I'll have to wait for the next training session." I opened my car door, but the subtlety escaped her.

"Keiko mentioned it. She'd love to make an exception in your case, but our executive director is adamant about sticking to our policy. We have to be certain that our tutors are committed. Some of them sign up, but then lose interest and abandon their students." She frowned faintly and then brightened. "We'd love to have you volunteer in some other capacity. You're so well-known and respected in Farberville. Having you involved in the FLC would enhance our reputation in the community, as well as in the state organization. You're so intelligent and articulate."

I enjoy flattery, but she was shoveling it on. "If you have a bake sale, let me know and I'll whip up a batch of *profiteroles au chocolat.*" I waved as I got in my car and drove away at a speed appropriate for someone who was well-known, respected,

22

intelligent, and articulate. If I ever needed a letter of recommendation, I'd call Sonya.

In the meantime, I was all dressed up with nowhere to volunteer. I parked in the Book Depot lot and went inside. The clerk, Jacob, gazed morosely at me from his perch behind the counter. "Good morning, Ms. Malloy. A shipment came in Friday, paperbacks for the freshman lit classes. They sent fifty copies of *Omoo* instead of *Typee*. I've already sent them back. Everything else was as ordered. Shall we have a sale for the remaining stock of beach books? Perhaps twenty percent off or three for the price of two?" His lugubrious voice reminded me of a funeral director displaying pastel coffins to the mourners.

"Whatever you think, Jacob." I went into my office, which was disturbingly neat and sanitized. Even the cockroaches had lost interest. I thumbed through a pile of invoices, but nothing required my scrutiny. I toyed with the idea of stopping by the grocery store to pick up the ingredients for *profiteroles au chocolat* (after I found a recipe online), but I envisioned the mess I'd make and therefore be obliged to clean up. Volunteering at the public library was not an option; everything was computerized except me. I pulled out the telephone directory and found a list of organizations under the heading "Social Services." Safety Net, the battered women's shelter, declined my offer and suggested that I send a check. The Red Cross suggested that I take a class in first aid. The thrift stores suggested that I send gently used clothes and a check. Residential facilities for children and at-risk teenagers declined my offers — and, yes, suggested that I send a check.

It seemed as if my only option was to operate a charitable trust fund. I would have spare time to perfect *magret de canard* and *galette des rois.* Admitting failure to Peter would be painful. To distract myself, I called Caron and left a message on her voice mail, telling her what Leslie Barnes had said about making the calls. Which, I have to admit, sounded daunting even to Ms. Marroy.

Having devised no clever way in which to make a meaningful contribution to the community, I drove home and read a book by the pool.

Peter came home early and invited me for a swim. Since Caron wasn't around, we indulged in some adult hanky-panky in the shallow end. After we were more modestly attired and armed with wine in the chaise longues, I told Peter about my dismal excursion into volunteerism. He commiserated, although I detected an undertone of amusement. I gave him a cool look and said, "I think I'll talk to the police chief about setting up a victims advocacy program at the department. Someone needs to listen to them and steer them to the proper agencies. We can have lunch together. Is there a vacant office next to yours?"

"Not one in the entire building," he said in a strangled voice.

I used my napkin to blot wine off his chin. "Maybe we can share yours. All I need is a tiny little desk, a computer, and a separate telephone line. I promise I won't eavesdrop when you're interviewing suspects. By the way, we're having leftover quiche for dinner. Tomorrow I'm going to try to make *avocat et oeufs à la mousse de crabe.* That's avocados and eggs with crab mousse. Sounds yummy, doesn't it?"

Peter poured himself another glass of wine.

Caron and Inez arrived as we were finishing dinner. "We already ate," Caron said as she went into the kitchen and returned with two cans of soda and a bag of corn chips. Inez nodded and sat down at the table.

"Did you talk to your students?" I asked them.

"Sort of," Caron said through a mouthful of chips. "We went to the Literacy Council and let Keiko help. It was weird. She understood everybody — or pretended she did, anyway. Ludmila, who's this ninety-year-old obese woman from Poland, about five feet tall, with squinty little eyes and a voice like a leaf blower, came in the office. Guess what? She happens to be my student. Lucky me."

"She was kind of hard to understand," added Inez. "Maybe because she was so upset about something. Keiko took her to the break room for tea. I met my two students from Mexico, Graciela and Aladino. They both speak some English."

"As opposed to my students," Caron cut in deftly. "Besides Ludmila, I got to meet Jiang, who's from China and in his twenties. He talks really fast. I smiled and nodded, but I didn't have the faintest idea what he was saying. For all I know, he was telling me where he buried the bodies or what he did with the extraterrestrials in his attic. The Russian woman's English is pretty good. Anyway, we both have our teaching schedules. C'mon, Inez, let's go to the pizza place in the mall."

26

"I thought you'd already eaten," I said.

Inez lowered her eyes, but my daughter had no reservations about mendacity. "We did, Mother. Joel and some of his chess club friends are celebrating their victory at a tournament in Oklahoma. Inez has a crush on this guy who turns red when you look at him."

"Rory's shy," Inez protested. "Why do you always stare at him, anyway? He thinks that you're going to scream at him."

"That's absurd. I am merely waiting for him to say something coherent, which may take years."

Peter produced a twenty-dollar bill. "Have a good time."

After they scurried away, he insisted on cleaning up the kitchen. I sat on a stool at the island, admiring his dexterous way with plates and silverware. We were idly speculating about Inez's potential boyfriend when the phone rang. Since Peter's hands were soapy, I answered it.

"Is this Claire Malloy?"

"Yes," I admitted.

"I don't believe we've met, but I have encountered Deputy Chief Rosen several times," the woman continued. "My name is Wilhelmina Constantine. I'm a member of the Farberville Literacy Council board of directors, and I was told that you might be interested in volunteering for our organization. We're delighted."

"I was told that I have to wait for the next training session before I can be a tutor."

"To be a tutor, yes. However, I'd like you to consider becoming a member of the board. You're well-known in the community and have a background in retail. Although the FLC is a nonprofit, we're forced to run a business as well. Raising funds, making payroll, dealing with vendors, all those petty nuisances. Your experience will be invaluable."

"I doubt that," I said. "Today was the first time I've set foot in the building. After I've been trained and have tutored for a few months, I'll think about the board. You may not want me. Thank you for asking, Ms. Constantine."

"I wish you'd reconsider, Ms. Malloy. If this wasn't an emergency, I wouldn't be asking. I'm afraid it is, and we're desperate."

I made a face at Peter, who was watching me. "An emergency?"

She remained silent for a moment, then said, "I really can't discuss it on the telephone. We have an informal board meeting tomorrow night at seven o'clock. Would you please at least attend?" Her voice began to quaver. "Otherwise, the FLC may not survive the summer. Our students will have no place to go."

"I'll attend the meeting," I said, aware that I was capitulating to emotional blackmail, "but only as an observer."

"Wonderful." She hung up abruptly.

"Ms. Constantine?" Peter murmured. "As in Wilhelmina Constantine, better known as Willie?" I nodded. "She's a federal judge. Tough lady."

"Her name is familiar, but I'm not sure why."

"She made a controversial ruling a few years ago, but at the time you were distracted by Azalea Twilight's unseemly death."

"I was distracted because I'd been accused of murder and was being stalked by a certain member of the police department."

"You were never accused of murder," Peter said.

"Well, I was most definitively stalked. No matter where I went, you were lurking in the bushes, spying on me."

The certain member of the police department raised his eyebrows. "I was not lurking. You went to extremes to make yourself unavailable for interviews, and the few times I cornered you, you flounced away like

29

Scarlett O'Hara."

"Fiddle-dee-dee," I said. "I have never flounced in my life."

"And I've never lurked."

I thought about it for a moment. "Deal."

2

Thursday evening I arrived at the Farberville Literacy Council building a few minutes before seven. Students were chattering
as they came out to the parking lot. Keiko
waved at me as she climbed into a turquoise
VW. Two women wearing hijab headscarves
drove out of the parking lot in a silver
Jaguar, followed by a carload of boisterous
Latino men. A dozen students walked
toward the bus stop on the corner. Sonya
swooped in on me as soon as I stepped
inside and, babbling with delight about my
limitless virtues, escorted me into a classroom with tables arranged in a U forma-
tion. In one corner was a counter with a
coffeepot, a minirefrigerator, and a sink. A
chalkboard in the front of the room was
covered with words, phrases, and primitive
drawings that might have been found in
caves in northern Spain. Maybe some of
the students were neo-Neanderthals (al-

though I hadn't seen any woolly mammoths tethered outside).

"You must be Claire Malloy," said a sixty-ish woman carrying a coffee mug in one hand and several papers in the other. "I'm Wilhelmina Constantine, and I do want to thank you for coming. Please call me Willie." I'd expected someone tall and regal, as befitting her lofty position in the judiciary, but she was short, pear-shaped, and, well, a tad frumpy. She was wearing a pink blouse that was missing a button, and her skirt reminded me of a washboard. Her frizzy gray hair had not withstood outbursts from prosecutors and defense attorneys. Her eyes were close-set, and her nose was as sharp as a beak. Despite her smile, she had the look of an offended songbird.

"I don't know how I can be of help," I said, resisting the impulse to chirp.

"We'll get to that in a minute. Sonya, introduce Ms. Malloy to the others so we can get started. I've been on the bench all day and haven't had a martini, much less dinner."

Sonya assessed the situation and gestured to a thirty-something-year-old man, who promptly stood up. He was attractive and expensively packaged, with broad shoulders, a clean jaw, and a friendly expression. His light brown hair was carefully tousled. I wondered if he might be MBA Ken. "Ms. Malloy, this is Rick Lester. He's a recent addition to the board." The lack of warmth in her voice caused me to scratch my theory.

Rick's blue eyes met mine as if he were auditioning for the role of earnest young man of impeccable integrity. "I'm Claire," I said.

"The fabled sleuth of Farberville," he said with a bow. "I'm delighted to meet you, Claire."

"Ah, thank you."

"I've only lived in Farberville for a couple of months, but I've heard of your exploits." He smiled at Sonya, but she turned her back to speak to Wilhelmina. "Are you working on a case now?"

"Not that I know of," I replied. "Are you enjoying Farberville?"

Rick chuckled. "It's quieter than Hong Kong. It's hard to fall asleep without the incessant cacophony of horns blaring and neon lights flashing. Before that, I was in Manila, also a busy place. I worked for an international financial outfit. Now I'm only a small-town banker."

"Why Farberville?"

"I know some people who used to live here, and they loved it. I'm still adjusting to the pace. My previous jobs came with a chauffeur and full-time help, so I haven't owned a car since I was in college — or scrubbed a toilet. Now I'm learning how to drive myself around town. It seems to be a nice place to settle down."

Sonya swooped in once again and said, "Let me continue the introductions." We approached a middle-aged man wearing dark-framed glasses, slacks, and a beige cotton sweater. "This is Drake Whitbream, our vice president. He's the dean of the business school at Farber College. Perhaps you've already met him."

He held out his hand. "Ms. Malloy and I have met at a few functions. It's so kind of you to join us." He was a big man who'd probably been an athlete in decades past. Years in academia had softened him and added a sprinkling of gray hair.

He was somewhat familiar, I thought, trying to find his face in a memory. "Yes, at a reception at the Performing Arts Center. You and your wife . . . ?"

"Becky," he supplied promptly. "Aren't you married to a police detective?"

"Something like that. Your son plays football at the high school. My daughter and her friend are big fans."

His face tightened briefly. "Toby will be

the starting quarterback this season. He's determined to get a football scholarship at one of the big universities and then go pro. With his grades, an athletic scholarship is the only way he'll get accepted."

I shrugged for lack of a better response.

"Can we get started?" asked a woman who'd entered the room and was now seated at the head table. She spoke with such authority that everyone hastily found a chair. "Where's Austin? Has anyone heard from him today? Sonya, call his cell." She looked at me as if I were responsible for Austin's absence. Her firmly curled hair and predominant chin made her face look round, but far from jolly. Saggy jowls gave her an air of perpetual dissatisfaction. None of her buttons would dare go missing. "Welcome, Ms. Malloy. I am Frances North, the president of the board. It is very kind of you to join us on such short notice."

"Austin will be here in five," Sonya reported as she put down her cell phone.

"I'll bet he stopped at a liquor store," Rick said, lacing his fingers behind his neck. He smiled at me. "Austin is our bad boy. Frances would love to kick him off the board, but she needs his vote."

Frances was not amused. "Don't be ridiculous. Austin has done an excellent job publicizing the Literacy Council's programs and events. I certainly do not dictate his vote. Now let's get started." She shifted the papers and files in front of her for a moment. "Here is the situation, Ms. Malloy. Currently there are twelve members on the board. Due to illness and vacations, only six of us are active this summer. According to the bylaws, this does not constitute a quorum, which means we can take no action in regard to certain sensitive issues. However, we do not require a quorum to increase the size of the board. If you agree, we will vote to add your name to the board. With thirteen members, seven will make a quorum. All you'll have to do is attend any meeting that requires your vote. You needn't concern yourself with these issues."

"I haven't agreed to anything," I said, "and I certainly won't unless I know what I'm getting myself into. Why can't this be resolved when the other board members are back?" I began to wish I'd sat closer to the door.

Frances shook her head. "It's time-sensitive, and we cannot risk any leaks if the FLC is going to survive. That's why we're here — and why we need you. Where is Austin?"

"At your service," a young man said as he

entered the room, a bottle of wine in each hand. "Rick, will you get the cups out of the cabinet? Good evening, everyone. Willie, you're looking especially fine. I hope this doesn't mean you've been frolicking with your clerk." He wore pale blue slacks with pink suspenders, a short-sleeved dress shirt, and a pink bow tie. His teeth were very white against his dark skin. A metrosexual nerd, I concluded, although I was aware that snap judgments were unreliable. Other people's, anyway.

Willie sputtered while Austin opened both bottles of wine, but she eventually accepted a cup of white wine, as did Sonya and I. Drake declined. Frances North sat in silence, emanating disapproval until Rick and Austin sat down. I was relieved that I was not a member of their oenological conspiracy.

"Claire, this is Austin Rodgers." Sonya said, tersely. He and I nodded at each other — tersely.

"Austin, I informed you at the last meeting that we would no longer have wine," Frances said. "Keiko told me that some of the Muslim students were upset when they found empty bottles in the trash. Our primary concern is our students."

He took a sip of wine. "So I'll take the

empty bottles home with me. If there's to be no wine, then there's to be no Austin. I didn't get away from my office until six thirty, and I need a fix. Why do you have your pantyhose in a knot, Frances? Did the third graders march on your office, protesting cafeteria food?"

Frances stood up. "Shall we proceed? Do I hear a motion to nominate Ms. Malloy for membership in the Farberville Literacy Council board of directors, pursuant to article six, paragraph four of the bylaws?"

"Wait just a minute —" I began.

"I so move," Sonya said quickly.

"Second," Drake said even more quickly.

"All in favor please raise your hand." Frances avoided looking at me as she glanced around the table. "The motion passes unanimously. Welcome to the board, Ms. Malloy. If you choose, you may resign at the first official meeting in September, but of course we'll be delighted to keep you."

I wondered if I was supposed to give an acceptance speech. "I'm honored," I said without enthusiasm. They could elect me in a nanosecond, but I could always resign in half of one.

"Why wouldn't you be honored?" Austin refilled my cup. "I propose a toast to Ms.

Claire Malloy for her courage. Not everyone would willingly embroil herself in such a maelstrom."

"Don't exaggerate, Austin," Willie said. "It's more of a bother than anything else, and Claire needn't worry about it."

"Until she gets sued," he said.

I found my voice. "Wait just a minute! I'm going to be sued? What's this about?"

Drake stood up and closed the door. "She deserves to know, people."

That was the first sensible thing anyone had said since my arrival. I placed my hands on the table and looked at Frances. "Well?"

"A small problem with our finances," she said. "Rick?"

Rick cleared his throat. "I joined the board this spring. Although Willie is our treasurer, I looked into the grants, expenditures, and so forth. There are some subtle discrepancies that suggested further analysis. The FLC hasn't had a full audit in five years, and the board budgets according to Gregory's monthly reports."

"He's talking about embezzlement," Austin said as he winked at me. "Bankers are incapable of using the word. It sticks in their throats like a whalebone."

"We will not use *that* word," Frances said. "The books are a mess, and the bank statements are confusing. Right now Willie, Keiko, Gregory, and I are authorized to write checks. Some of us are sloppy about noting the details of the expenditures. I received a notice earlier this week that we were in arrears with the electric company. I paid it from my personal account so they wouldn't turn off the lights. Gregory swears that Keiko is responsible for the bills, but she said that he takes them into his office and loses them in the clutter. As for the credit card statements . . ."

"We might as well shred them," Sonya said. "The real problem is that those of you who write checks reimburse yourselves without, as you said, noting the details of the expenditures. Gregory can't keep the accounts organized without receipts."

Willie did not look pleased with the discussion. "I bought office supplies because they were on sale. I did not have an FLC credit card or checkbook with me, and I wasn't about to drive all the way over here. I felt entitled to reimburse myself. If you have a problem with that, you can reimburse me the seventy-nine dollars I spent."

"Don't push your luck," Sonya replied. "Seventy-nine dollars is a drop in the bucket — or should I say, your budget?"

Surprised at Sonya's flippancy, I waited

for Willie to bash her with a concealed gavel, but she sat back and picked up her cup of wine. I decided to take my new position seriously. "Why not have an audit? That should identify the source of the discrepancies. Aren't nonprofits obliged to have yearly audits?"

"Full audits cost thousands," Drake said. "We don't have enough cash in the account to pay for the audit and stay open this summer. Because of the economy, our grants are shrinking, and they have to be used for specified programs. A few of our benefactors have told us that we won't be receiving anything from them."

"Then a bake sale it is!" said Austin. "And the next weekend, a car wash. After that, we can rent out students for housecleaning and yard work."

"Your suggestions will not be noted in the minutes," Frances said coldly.

Rick waggled his fingers. "I could use a chauffeur and a houseboy."

"While Willie," Austin added, "definitely could use a lady's maid to stitch on buttons. It's a good thing that you cover yourself with a long black robe, Your Honor."

"You'd better pray you never end up in my courtroom, young man."

"Enough." Frances thumped her fist on

the table. "This meeting was called to elect Ms. Malloy to the board. Our official meeting is next Monday at five o'clock. Austin, you need to arrange to leave work early. Sonya, please have the minutes typed up. Do your best with a financial report, Willie. Let us hope that we can behave in a more decorous fashion. Meeting adjourned."

She scooped up her papers and left the room. Sonya and Willie retreated to a corner to speak in hushed tones. Neither of them appeared amicable. Drake wished me a pleasant evening and left. I looked across the table at Austin. "Where do you work?"

"At a local TV station, in the advertising department. I produce some of those memorable messages from used car dealerships and carpet stores."

Rick laughed. "Last night I caught the one with the flying sheep, and I must say it was brilliant, my friend."

"I agree," he said, handing Rick one of the wine bottles. "Where do you work, Ms. Malloy? I envision you as a medical examiner, or perhaps an insurance appraiser." He squinted at me for a moment. "No, neither of those. Are you a covert agent for the CIA?"

His crack about the CIA startled me, since Peter did have some sort of relationship with the agency. He'd never explained, and I'd long since given up asking him. "I own a bookstore on Thurber Street called the Book Depot. My degree is in English literature, and the sight of blood makes me dizzy. I have also been described as 'a loose cannon,' rendering me useless as a covert anything." I picked up my purse. "I'll see you on Monday."

Now the main room was lit only by a dim light over the receptionist's desk. Although there was daylight outside, the scarcity of windows left the interior gloomy. The cubicles looked like dark stairways into the basement, if there was one. I made my way around them, mindful of the boxes piled on top of file cabinets that lined the wall. I may have been a bit nervous, but I could hear voices from the room behind me. If I'd been alone in the building, I would have been more than a bit nervous — but only because I was unfamiliar with the floor plan. I was pleased to arrive at the exit, and was scolding myself for being a ninny when the door opened abruptly.

I gulped at the towering figure, his face obscured by shadows. "Good evening," I managed to say.

The figure moved into the light. He was, I realized, a teenager with floppy hair and a sprinkle of freckles who might live on the Jersey Shore. He wore tattered denim shorts and a T-shirt emblazoned with an advertisement for a brand of beer. His grin was lopsided and disarming. "Good evening. Who are you?"

"I'm here for the board meeting."

"Shit, nobody told me or I would have waited."

"Are you a tutor?"

"I'm the janitor, four nights a week. I clean the toilets and mop the floors and empty the trash — and I don't even get paid. It sucks, lemme tell you. The students toss banana peels and half-eaten oranges in the waste-baskets. I found a moldy tangerine in a cabinet in the women's restroom. I about barfed."

"It must be a brutal job," I said, more interested in getting past him to the parking lot. "I guess somebody has to do it."

"Well, I'm that lucky somebody."

"Perhaps you should quit." I sidled to my right, hoping to dart around him. I'd listened to more than my fair share of whiny teenagers. Caron, precocious child that she is, stormed home from first grade to demand that I have her teacher fired for tyranny. By middle school, she was filing complaints in the principal's office.

44

"Like I can quit? That's a joke."

"Toby," Sonya said as she emerged from the maze, "enough of this. You're wasting Claire's time — and yours. Keiko told me that you haven't vacuumed the classrooms this week. Make sure you do the offices, too." She reached up to brush a lock of hair out of his eyes. "And no more pouting, okay?"

He flashed us a quick grin, then continued on his way. I gazed at Sonya until she finally said, "Drake's son. He had, uh, a spot of trouble with the police and was sentenced to a hundred hours of community service. Drake arranged for him to work it off here instead of picking up trash along the highway. Toby's a good kid, just clunky and rebellious like all teenagers these days."

"I'm sure he is," I said, then smiled and went out the front door. To my annoyance, she stayed on my heels like a nascent blister, asking me what I thought of the board of directors and "interpersonal dynamics."

I opened my car door. "To be honest, I didn't pay that much attention. I was too busy being manipulated. At the first hint that I'm somehow personally liable for this financial mess, I'll nail my resignation to the door."

"Don't worry about it. I'm so glad you

came, Claire."

She may have said more, but she would have been talking to my tail-lights. When I was safely out of sight, I decided to stop for coffee before I went home. Peter was at yet another meeting in Little Rock, and Caron and Inez were off with their friends. I wondered if they knew that their idol was working off his community service at the Literacy Council. Quarterback, in the restroom, with the mop. I'd barely seen the girls in the last few days. They'd managed to schedule their students between eleven and two, which meant they could sleep late, grab breakfast on the way out the door, and drag home from the lake just in time for a shower before heading for the mall or a pizza place. I'd not heard complaints about their tutoring sessions — or much of anything else.

I parked at Mucha Mocha and went to the counter. The menu board was so complicated that I ordered unadulterated coffee, to the barista's disdain, and then sat down on the back patio. I'd hedged the truth with Sonya; I'd been quite interested in the so-called interpersonal dynamics. Only out of curiosity, I assured myself. I'd already encountered more than enough murders for the summer, and embezzlement was entirely too mundane.

The patrons did not provide much entertainment. Most of the students were entranced with their laptops, their hands flickering over the keyboards like dragonflies over a pond. A few were engrossed by electronic readers and cell phones. They might glance up if a bomb exploded nearby, but I doubted I could gain their attention by standing on a table and ripping off my clothes. The coffee shops of my college days were loud and raucous places where philosophical arguments competed with poetry slams and subversion. This place resounded with clicks.

I glanced up when a voice said, "Do you mind if I join you?"

It took me a few seconds to recognize Gregory Whistler, the executive director of the Literacy Council. Flustered, I said, "Please do."

He introduced himself, requiring me to do likewise, and then said, "I saw you the other day, and then at seven o'clock, going into the building. Keiko told me that you wanted to become one of our tutors. We'll look forward to having you once you've gone through the training. I know it's silly, but the state Literacy Council insists. Were you dropping off the application form?"

"No one has mentioned an application

form," I said. I knew precisely what information he was after, but I wasn't in the mood to enlighten him. "My daughter is a tutor. Although it's hardly urgent, I'll ask her to pick up one for me. The next training session is at the end of the summer."

"Yes, good point. I was leaving when you arrived. Did you want to speak to me about volunteering in another capacity? Next month we're having a potluck picnic for the students, their families, and the tutors. We need all the help we can get. A lot of the students have large families, and they allow their kids to run wild. Last year we had an unfortunate incident involving alcohol, sushi, mustard, and couscous. No one was arrested, but I'm afraid that we might have a repeat this year."

"I'll have to check my calendar." I was aware that I was being uncooperative, but I'm always in the mood to outwit the witless. I finished my coffee. "It's been lovely chatting with you, Gregory. Perhaps I'll see you at the FLC sometime in the future."

"Please let me offer you another cup of coffee," he said. Before I could decline, he added, "I'm aware of your reputation, Claire, and I'd be deeply appreciative if you'll hear me out. Something's going on at the Literacy Council, and I'm afraid." He reached for my mug. "Ten minutes, okay?"

I nodded and sat down. Gregory took our cups inside for refills. If what I'd heard at the meeting implicated him in an embezzlement scheme, he had every right to be anxious. I could think of no reason why he might want to share this with me. He had come to the obvious conclusion that I'd attended the board meeting in some capacity, and surely he'd realized by now that I wasn't going to pass along what had been said. If he was hoping to buy my allegiance with overpriced coffee, he was out of luck.

He eventually returned, bearing two cups, and resumed his seat. "Thank you, Claire. This has nothing to do with whatever took place at the board meeting." He paused for a long moment. "This may sound paranoid. I've been the executive director for four years, and until recently, there have been no problems. I've pulled in a lot of grant money and donations, and done my best to see that the funds are allocated to the proper programs. Our immediate financial situation is grim, but I'm confident we can continue to operate on a reduced level until the economy improves. We've cut back on evening classes and close at one on Fridays."

"That seems reasonable," I said.

"I think so, but apparently I've stirred up

resentment from an unknown person or persons. A couple of months ago I went into my office and found red splatters on my desk and the files I'd set out the previous evening." He held up his palm. "No, not blood. It was paint, but meant to convey the message that it might be my blood the next time."

"Are you sure? Were there painters in the building? One of them might have wandered into your office and made the mess. Or what about Toby's cleaning supplies?" Not that I could truly believe either scenario, since cleaning solutions are rarely bright red.

Gregory shook his head. "It was a message, the first one. The second was a dead bird in my wastebasket. It didn't open a window and fly inside." He crossed his arms and stared at the tabletop, his forehead creased. When he finally picked up his cup, his hands were trembling. "Maybe I'm paranoid, but I'll be damned if I can come up with a reasonable explanation. Last week my name plaque disappeared. Yesterday someone got into one of my desk drawers and made off with my flask and a box of antacids. That may be nothing more than petty theft by one of the students. I don't know."

Toby sprang to mind as the culprit. He

might have taken the flask, but I couldn't envision him pocketing the antacids. If he had a grudge against Gregory, he was capable of mischief. However, it seemed more likely that he was angry at his father for forcing him into menial labor.

"Have you told the board?" I asked.

"I asked Keiko about the paint, but she was mystified. I didn't see any point in mentioning these nasty pranks to any of the board members. I'm in enough trouble with them without being perceived as a whiner."

"Trouble over receipts? When I dropped by yesterday morning, I overheard the conversation between you and Sonya."

He rolled his eyes. "That's the reason, for the most part. I admit I can be disorganized when I'm up to my chin in paperwork, but I have saved all of my receipts in manila envelopes labeled accordingly. Either I misplaced them or they've vanished. It shouldn't be Sonya's problem, anyway. Willie is the treasurer." He stirred his coffee with a wooden stick as he sighed. "Someone is out to get me."

"Why?"

"I wish I knew, Claire. My position is hardly prestigious or lucrative. I suppose I could find a management position else-where, but I want to make a contribution to

51

the community. With our assistance, our students are able to get better jobs, communicate with their children's schools and doctors, and integrate into the culture."

I noted that his eyes were moist. He was either very sincere or very talented. "That's admirable, Gregory." My reply was lame, so I tried to rally. "Your background is in management?"

"After I graduated, I worked for my father's company, a medium-sized pharmaceutical manufacturer headquartered in Europe. Ten years ago Father retired to a tropical island to continue his campaign to hold the record for most marriages and divorces in one lifetime. His current wife is twelve years younger than I, and never met a mirror that didn't love her. I can't recall her name offhand."

"How did you end up in Farberville?"

"My wife went to college here, and she loved it. She — well, she died two years ago. I'm still trying to deal with it. Rosie was such a wonderful person, generous, caring, and very sensitive. She taught math at a middle school, but she was looking forward to having a houseful of children. We agreed to wait for a few years so we could settle into the community. When I went through her things, I found a folder filled with magazine articles about decorating nurseries and making baby clothes."

"I'm sorry for your loss," I said.

"Thank you."

We sat in silence for a few minutes. I finished my coffee and gathered up the torn sugar packets and stirrers. Gregory looked up, almost startled, when I said, "I need to go home now. I suggest you keep your office door locked when you're not there. These pranks seem juvenile at best."

"Yeah, I suppose so," Gregory said as he stood up. "I shouldn't have bothered you with my petty problems. Our students are adults, but they bring their children from time to time. I'll take your advice and lock my door. If that offends anyone, he or she will have to get over it. Thanks for hearing me out, Claire. I don't seem to have any friends these days. Rosie was the one who drew friends like a magnet. They tolerated me." He tried to chuckle. "Not that I'm a total bore. I just don't seem to have the energy to make an effort to get back out there and start dating."

If he was hitting on me, he was miles away from making contact. I smiled and went back into the café. As I squirmed through the crowd, I saw Rick seated alone at a table in a corner. He looked away, but not before we'd made fleeting eye contact. I continued out to my car and fished in my purse for my keys, feeling a sudden urge to leave before any other members of the board popped up behind a bush — or slid into my backseat. While I drove home, I composed a letter of resignation to the board, replete with gratitude for the honor of being elected and expressing dismay that I'd suddenly remembered I had to wash my hair on Monday night. I had no desire to embroil myself in their skullduggery and angst and pettiness. I wondered if Meals on Wheels would allow me to deliver *bouillabaisse* to the elderly and disabled. I would be an adorable candy striper. It might not be too late to enroll in summer school and take a class in nineteenth-century poetry. I'd always wanted to take up pottery. Pottery and poetry could be my salvation.

Or there was always culinary school.

3

The following morning I was sipping my first cup of coffee while I flipped through the pages of a cookbook extolling the delights of *la nouvelle cuisine de Haute Bordeaux* when the phone rang. I eyed it with suspicion, since Peter had told me the previous night that he would be in a meeting long before any *patisserie* pulled its first croissant out of the oven. Caron was asleep upstairs. My best friend, Luanne, was stalking bimboys on the beaches of southern Spain.

I reluctantly picked up the receiver. "Hello?"

"Oh, Ms. Marroy, I hope I am not disturbing you, but I know how much you want to volunteer and how bad I felt that you could not tutor and now I can think of —"

"Good morning, Keiko. How are you?" I said soothingly, given that she sounded like a canary frantically beating its wings against the bars of its cage.

"I would not bother you with such an early call, but —"

"Breathe in, breathe out. Think of cherry blossoms and tiny waves lapping on the beach. Take a deep breath and let it out in a gentle breeze. You can do it."

There was a moment of such silence that I wondered if she'd stopped breathing altogether. Finally she said, "I am sorry, Ms. Marroy. I am not so comfortable talking on the telephone with someone important like you. I get excited. I am breathing with calmness now. May I speak?"

"Is there an emergency, Keiko? Is someone hurt? Should you be calling nine-one-one for an ambulance?"

"Oh, no, Ms. Marroy," she said earnestly, "no one is breeding. Our receptionist, who is a volunteer, called to say that she cannot come here this morning. It would not be a problem except for that it is a problem. Not a terrible problem, but a very big problem. This nice old woman who gives us money wants to come here to show her friends that we are worthwhile. We will not be so worthwhile if I have to run away and answer the telephone every time it rings. Gregory never comes in before eleven o'clock."

"What about the other board members?"

"They are busy people who cannot leave their jobs. You did say that you wished to volunteer, didn't you?"

"I did," I admitted, sadly aware that I was not among the "busy people." Added to my abrupt addition to the board of directors, I'd have more volunteer hours by the end of the summer than Caron and Inez. "I'll be there in half an hour. Shall I bring doughnuts?"

"No, there is no time. Mrs. Slater will be here at ten. Thank you so much, Ms. Marroy."

I opted for casual Friday attire and arrived at the FLC with minutes to spare. There was no indication of high anxiety among the students in the lounge area, who were pretty much lounging. I could hear the teacher in one of the classrooms, conjugating verbs in a monotonous voice. Keiko bounced out of her office before I could take refuge behind the receptionist's desk.

"You are saving my rife, Ms. Marroy," she said.

"I doubt that very much, Keiko." I looked down at the phone with many buttons. "What am I supposed to do if someone calls?"

"Take messages. If new students come, give them this form and tell them to come back after lunch or next week. You are so kind to do this, Ms. Marroy. I didn't know who else to —"

"Your lipstick is smudged," I said mendaciously. "You don't want this donor to think badly of you, do you?" As I'd anticipated, she squealed and hurried into the ladies' room. I sat down and regarded my domain. I had a pad of paper and a pen. The buttons on the phone were unlit. I checked the folder with the forms for new students. All that my desk lacked was a potted plant and a photo of Peter and Caron. All I lacked was something to do while Keiko gave a tour to Mrs. Slater and her friends. I shot a warning glare at the phone, then emerged from behind the desk in search of a newspaper and, if I was lucky, a cup of coffee.

The coffeepot was in the room where the board had met. I took a cup out of the cabinet and filled it, noting that someone had added a mustache to one of the cave drawings on the chalkboard. The trio of Asian girls giggled as I picked up a crinkled newspaper from one of the tables, but they declined to share the source of their mirth. I resumed my post with dignity and engrossed myself in the antics of local politicians.

A shaggy man in a khaki jacket came

inside, nodded at me, and beckoned to a
Latino man. The two of them disappeared
into a cubicle. Minutes later, a grim young
woman appeared and took her student, a
stout woman with a headscarf, into another
cubicle. My trio of fans relocated to a table
where they had a better view of me. An
elderly man wearing a baseball cap waved
to his student, who was Latino and as old
as his tutor. I turned to the editorial page.
The phone rang. I punched the blinking
button and informed a siding salesman that
the FLC was not interested. The next call
was for Gregory. I dutifully wrote down a
name and telephone number and secured
the note under a stapler. A man with a thick
guttural accent called and asked for Leslie;
it took several minutes for me to ascertain
his callback number (if I did with any ac-
curacy). Keiko came out of her office several
times to hover briefly by the front door
before retreating. Dealing with important
donors should be Gregory's job, I thought
as I aligned stray paper clips, but his forty-
hour week might include late afternoon and
evening networking. It seemed the Farberville Literacy Council was in desperate need
of funds. Checkbooks might open more
readily after a few cocktails.

There was a second caller for Leslie, this

one a snap since the speaker had graduated to ESL 102. I was feeling confident that I was keeping a steady hand on the helm when the front door opened and a familiar figure tottled into view and beamed at me. My steady hand slipped. "Miss Parchester," I said weakly. "How have you been?"

"Goodness, Claire, I wasn't aware that you were one of our volunteers. What a charming surprise."

As she came around the corner of the desk, I was relieved to see that she was wearing sensible shoes rather than fuzzy pink slippers. We'd met when she had been accused of embezzling money from the high school journalism department. I'd cleared her name and, due to certain behavior on her part that is best left unspecified, persuaded her to retire. We'd had a few encounters since then, but I was too befuddled to recall any of them.

"I'm just helping out this morning," I said, resisting the urge to fan myself with a folder. "And you?"

"I've been a tutor for several years. I do so enjoy it. After my session with Miao, you and I must catch up over tea. I clipped all the articles about your latest case, but I'd adore to hear the details about those nasty people. You're always so clever, Claire."

"Meow?"

Miss Parchester was still beaming at me. "Isn't that a lovely name? I think of her as my little Chinese kitten. Such a dear girl, very bright but too shy for her own good. She's working on a graduate degree in mathematics. Her English isn't very good, I must say, but she's making wonderful progress." She beckoned to a slim and exquisitely beautiful young woman, who was waiting near the windows. "*Ni shang hao,* Miao. *Ni hao ma?*"

"Good morning," the woman whispered, her eyes downcast.

"This is my friend, Claire Malloy," Miss Parchester continued.

I smiled at Miao, who managed to glance up for a few seconds. "Miss Parchester told me that you're a student at the college. It must be quite a challenge because of the language barrier."

"Yes, but numbers . . . they are . . ." She looked at her tutor for help. When Miss Parchester merely nodded, she gulped and added, "The same. Only the words."

I watched the two of them retreat to a cubicle. I was pleased that Miss Parchester had found a hobby that was harmless and benevolent. I had no doubt that she was an excellent tutor, unlike my daughter, who could be impatient. The telephone interrupted my musing. I dealt briskly with a lawn service, suggesting they send their brochure via the mail. Another call for Gregory, followed by yet another for Leslie. A middle-aged couple came in and gazed expectantly at me. I quickly ascertained that they were potential students, in that I could understand neither of them, and handed them the appropriate forms. They gave me bewildered looks as they left.

Eastern European languages are not my forte.

Keiko's visitors arrived just as the class ended. Collisions were avoided as students found seats in the lounge area, jostled each other in front of the soda and snack machines, went into the restrooms, or departed. Keiko shepherded four well-endowed (in both senses) women into her office. Leslie gave me the same harried smile as she took the slips of paper from me and headed for her office. It occurred to me that she might have taken Gregory's flask after a particularly frustrating class in which malapropisms and mangled English had competed with the recitation of the past and present tenses. It was not anything I planned to pursue.

I wanted to fetch another cup of coffee,

but I could not abandon my post while the donors were present. My expression must have been plaintive, because a dark-haired woman came to the desk and said, "Hello. Can I help you?"

"No, but thank you. My name is Claire."

"Is a good name. I do not know how to say in Russian, but I will learn. My name is Yelena. I was famous actress in Moscow before I come to America. You are new tutor, yes?"

"I hope to become one. How long have you been coming here?"

"One year and four months. My English is not so good, but is getting better. My old tutor, a lady named Sara, has gone home to have baby, so now I have new tutor. My tutor is not so good, but she tries." She laughed so loudly that heads popped up from the cubicles. "I tell her I am of Cossack blood, so she must be careful or I will bounce on her with scimitar!"

With orange highlights in her hair, she would make a fine Siberian tiger. I had no desire to be her next meal, although it would be fun to be her tutor. Caron might think differently. The girls should arrive shortly, I realized as I glanced at the clock on the desk. I looked up at Yelena. "I have to take the tutor training session at the end

63

of the summer. Perhaps we can work together. My Russian is limited to *da, nyet,* and vodka. Maybe you can teach me as well."

"Then I will teach you new word: *spaseebo.* It means thank you."

We grinned at each other. Leslie emerged from her office and went back into the classroom. Yelena and most of the other students followed dutifully, including the pesky trio. I shirked my responsibilities and dashed into the classroom to refill my coffee cup. When I returned, Keiko was showing her entourage the computer in one of the cubicles. As she glanced in my direction, her eyes widened and she frowned. I would have been annoyed had I not realized that her displeasure was aimed at an obese elderly woman who'd arrived during my brief absence. Despite the mild weather, the woman wore a stained jacket over an equally stained shirt, a long skirt, and boots. Had someone been filming a movie set during World War II, she would have been cast as the peasant woman who was the mastermind behind the resistance cell.

"May I help you?" I asked her as I resumed the helm with renewed resolve.

The woman's mouth puckered and her eyebrows lowered as though I'd said something offensive. "Who be you?"

"A volunteer," I said. "And you?"

"Ludmila Grabowski." Her voice resonated like a gong. "I from Bialystok, Poland. Grandson professor at Farber College." She paused, daring me to contradict her or cast aspersions on Bialystok, Poland, or her grandson. "I know not why you here, but what matters? It bad day for *swistak* I came here. *Dupek!* Nowhere safe to hide from sins of father." Despite my aversion to sweat, I may have been a bit damp as she continued to blister me with an unrelenting glare. When I remained mute, she said, "You know nothing. Where is tutor?"

"I don't know." It seemed like the appropriate reply.

Ludmila snorted, then stomped over to a table and plopped down with a loud sigh. My hand may have wobbled as I took a gulp of coffee, but I reminded myself that I was not a sniveling child deserving of a lecture. I would have said as much to Ludmila had my Polish been up to par. I waggled my fingers at Keiko, who looked very much as though she might snivel at any moment, and turned my attention to the crossword puzzle in the newspaper.

I'd finished it (in ink, naturally) when Leslie's class ended and once again students streamed out the door. Keiko hastily led the ladies into her office before they were trampled. Miss Parchester waved merrily to me as she left; Miao glided by on her way to the restroom. The shaggy tutor and his student left together, talking loudly about Latino music. Gregory appeared, gave me a puzzled look, and continued into his office. The telephone, which had been behaving nicely, rang. In the lounge area, cell phones produced a chorus of blips, chirps, and jingles. The majority of the students responded in their native languages, doing their best to be heard over the polyglot explosion. Yelena winked at me as she followed Leslie into her office. The caller's heavy accent suggested that English was not his first, second, or even third language, and I was begging him to speak more slowly when Caron and Inez strolled in. Even from a distance I could smell doughnuts on their breath.

Caron's eyebrows rose as she spotted me. Inez blinked. After I gave up on the caller and hung up, my darling daughter said, "Whoa, who opened this can of crazy?"

"Not I," I assured her. "Keiko needed a volunteer to handle the receptionist's desk this morning. If you'd been up, I would have mentioned it to you."

"You mean you would have stuck me with it."

"No, that didn't cross my mind, but it should have. I don't need to pad my college applications. You might have received extra credit."

"Very funny."

Inez gazed at me in awe. "Wow, Ms. Malloy. I don't think I could handle all these students and answer the phone. You must know a lot of languages."

"Right," Caron said, rolling her eyes in a manner I found less than enchanting. I should have been inured to it; she'd been perfecting it for the last five years. "Go ahead and ask her something in Cantonese, Inez."

"Aren't you supposed to be tutoring some innocent victim?" I asked.

Inez scurried to the lounge area and zeroed in on a swarthy young woman in a headscarf. Caron shot a final look at the ceiling, groaned, and waved at Ludmila, who was still glowering. In a melodramatic whisper, she said, "If I don't survive, go ahead and send in my application to Vassar. Maybe they'll accept me posthumously."

"I guess that'll save on room and board," I said without sympathy.

"Yeah, but you'll have to hire pallbearers

to take me to my classes." She turned to Ludmila and said, "Good morning. How are you today?"

Ludmila muttered something, trudged past us, and went to a cubicle. Caron took a deep breath as she followed her. I wished them well. Most of the students were leaving. Yelena stopped by the desk to clasp my hand, her cell phone plastered to her ear, then joined the grand exit. Miao was seated at a table, her back straight and her feet crossed at the ankles, peering at a notebook. Keiko came out of her office with Mrs. Slater and the three potential donors, and gushed with gratitude until they went out the front door. Once the door closed, she fled back to her office.

Only then did Gregory appear. He glanced over his shoulder as he approached the desk. "Is it safe?" he asked me as if we were coconspirators.

"I haven't seen any lions, tigers, or bears since I arrived."

"I thought I heard Ludmila," he said.

"She's in a cubicle with my daughter. Is there a problem?"

He rubbed his face. "No, not really. Well, she has a problem, but none of us can figure it out. When she gets upset, she lapses into Polish, and she's upset most of the time. We have the pleasure of entertaining her several times a week. Her grandson's afraid to leave her home alone for more than a few hours. She doesn't get along well with the neighbors. He tried to park her at a senior citizens center. That lasted three weeks."

"If she's not happy here, then why let her come?"

"We have to be very careful to avoid any hint of discrimination. Her grandson's a professor and may have friends at the law school. She could qualify under several categories: age, disability, and country of origin." Gregory pulled down his mouth and widened his eyes, making a wickedly funny face. "Even Notre Dame has its gargoyles. Just smile and nod, and don't pay attention to anything she says." He went into Keiko's office.

It was tempting to eavesdrop near the cubicle where Ludmila was berating Caron, but I'd done my good deed for the day. That, and I'd only had a muffin for breakfast. I folded up the newspaper, washed the cup and put it away, and was collecting my purse when Keiko caught me. She thanked me profusely, and I made polite responses while I eased out of her clutches. I'd almost made good on my escape when I heard Ludmila's voice bellow, *Dupek!*

I froze and then looked over my shoulder, hoping she wasn't physically assaulting Caron. I still was burdened with a few maternal obligations, one of which was packing my offspring off to college intact. Ludmila was pointing her finger at Gregory, who looked like a deer caught in the headlights of a Sherman tank. Caron was peeping over the wall of the cubicle, as were Inez and her student. Keiko stumbled out of her office. Leslie appeared in the doorway of her office, a half-eaten sandwich in her hand. Miao cowered behind her notebook.

It was a splendidly melodramatic scene. I replayed it several times as I drove home, chuckling at the images of stunned faces and ungainly poses. Once I was inside my perfect house, however, I dismissed it and curled up with a cookbook. Peter would be home in time for dinner, and I didn't want to disappoint him.

4

Peter and I had a lovely time Friday evening, despite a small problem with the *Emincé de Volaille sauce Roquefort* (my sauce refused to homogenize properly). We dawdled in bed the next morning, and had breakfast on the terrace. Caron had rescheduled her pool party for the afternoon, and shortly after noon a horde of hormonally addled teenagers descended. Peter conveniently remembered that he had paperwork at the PD and deserted me. I spent the rest of the afternoon playing on the rolling ladder in my library, with occasional forays to the pool area to keep an eye out for pot, beer, and/or undue rowdiness. I did not anticipate any problems, since they all knew that Peter was a cop. Later, I was able to assure him that there'd been no felonies committed under my watchful scrutiny. I did not comment on the likelihood of misdemeanors in the demilitarized zone.

On Sunday morning Peter and I were sharing the newspaper when Caron dragged herself out to the terrace and grabbed a bagel. I handed her the comics. After she'd had time to compose herself, I said, "Everyone seemed to have had a nice time yesterday."

"Yes, I know I left a mess in the kitchen. I'll clean it up, so don't bother to —"

"I already took care of it," Peter said from behind the sports section. "The trash bags are in the trunk of your car. You can put them in the Dumpster behind the PD, unless you want to keep them as souvenirs. There's a red bikini top on the dryer in the laundry room."

Caron frowned. "Red?"

I did not want to hear any details. "I noticed you didn't invite Toby Whitbream to your party."

"I didn't invite the French ambassador, either. What's your point?"

"You're volunteering together," I said. "I ran into him at the Literacy Council Thursday evening."

"Toby Whitbream?" She looked so astonished that I might as well have made the same claim about the French ambassador. "Why didn't you tell me?"

"Why didn't you tell me that Miss

Parchester is a tutor?"

"You didn't ask."

I heard muffled laughter from behind the newsprint, but I opted to ignore it. "No, I didn't ask you if Miss Parchester is a tutor. You didn't ask me if I encountered Toby Whitbream on Thursday. Let's think of all the things we didn't ask each other, shall we? Are those my sandals on your feet? Did you ever repay me for the last advance on your allowance? How long do you plan to go without making your bed? Do you honestly believe that I wouldn't notice the stain on —"

"Okay, okay," Caron said. "I meant to mention it, but I forgot. It's not like she's going to cause trouble like she did before. It's kind of funny. She has two students, one a skinny Chinese girl and the other this six-foot-seven black guy from Africa. She doesn't come up to his armpit. One day last week he hadn't done his homework, and she scolded him like he was a little kid. If he wanted to, he could crush her head in one hand. Instead, he got all teary and apologized." She nibbled on the bagel for a moment. "Toby Whitbream is a tutor?"

"Not exactly. He cleans the building in the evenings."

"The janitor?"

"I suppose you could call him that. His father's on the board of directors. Apparently Toby got into trouble with the police and was ordered to do a hundred hours of community service." I flicked my finger on a photograph of a gentleman in a baseball uniform. "You know anything about that, Sherlock?"

"Nope."

"This is rich," Caron said as she stood up. "Inez will totally freak when she hears this. Imagine the great Toby Whitbream scrubbing toilets! I Love It! He thinks he's the meanest dude at school, just because he's the star quarterback. Rhonda's been panting after him for three solid years."

I waited until she was out of earshot before saying, "Caron seems to have forgotten that she's been panting herself."

"What about that boyfriend of hers? What's his name? The gawky kid who stutters."

"Teenagers are capable of multitasking. Her crush on Toby is an idle fantasy. And by the way, Joel does not stutter. You go out of your way to terrify him."

"Do not."

I flicked the paper once more, then picked up the other half of Caron's bagel and settled back with the editorial section of the paper. I was gritting my teeth over a particularly absurd column when I heard shrill giggles from Caron's bedroom.

Juicy gossip travels at the speed of light, and then some.

Monday evening arrived, to my regret. The parking lot at the Literacy Council was nearly full. I deftly maneuvered into a narrow space. I assumed the students taking classes after work were likely to be unfamiliar to me, but I was wrong. Miao was there, as were Yelena, Ludmila, and Inez's Egyptian student. I recognized several other faces. I smiled and nodded as I made my way to the classroom at the back, where Frances North was making notes and Sonya was distributing papers in front of each chair. Willie was seated at the end on one table, dozing. I sat down and pretended to be engrossed in what proved to be a monthly financial report. After all, what can be more intriguing than utility bills, office expenditures, insurance payments, and the ever so fascinating cost of paper towels?

"Thank you for coming, Claire," Frances said. "This shouldn't take too long. There's a copy of the agenda among those papers. Old business, committee reports, new business, and then we can all go home. Isn't that right, Willie?"

"Hallelujah."

Sonya came up behind me and patted my shoulder. "We're so grateful, Claire. You must be very busy solving crimes, and it's so wonderful of you to take the time to serve on the board."

Frances gave me a sharp look. "Crimes?"

"The only crimes I'm aware of are happening in my own kitchen, and I'm the perpetrator. Ask my husband."

"Claire's husband is the deputy chief at the Farberville Police Department," Sonya explained to Frances, who seemed unsettled. "Claire has helped them solve all sorts of murders."

Frances's eyes narrowed. "Murders?"

I was relieved when Rick and Austin came into the room. Austin was carrying bottles of gin, vodka, and vermouth. Rick had a silver cocktail shaker, an ice bucket, and a stack of plastic cups. "No wine," Austin announced as he set the bottles down on the counter. "We wouldn't want to upset the Muslim students, would we?"

"That is not what I meant!" Frances forgot about me as she pointed her finger at the miscreants. "Rick, I thought you had a smidgen of common sense."

"I do," he murmured, "but no olives.

Would you prefer a gin or vodka martini, Your Honor?"

Willie was wide-awake. "Gin, thank you, and go easy on the vermouth."

Sonya wiggled her fingers. "Me, too."

I admitted a preference for vodka. Frances continued to mutter under her breath as Austin mixed martinis and Rick delivered them. When Drake arrived, he chose gin. I decided I could survive the meeting.

The minutes were approved without comment. An addendum acknowledged my election to the board. Nobody bothered to vote. The old business included the dismal attendance at the last open house, the inconclusive results of a student poll on night classes, and generalized rumbling from those present. I was toying with the idea of a refill when Keiko and Gregory came into the room. Keiko twinkled as best she could as she rattled off the numbers concerning students, tutors, volunteers, and recent library acquisitions. When no one had any questions, she left the room with an audible sigh.

Gregory smiled broadly, but his face was flushed. "I spoke to a Rotary Club last week and came away with checks totaling three hundred dollars and change. The United Way is demanding more paperwork before they decide on the grant. The Otto Foundation will give us another eight thousand dollars, but money has to be used for an in-school program for non-English-speaking mothers of elementary school children. Leslie says she doesn't have time. None of our tutors are certified to teach ESL."

"What did we do last year with their money?" asked Rick.

"We did our best to comply."

Sonya was flipping through the financial report. "I don't see how we're going to stay open this summer. If anything breaks — the air conditioner, the hot water heater, the vacuum cleaner — we're broke, too. I don't understand, Gregory. Money is evaporating. When we set the budget at the first of the year, we had all the anticipated expenses covered."

Frances nodded. "I'd like an explanation."

"This happened last year," Gregory said. "A lot of our grants come in the fall, along with our annual fund-raiser. Summers have been a problem since I started here. We'll survive the next ten weeks."

"You didn't answer my question," Rick said.

Willie rapped on the table with her knuckles. "He said that we did our best. That's all we can do, unless you'd like to get certified to teach ESL."

He held up his hands, feigning contrition, but his voice was chilly. "I'm just saying that if we accept money from this foundation, we have to comply with their restrictions."

"Hey, I don't want them breathing down my neck," Austin said. "My karma's shaky enough already on account of the untimely demise of one of the flying sheep in that furniture store commercial. Dumb creature ran bleating into the street."

Rick refused to be distracted. "So we're going to take their money under false pretenses? What are you going to do if a representative from the foundation wants to observe a nonexistent class?"

At that point, everyone except me felt the need to voice an opinion loudly and adamantly. Even Drake joined in, banging his fist on the table. Gregory rose to his feet, as did Rick and Austin. Sonya shrieked at them to behave. Frances shrieked at Sonya to stop shrieking. Willie demanded order in the court. Rick and Gregory were almost nose to nose, their hands clenched. I watched in awe. I'd expected a lot of polite dissension, not a vociferous uprising. Several Latino students came to the doorway, their eyes wide as they took in what might evolve into a bullfight. *Olé!*

Frances was literally hopping as she howled for order. After another basically incoherent exchange involving improbable lineage, Rick and Gregory backed away from each other. Austin hastily began to make another round of martinis. Sonya took out a compact and checked her lipstick. Willie grimaced before downing her last few drops. Drake's arms were crossed as he watched Gregory leave. I felt sorry for the amigos in the doorway, who'd had such high hopes.

Frances found her voice. "The executive committee will meet Thursday at five o'clock at my house, when we will delve into these matters more thoroughly. Austin, I suggest you recruit Claire for the fund-raising committee. Any new business?" Rick waved his arm, but she ignored him. "If not, we're adjourned. Please excuse me, but I've developed a dreadful headache and I cannot stay here another minute. Our next meeting is . . . hell, I don't know. Ask Keiko." She gathered up her things and marched out the door.

Sonya fanned herself with the sheaf of papers. "You must think we're terrible, Claire. Our meetings are usually short and boring. The financial situation has everyone on edge, I suppose. Gregory's doing his best."

"You're defending him?" Rick asked. "Did corporate suck out your brains today as part of a new restructuring plan?"

She quivered with anger. "You're a damn bully, that's what you are! Willie, don't you agree that Gregory's doing his best?"

"Whatever." Willie arose and picked up her purse. "This nonsense is too much for my aged bladder."

She left the room. Drake followed her, his expression rigid. I grabbed my purse, but before I could bolt, Sonya snagged me. "Please don't resign, Claire. This won't happen again, I promise. We all care about the Farberville Literacy Council, maybe too much, and so do the students. We can't let them down."

I removed her hand. "I've been in faculty meetings where certain professors were threatened with defenestration. This was mild in comparison."

Austin's laugh sounded like a bray. "From the top floor of the ivy tower?"

"Academians make a very fine splat, or so I've been told." I escaped and went into the main room. In one of the classrooms, an elderly man was talking to a dozen students about bank deposit slips. Several of the cubicles were occupied by tutors and their students, while other students in the lounge cribbed off each other's workbooks. Keiko was in her office, conversing with a man in a dashiki. Drake stood in the corner, still grim. Sonya and Frances were talking together in the lounge area. As I paused, Willie came out of the ladies' room and, with a bewildered expression, went into the classroom. If Gregory had the slightest sense, he was either holed up in his office or long gone.

I chose to be long gone.

Peter had slipped away when I woke up the next morning. The previous night we'd had a very pleasant marital interlude that had almost erased the ugly scene at the board meeting, and I was feeling chipper as I fixed a bowl of cereal. Before I could pick up a spoon, the telephone rang. I thought of a long list of people with whom I had no desire to speak, so I opted to let the answering machine deal with it. I'd managed one bite when Peter's voice said, "Claire, I need to talk to you. It's urgent. Call me back as soon as you can, okay?"

I snatched up the receiver. "What's so urgent?"

"There's been a death at the Literacy

82

Council. I'm surrounded by people speaking so many languages I might as well be in the United Nations cafeteria. The person in charge is in her office, sobbing — I think in Japanese, but it could be Korean. The director's not here."

"Who's dead?" I demanded.

"One of the students. Will you please get here as quickly as you can?"

I felt a tingle of self-satisfaction. In every case I'd been involved in, Peter had done everything within his power to keep me out of it. He'd had my car towed. He'd put me under house arrest (or so he'd thought). He'd threatened and cajoled in a most endearing fashion. Now he was begging for my help. I deigned to be magnanimous.

"I'll be there in half an hour," I said sweetly.

My smugness faded as I went out to my car. The death of a student was tragic, no matter who it was. The ones I'd encountered were good people, struggling to fit into their adopted country. I recalled the terror of my French classes in high school, where I'd crouched behind my textbook and prayed that I wouldn't be called on to read or recite. I'd been obliged to take a foreign language, but the students at the Literacy Council did so voluntarily.

The parking lot was jammed with civilian and police vehicles. An ambulance blocked the entrance. I parked across the street and was approaching the door when two paramedics wheeled out a gurney. The body was in a black bag, but from the bulge, I had an idea who it might be. A uniformed officer lifted the yellow crime scene tape and waved me in. Forty or so students were milling about in Leslie's classroom. I knew that some of them had come from countries with oppressive governments and brutal police forces. I hoped Peter had been gentle with them.

Lieutenant Jorgeson joined me. "Good morning, Ms. Malloy. I understand that you were invited to the crime scene."

"For once," I said, finishing his unspoken sentiment. "What happened?"

"A woman's body was discovered in a storage room in the back. It looks as if she fell against the copy machine and cracked her skull. The medical examiner concurs. The girl in the office is trying to contact the woman's next of kin, but she's . . . upset. Do you think you can calm her down?"

"I'll try after you explain why this is being treated like a homicide. If the woman fell against the machine, why isn't it an accident?"

"It may have been an accident, but someone dragged the body into a corner and tried to conceal it. The medical examiner said that the woman would have been incapable of crawling."

"We're talking about a Polish woman, right?"

Jorgeson opened his notebook. "Ludmila Grabowski. Her grandson is —"

"A professor at the college," I said. "I met her Friday morning. She wasn't what I'd describe as likable. She may have made some enemies."

Jorgeson gave me a glum look that I'd seen numerous times in the past. "Would you please do something about the girl in the office, Ms. Malloy?"

I dutifully went to the office. Keiko was no longer hysterical, but her face was streaked with mascara. She was clutching a tissue to her nose and hiccupping with such force that her whole body shuddered. "Ms. Marroy," she said, "this is so very dreadful! What should I do? I try to call Gregory, but he no answer. How do I call college? How do I find Grabowskisan? *Tetsudatte kurema-suka?*"

Her English was slipping away like an elusive tide. I went around her desk, pulled her to her feet, and hugged her. She began

85

to sob. I tried not to wince as my shoulder became increasingly clammy. After several minutes, she calmed down, and I released her cautiously. "Do you have a file for Ludmila? That's likely to have her grandson's contact information."

She opened a drawer and extracted a manila folder. I scanned the pages until I found her grandson's name and telephone number. Since Keiko was in no shape to talk on the phone, I dialed the number. I was immediately informed that Bartek Grabowski was unable to take my call. I left a message with my name, the number of the Literacy Council, and a vague reference to an accident involving his grandmother.

Keiko produced a feeble smile. I suggested that she clean her face, and she was staring in horror into a compact mirror as I went to find Deputy Chief Peter Rosen of the Farberville PD. He and several officers were outside a small corner room. The CSI team was taking photographs, measuring the floor, and crawling about like large beetles. Peter nodded at me, quite officiously in my opinion. "Thanks for coming," he said. "Is there someone on the board that we should call first?"

"Frances North is the president. Keiko will have her number."

"Is she still upset?"

"She's recovering." I did not offer to run to ask her to find the number. "May I see the crime scene?"

He started to protest, then shut his mouth and gestured at the doorway. I interpreted it as an affirmative and peered into the room. It was small and crowded with the copy machine, boxes, stacks of folders, a collection of umbrellas and oddments of clothing in a bin marked LOST AND FOUND, and a decrepit office chair tilted at a perilous angle. The worn rug was stained with a large blotch of blood. The dirty window allowed in enough light to illuminate the overall dustiness. I sneezed as I stepped back.

"Do you know when she died?" I asked Peter.

"What I need you to do is help us communicate with the students. We're trying to get a list of everyone who was in the building last night. I've sent for a translator for the Latinos. Jorgeson speaks a little German. As for Chinese, Japanese, Korean, Arabic, Thai, Russian . . ."

"You called your wife, the multilingual? I'm afraid my Farsi is a bit rusty. Besides, all of the students speak some English, or so I was told. Where's Leslie? She can help."

Peter glanced at a minion, who consulted

her notebook and said, "Leslie Barnes teaches from three to five classes every day, and a couple of night classes. She was supposed to teach an intermediate conversation class at nine this morning, but she hasn't shown up."

"Go find her and bring her here," Peter said, annoyed. "Did anyone else not show up this morning?"

The minion, clearly a rookie, blushed to her roots. "No, sir, not that we know about. The director usually doesn't come in until eleven."

"Why don't we invite him to break tradition and come in early?"

"Yes, sir. Right away, sir." The poor creature fled toward the entrance.

Peter asked for a description of the daily operation. I obliged as best I could, having been involved for less than a week. After my brief recitation, he asked me to elaborate about the previous evening's board meeting. I'd already given him a synopsis, so I filled in some details and then added, "It was hard to figure out who was angry at whom, although Rick was close to punching Gregory. Sonya and Frances seemed to be on Gregory's side. Willie was demanding order in the court. I suspect she'd already had a cocktail or two before she arrived at the meeting. Austin's just a fan of drama, as far as I can tell. Drake was smoldering." I paused for a moment. "That's all irrelevant, if Ludmila died hours after the meeting was adjourned."

"You didn't see them leave, did you?" Peter asked.

I made a vague gesture. "No, but I doubt any of them had ever encountered Ludmila, with the exception of Gregory and Keiko — and perhaps Sonya, who was here last Wednesday morning when I came by to volunteer. The board members have day jobs. Shouldn't you be questioning the students?"

"We're trying to sort out who was here last night. According to the medical examiner's unofficial estimate, the victim died sometime before midnight. She was seen eating a meal she'd brought with her at six o'clock. Once the medical examiner's done the autopsy, he can be more precise." He put his hand on my back and led me to the reception area. "Would you please see if that girl can find the class roster and a list of tutors and their students? Every time I look at her, she bursts into tears."

"Look at her — or glare at her?"

"I don't glare."

"And I never interfere in police investiga-

89

tions. I certainly don't want to risk tarnishing my record by interfering now," I said.

"Do I have to say it?" he asked in a pained voice. I nodded. He took a breath, no doubt considering his options, then said, "My darling Claire, you have never interfered in a police investigation. Your eagerness to assist the police is admirable. Now will you please get the damn list?"

I patted his cheek. "All you had to do was ask. I'll help Keiko find the information and be right back."

Gloating does not become me, so I contained my elation and went back to Keiko's office. She'd repaired her makeup and was able to give me a low-wattage twinkle. I told her what Peter wanted, and she and I sorted through the folders on her desk until we found the information. I was relieved that Miss Parchester only tutored in the mornings. It wasn't that I suspected her of anything whatsoever, but her presence had often complicated the situation.

Keiko offered to make copies of the pages, then remembered what had happened and burst into tears. I handed her the box of tissues and took the pages to Peter. He'd moved to the doorway of the classroom, where the tension in the room had escalated. I peeked over his shoulder at students wailing, gabbing wildly on their cell phones, and exchanging hostile remarks in their native languages. I tried to recall what I knew from Sunday school about the Tower of Babel. What came to mind was a fragment of a quote about how the Lord had confounded the language of all the earth. He'd done a fine job.

I squirmed past Peter and said, "Hey, everybody, I'm Claire Malloy. Please listen to me. If you want to leave anytime soon, you're going to have to be quiet." I clapped my hands. "Really. Just sit down and look at me." To my surprise, the majority of them did. I shot a stern look at the cluster of Asian girls until they complied. I found a notebook on the podium and began to rip out pages. "I want you to write down your name and telephone number. After you've done that, write down the specific times you were here yesterday. Okay?"

There were a lot of blank stares as I passed out pieces of paper. It was possible that I'd overestimated their competency in English. I repeated my instructions more slowly and rephrased them in simple sentences. Eventually everyone began to write, although I wasn't confident that whatever they wrote would be of much help. At least I'd calmed them down, I assured myself — something

91

Deputy Chief Rosen had been unable to do. "Thank you so much," I said. "Be sure to write down what time you left if you were here last night. Okay?" When they were done, I collected the papers.

"When can we leave?" asked Yelena, the Russian actress, her back arched and one hand lifted in a graceful pose. I hoped she was not about to launch into a melodramatic monologue by Pushkin or Chekhov.

"I don't know. The police have to sort this out before any of us can leave." This wasn't true, since I could leave whenever I wished. I was not inclined to share this. The students were still distressed and capable of another uprising. "Go ahead and use your cell phones," I said cheerfully. "Would anyone like to make coffee and tea?"

Inez's Mexican student and two women clad in headscarves volunteered and left for the other classroom. Several of the others asked me questions, but I smiled vaguely and took refuge in a chair behind the podium. Miss Marple never babysat while the police investigated, I thought irritably, but I knew that questioning the potential suspects would not sit well with a certain cop. I realized that I was clutching papers that might be vital to the investigation. I looked through them, noting that about twenty of those present had been here the night before. Although I had doubts, I wondered if any of them might have been on a friendly basis with Ludmila.

Peter was no longer in the doorway. A pimply uniformed officer was standing by the water fountain, doing his best to look stern. I gave the papers to him and asked him to take them to the deputy chief, then went back inside the classroom and sat down next to Yelena. "We won't have to stay much longer," I said. "The police are more concerned with the people who were here last night."

"I was here. Am I suspected of crime? I did not like Ludmila, but I did not hurt her. She had big mouth, all the time talking loudly."

"I noticed that when I was here yesterday. Did she have any friends?"

Yelena shook her head. "She call me stinking Communist. She says Muslims are devils, Mexicans are dirty; Asians are yellow spies. All the time she yells *dupek* at people. I do not know meaning, but I think not very nice."

"I agree with you," I said. "So you didn't ever talk to her?"

"I tried. We have potluck lunches on first Friday of month. Ludmila brought pastries

called *paczki,* like what you call jelly doughnuts. I told her they were delicious. She said
she learned to make them when she was
little girl. It was not so easy to imagine her
as ever being little. Then I ask her when she
came to this country. She says her grandson,
who is very important professor, brought
her to live with him one year ago. She did
not like this. He wanted her to cook and
clean his fancy house, but she told him she
was too old. She was not too old to make
strudel and poppy-seed cake and eat it all
before he came home. She laughed when
she tells me this."

At least Ludmila had a few happy moments, I thought. "Did you see her talk to
anyone else?"

"I see her yell at everyone else," Yelena
said with a smile. "Whistler was frightened
of her, I think. Maybe not frightened — that
is wrong word. When he saw her, he would
rush into office like it was urinal and he
needed to piss. He would peek out door to
see if coast was clean."

Peter came into the room and cleared his
throat. I shrank down and tried to look like
a student. "May I have your attention,
please?" he asked. "If you were not here last
night, you are free to leave. We may have
some questions for you later, but we'll let

94

you know. The Farberville Literacy Council will be closed for now, but it might be open in a day or two. If not, I apologize for the inconvenience." He tried to appear avuncular as half of the students streaked out the door as though the prison gates had burst open. "I'm very sorry to keep the rest of you here. We'll question you as quickly as possible. Please try to remember the details of any interactions you had with the victim."

As soon as he'd left, Yelena said, "What is 'interactions'?"

She was not the only one with a mystified expression. "If you talked to Ludmila, or noticed anything about her that seemed different," I explained to my international charges. "I'd like to know your first names."

"Graciela. My English not good," said a Latina woman.

"My English no good, very bad," chimed in an Asian girl, not the least bit giggly. "I named Sammie."

"Where is Miss Leslie?" asked a man with dark chocolate skin. I suspected he was Miss Parchester's student. He was exceedingly tall and certainly large enough to pick her up with one hand.

"She hasn't come in this morning," I said. "Was she here last night?"

A scowling young Asian man flipped his

hand. "I am Jiang. No, Miss Leslie has night classes on Tuesday and Thursday. Last night a woman talked about first aid and a man talked about bank accounts. Waste of time." I remembered that he was one of Caron's students.

Not everyone agreed with Jiang, and they voiced their opinions. As the volume rose, I considered slipping away to find out what Peter was doing. I was on the verge of attempting my great escape when Yelena stood up and said, "This is not time for fighting. Ludmila is dead. She was one of us, even if we did not like her. Do you want police to find out who killed her? Sit down and be quiet!"

They all resumed whispering, punching buttons on their cell phones, or brooding. I patted Yelena on the back. "Good job. Did Leslie say anything yesterday that might explain why she hasn't shown up this morning?"

Yelena chewed on her lip. "I do not think so. She gave us homework to bring to class today. Would you like to see?"

"Maybe later," I said. "Why don't you get everyone to talk about some sort of memorial service?"

Yelena did not look excited, but she promised to do her best. I hastily left the room and was heading for Keiko's office when a man came into the building. He had pale blond hair, a trimmed mustache, and a minimal beard. Even from across the room I could see the tweediness of his coat, replete with leather patches on the elbows. Clearly, a professional professor. He stopped and looked around, as if expecting a multitude of uniformed police officers to swarm in on him.

"Professor Grabowski?" I approached him and held out my hand. "I'm Claire Malloy, the person who left the message for you. I'm sorry to tell you that your grandmother died sometime last night."

"Babcia had a heart condition." Any trace of an accent came from the Midwest. "Why wasn't I notified when it happened? I've been worried out of my mind about her. I was supposed to pick her up at eight o'clock last night, but I was delayed by some colleagues. When I arrived here, the building was lit but locked, and no one appeared when I rapped my keys on the glass. Sometimes when I'm late, she takes the bus. I expected to find her at home, but she wasn't there."

"Did you call the police?"

"I thought about it, yes. Then I decided she must have gone to stay with a friend, and was too angry at me to call. Babcia had a temper . . ." He was doing his best to sound upset, but I wasn't fooled. He pretended to blink back tears, then took out a perfectly ironed handkerchief and wiped his eyes. "Where is she? I need to talk to someone. I saw police cars outside. Why are the police involved?"

"I'm sure they'll want to talk to you," I said. "Let me find Deputy Chief Rosen and let him know you're here." I gave myself bonus points for not interrogating Bartek while I had the chance, but I was never one to interfere with official police investigations.

Peter and Jorgeson had taken refuge in the back classroom. I told them about Grabowski's arrival. After Peter left, I said to Jorgeson, "How's it going? Any updates from the medical examiner?"

Jorgeson squirmed. "Well, Ms. Malloy, it's kind of early to establish the time of death. There are some recent bruises on her upper arms, like she was grabbed."

"So there was a struggle," I said. "Ludmila didn't lose her balance and fall against the copy machine. She was shoved."

"We don't know that, Ms. Malloy. That's why we investigate."

"Oh, Jorgeson, you're such a nice man. Of

course there was a struggle. Ludmila was old. I probably could have done it — or anybody else in the building at the time. I don't know why anyone would have a motive, though. Her fellow students didn't like her, but I didn't get the sense that any of them hated her. They're planning a memorial service as we speak." My cell phone rang before I could expound on the sharing of grief in the front classroom. I dug out the blasted thing and said, "Hello?"

"What is going on, Mother? The parking lot is full and there are cops at the front door. Did you Do Something?"

I glanced at the clock on the wall. It was nearly eleven o'clock, time for Caron and Inez to report for tutoring. "There's been a possible homicide. I had absolutely nothing to do with it. Peter asked me to help with the students."

"Peter asked you to help? Did you spike your orange juice this morning?" Caron said. "That's a sign of alcoholism, you know. I wish you'd wait until I go off to college before you turn into a lush."

My gaze flitted to the wastebasket. I was relieved to see only wadded paper towels and disposable cups. Austin had kept his word and taken away the gin, vodka, and vermouth bottles. "I am not going to turn into a lush anytime soon," I said haughtily, aware of Jorgeson's raised eyebrows. "You will not be tutoring today, so I suggest you trot on to the lake or the mall or wherever. Maybe you can find an Al-Anon meeting in a church basement."

"Who got killed?"

"Ludmila. Her body was discovered this morning."

Caron was silent for a moment. "She was one of my students. She was a real pain in the butt, but I'm sorry she's dead."

"I know you are, dear," I said. "Peter will want to ask you some questions about your sessions with her, but he's too busy now. We can talk over dinner."

"What are we having?"

I recognize a trick question when I hear it. If I so much as mentioned *boeuf,* she would claim to have plans to eat at Inez's house, the pizzeria, or possibly the White House. "I'll pick up some fried chicken and biscuits on my way home."

We settled on seven o'clock and ended the call. Jorgeson, who has a vague resemblance to a bulldog, was watching me with an innocent smile. I took the high road and ignored it. "How many suspects do you have? There were at least thirty students here, as well as the board members and staff."

"I could not say, Ms. Malloy. No one has been ruled out."

"I trust that I have," I said.

Once again he gave me that damn smile.

5

Peter was talking to Bartek Grabowski in the back of the lounge. I kept my head down as I went into Keiko's office. Her cheeks were flushed, but she appeared to be over the bouts of emotional outbursts. "Do you know if the police located Gregory?" I asked her.

"I gave them telephone number and address. I also call all the board members. I spoke with Austin, Rick, and Sonya and left messages for the others. What will happen now, Ms. Marroy? Will the police make us closed? What do I tell the students and tutors who will come today?" She began to shred a tissue to add to the pile on her desk.

"The officers outside will explain, and I don't know how long the Literacy Council will be closed. Several days, most likely. One of the students told me that Gregory was afraid of Ludmila. Did you see anything happen between them?"

Keiko's eyes widened as she looked over my shoulder. I reluctantly turned around. Peter was in the doorway, his expression a trifle annoyed. I smiled brightly and said, "Do you need more folders? There might be a sign-in sheet from last night."

"I came to thank you for your assistance, and to let you know that you can leave now. We've found translators. I don't know if I'll be home for dinner." He gave me a little wave as he walked away.

"Home for dinner?" asked Keiko. "I thought he said his name Deputy Chief Losen." She covered her mouth with her hand. "I do not have right to ask you questions, Mrs. Marroy. Please excuse me."

"We're married. I chose not to change my name at this stage of my life." I did not add that at the moment he was Deputy Chief Loser, at least in my mind. "I guess I'll run along. Call me if you need me."

I strolled out into the open area and looked for an excuse to linger. Calmness had settled in after the storm. Unless this was the eye of the hurricane. As I went out to my car, the police officer lifted the yellow tape and told me to have a nice day, ma'am. After a small series of escapades involving the police force, I recognized some of them. They recognized me as well. I was renowned or infamous, depending on one's point of view.

I was too keyed up to go home and curl up with a book. There was no reason to tackle another culinary challenge. My fair-weather husband had so many potential witnesses to question that he might not be home until midnight. I sat in my car until an officer began to approach.

I went to Mucha Mocha for coffee, a blueberry scone, and serious thought. The scattering of occupants on the patio were all texting or tapping on laptops. Gregory, wherever he was, was not skulking in a corner. I sat at a table in the shade. I'd been inside the Farberville Literacy Council four times in less than a week, but I still had very little idea about the dynamics. The structure of the daily schedule was straightforward. Students came and went, as did their tutors. Leslie taught classes and retreated to her office during breaks. Keiko interviewed new students, did the paperwork, and oversaw the program. Gregory came in late but raised money after hours. The board members were hardly omnipresent. I'd seen Sonya there. It had been mentioned that Rick was examining the books, presumably in Gregory's office — which brought me back to what Gregory had told me about the nasty jokes and petty theft. I'd forgotten about it, but I began to wonder if the perp was somehow involved in Ludmila's death. Being an upright citizen devoted to assisting the police whenever possible, I made a mental note to tell Peter about it.

My coffee had cooled by the time I came up with an idea. I have to admit it wasn't among my most brilliant ideas, but I needed to do something. I drove up Thurber Street and turned into the historic district. Miss Parchester's house, shabby but dignified, sat between a restored antebellum manor and a grubby boardinghouse. I went to the front door, smiled as I saw a handwritten sign that advised me to beware of the cats, and knocked. When she didn't answer, I tried to peer through a window, but it was covered with sheers and allowed only a vague view of the dim living room. I knocked again and had started down the steps when the door opened.

"Why, Claire," trilled Miss Parchester, "I wasn't expecting company. Do come in and have some tea. I believe I have some cookies in the pantry. Or would you rather have lunch? I may need to trot to the store unless you have a fondness for canned tomato soup. Do you?"

She was aglow with pleasure, her hands

fluttery and her eyes bright. I felt a pang of guilt, since I'd come to weasel information out of her. I made a second mental note to visit her on a regular basis (monthly, not weekly). "You're so kind, Miss Parchester, but I just wanted to talk with you. I hope I'm not interrupting. I can always come back later."

"I won't hear of it," she said. "Come right in and I'll put on the kettle. There's nothing like a nice cup of tea, is there? Papa preferred his manly drink, of course, but Mama and I loved our tea. You may have to help me find the package of cookies. I don't recall seeing them since before Christmas. Watch out for the cats, dearie. Some of them are skittish."

She continued blithering as I came in and shared the sofa with a limp gray cat. I suggested that we skip the cookies, and then flipped through an old issue of *National Geographic* while she bustled about in the kitchen. A tabby wound around my ankles and sashayed away, swishing its tail. There was a sense of movement in the room that was unnerving, as shadows glided behind furniture and settled in dark corners. I wasn't ailurophobic, but I wasn't overly fond of cats. I forced myself to gaze at a photograph of a tribe of headhunters in

106

Indonesia when I heard an odd noise upstairs. I debated the possibility that Miss Parchester had stashed a gentleman caller in one of the bedrooms, but I had to admit the idea was ludicrous. To the best of my limited knowledge in the field of felinology, cats were incapable of turning doorknobs. I glanced at the top of the staircase. A large black cat with pure evil shining in its eyes stalked to the landing and regarded me as if I were a crunchy chipmunk. It looked capable of anything.

"Is Puddy bothering you?" asked Miss Parchester as she came into the room and set a tea tray on the coffee table. "He awoke in a foul mood this morning. He yowled when I offered him breakfast and has been lurking upstairs ever since. He imagines himself to be a panther on the prowl, but he hasn't had much practice since the exterminator came last month. Lemon or milk, Claire?"

I requested lemon. Once she'd done the hostess routine, I balanced the saucer on my knee and said, "There was a tragedy at the Literacy Council last night. Ludmila Grabowski died after hitting her head on the copy machine. Did you know her?"

"Oh, how sad." She took a sip of tea. "Her grandson must be devastated. The woman was not very nice, I'm sorry to say. She was a bully. Poor little Miao was terrified of her. Ludmila had it in her head that the girl was a spy for the Chinese government. When I came in one morning, Ludmila had Miao backed into a corner and was berating her in Polish. I almost whacked her on the head with my handbag. She deserved it."

My hand quivered as I felt a chill curl down my back. I swallowed and said, "You weren't at the Literacy Council last night, were you? I thought you told me that you tutor in the mornings."

Miss Parchester wasn't all blither, although she seemed to prefer to come across as a genteel Southern lady of a particular age. I knew from past events that she had a keen mind. Her eyes bored into me as she said, "You're absolutely correct, Claire. I tutor Tuesday, Wednesday, and Friday mornings. Miao comes all three mornings. Mudada can only make it once a week, although he attends classes in the evening. He works at an auto repair shop. You haven't met him, have you? He's from Zimbabwe, which I believe used to be Rhodesia. The Limpopo River runs through it." She clasped her hands. "I shall never forget how the Elephant's Child got his trunk on the banks of the great, gray-green, greasy Limpopo River!"

I gave her points for turning the topic from the Farberville Literacy Council to Kipling in less than thirty seconds. "If you were supposed to tutor this morning, why didn't you go?"

"Would you like more tea, Claire? I do feel bad that I cannot offer you a cookie or a biscuit."

"Why didn't you go to the Literacy Council this morning?" I persisted, hoping she would not toss out a diversion about how the camel got its hump or the leopard got his spots.

She refilled her cup and set down the pot. "Miao called earlier and canceled our session. She had some disturbing news from home. She's somewhat hard to understand on the telephone, but I gathered that her grandfather died over the weekend. She's from a village called Tai Po and is making arrangements to go home. The family is Buddhist, so the funeral can go on for forty-nine days. That sounds exhausting."

"Will you take a new student?"

"I doubt it," she said. "I'm an old lady, as much as I hate to say it. I have my garden club and my book club, and I mustn't forget my monthly happy hour with the ladies from my church. Last time we met at the bar across from the Performing Arts Center, and were asked to leave. Ruthie and Adele got into a frightful argument about same-sex marriage. I wish we hadn't ordered that third pitcher of margaritas . . ."

I steeled myself not to envision the scene. I thanked Miss Parchester for the tea and went out to my car, aware I hadn't learned a damn thing except the location of the Limpopo River — the great, gray-green, greasy Limpopo River. I hesitated for a moment, wondering if in some obscure way Miss Parchester had given me a warning not to poke my nose (or trunk) into the investigation.

Surely not.

It was frustrating to be across town from the ongoing activity. Peter would be shuffling people in and out of a makeshift interrogation room. Jorgeson was likely to be in Keiko's office gleaning information from the paperwork. By now officers would have located Gregory and Leslie and brought them in. Caron and Inez would be at the lake. The board members who weren't chained to their desks would be arriving at the Literacy Council. I had a feeling Sonya would handle damage control. Peter would not be pleased if I showed up again.

The library was only a block away. I

decided to assist the police by doing background research on whatever seemed remotely pertinent. I left my car parked in front of Miss Parchester's house and walked down the sidewalk, appreciating the maple trees and fiercely planted flower beds. Once inside, I sat down at a computer and stared at the blank screen.

A white-haired lady in a cardigan appeared beside me. "Having trouble? Perhaps I can be of help." She leaned over me and hit the space bar on the keyboard. "Now I've got you started. Call if you need more help." She wandered away in search of more techno-dummies.

The only help I'd needed was a clue where to start. Earlier in the summer I'd mastered the art of Googling. I started with myself, just as a refresher. After a highly enjoyable half hour of reading about my prowess, I focused on the board members. Austin had rated a photograph in the local newspaper upon being presented with an ADDY Award two years ago for an especially creative series of commercials. Frances North had been named Principal of the Year five years ago and been runner-up twice since then. Drake Whitbream and his wife, Becky, were quite the socialites, meriting photographs at pricey fund-raising events. Rick Lester and

Sonya Emerson had yet to make themselves known to the newspaper's readership.

Wilhelmina Constantine won, hands down, for the most Google hits. She had presided over a trial involving millions of dollars of real estate, ruled in favor of the plaintiffs of a class-action suit over school taxes, dismissed a negligence case against Farber College, and shot down another class action for sexual discrimination at Sell-Mart, the local merchandising behemoth. I doubted that I would agree with her politics.

I moved on to Gregory Whistler. There were plenty of photographs of him accepting checks from civic clubs. He was in a group shot of the board members holding an oversized faux check from the United Way. There were several unfamiliar faces, presumably the board members who were taking summer vacations. Everybody beamed except for Austin, who had his hands in his pockets and a goofy grin on his face. A feature article on the Literacy Council noted the hiring of Gregory Whistler as executive director.

I kept digging until I found the obituary of Rosalind Whistler. The cause of death had been ruled an accident. She'd attended Farber College, as Gregory had mentioned. Her parents were deceased, and she had two siblings, a brother in Oregon and a sister in Iowa. The funeral had been held in a Presbyterian church. That was about it. I was curious about the "accident," which covered everything from falling down the stairs to discovering one's parachute was shredded. It was more likely to be a car wreck.

Going to the library was not among my most brilliant ideas. I walked back to my car and tried to come up with something with more potential. After fifteen minutes of convoluted and useless ideas, it occurred to me that only mad dogs and Englishmen sat in their cars in the midday sun, and I was in danger of perspiring. I prefer blood to sweat. I found a brochure that I'd picked up at the Literacy Council and called the number on my cell phone.

As soon as Keiko chirped, I said, "This is Claire Malloy, but don't say my name out loud, okay?"

"Whatever you say, Mrs. Marroy. You are a kind lady."

I winced. "What's going on there?"

"Much less confusion, but students are not happy. Gregory is not happy, either. He is in his office with Chief Deputy Losen."

"Did the police locate Leslie?"

"No, Mrs. Marroy. They went to her house, but she was not home. Do you think

113

something bad happened to her? She is our best teacher." Keiko sighed. "She is also our only teacher this summer. In the fall we get graduate students from the Education Department at college. It is very funny to watch them sometimes."

"I'm sure it is," I said before she could elaborate. "Do you have Leslie's address? I'll stop by and see if she's home now."

"Yes, Mrs. Marroy. I will have to look for it on my desk. The police wanted much information, and I had to pull many folders out of the drawer." During the lull, I could hear paper shuffling and a word in Japanese that required no translation. "Okay, Mrs. Marroy, I have it. I hope she is not sick." She told me the address, and would have continued had not a male voice asked her a question.

"Thanks." I ended the call before she blurted out my name again, although I had little faith that she wouldn't if anyone asked. The address was in the neighborhood where Caron and I had lived before Prince Charming sprang for my dream castle. I drove by the small yellow house, keeping an eye out for a patrol car in the vicinity. The coast appeared to be clear, but I parked around the corner anyway. It was improbable that Peter would have assigned a plainclothes detec-

tive to stake out her house. She hadn't been at the Literacy Council the previous night.

No car was parked in front of the house or in the driveway, and no one responded to the doorbell. I walked down the driveway to a detached garage with padlocked doors. No windows, but enough weeds to suggest that Leslie had not kept her car inside it. I went back to the porch and pushed the doorbell button. After several more tries, I gave up. As I came down the steps, I saw a young man watching me from the curb. He had long, stringy hair and dirty feet.

He cut me off when I reached the sidewalk. "Who are you?"

"Would you believe me if I said I was a census taker?"

"No," he said. "There have been some burglaries around here lately, some during the day. Why don't you just tell me who you are? Are you a friend of the lady who lives here?"

Not exactly. "Yes," I said firmly, "and I'm worried about her. She didn't show up at the Farberville Literacy Council this morning to teach her classes. Have you seen her?"

He still seemed skeptical. "No. The cops were here earlier, looking for her. I've never seen you around here."

"I'm not a burglar, for pity's sake! I'm a

115

friend of hers. Did you see her last night?"

"Somebody was banging on her door about ten thirty."

"Did you see who it was?" I asked, doing my best not to sound excited. "Male or female, anything like that?"

"I don't spy on my neighbors. Do you think I'd go out to the front yard so I could see who it was? I don't even know the woman, except to say hello when we meet on the sidewalk. For all I know, it could have been you."

"Casing the joint? If I were a burglar, I wouldn't announce my presence, would I? Why don't you run along and snoop around at someone else's house?"

We were not destined to be best friends. He walked across the yard of the house next door, went inside, and slammed the door. I fumed for a moment, thinking of all the amazingly barbed retorts I could have used to squelch him like a bug. A grimy little bug. Once I'd cooled off, I went back down the driveway and into the backyard. Leslie had not been a gardener. The grass was skimpy, and large bushes stood on either side of the back door stoop. I knocked on the door without success. I had no reason to think Leslie was home and merely unwilling to answer the door. Although, I told myself,

she could be inside, so ill that she couldn't get out of bed. She could be crumpled on the floor with a broken leg or even unconscious. On the other hand, her car was missing, which implied that she'd gone somewhere for whatever reason. One possibility was obvious — she was responsible for Ludmila's death. She might be driving toward Mexico or Canada, depending on whether she preferred searing summers or freezing winters. Or her car could be in a chop shop.

The door was locked, and I was not skilled in the genteel art of picking locks with a hairpin (if I'd had such a thing). I looked at the windows. One was slightly open, clearly an invitation to make sure that Leslie was not in a puddle of blood. I dragged a garbage can under the window, did what I could to secure the lid, and then managed to crawl onto it. I finally made it to my feet, clung to the sill until I had my balance, and shoved open the window. Had the garbage can not flipped over under my weight, it would have been quite a display of ingenuity. As it was, I kicked and squirmed my way across the sill and flopped face-first onto a bed, bounced, and rolled onto the floor. I lay still for a moment, listening for gasps from either Leslie or myself. I decided I was unharmed and, I dearly hoped, alone.

Such entrances can be tricky to explain.

Leslie's bedroom was tidy, the bed made and a stack of books aligned on the bedside table. Most people in the act of fleeing don't dally to close drawers or empty the wastebasket. The closet contained dresses, blouses, suits, and a few bare coat hangers. Shoes were in neat pairs on the floor. The only anomaly was one large, worn athletic shoe in a back corner. Leslie had two feet, and neither was apt to fit it. I concluded it had been left by a previous tenant. I declined to examine it, since brown recluse spiders were fond of such residences.

I went out to the hall. The bathroom was as tidy as the bedroom, and there were no splatters of blood in the bathtub or on the floor. Her makeup, toothbrush and toothpaste, and similar items were next to the sink. The living room held no surprises, nor did the kitchen or the small dining room. I returned to the hall and went into the second bedroom, which had been converted into an office. The bookcase held heavy tomes, boxes of supplies, and packages of printer paper. I sat down at the desk and picked up the top folder from a stack of perhaps a dozen. A photograph of a thirty-ish, ebony-skinned man had been stapled to what appeared to be a résumé. I noticed that he was from Zaire and was a graduate student in astrophysics at a university in Arizona. I put aside his folder and picked up the next one. It, too, had a photograph, this one of a swarthy man from Egypt. He was working on a degree in mechanical engineering.

Leslie might be trolling for a husband, I thought, in this case a mail-order groom. As I reached for another folder, I heard the front door open. I reminded myself that I was on a mission of mercy, motivated solely by concern for her welfare. And since there was no place to hide, I was going to have to sell it to Leslie herself. I straightened the folders and hurried out of the office. Leslie stood in the living room, understandably shocked.

"I'm so glad you're okay," I said with an exaggerated sigh of relief. "We were all worried when you didn't come into the Literacy Council this morning, especially after what happened last night. Dreadful, wasn't it? Poor Keiko has been hysterical all morning, and the students —"

"Why are you in my house?"

It was not an unreasonable question. I took a breath, exhaled slowly, and said, "I apologize for sounding like a gibberish monkey. I'm Claire Malloy, Caron's mother.

We met last week when I came in to see about volunteering."

"So why are you in my house?" She sounded more curious than angry.

"As I said, we were worried. My imagination can be overactive at times. I was afraid you were ill or injured and unable to reach a phone."

"So you broke into my house?"

"The doors were locked."

"Yes, I'm always careful about that," she said. "There have been daytime burglaries in the area. I left the window slightly open, didn't I?" I nodded. "How foolish of me. My house isn't packed with expensive electronics, but I'd hate to lose my TV and computer — and my grandmother's silver ice tongs. You never know when you might need silver ice tongs. Come sit down. I'd like to know why everyone is so worried about me."

I told her about Ludmila. "I realize you weren't there last night, but you were scheduled to teach classes this morning. The detectives sent someone earlier to check on you. You weren't here. It was worrisome."

"Or suspicious." Leslie's smile was tepid. "Ludmila was very difficult. I don't know how many times I took her aside after class and warned her that she would not be allowed in my classroom unless she showed respect for her fellow students. Her response was to lapse into Polish and spew out venomous rants. Once she told me I was a slut because I met with one of my private students in my office — with the door closed. I disliked her, but I didn't kill her. Why would I? All I had to do was ban her from my classes. Gregory assured me that I had the right to do so if I chose."

"You have private students?"

"I can't live on my pitiful salary at the Literacy Council. I've been promised a raise when the finances are healthier, but promises don't pay the rent. I teach classes on the Internet, mostly prep for the citizenship test, and a class for grad students to be certified in TESOL. Teaching English to Speakers of Other Languages. I also provide information about the necessary paperwork to extend work and student visas and apply for green cards. I do this from home, but occasionally a local student needs immediate help."

Which explained the folders by her computer, I thought, reluctantly giving up my mail-order-groom theory. "Did someone have an emergency this morning?" I asked.

She grimaced. "I had to go to court this morning. I didn't find out until I got home yesterday afternoon. I called Keiko and left a message on her voice mail." She caught my inquisitive look and added, "I'm in the final stages of a divorce. Amicable, but complicated." She pulled a gold band off her finger and let it clatter on the tabletop. "I haven't worn this for months, but it seemed appropriate today. I haven't decided whether to sell it or throw it in a pond."

"Divorce can be stressful," I said.

"You say this from experience?"

"My first husband saved me the bother by driving off a mountain road. My second is a keeper."

"Good for you." She stood up. "I'd better make an appearance at the Literacy Council so I can be interrogated with rubber hoses and bamboo slivers. I wish I knew something useful, but Ludmila had more enemies than Keiko has shades of fingernail polish."

I hoped I would be ushered out the front door rather than the rear window. As I rose, I tried to come up with a clever way to ask her about her late-night visitor. Cleverness failed me. "Leslie, when I was in your front yard, your neighbor came over and accused me of banging on your door last night at about ten thirty. I assured him that burglars do not case the joint so loudly."

"Charles is paranoid that someone will

122

steal his vintage tie-dyed T-shirts," she said, shaking her head. "If you're asking who came by last night, I might as well tell you. My husband wanted to dissuade me from going through with the divorce. I didn't want to talk to him, so I stayed in my office." She opened the door for me. "Let's have lunch sometime."

"Sure," I said, although I doubted either of us would pursue it.

I went back to my car and sat. Minutes later, Leslie drove by. Students were walking both toward the campus and away from it as the bell tower began to chime. Ninety percent of them had cell phones plastered to their heads. I tried to imagine how they'd react if they had to entertain themselves with only their thoughts.

My wry smile vanished when I saw red and blue lights flashing in the rearview mirror. I turned around and saw a police car parked behind me. An unfamiliar officer, a stocky man with beady eyes, approached cautiously, his hand on the holster of his gun. I stuck my head out the window and said, "Is something wrong, Officer? The only things I might be guilty of are reckless daydreaming and failure to yield to technology."

He did not appreciate my wit. "License

and registration, ma'am."

I was bewildered, to say the least. "Have I done something wrong? This is a legal parking space, and all I was doing was sitting here." His lips pinched, so I pulled out my registration and insurance card, and then fumbled in my purse for my wallet. "Here," I said as I handed them to him. "What's this about?"

"A citizen reported that you were behaving in a suspicious manner. There have been some —"

"Burglaries in the neighborhood," I cut in. "Please explain precisely what I did that can be construed as 'behaving in a suspicious manner.' I stopped by to visit an acquaintance. After she left for her office, I returned here and was pondering what to fix for dinner. Feel free to search my car for lock picks, skeleton keys, crowbars, and whatever else burglars need to ply their trade."

"You need to come down to the station, ma'am. Please get out of your vehicle."

"I most certainly will not," I said, "until you tell me on what grounds you're dragging me to the police station."

His lips pinched tighter. "I have no intention of dragging you anywhere. Why don't you get out of your car so that I can drive you to the station? If necessary, I will arrest you for failure to comply with my directive. I've been told that our handcuffs are uncomfortable."

I bit my lower lip to stop myself from saying, "Do you know who I am?" in a voice so laden with ice that the officer might be in danger of frostbite. However, I had vowed to myself before I married Peter that I would never play the role of Her Ladyship in these situations. "All right," I said as I got out of the car, made sure it was locked, and allowed the officer to open the back door of his vehicle. The redolence was a revolting miasma of vomit, urine, and sweat.

"Have you been with the Farberville Police Department long?" I asked pleasantly through the mesh.

"Couple of weeks. Transferred here from Speevy when my daughter got accepted at the college. She's gonna live at home so she doesn't get into trouble."

It occurred to me that the officer might get into a spot of trouble at the PD. He was not the only one in peril. Someone might feel obliged to call Deputy Chief Rosen. Or worse, Deputy Chief Rosen would be at the PD. I had a feeling he would not buy my story of stopping by the old neighborhood to drink in the nostalgia. On the day we moved, I'd practically loaded the moving van by myself. One thing would lead to another, and when we got around to breaking into Leslie's house, it would not be jovial.

"Officer, would you please pull over for a moment? I'd like to talk to you before we arrive at the police department," I said.

"You're saying you want to talk? Maybe you mean negotiate."

"Yes, that's the word. You see, I have this sort of relationship with —"

"You want me to run you in for solicitation and attempted bribery?" he asked in a very unfriendly voice. "I don't know how they do things around here, but no officer in Speevy accepted sexual favors in exchange for dismissing charges. You ought to be ashamed of yourself!"

"I said no such thing!" I sputtered, my face hot with indignation. "How dare you accuse me of solicitation! I should sue you for slander, Officer Speevy!"

"You just do that, little lady." Snickering, he pulled into the parking lot of the PD. As soon as he opened the back door, I scrambled out and marched toward the entrance. He yelled something at me as I went inside, but I was in no mood for further conversation with him.

The desk sergeant glanced up at me. I saw the recognition in her eyes as she stepped back, as though my visage adorned a MOST WANTED poster on the wall behind her. "Ms. Malloy," she squeaked. "Can I help you?"

"Book her for resisting arrest and stick her in the cage until I write up the report," said my chauffeur. "Yeah, and do a strip search while you're at it. I'll bet you ten bucks she has a record longer than my arm."

I remained silent. The desk sergeant licked her lips, cleared her throat, and at last said, "Ms. Malloy, would you mind having a seat on the bench for just a moment? Officer, I need to have a word in private with you. Let's use the office behind me."

That was the last time I saw Officer Speevy.

6

A taciturn officer gave me a ride back to my car. Leslie's nosy neighbor had retreated under his rock. I drove slowly by his house in hopes of spotting something remotely felonious. Alas, there was nary a scrap of litter in the stubby brown grass. I reminded myself that I was not a vengeful person, tossed my chin, and headed to the Book Depot.

Jacob had arranged the front window with a beach umbrella, a plastic bucket and shovel, a poster that offered half price on "summer blockbusters," and said books propped on brightly colored beach towels. He was dusting a rack of paperbacks as I sailed by and into my office. I thumbed through a couple of publishers' catalogs but found nothing that intrigued me. Eventually, Jacob would study them intently, fill out an order form, and, after a shrug from me, order the books online. I was peripheral.

To my annoyance, I was also on the periphery of the murder investigation. Under duress, Peter had said that I'd never interfered, but we both knew his statement might as well have been written on an ice cube. I couldn't return to the Literacy Council under any circumstances. Had it been on fire, I would not be admitted if I were carrying a fire extinguisher. If it flooded, there was no point in showing up with a mop and a bucket.

I did know who had a mop and bucket, though. Toby Whitbream, the indentured janitor, might have been the last person to leave the Literacy Council — with the conspicuous exception of Ludmila Grabowski. Peter would already have that information and would have sent someone to collect Toby, so there was no reason for me to drive by the high school football field on the obscure chance the illustrious quarterback was throwing passes to phantom teammates.

Everyone who might be involved in Ludmila's death was unavailable. My attempt to run background checks had resulted in superficial information. To get specifics, I needed to ask questions. At which point I asked myself the obvious one: Why was I so determined to solve the murder? I hadn't liked the victim, and I didn't especially care about any of the suspects. The crime itself had probably been an accident. Ludmila encountered someone in the copy room. An argument escalated into a shoving match. Ludmila bounced off the copy machine, smashing her skull. The second party panicked and tried to hide the body. It was a credible scenario, as long as I could concoct a reason for either of them to be in the dusty little room.

I forced myself to return to the question I'd posed. I tried the high road: Murder was a despicable crime and justice must prevail. I moved along to the middle road: The Literacy Council provided invaluable help to nonnative speakers and promoted community harmony. Caron and Inez were volunteers, and so was I (although I'd been railroaded). The low road was rocky: The glamour of French cuisine was fading fast, and I could read only so much poetry in the meadow before I started stalking field mice.

Jacob came to the office doorway. "Is there anything I can do for you, Ms. Malloy? Would you like me to fetch you a salad or sandwich from the café up the block?"

"No, thank you." I stood up and picked up my purse. "Good job on the window,

Jacob. I'll stop by later in the week." I went out to my car. Food had more uses than appeasing a rumbling stomach, I thought as I started the car. It could provide an excellent excuse for intrusion.

I stopped at the grocery store, drove home, and settled down to create a masterful rendition of *coq au vin.* Once I'd stuck it in the oven, I indulged in a long bath. Afterward, I applied makeup and dressed in an appropriately subdued blouse and skirt. I took the dish out of the oven and let it cool, then transferred it to a ceramic serving bowl with a lid, sprinkled some parsley, and stepped back to admire my work. By now, it was late afternoon, the decorous time to make a condolence call.

I knew from reading Ludmila's folder that Bartek Grabowski lived near the college football stadium, a popular area for faculty and retirees. The house was located on a wooded side street but within earshot of Saturday afternoon stadium pandemonium. Clutching the dish, I went to the front porch and rang the bell. Moments later, Professor Grabowski opened the door. He was dressed in a T-shirt and shorts, his feet bare, and was holding a highball glass.

"I've seen you somewhere," he said, confused. "Are you in one of my classes?

No, that's not right. Were you at Pashaw's party last month?"

Had my ego been vulnerable, I would have been deflated. "We spoke this morning at the Literacy Council. I'm the one who called your cell phone and left the message about your grandmother."

"That's it!" He smiled at me. "Please come in. I'm afraid I don't remember your name."

"I'm Claire Malloy, a member of the board of directors." It was true, although hardly as impressive as it sounded. "I came by to express our condolences on the death of your grandmother. This is *coq au vin.*"

"How kind of you, Claire." He took the dish and led me through the living room and kitchen to a screened-in porch. "Please make yourself comfortable on the wicker sofa. May I offer you a glass of wine or something hardier? What would you prefer?"

"Iced tea, if you have it," I said. During my illustrious endeavors to solve crimes, I had been met on doorsteps with animosity. Gaining entrance to his house seemed almost too easy. If he was mourning the loss of his grandmother, he was disguising his grief very well. I suspected that the cocktail in his hand had not been his first, nor would it be his last. Maybe it was a Polish tradition to drown one's sorrow.

"Here we go," Bartek said as he put down a glass and sat down across from me. "I often see deer at this time of day. It's so peaceful here."

"But perhaps not as peaceful after your grandmother arrived from Poland."

He grimaced. "That is an understatement worthy of a gold medal. She yapped and griped and lectured me morning and night. Luckily, it was all in Polish so I never understood a word of it." He took a sip of his drink and leaned back. "I pretended I had office hours and faculty meetings every night just so I wouldn't have to put up with Babcia. I suppose I should shed a tear."

"Why did you bring her over from Poland?" I asked.

"The last of her old friends died. They were sharing an apartment, and Babcia could no longer pay the rent. I was her only living relative, she informed me in a convoluted letter, and therefore had an obligation to take care of her. I fell for it. Of course, I hadn't seen her for thirty-odd years. I was ten or eleven when my parents took me to Bialystok to meet the family. I remembered that Babcia was brusque, but I didn't remember being frightened of her. I must have been one dumb kid. Anyway, after I made her flight reservations, I flew to New York to meet her. I could hear her squawking as she went through customs." He looked down and shook his head. "What an idiot I was. I should have sent her money every month so she could keep the apartment. No, I decided to do the noble thing and take care of her in her old age. My life has been hell for the last year."

"Well, it was the noble thing," I said, "if not the brightest. Why do you think she was so angry at everybody? Could it have been an early sign of dementia?" I figured I might as well be blunt.

"I thought of that. You wouldn't believe how hard it is to find a gerontologist who speaks Polish. I finally found a woman in Tulsa and dragged Babcia to see her. I sat in the waiting room. Later the doctor told me that Babcia was angry because she felt isolated, and prescribed an antidepressant." He laughed. "She might as well have suggested Babcia take up tennis or ballet. Even when Babcia complained about her arthritis, she refused to take an aspirin. She accused me of trying to poison her when I gave her the antidepressants. I did what I could to find ways for her to occupy her time, with mixed results. Did you hear about the senior citizens center?" Without waiting for a response, he took our glasses into the house for refills.

I watched a mockingbird attack a squirrel. As loath as I was to anthropomorphize nature's nasty little creatures, I couldn't help remembering Ludmila's reputed hostility toward Gregory. When Bartek returned, I said, "Why did your grandmother have it in for the Literacy Council director? From what I heard, she verbally assaulted him whenever she saw him."

He frowned. "Whistler, right? I have no clue. Keep in mind that Babcia almost always spoke to me in Polish. My father was a biochemist and moved here for a postgrad degree. My mother was American. I was born in Philadelphia and studied French in high school. Since I know about ten words in Polish, Babcia and I did not communicate well. Yeah, I saw her shouting at him when I picked her up in the late afternoon. She sputtered and cursed all the way home."

"Did she have any friends?"

Bartek thought for a minute. "There was one old guy at the senior citizens center who spoke some Polish. I don't know his name. Sometimes they would be playing dominoes when I arrived. White hair, cane, thick glasses with black rims. I had visions of them shacked up in a nursing home, terrorizing the staff, hording denture cream, and copulating like crazy."

I willed myself not to share his vision. "Maybe Ludmila confided in him."

"Maybe."

I was about to ask him about the previous evening when the doorbell rang. Bartek nodded at me, then went inside. I heard voices as he admitted visitors — female voices. I was relieved. It might have been uncomfortable if Peter had come by and discovered me drinking Bartek's iced tea on the deck. He would not have been diverted by the *coq au vin* on the kitchen counter. I stood up as Bartek escorted two women out to the deck. He introduced them as a colleague and his secretary. Each was bearing a covered dish, although I assumed the dishes were more likely to be commonplace casseroles than *haute cuisine.* The doorbell rang again. I patted Bartek on the arm before I slipped through the arriving visitors and made it to my car. I noticed that the majority of them were women. With Babcia out of the picture, Bartek might have become the most eligible man in the department.

I dutifully picked up a bucket of fried chicken on my way home. Caron and Inez were in the pool, conversing in low voices. I announced my arrival, changed into a caftan, and took the newspaper out to my chaise longue. I was sighing over the sorry state of the country when the girls joined me.

"Well?" demanded Caron. "What happened?"

I told them the basic story. "You two are in the clear unless you snuck into the Literacy Council to search the files for lesson plans. The board of directors met and adjourned, but I didn't see any of them leave the building. Students and tutors were in cubicles. There was a class in session and activity in the lounge. Fifty people could have been there, for all I know."

Inez regarded me with the solemnity of an owlet. "So somebody stayed behind after the closing time."

"Or came in a few minutes later," I said.

Caron gasped. "You mean Toby Whitbream? Why would he murder some old Polish lady? He wouldn't have paid any attention if she was screaming at him in Polish. I didn't — not that she screamed at me. She tended to get sort of excited when I didn't understand her English. A couple of times her face turned so red that I waited for her head to explode. Like I wanted to be covered in blood and brains."

137

"Perhaps Toby isn't as patient as you," I said evenly.

My daughter deigned to overlook my jibe. "She criticized the way he vacuumed, so he waited until she went into the copy room to steal an umbrella from the lost and found, then tackled her. Gee, I wonder why Peter hasn't figured it out by now. Shall I call him?"

"It wasn't raining," Inez volunteered.

"No, it wasn't," I said, "and it was obvious that Toby didn't consider the copy room to be part of his nightly routine. The only thing in there that isn't covered with dust is the copy machine."

"Everybody uses it," Inez said. "Not the students, but the tutors, Leslie, and Keiko are in there all the time. I made copies of some recipes because Graciela loves to cook. Aladino is reading a Hardy Boys book. I make an enlarged copy of each page so he can make notes. I'm sure Caron does that sort of thing, too."

"Yeah, all the time," Caron said. "But there's no reason to suspect Toby of anything. He's the starting quarterback this fall. He made some All-American high school football players list last year. Ashley heard that college scouts will be at our games. Is that not cool?"

"Very cool." I picked up the newspaper, and the girls went upstairs to Caron's room. After a while, I began to feel hungry. I set out food and called the girls. Since they had no plans (Joel was visiting his grandmother), we carried our plates into the living room and wept companionably through an old movie.

"At least I don't have to tutor today," Caron said as she joined me on the terrace the next morning. "Plus I'm down to three students unless Leslie sticks me with somebody else. Nobody can be more of a pain in the butt than Ludmila. I know I shouldn't talk about her like that, but every minute with her was like tiptoeing on lava. Well, not every minute. Once she was nice."

"She was?"

"I think, and I might have been wrong, that it was somebody's birthday. She had some photos of a kid in a silly hat, blowing out two candles. The photos were really old and faded. The same kid with a stuffed animal, another with him asleep in an old lady's arms. I asked Ludmila if these were of her grandson, but she said no. What she really said was *nie,* but I figured it out. Just think, my first Polish word. I picked up some other ones, but they're apt to be obscenities. I guess I could get away with them as long as I don't run into any Poles. 'Rhonda, you are a *gwizdek*!' "

"What's the fun in that if she doesn't know what you're calling her? She might think it's Polish for 'gorgeous model.' Let's go back to these photographs. Could the old lady have been Ludmila?"

"If she'd shrunk six inches and lost a hundred pounds since the photo was taken. Oh, and had a mole on her chin removed — and rhinoplasty. No, Mother, it was somebody else. Ludmila got all teary, though. She started crooning to the picture of the baby. It was creepy."

"Sounds like it," I said. "Do you remember anything else she said?"

Caron looked at me. "It was in Polish. How much would you remember?"

"Not much," I said with a sigh. "Is Inez still asleep?"

"She left an hour ago. She has an appointment with an optometrist to get contacts. I didn't know contacts could be half an inch thick. It's really annoying. We've got the whole day ahead of us, and she'll be tied up all morning. I guess I'll text Carrie and Ashley." She trudged inside on her way to the dungeon on the second floor, doomed to several hours of potential solitude.

140

I pondered her story about Ludmila and the photos of a young child. Bartek had told me he was her only living relative. From Caron's description of Ludmila's behavior, it seemed likely that the small child had not thrived. It might not be relevant, I thought as I sipped coffee. I doubted that Peter, who'd come home at midnight and departed seven hours later, would have given the photos a second glance. He had witnesses and evidence from the crime scene, as well as the ability to run background checks. I had an anonymous old man who spoke some Polish. For lack of anything more promising, I concluded it was time to track down Ludmila's only friend.

The senior citizens center was housed in a stark concrete-block building painted beige. Armed with a description that probably fit ninety percent of the male patrons, I charged ahead. The large, open room was dotted with card tables and chairs. Sofas and easy chairs were arranged in front of a TV set. A dozen people were yelling at a game show contestant who was floundering. Their language was colorful. In another corner, a tense game of bingo was in progress. There were a couple of checkers games being waged, and a bridge game in one corner. It was a busy place.

141

I went into the office by the door. The woman seated at a desk looked up and said, "Can I help you?"

"I'm looking for an elderly gentleman with white hair, glasses, and a cane," I said. "I don't know his name, but he speaks Polish."

"Why?"

I'd been hoping for a warmer reception. "A friend of his passed away yesterday. I thought he would want to know."

She made a vague gesture with her hand. "If you knew his name, I could check the list to see if he's here today. In case you didn't notice, there are at least a dozen men with glasses and canes. I've never heard any Polish spoken here."

"I know he was using this facility a year ago. I'm hoping he's still around."

"You mean alive?" she said, her eyebrows raised.

I'd kept that possibility buried in the back of my mind. "Yes, I guess that's what I mean."

"Even if I knew the man, I wouldn't give you his name. We protect the privacy of our patrons. However, I've only worked here for three months, and we don't keep files on who comes on a regular basis." She picked up a pen and looked at me. "Now I really must work on these invoices. It's clear that we're being overcharged for fresh produce, and I need to get to the bottom of it before we put in next week's order."

I had been dismissed. I returned to the main room and assessed my chances of finding someone more helpful than the woman in the office. The TV viewers were infuriated at the game show contestant; their children would have been appalled at their language. Those playing checkers and bridge were stony-faced. I ambled over to the bingo tables and sat down next to a woman in a bright orange dress, matching hair, dangly earrings, and a half-dozen bracelets on each arm. She had four bingo cards in front of her and a tubular object in her hand.

"Shit!" she said as the caller announced an apparently ineffectual number. "You'd think there's a ball with B-twelve on it, but it must be buried at the bottom. Look at this — I can make two bingos with one lousy B-twelve. But no, it's B-eleven and B-thirteen and B-three." The caller announced another number, and the woman smacked two of her cards with what I realized was a stamper.

A birdlike woman at the next table shouted, "Bingo! I win, I win!"

My newfound best friend put down her weapon. "Now we wait for a ten-minute bathroom break. My name's Shirley. You're a little young to be hanging around here, aren't you?"

I introduced myself. "I'm trying to find someone who was here last year. The woman in the office wasn't any help."

"Her name is Mrs. Bell," Shirley said, "but we call her Bela Lugosi. She gets a constipated look on her face if someone dares to ask her the time. She's lasted longer than we expected. I lost ten bucks when she made it to six weeks. In another week, she'll have been here three months. Old Carlyle is going to win because he's a damn fool."

"What about Mrs. Bell's predecessor?"

"Four weeks."

"Do you happen to know who the director was a year ago?"

Shirley laughed. "Good Lord, no. They come and go, rarely speaking of Michelangelo. Sorry, I was a high school English teacher before I retired. I've been coming here on and off for five or six years, but only for the bingo tournaments. We all buy our cards, and the money goes to the winners. Last week I won fifty bucks."

I hoped no one on the vice squad retired soon. "Do you recall a short Polish woman named Ludmila? She did not play well with others and was told not to come back."

"I encountered her once, and that was once too often. What a bitch." She looked at the patrons milling around the bingo tables. "Simon! Haul your sorry ass over here. This woman needs information."

Simon was lanky and frail, but he moved quickly. "Shirley, still your charming self. If you meet me in the broom closet for a quickie, I'll give you a dollar. Now if this lady" — he pointed at me — "is willing, I'll give her ten. She's a hottie."

"Hush, you old goat. Do you remember a Polish woman named Ludmila who was here a while back? She got expelled for bad behavior."

Simon sat down with us. "I do. I accidentally brushed up against her butt, and I thought she was gonna rip off my ears. I hid in the men's room for over an hour, till Farley came in and told me she was gone. I stayed another half hour on account of Farley being such a liar. And don't ever play checkers with him. Every time I glance away, two or three of his men have hopped across the board like big round fleas."

"I was told that Ludmila had a friend here," I said before we delved further into Farley's devilish deeds. "A man with glasses, white hair, and a cane. They played dominoes together."

Shirley whacked Simon on the arm. "Don't go whining that you don't remember. You don't have any problems remembering every last nickel you won from me playing cribbage."

"Let me think about it, okay?" Simon hobbled toward the men's room.

"Old goat," Shirley said with a sniff. "Why are you so all-fired interested in this Ludmila woman? Instead of finding her, you'd be better off hiding from her."

"She died Monday night," I said, "and I'd like to break the news to her friend. Her only friend. I feel sorry for her, in a way. Her old friends in Poland all died, so she moved to Farberville to live with her grandson. He couldn't stand her, either. Her anger must have come from a painful sense of isolation and loneliness."

"That's all very touching, but she didn't smack you on the rear end with an umbrella. She bawled me out for blocking the door. I wasn't anywhere near the door. She was damn lucky I restrained myself." She curled one arm behind her head and jabbed the stamp at me. "I took fencing in college."

Simon rejoined us. "Yeah, I recollect the man. Name was Duke, Duke Kovac, but he wasn't Polish. One of those other Slavic countries or Russia. He was about the only person she didn't try to bully. Maybe that's why he put up with her. God only knows what they talked about, the two of them. He was a regular guy, friendly, helluva poker player."

My tummy tightened as he continued to speak of good old Duke in the past tense. I moistened my lips and said, "Is he still alive?"

"Far as I know," Simon said. "Not long ago he upped and married a waitress with some ridiculous name like Bunny or Fluffy. Haven't seen him since, but I got a Christmas card last year. He enclosed a photo of the two of them on a ski slope. His face was redder than a candy apple."

I dearly hoped Duke's health had not deteriorated over the last several months. I squeezed Shirley's hand, then leaned over and kissed Simon on the cheek. My superior reflexes saved me from his unexpected lunge for my bosom. Shirley was scolding him as I left the senior citizens center with a grin on my face. I had a name. What's more, I had no reason to share it with Peter. He would merely look at me if I proposed he investigate the cause of Ludmila's anger. Fingerprints and hair follicles were tangible clues; emotions were irrelevant. I would receive nary a word of praise for my diligence.

On to the next step, which was hunting down Duke Kovac and his wife. I drove by the Literacy Council, still barricaded with yellow tape. The lights were on inside, and I could see movement in Keiko's office. One of the cars was an official police vehicle, the other nondescript. Detectives used their own cars. I weighed my chances of being permitted inside and decided the odds were very, very poor. I continued on to the Book Depot, waved at Jacob as I went to my office, and pulled out the telephone directory. Caron had scoffed when I'd used one in the past, pointing out the information was readily available online. I preferred my reading material to involve paper and ink.

I found a listing for Dusan Kovac, clearly my man (since there were no other Kovacs in the directory). The address was on the mountain flanking the east side of town, where the swankier houses were nestled among vast lawns and flowering trees. Duke must have done well for himself, I thought as I copied down the address. I wasn't quite sure which winding lane I wanted, so I went into the front of the store. Jacob watched me from behind a thick tome.

"Will you please pull up a map online that shows this address?" I asked.

"I would prefer not to."

I sucked in a deep breath and exhaled slowly, struggling to control my temper. Jacob had pulled that nonsense on me in the past, and it was getting stale. "I have no interest in what you would or would not prefer to do," I said carefully. "I can promise you that if you ever say that phrase again, there will be an ad in the classifieds seeking a new clerk. I'm not kidding, Jacob. I am trying to assist the police by locating a potential witness, and I'm not in the mood to play games." I stared at him until he blinked.

"What's the address?" He moved in front of the computer.

I read it aloud, and he clicked on this and that for a brief moment. "Here," he said, "the blinking dot."

It would have been rude to chortle at the defeat in his voice. I came around the counter, traced the streets that led up the mountainside, and determined the quickest route. "Thank you," I said.

"Anytime, Ms. Malloy," he said in utter despondency, as if he'd betrayed every member of his family from great-grandmother to newborn nephew. I probably should have lingered to console him, but I was on a mission and dared not break my momentum. It had taken less than an hour to acquire Duke's name, and a fraction of that for his address.

I maneuvered through the streets and headed for the mountain. The roads curled this way and that, but there was no traffic. The husbands were at their offices, and their wives at their health clubs. The children who were not at camps were scattered across town for their swimming lessons, music lessons, golf lessons, tennis lessons, and any other lessons their mothers could find to keep them occupied elsewhere. After a couple of spontaneous explorations that led to cul-de-sacs, I found Duke's house on top of the mountain.

It was far from modest. I noticed a double garage with a smaller garage beside it. I envisioned a golf cart careening across the immense yard, swerving around the trees and brick-lined flower beds. I parked in the empty driveway and went to the porch. Fingers crossed, I rang the doorbell. The opening notes of Beethoven's Fifth reverberated inside. I waited a moment and pushed the doorbell again and was treated to the same sonorous melody.

I had been too excited to prepare myself

for a major setback. In TV series, the suspects always answered the door. Duke wasn't a suspect, granted, but he should have answered the door all the same. Irritated, I tried again. Duke was retired, I told myself in a grumpy voice, and I doubted his wife was still waiting tables. The neighbors' houses were so far away that I would have required the golf cart to borrow a cup of sugar. Clearly, my witness had chosen to be uncooperative. I went to my car and found a piece of paper. I wrote a message telling him that I had some news about Ludmila and asking him to call me, added my name and telephone number, and stuck it between the screen and the door.

Having run out of leads, I went home. Caron came downstairs while I was fixing myself a sandwich. "Want one?" I asked.

"What is it — fish eggs and watercress? Yuck." She opened the refrigerator and took out the leftover chicken. "Is there any chance you'll get into Italian cooking? Spaghetti's pretty hard to mess up. So's pizza, but you'd put all sorts of weird stuff like zucchini, radishes, and truffles on it. Forget I said anything."

We sat at the marble-topped island and ate. I was trying to come up with a theory that was remotely plausible, but I would have had more success doing a crossword puzzle in Polish. It boiled down to who was at the Literacy Council after it closed. Ludmila, obviously. Bartek said that when he got there to pick up his grandmother, the building was lit but unoccupied.

"You're not planning dinner, are you?" asked Caron.

"Just thinking about Ludmila's murder." The previous evening when I'd told the girls about the crime, I'd omitted my visit to Bartek's house. I repeated as much of the conversation as I could, then described my adventure at the senior citizens center. "I was lucky that I sat down next to Shirley," I continued.

"Orange hair? Really?" Caron wrinkled her nose. "I would have run the other way. Some horny old guy tried to feel you up? That place doesn't sound very wholesome, if you ask me. They should all be sedated."

"And sit in a stupor watching soap operas? Think of the money the center could save if it served only gruel and little cups of gelatin."

Caron's eyes narrowed. "That's not what I meant."

"I think it is," I said. "Why don't you go offer to volunteer until the Literacy Council is open? You might discover that life doesn't end at sixty-five or seventy-five or ninety or a hundred and three."

"Or so you hope." She put her plate in the sink. "What's the name of this guy you're looking for? Maybe I can help."

I realized her offer was an apology. "Dusan Kovac, also known as Duke. He lives on Belvedere Drive."

She scampered upstairs. I put away food and stuck the plates in the dishwasher. I was refilling my glass with iced tea when Caron bounded downstairs like an overgrown puppy. "Got it!" she said. "I know where you can find the Duke guy."

I must admit I was impressed.

7

According to something Caron called Face-
book, Duke Kovac played in a darts tournament every Wednesday afternoon at Farberville's ersatz British pub. I parked behind
Luanne's vintage clothing store and walked
down the alley to the front entrance of the
Tainted Frog. Since summer school was in
session at Farber College, there were only a
few students at the bar. I heard loud laughter from the back of the room. The booths
were crowded and the tabletops littered
with mugs and bottles. The middle area was
clear so that the dart players were less likely
to do physical damage to the onlookers.
Several of said dart players were swaying as
they stood behind a man with a plaid cap. I
spotted an unoccupied table in the corner
and hastily took refuge. Darts and drinks
seemed like a potentially lethal combina-
tion.

I watched as the players, mostly older men

with white hair and glasses, threw darts at a pockmarked dartboard. A couple of college boys attempted to show off their skill, resulting in brays of laughter and derisive hoots. One woman with waist-length gray hair nailed her dart, to laudatory whoops. I became aware that bull's-eyes were less vital than other spots, but the rules were as elusive as those of cricket. I doubted anyone wanted to explain them to me. Which is not to imply I wanted them explained.

I was considering how best to determine which player was Duke when the man in the plaid cap sat down. He had shaggy white hair, glasses, a red nose, and yellowed teeth below his trimmed mustache. "Looking for me?" he asked, grinning.

"I don't know."

"I'm Duke, and you're a friend of Ludmila's, right? I found your note. What's the poor cow been up to these days? Don't tell me she wrote a threatening letter to the president. I warned her about that."

"I'm afraid I have some bad news," I said. "Ludmila died Monday night."

He winced. "I'm sorry to hear that. Excuse me for a minute. I'm up after this guy from the Ukraine. He fancies himself to be the best in town, so I need to teach him a lesson."

155

I paid more attention to the spectators. Most of them were elderly, dressed shabbily, and spoke with heavy accents. Farberville seemed to be a popular destination for immigrants of all ages, from the cheeky Asian girls at the Literacy Council to Duke and his buddies. I realized how insulated I was. The only books in a foreign language available at the Book Depot were on the reading lists at the college. Requests for them were almost always followed by pleas for the translations.

Duke plopped back down in the chair. "Nikita is only pretending to be drunk, damn his soul. Now what's this about Ludmila? What happened? Did she have a heart attack or a stroke?"

"The police suspect she was murdered."

He mulled this over for a minute. "Why would I be surprised? Ludmila was very difficult to get along with. Somewhere deep in her subconscious she believed that everyone spoke Polish, but we'd all conspired to pretend we didn't. It's not so crazy as it sounds. When I came to this country fifty-three years ago, I spoke only Slovakian. I couldn't understand anybody, or read a newspaper, or go to a movie. I was convinced that as soon as I left the room, everybody reverted to Slovakian. I used to put down the newspaper, then snatch it up to catch it before it changed. When my English got better, so did I. Ludmila didn't want to learn more English. She thought she was too old. Maybe she was."

I smiled sympathetically, but I was much more interested in what she had told him over the domino games. "Did she ever show you some photos?"

"One moment, please." He returned to the dart game. This time he was cheerful when he resumed his seat. "My weary old eyes have not failed me. What were you asking me?"

"Old photos of a young child, possibly two years of age."

"Little Jozef," he said, nodding. "He was her friend's great-grandson back in Bialystok. The child died at a young age." Duke pulled off his hat to scratch his head. "Some disease. I can't remember exactly what she said, and keep in mind that I don't speak Polish. Slovakian has many similar words. I got maybe seventy percent of what she said. I didn't recognize the word for this disease." A group in front of the dart board began cheering, stomping their feet and poking other competitors. "It seems my team has won, so I must drink toasts and say rude things to the losers. Thank you for telling me about Ludmila. Is there to be a funeral?"

"I don't know, but I will get in touch with you if I find out." I watched him join his teammates, who were as thrilled as Olympic gold medalists, and went back through the bar. I'd wasted most of the day trying to find out more about Ludmila and the source of her bad temper. I'd gotten nowhere. Maybe she was just plain mean.

It was the middle of the afternoon. I went into a coffee shop and emerged with a bag of pastries. I parked in the visitors lot at the Farberville Police Department and carried my offering inside. The desk sergeant gave me a startled look.

"Is there another problem, Ms. Malloy?" she asked.

"I dropped by to see my husband," I said cheerfully. "I saw his car outside. Is he in his office?" She nodded. I walked to the back of the building, where the bigwigs had their offices. Middlewigs did not merit windows. Peter's door was closed, and he looked annoyed when I came inside.

"I thought you might need a break," I said. "The pastries may be stale, but they're better than those chemical things in the vending machine."

"You went to see Bartek Grabowski."

I made myself as comfortable as possible

in a straight-backed chair. "It was a condolence call. I took a covered dish and expressed my sympathy for his loss. Shortly after that, friends from his department began to arrive, so I left. Do you want the blueberry scone or the banana nut muffin?"

"Since when do you make condolence calls on strangers?" Peter said, waving away the bag. "You spoke to the man for all of two minutes yesterday morning."

I was not amused. "I went there as a representative of the Literacy Council. I *am* on the board of directors, as you know. Do you have a problem with this?" It was a silly question, in that he was frowning at me in a most unfriendly fashion. I took the blueberry scone out of the bag and began to nibble on it.

"All you said was that you were sorry for his loss? I know you better than that, Claire. A lot better than that. Did you learn anything you might want to pass along?"

"He loathed his grandmother, but so did pretty much everybody else. Could he have killed her? He claimed he arrived at the Literacy Council after it had closed, assumed Ludmila took the bus home, and when she wasn't there, thought she had spent the night with a friend. I'd be curious to know who he had in mind. Ludmila wasn't up for any awards for congeniality. From what I've gathered, she was a holy terror."

Peter relented enough to extract a muffin. "Leaving anything out?"

I shot back an offended look. "Why would you accuse me of that? Yesterday morning you admitted that I never interfere and have been quite helpful. Now you're asking me if I'm impeding the investigation?" I kept my chin up in a display of indignation until he began to chuckle. My facade collapsed. "Okay, she had a friend from the senior citizens center. His name is Dusan Kovac, and he goes by Duke. I have his address in my purse." I fluttered my eyelashes at him. "Surely Farberville's finest already know about Duke. That's why I didn't bother to mention him."

"But you bothered to hunt him down," Peter said.

"Well, yes, I wanted to save you the trouble. All he told me was Ludmila was very unhappy, which we already knew, and that she carries around old photos of a child who died in Poland years ago."

"Her son?"

"The great-grandson of one of her friends. The child's name was Jozef. He died of an illness, but Duke couldn't translate the Polish word. I don't see how it can have anything to do with the murder, unless Jozef rose from the dead, applied for a travel visa, and found a fake passport."

"Homeland Security would not allow an unescorted zombie toddler into the country. Those guys have no sense of whimsy. I need to get back to these statements. It's going to be another long night, so don't wait up."

I went around the desk and sat down in his lap. A moment later he disengaged my arms and said, "Run along, Claire. By that, I mean go home, have a nice dinner, and pine for me until I stumble in at midnight."

"Sounds like a plan." I left the remaining pastries for him, smiled at the desk clerk, and went out to my car. It was too early to put on pajamas, I thought as I drove up Thurber Street. Since my husband was occupied, it might be time for a dalliance.

I took out my cell phone and the FLC brochure.

Rick Lester had an understandably puzzled expression as he sat down across from me at a picnic table in the beer garden. We exchanged greetings and then waited while he ordered a pitcher from the waitress. "This doesn't seem like your kind of place," he said. "I can picture you in the bar of a fancy restaurant, drinking something pastel and eating caviar on toast points." He traced a peace sign carved in the tabletop. "Is it possible you don't want any of your friends to see you drinking with an incredibly handsome younger man?"

I politely overlooked his presumption that I would be categorized as an older woman. "My husband happens to be an incredibly handsome man of a perfect age," I said. "You might have met him if you went to the Literacy Council on Tuesday. Tall, curly hair, golden-brown eyes — and a shiny badge."

"Deputy Chief Rosen? I had no idea." He picked up the pitcher and filled the two mugs. "I agree with you about his looks. What's more, he was wearing very expensive Italian shoes. I was impressed. There was a time when I bought shoes in Milan and had my suits made on Savile Row. Now I'm living on an adequate salary, but I shop at the mall."

"Because you want a picket fence and the chance to coach a T-ball team?"

"Maybe. In Hong Kong I met either executive cougars or agreeable Chinese women who wanted to get married and move to the United States. I hung out with the Brits. The eligible young women had titles and talked incessantly about polo and yachts. I was included because I play a mean game of bridge." Rick held up his mug. "You didn't invite me here to talk about my shallow dreams, did you?" He gulped down the beer. "I don't know anything about what happened to the Polish woman. Austin and I left after the meeting was adjourned and went across the street for a beer. I was home in bed by ten."

"I don't believe you," I blurted out, then put my hand over my mouth. "Oops, I didn't mean to say that, but there's something fishy about your whole story."

Rick propped his elbows on the table and cradled his face. "This is serious. We need to determine what it is that you don't believe. Immediately after I graduated from Harvard, I was offered a position in an international finance company. After eight years, I got tired of living overseas. I was extremely fond of a second cousin who lived here. She and I spent summers together at my grandparents' house on Nantucket. We were hooligans from the age of six. One summer we spray-painted mailboxes purple and pink. When we were teenagers, we scattered marijuana seeds in the flower beds of all the rich people. When she told me about Farberville, she made it sound idyllic. I made the decision to settle down. Better?"

I nodded, but without conviction. "Does she still live here? What's her name?"

"It doesn't matter," he said grimly. "She committed suicide. We wrote each other letters on a regular basis, and e-mails later. I knew she was depressed, and I tried to convince her to seek counseling. I felt so damn helpless on the opposite side of the planet. Coming to Farberville is bittersweet, but I feel as though I'm doing it to honor her memory."

"Was she living here when she . . . died?"

"Some place on the West Coast. I don't remember because it didn't make any difference at the time." He gave me a rueful look. "Has my credibility score gone up a few points?"

I'd seen his eyes well with tears when he told me the story. "Yes, Rick. I'm sorry about your cousin. Sometimes there's nothing you can do."

He tapped his glass with a manicured fingernail. "And sometimes there is. If you'll excuse me, what goes in must come out. I'll be back shortly."

At least I knew his story, I thought, but it didn't seem to have anything to do with Ludmila. She'd come to Farberville via New York, with no detours to the Northwest. It was highly implausible that Rick's cousin had visited Bialystok. I made a note to Google it in case it was home to the eighth wonder of the world. Even my highly imaginative mind could not make the leap.

Rick returned with a bowl of pretzels. "Have I answered all your questions?"

"Oh, no," I said. "Why did you want to be on the FLC board of directors? I have my excuse. What's yours?"

"I think it's worthwhile. If you've ever lived in a foreign country, you'd understand how frustrating it can be. Hong Kong is a worldwide commerce market, so most of the educated locals speak English and three or four other languages, but I'd go in a shop where all the signs were in Cantonese and everybody stared at me. I felt like a hairy, unwashed Mongol. They may have considered me to be a mongrel."

Duke had conveyed the same sentiment. I had no desire to move to Algeria or Albania to confirm their invasive sense of paranoia. I began to understand Ludmila's outbursts and depression. That did not justify her verbal abuse, however. I gazed at Rick. "So you were motivated by altruism?"

"I love that word, but it's an exaggeration. I wanted to help, and, to be candid, young bank executives need to display their involvement in the community. You never know what programs the presidents of banks support. Mine always buys a table at the Literacy Council fund-raiser in the fall, and his wife is rumored to spend a great deal of money during the silent auction. Disillusioned?"

"Merely disappointed," I said. "So what's the problem with you and Gregory? I realize you suspect him of embezzlement, but I was worried that you two were going to start throwing punches. I was ready to duck under the table."

Rick's eyes slitted. "The idea of him stealing money from a nonprofit pisses me off. We may not feed the homeless or provide vaccinations for indigent children, but we are helping the community. If Gregory wants to hold up a liquor store, that's fine with me. I don't care if he's never returned a library book in his life." His fist slammed against the table. "I'm going to nail that bastard! Once I have proof, I can bring in the FBI. We get funds from the state, and the state gets funds from the federal government."

"Whoa, Lone Ranger," I interrupted. His voice had become so loud that customers were staring and the waitress was watching from the doorway. I could hear clicks as we were captured on cell phones, doomed to be displayed on Internet sites. "Gregory may be committing a felony, but it won't warrant the death penalty. If he's guilty, the feds will deal with him. Do you have proof?"

"Not without a full audit that goes back five years. Frances won't even allow discussion. She, Sonya, Drake, and Willie have had what they call 'executive' meetings. The rest of us have no input. Frances would prefer to squelch the whole thing rather than acknowledge a scandal during her reign. I want to see Gregory hauled off in handcuffs and convicted."

"How much do you believe he's embezzled?" I asked.

"It's impossible to tell because of the way the books are kept. From what I can estimate thus far, as much as forty thousand dollars."

I was taken aback. "That's not exactly a fortune, Rick."

"It's the principle of the thing." His voice began to rise again. "It doesn't matter if it's a hundred dollars or a hundred thousand dollars. The man is a criminal!"

Austin slid in beside me. "I hope you're not talking about me."

I started in surprise. "Austin, please feel free to join us."

"I believe I did," he said, flashing his teeth. He was dressed in a pale blue shirt, white suspenders, and a red bow tie — a patriotic motif of dubious taste. He held up his palm. "Rick, my man, how's it going? You didn't tell me that you and the alluring Ms. Malloy were having a little something on the side. You rock, bro!"

Rick slapped Austin's palm. "Only in my dreams, alas. Claire and I were discussing my problem with Gregory. I'm afraid she thinks I'm overreacting to a minor indiscretion. She's off my list for the lynch party."

Austin draped his arm around my shoulders. "Don't you worry, Claire. We'll invite you to the reception afterward. We'd better not hold it at the Literacy Council. We'll be drinking champagne, and Frances is obsessed with our stodgy Muslim students."

"I thought you had to work late every day," I said to Austin. "Have I forgotten an obscure holiday?"

"We finished shooting a commercial a couple of hours ago. You would not believe how difficult it is to keep penguins from pooping. They never poop in documentaries, but they were doing their business nonstop. You try to shoo them away, they attack. I have bruises all over my legs." He winked at the waitress as she put down a mug. "Let's have another pitcher, Angelina, and some chips."

"And you just happened to drop by here? What a coincidence."

"Coincidence? This happens to be my second home, my happy hunting ground. See that sweet brown thing over there in the corner? She hasn't taken her eyes off me since I came through the gate." He grinned broadly. "If she could ditch that brute, she'd be sitting here in a split second."

"The brute looks as though he plays varsity football," I pointed out. "Did Rick call you earlier and tell you to come rescue him? I can't believe I'm quite so scary."

Rick turned back when he heard his name. "Why would I be scared of you? You're charming, attractive, intelligent, and witty. I may be a little nervous when Frances comes at me like a condor, but I'm beginning to adore you." He was also beginning to get a teensy bit drunk, having consumed most of the first pitcher.

"As am I." Austin gave me a sloppy kiss on the cheek. "Ditch your husband and we'll escape to a deserted island on the woolly backs of flying sheep."

"I prefer to fly first class." I had to clamp down on my lip to keep from laughing. "How long have you two been friends?"

"A long time," said Rick.

"Not that long," said Austin.

They looked at each other, grinned, and slapped palms. Austin grabbed the pitcher to refill their mugs and top off mine. "Somewhere between a long time and not that long," he said. "We met when Rick joined the board of directors. Before that, Sonya and I were the only members under the age of fifty. She's the personification of bitchiness behind her sugary facade. I don't know what happened between her and Willie, but if Sonya ordered Willie to jump, we'd have to peel her honor off the ceiling."

I tucked that tidbit into a corner of my mind. "So both of you are convinced that Gregory has been stealing funds? Why not call the police and ask them to do an audit? They have a forensic accountant on standby."

"Because," Rick said in a lugubrious voice, confirming my suspicion about his flagging sobriety, "it would take months for an outsider to decipher the books. All the grants, the endowments, and contributions are comingled with the profits from the fund-raisers and membership drives, and half the checks don't have notations. As you heard at the meeting, the board members with checkbooks reimburse themselves and

170

write checks without consulting each other. Sometimes Keiko will pay a utility bill, then Gregory will pay the same bill because Keiko forgot to mark it as paid. That means we get bills and checks from almost everyone. At any given moment, half the checks are still outstanding. It's his fault!"

To avoid another outburst, I said, "You've been trying to sort out the books in the evenings." I thought about the pranks that had taken place in Gregory's office. The obvious candidate was seated across from me. "I presume you prefer to work when Gregory isn't around."

"So?" Rick said defiantly.

Austin came to his rescue. "You're not accusing my good brother Rick of pilfering money from the petty cash box, are you?"

"Good heavens, no," I said. "I've heard some rumors about some mischief in Gregory's office. Little stuff."

"He claims I hide things," Rick said, "but that's absurd. Have you looked in his office, Claire? He stacks folders on the floor until they topple over. Despite the nonsmoking policy, the room stinks of cigars. He brings in fast food and leaves half-eaten burgers in bags."

"Toby doesn't clean in there?" I asked.

Austin laughed as if I'd said something

hilarious. "Master Toby went in there one time and then came out and asked if he could rent a bulldozer. Gregory told him to never set foot in there again. That resolved the issue."

Rick splashed beer on the table as he tried to refill his mug. "Wish I had a bulldozer," he growled. "I'd chase Gregory around the parking lot until I'd flattened him like a crepe." His eyes filled with tears as he gave me a blurry look. "I loved my cousin, I really did. She was my best friend. We told each other everything." Tears dribbled down his face as he leaned forward. "Do you understand? Do you?"

I nudged Austin, who stood up and said, "Guess what, bro? It's time to go home. We'll pick up a pizza on the way." He went around the picnic table, slid his arms under Rick's armpits, and pulled him up. "Put your arm over my shoulder. I'm going to help you out the gate and into my car. We'll figure out how to fetch your car later."

Rick was mumbling as Austin took him to the parking lot. I sat back, trying to make sense of what had happened. There was no question that Rick was drunk, and for good reason, having gone through a pitcher and a half of beer at the speed of light. He was still mourning his cousin's death. He loathed Gregory, but luckily for him, Gregory was not the murder victim. But why had he called Austin to chaperone us? The obvious answer was that Rick knew he had a drinking problem and was afraid he might blurt out something to me. I had no reason to think he might be involved in Ludmila's death. If he'd met her, odds were excellent that he hadn't felt any fondness for her. No one whom I'd encountered thus far had expressed any kind words about her, with the exception of Duke.

I hadn't had the opportunity to ask Duke when he had last seen Ludmila. She'd been expelled from the senior citizens center, but they could have stayed in touch. Duke had married a waitress, presumably a good deal younger than he. Maybe Ludmila had been harboring romantic fantasies. The image was so unsettling that I had to take a sip of the tepid beer. Maybe Duke's wife was not pleased with a ménage à trois. Beer spewed out of my mouth as I imagined Ludmila standing on the end of the bed, shouting at her consorts. *Please, no,* I thought as I realized everyone was staring at me. Happy hour at the beer garden on a sunny afternoon.

It didn't seem tactful to drop in on Duke and his wife to discuss Ludmila. The Literacy Council was off-limits, and I was leery of visiting Bartek again. I wondered if he'd said something to Peter or if his house was under surveillance. Murders were often committed by family members or spouses. "Parenticide" was in the dictionary. I was less sure about "grandparenticide," although it certainly deserved inclusion.

The waitress interrupted my aimless and meandering thoughts. "You done, honey?" I nodded. "That'll be sixteen fifty-five, not including tip."

Not only had I been deserted, I'd been stiffed.

8

When I arrived home, I found Caron sprawled on the sofa. She, her clothes, the sofa, and the floor were sprinkled with crumbs. From the evidence on the coffee table, she'd swilled three cans of soda, emptied a jar of salsa dip and a bag of chips, and finished the last of the leftover chicken. The TV was turned to a game show but muted. I hoped the EPA was on high alert for a potential meltdown.

"Hello, dear." I entered the room with the same trepidation I'd feel if I'd been sent into the cage to feed the lions.

"I have to tutor tomorrow."

"That's the cause of the display of abject misery and despair? You knew the Literacy Council would open in a couple of days. Where's Inez?"

"How would I know? She hasn't called or answered a text all afternoon."

"So you're worried that she was abducted

by aliens and whisked away to a distant galaxy. Now I understand."

Caron lifted her head long enough to douse me with radiation. "Why do you insist on trying to be funny, Mother? Trust me — you're not. Anyway, Annabelle saw her at the movie theater in the mall with a guy from the Latin Club. What's more, she wasn't wearing her glasses. She was dressed in really short cutoffs and a tight T-shirt and swaggering like a model. Then again, Annabelle failed home ec in ninth grade. She *flambéed* her brownies."

"Good for Inez," I said.

"Why did I know you'd say that? I must be omniscient! Wait until I tell everybody. Nostradamus must be rotating in his grave."

"You don't think twice about abandoning Inez when you have a date with Joel," I said, refusing to react to her sarcasm.

"That's not fair," Caron retorted. "We all hang out together at the mall. Inez tags along, just like everybody else."

"Did Inez tag along when Joel took you out to dinner to celebrate your three-month anniversary? How about when you two went to the play at the college?"

Caron stood up. "That is so Not The Point. I need to go call Jiang, Nasreen, and Yelena. At least I don't have to call Ludmila." She marched toward the staircase, her shoulders quivering with indignation. "Oh, and Keiko left a message for you on the answering machine. The receptionist quit, and Keiko wants to know if you can cover until they find somebody else."

"Wait," I said as she started upstairs. "Have you given your statement to the police yet?"

"Yeah, after you left, Jorgeson called, and I went to the PD. Some guy with a beer gut asked me a bunch of questions. It took all of fifteen minutes, since I don't know anything useful. Ludmila didn't exactly confide in me. Afterward I went by Peter's office to see if the PD wanted to reimburse my travel expenses with enough money for lunch. He gave me ten bucks."

"Did the two of you talk?"

"Do you think we used sign language?"

"Did he ask you about me?" It was increasingly difficult to hide my annoyance.

"He just wanted to know if you were upset about what happened at the Literacy Council. I said that if you were, you were doing a fine job of hiding it and were running around trying to solve the case under his nose, thereby embarrassing him and the Farberville Police Department for the umpteenth time. That pretty much covers it, Mother. I need to make those calls. Go make *boeuf* à la barf or whatever. I guess I'll be here for dinner every night until Joel gets back."

Now I knew why Peter was so well informed about my activities. I'd reared a freckled Mata Hari and married a man who had no scruples about coaxing information out of her for a measly ten dollars. Caron, at least for the last month, was planning to major in political science. She would never succeed in politics unless she learned how to negotiate. I would have given her fifteen dollars *not* to blab to Peter.

On a brighter note, Bartek's house was not under surveillance. I had a legitimate excuse to spend the day at the Literacy Council. I would find a reason to go to Duke's house and continue our conversation about Ludmila. Feeling much better, I took a package of ground beef out of the freezer and stuck it in the microwave to thaw. Caron and I would dine on *boeuf avec fromage* on buns, with fries, salad, and the Key lime pie I'd hidden in the darkest corner of the freezer.

La vie — c'est belle.

I appeared at the Literacy Council at nine o'clock. Keiko must have seen me through

178

her office window, because she came bounding out of her office to throw her arms around me and squeal, "Oh, thank you, Ms. Marroy! You are so very wonderful to come and help. Everything is a big mess. The police went through all the files and left them in piles. I need to contact all the students and let them know we can have classes again. I cannot find the files for the tutors. I put a message on our Web site, but nobody looks at it."

I disengaged myself and looked around. There were only a few students in the lounge area. Leslie came out of her office, gathered them up, and took them into her classroom. I had not blipped on her radar screen. I went to the doorway.

"We are all very upset about what happened to Ludmila," Leslie was saying. "I know that in some cultures, it's considered best not to speak about tragedy. In this country, it's encouraged. Does anyone want to say something?" She waited for a moment. "Then I'll start. I feel as though the Literacy Council has been tarnished by this crime."

An Asian girl waved her arm. "What is 'tarnished'?"

"Made dirty!" said Jiang. When I'd seen him earlier, he seemed to be simmering with anger. Someone or something had turned up the heat, because he was near his boiling point. Even Leslie was unnerved.

"That's right, Jiang," she said. "Would you like to add to that?"

His arms crossed, he shook his head and slunk down in his chair. I hoped he wasn't a closet samurai. Keiko, Leslie, and I were not going to subdue him if he pulled out a razor-sharp sword and began slashing. I eased back and found Keiko in her office.

"Same drill as last time?" I asked. "Answer the phone, take messages, hand out forms?"

Her eyes were wet. "Oh, Ms. Marroy, this is too much for me. No one is telling me anything. The board members came on Tuesday and stood around talking to each other. Gregory came in and talked to your husband, and then Leslie came in and did the same. No one is talking to me except to demand that I find files and folders and time sheets for the tutors. The schedule is different every day. I don't know who is here on Monday evening or Wednesday morning or anytime!" She grabbed a tissue from the box on her desk. "I think that I will quit. I will stay at home and make sushi for my children."

I stared at her. "You have children? How old are you, Keiko?"

She recovered from her emotional outburst and smiled at me. "How old do you think I am, Mrs. Marroy?"

"You look like you're about fifteen," I said.

"I am two times that. Kazu is eight and Rie is six. My husband is Australian. We are here because he is putting in a new computer system at the Sell-Mart corporate headquarters. He works for a big company in Tokyo. We will be here for two more years, since he has to fly to distribution centers all over the country and teach the new system. After that, he will be transferred to a European center to do the same. I took this job to keep myself from getting lonesome. Now I want to be lonesome all by myself."

"I understand, but you should probably wait a few days before you make a decision. The police will determine what happened to Ludmila. The students will drift back, and everything will be back to normal."

"Like hell it will," said Keiko. "Please excuse my language, Mrs. Marroy. Most of the students have e-mail addresses, and I have notified them. Then there are some who don't. This is a list of their telephone numbers. You need to call and tell them that the Literacy Council is open. I need to look for the tutors." She dropped to her knees and began to sort through files. "I know you are here, my lovely tutors. Where are you hiding?"

I poured myself a cup of coffee in the back classroom, noting that the door to the copy room was festooned with yellow tape, and took a seat at the receptionist's desk. I located a pen and a notepad. I made sure the stapler was armed. I listened to Leslie leading a conjugation drill: I swim, you swim, he swims, etc. Keiko's list seemed to grow longer as I looked at it with a sour taste in my mouth. I had felt no sympathy when Caron and Inez had to call their respective students. Faced with the same dilemma, I wanted to crawl under the desk and stay there until everyone went home. Which would make for a long day, I told myself. Leslie had assured the girls that all the students spoke some English, but she assumed that the students would answer the telephone.

As it turned out, half of my calls went unanswered. Those who answered seemed to understand me, although I was just as willing as they were to pretend they did. There were about forty names and numbers on the list. When Gregory came in, I was down to the last ten. I decided they could wait.

"Good morning," I said.

He stopped. "Good morning, Claire. Are you the permanent receptionist? Seems rather menial for someone with your talents."

"I'm volunteering until Keiko finds someone else. Have you recovered from Tuesday morning's tragedy? Such a shock."

"It was a nightmare." His face was pale, and there were dark half-moons under his eyes. "The detectives kept me here all day, asking questions and searching my office. I don't know what they thought they'd find. At least they didn't come across another dead bird or a death threat. I'd have a hard time explaining that."

Students and tutors began to come into the building. Gregory seemed panicky as he said, "Let's continue this in my office, Claire. I detest being stared at as if I were a monster."

"Okay," I said, although those staring in our direction seemed to be focused on me. I doubted any of them had figured out what my role had been after Ludmila's body was found. I wasn't sure myself.

Gregory's office was as chaotic as Rick had told me. Papers, files, folders, booklets, and envelopes were piled haphazardly on the floor. I moved a stack of papers off the chair while Gregory found a path behind his desk. The room reeked of cigar smoke. The blinds were closed, the light minimal. I am not claustrophobic, but I was uncomfortable.

"It may look disorganized to you," Gregory said, "but I can find things — unless someone moves them. Since our conversation last week at the café, I've been careful to lock the door when I leave." He gave me a plaintive look. "I don't know if the police took anything, and, frankly, I don't care. I was exhausted when they let me leave. Someone must have told them about Ludmila's vendetta against me. I don't know why the woman despised me. When she first began coming here, she ignored me. Then one day she stormed in like a Valkyrie on steroids and started shouting at me. All I could think of was that she didn't like my tie. Silly, I know, but I was stunned. By the way, it was a very nice silk tie from Hermès in Paris."

"I'm sure it was," I said lamely. "I suppose the police asked you about Monday night. That was quite a scene at the board meeting, wasn't it?"

Gregory shook his head. "I toyed with the idea that Rick was Ludmila's evil pawn. I don't know what Rick's problem is. Yes, I know he's been accusing me of embezzlement. If he had any proof, he wouldn't have to resort to this deceitful attack on my character. I've spoken to a lawyer about filing a suit for slander."

And I'd volunteered to spend time in this minefield. There was no reason why I couldn't take on Italian cooking and learn how to make pasta by hand. Somewhere in my kitchen there was apt to be a contraption for that specific purpose. I could make cute little ravioli and tortellini. Ditch the truffle oil in favor of olive oil. I was in the middle of a whimsical vision of my private olive grove when I realized Gregory was watching me. "A lawsuit can be played on the front page of the newspaper," I said. "It might do a great deal of harm to the Literacy Council's reputation. Even if you're exonerated, your donors may have reservations. Where there's smoke . . ."

"Would you talk to him, Claire? He'd spit in my face before I could get out a word. If I offer to show him my personal bank statements, he'll accuse me of having an account in the Caymans. There's an old political joke: If a candidate walked on water, his opponent would claim he couldn't swim. If Rick can't find any evidence against me, he'll say that proves I've hidden it."

I held up my hands. "I'm not getting in

the middle of this. Talk to Frances. She's the president of the board of directors. I've been on the board for less than a week, and nobody listens to me. I'm not complaining, mind you. I may take the training session so I can tutor, but I'm going to resign my position as soon as enough of the absent board members return to make up a quorum. There's a reason why I majored in English instead of business. I prefer to deal with characters on a page, not in my face." I stood up and repositioned the papers on the chair. "I have more phone calls to make. Good luck, Gregory, with whatever you decide to do."

I went back to my desk and finished calling the names on the list. Leslie's class was now chanting about those who sing, sang, and had sung. More students were in the lounge, and I could hear tutors in the cubicles. The telephone rang. The caller asked to speak to Gregory, and after a few false tries, I managed to transfer the call to his office. A UPS man delivered a box and allowed me to sign for it.

Then, as though a thunderstorm had moved in just above the building, the phone began to ring and ring and ring. Most of the callers were students who wanted to know if the class schedule had been revised or if their tutors had been notified. To those whom I could not understand, I repeated the word "yes" until they hung up. I might have said the same thing to Jorgeson if he called to ask if another body had been discovered. Caron and Inez appeared at eleven, both texting intently. When Leslie's class emerged, Inez plucked her Mexican student from the throng and took him into a cubicle. Caron sighed as she did the same with Jiang. I hoped she was prepared for a bumpy ride.

The phone kept ringing and I kept answering it. There was no way I could get a cup of coffee or even make a dash to the ladies' room. I scribbled messages for Leslie and did my best to transfer calls to Gregory's office and Keiko's. Sometimes it appeared to work; other times the light went off. I did not care. Gregory had dismissed my job as menial, but it required the appendages of an octopus to grab the receiver, deal with the students in front of me, and make indecipherable marks on scraps of paper. I was aware my performance was subpar, but one gets what one pays for.

Caron gave me a desultory wave as she left. Inez emerged with Aladino, patted him on the back, and headed for the lounge to find her next student. Aladino watched her with a dopey grin. I could see why. Inez had not only ditched her glasses for contact lenses, she'd also done something to her hair to make it soft and shiny. Her shorts fit snugly, and her knit top displayed a hint of cleavage that I'd never realized she had.

It was noon, and I was exhausted. Keiko had said nothing about how long she expected me to stay. When the phone rang, I merely looked at it. Instead of saying, "yes, yes, yes," I was perilously close to saying, "no, no, no," to every last blasted question. I was wondering what I was supposed to do about lunch when Keiko and Gregory came out of their respective offices.

Keiko patted her hair. "How do I look?"

"Fine," Gregory said as he took her arm. "You have your story straight?"

"Do you?" she countered. I sucked in breath as I waited for him to respond to her flippant tone.

After a long, uncomfortable moment, he propelled her out the front door. I followed them and was not especially surprised to see the local TV station van. The cameraman and the soundman fiddled with their equipment while a middle-aged woman in a suit tried to hide her wrinkles with a thick layer of makeup. There were photographers and reporters from the regional newspapers.

A group of students huddled at the far side of the parking lot, unsure what to do. I backed toward the door, but I was too late.

"Claire Malloy!" shouted a reporter. "Are you assisting the police? What can you tell us about the victim?"

"Are there any persons of interest?" shouted another one.

The camera was pointed at me as the TV reporter hastily brushed powder off her lapels and said, "Was this a terrorist attack? These students are from countries like Iran, the Sudan, and Indonesia. Is Homeland Security investigating their backgrounds?"

"I don't think so," I said.

Gregory nudged me aside and introduced himself. "What happened involved an attempted burglary, not an act of terrorism. Police suspect that the victim, Mrs. Ludmila Grabowski, encountered the burglar and was shoved so violently that she took a fatal fall. This has nothing to do with international anything."

Keiko stepped forward. "I am the program director, and I am personally acquainted with all of our students. They are good people who wish to find better jobs, communicate with their children's teachers and doctors, pay taxes, and be members of this community. Please respect their privacy."

She twinkled at them.

Sonya appeared at Gregory's side like an apparition. I realized that it was possible that one of the phone calls I'd blithely transferred to Gregory might have been hers. I had been well beyond asking for any caller's identity. She showed all of her teeth to the reporters. "I'm a member of the Faberville Literacy Council board. Our president, Frances North, could not be here because of work-related responsibilities. She will be issuing a formal statement later in the day." Her smile faded. "On behalf of the board, I'd like to extend our deepest condolences to Bartek Grabowski for the loss of his beloved grandmother. She was a part of our little community and an enthusiastic participant. She will be missed. Contributions in her honor can be made on our Web site."

Gregory was displeased to be shuttled aside. Easing in front of Sonya, he said, "Thank you very much for coming. At this time, we are all distressed by this tragic accident, but we hope you can come back at a happier time so we can share our program with you and your viewers. Good-bye."

We all trooped inside. Sonya followed Keiko into her office. I looked at Gregory. "So, Ludmila was killed by a burglar? Have

190

the police determined what the burglar was after? The copy machine is hardly state-of-the-art, but there are a lot of computers. That doesn't explain why the burglar and Ludmila were in the copy room."

He snorted. "I had to say something. Do you want the villagers to descend on the castle with torches, intent on ridding Farberville of foreign terrorists? We have students from Iran, Egypt, Korea, and China, as well as the Latinos and Europeans. Have you met the Buddhist monk with the shaved head? What about the women in saris? Do you believe the rednecks know the difference between 'hijab' and 'jihad'? If you want, go ahead and shoot me."

"You're right," I said. "Congratulations on not choking when Sonya said Ludmila will be missed." He shrugged as he went into his office. I resumed my seat and gazed glumly at the telephone. I wished it would succumb to the fate of Salvador Dalí's melting pocket watches. In retaliation for my mean-spirited thoughts, it rang. As I picked up the receiver, the students who'd been in the parking lot came in, talking and gesticulating. They stopped in front of my desk and began to pepper me with questions about the TV van and reporters. The caller said something, but I couldn't hear enough to understand him. I covered my right ear with my hand and said, "You'll have to speak up. It's noisy here." He said something that sounded like "Leslie." I tried to shoo away the students without success. "Leslie is teaching," I replied. "Can you call back?"

"Waterford!" he shouted.

"Okay," I said and then hung up. Leslie might be collecting Waterford crystal, although I hadn't seen any pieces in her house. I wrote the word on a piece of paper, adding the time. I looked up and smiled. "What seems to be the problem?"

Half an hour later I had done my best to satisfy everyone's curiosity, handed Leslie the note about her crystal, and watched Sonya leave. I was most decidedly hungry, and I wasn't inclined to search the desk drawers for a granola bar. I went into Keiko's office. "The Fair Labor Standards Act gives me the right to a lunch break. I'm taking it now."

"Excellent idea, Mrs. Marroy. May I join you? We can go to bar across the street. They have good chili dogs."

"And leave Gregory in charge?"

She covered her mouth with her hand as she giggled. "Maybe his burglar will come back and Gregory will pounce on him like a tiger." She punched a button on the telephone. "Anyone who calls will have to leave a message. Let's go, Mrs. Marroy."

Only a few students were in the lounge, and no one seemed disconcerted when we went outside. We walked across the parking lot and made our way into what touted itself as a sports bar. Posters advertised upcoming pay-for-view boxing events. The prime decor consisted of TV sets, neon beer logos, and football paraphernalia on the walls. Two pool tables were in use. Keiko led me to a booth in a far corner.

"I am so happy to have lunch with you, Mrs. Marroy."

"Please call me Claire." I was very sincere. It occurred to me that I should have come up with a name that she couldn't mangle.

We picked up menus. When a waiter appeared, Keiko ordered a cheeseburger, fries, onion rings, and a chocolate milk shake. I opted for chicken salad. After the waiter wandered away, I leaned forward. "Will you promise not to get upset if we talk about Ludmila?" I asked, having made sure the napkin dispenser was filled.

"I promise. If I sniffle, you can kick me under the table, Claire-san."

"After the board meeting Monday night, I left. What happened then?"

She sat for a moment, frowning. "A former student came by to tell me about his new job and his twin boys. Mr. Whitbream was annoyed because he had to wait until Ngozi left before he could ask me about Toby. I told him Toby was doing okay. He acted like he didn't believe me and demanded to know how many hours Toby worked. I told him I didn't know, since I normally leave at five. I was there Monday night because of the board meeting. Other nights a volunteer sits at the reception desk in case someone has a problem. On Mondays and Wednesdays we close at eight, and on Tuesdays and Thursdays at nine."

"Who locks up?" I asked.

"Gregory, if he's there, or the volunteer. Leslie has a key. Most of the time Toby arrives before everyone is gone. He has a key so he can lock the door when he leaves."

"So closing time on Monday was eight," I said. "Who was there when you left?"

Keiko massaged her neck. "You sound like that detective, Claire-san. Questions and more questions. Gregory was still in his office. Mr. Sangine was in the classroom with a couple of students who were showing him their checkbooks. Ludmila sat at a table, her cane clutched in her fist and her face frozen. Miao and Jiang were in the lounge

194

area, arguing. I tried to listen while I gathered up the newspapers, but they were speaking Chinese. When I went into the parking lot, I saw a group of students walking toward the bus stop. I am told this happens every night."

I hadn't seen a hint of a tear or heard a crack in her voice. I pressed onward. "Were you the first person to arrive at the Literacy Council Tuesday morning?"

"I always come at seven forty-five. Some students meet with their tutors before they go to work. I unlocked the door, turned on lights, and made coffee. Mr. Rapetti often stops at the bakery on his way, and on that morning he brought me a cinnamon roll. It was so wonderful that I kissed him! I hope he doesn't tell Mrs. Rapetti."

I was going to have to phrase my questions carefully in order not to be inundated with too much information. "Was the door to the copy room closed?"

She wrinkled her nose. "It must have been. I walked by it when I went to make coffee."

"Then who discovered Ludmila's body?"

"A Chinese girl named Luo Shiwen. Everybody heard her scream. She was standing just outside the door, pointing at the blood. Mr. Rapetti entered the room and saw a foot sticking out from under boxes. He moved a box, saw that it was Ludmila, and told all of us to stay outside. I called the police, but I was very upset." She gave me a wry smile. "Maybe you already knew that."

"I suspected that was the case," I said. "Did Mr. Rapetti see anything else?"

Keiko shook her head. "He was in there for not as long as a minute, and he was too shocked to have noticed a clue. I was afraid he was going to have a heart attack. He is quite old. One of the students took him to the back classroom and made him a cup of tea. I am concerned because he has not come in today."

I thought for a moment. "Tell me about Luo."

"She is from Beijing and a student at the college, studying some sort of chemistry. She and Miao share an apartment. She told me they met at an International Students Association meeting on campus and liked each other. Luo is older, almost twenty-five. Her English is not good, but better than Miao's." Keiko paused. "Luo usually meets with her tutor late in the afternoon. She told me she has classes all day. Maybe her schedule is different now, since summer school has started."

"Do you know why she opened the door and looked in the copy room?"

"When we found the body, everything got crazy. Mr. Rapetti turned gray and almost collapsed. Two of the Korean girls started sobbing. I went to my office to call nine-one-one. I was too busy to talk to anybody after that."

The waiter appeared with our food. Keiko was undaunted by the quantity of her order and dove into her cheeseburger as if she'd emerged from the tower after a month of bread and water. I picked at the chicken salad and declined her offer of onion rings. Grease dribbled down her chin. In less than ten minutes, Keiko had consumed eight million calories and was looking at the dessert menu. I estimated her dress size to be a two, or maybe a four. I was awed by her metabolism.

I ordered coffee, and she ordered a brownie sundae. "You mentioned that Luo and Miao shared an apartment. Have you heard from Miao?"

"You know her grandfather died? Yes, she sent a note with Luo that she was returning to China. Jiang is angry because she did not tell him. She told me that they met in college, and he followed her here. He wants to get married, but she wants to wait until they finish school. I think he is studying engineering. Is that important?"

"No, I think it's romantic. I'm still curious why Luo would go into the copy room. Did she come in this morning?"

Keiko was distracted by the arrival of her dessert. After wolfing down a goodly portion of it, she said, "I did not see her, but I was in my office. I wish I'd stayed there during the press conference. It was Gregory's idea, but we don't need that kind of publicity."

"The story was out there," I said, "and needed to be addressed. I have to say that I was surprised when you spoke to Gregory in that tone of voice."

"He won't fire me because he knows he can't replace me. I am paid slightly more than minimum wage, and no overtime. Gregory is an annoying little dictator who can't be bothered with petty things like utility bills. He doesn't know the names of the students — except for Ludmila. He never observes a class or a tutoring session. He has no idea where to find paper towels or toilet paper. When he's there, he prowls around with a smirk on his face."

"Oh," I said, leaning back against the bench. I'd made assumptions about her based on a stereotype. She was no anime teenager or repressed geisha. I took a drink of coffee. "I thought the press conference went well. Did Gregory call Sonya?"

"I didn't." She licked her spoon and waved at the waiter. "There may be a hundred messages by now. I will listen to them. If you want to leave, I will find a student to sit at the desk. Yelena is always offering." She handed a credit card to the waiter. "This is on the Literacy Council. I know you will solve this mystery quickly so we can continue to offer our program. Maybe the publicity will bring in a few donations."

I accompanied her across the street and into the building. I was eager to abandon my assignment so that I could talk to Luo Shiwen. Keiko looked inside Leslie's classroom and shook her head. I asked her to find Luo's file and followed her into her office. She wrote down an address on a slip of paper and handed it to me.

"Do you think Gregory's still here?" I asked.

Keiko batted her thick eyelashes. "Do you care?"

I didn't.

9

Luo and Miao lived in an apartment complex on the campus bus route. The two-story buildings, painted gray with blue trim, were crammed together along winding paved roads. Most of the balconies were crowded with aluminum chairs, grills, beer coolers, and hanging plants. Towels flapped on railings, and wind chimes jangled. It was afternoon, and I was surprised at the number of students lying beside the pool or lazing on their balconies. It was a busy place.

I cleverly deduced that I needed to find Building IX, since Luo and Miao lived in number 917. After several futile turns, I finally spotted the pertinent Roman numerals and parked. Their apartment was on the second floor. Luo was more likely to be out than in, and I prepared myself for disappointment as I rang the bell.

Locks clicked, and the door opened. Luo was as tall as I. Her face was broad, her features flat. She lacked Miao's delicacy. "Who are you?" she demanded, proving she also lacked Miao's timidity.

"I'm from the Literacy Council. I came by to make sure you're okay. Keiko said you were upset when you discovered Ludmila's body." When she blinked, I stepped forward. "May I come in?"

"Yes." She locked the door behind me.

I went into a small but nicely furnished living room. The few bits of pottery and artwork were Chinese. A plaster Buddha smiled down from a high shelf. I sat down and waited until Luo perched on the edge of a chair. "Have you recovered from the shock?" I asked.

"I fine now," she said haltingly. "I never see you at Literacy Council before."

A lovely opening, I thought. "That's right, Luo. I only come there in the mornings. Keiko told me that you meet with your tutor in the afternoons. Why were you there Tuesday morning?"

"I learn English there. Is important to talk better to professors. In China we study hard. Students here like children. They drink beer and make much noise."

"It's lucky that you met Miao," I said. I was aware she'd avoided my question, but I thought I'd have a better chance if I circled around it until she relaxed.

"Miao is good friend."

"I was sorry to hear that her grandfather died and she had to return home. Did she say how long she would be gone?"

Luo stared at me. "No, grandfather dead and must go to family. She cry when she tell me this. We burn incense and pray for him."

"That was Monday night?"

Her eyes began to shift back and forth. "Yes, Monday night."

"It must have been difficult for her to make airline reservations on the telephone," I said, pouring on the sympathy.

"Yes." Her hands were clenched so tightly her knuckles were white.

I considered my next move. Luo was a poor liar, which spoke well of her character. I needed to determine if her lies had significance. "I find it hard to believe Miao could deal with the airlines on the phone, since I always have to choose from the following options until I want to beat my head against the wall. Perhaps Miao got lucky."

"Yes, she lucky," Luo said. "She leave Tuesday morning for China. She take taxi to airport."

I resumed my tactful attack. "Why did you go to the Literacy Council that same morning, Luo?"

She stared at her hands. "Miao afraid she left notebook. I go to find it. Not there, but not important."

"If Keiko found it, she'll take care of it until Miao returns. I don't understand why you opened the door of the copy room."

"Someone tell me I can make cup of tea. I open wrong door."

Which was somewhat plausible, I supposed. The copy room was next to the classroom with the sink, counter, microwave, and coffeemaker. Luo's story was still flimsy. I couldn't imagine why Miao, while dealing with a family crisis, had even thought about a notebook she might have left at the Literacy Council. Unless it contained something of significance, I realized. Miao had no one with whom to chat between classes; she might have utilized the time to keep a journal of the interactions around her. Had she figured out why Ludmila despised Gregory, or noticed something that confirmed Rick's accusations of embezzlement?

Luo stood up. "I go to lab now. I not upset, so you not worry. Thank you for coming."

Once I was in the hall, I heard the locks click. She'd lied to me, of that I was sure. I just wasn't sure what was true and what wasn't. Someone must have helped Miao make reservations. The obvious suspect was Miss Parchester, but she'd told me Miao had merely informed her of her imminent departure. Jiang was purportedly angry that Miao had left the country without telling him. Luo's English was not adequate for leaping through the required hoops in order to speak to a live person.

Miao had been at the Literacy Council Monday night. She'd been unruffled when I saw her, which meant she'd received the call from her family after she was home. I'd never booked a flight at the last minute, but I knew the fare could be astronomical. Taxi fare to the airport was semiastronomical.

I made my way through the labyrinth of the apartment complex and drove back to the Literacy Council. The parking lot was only half full (or half empty, depending on one's philosophy). Most of the students were aware classes and tutoring had begun, but it might take another day or so before they all returned. Sitting in my car to think was beginning to pale, so I walked across the street to the sports bar.

After I ordered iced tea, I took a pen out of my purse and pulled a napkin out of the shiny dispenser. I wrote down the names of the members of the board and contemplated them. None of them appeared to have had a motive to kill Ludmila. On the next napkin, I wrote down the staff — Gregory, Keiko, and Leslie — and then slowly drew a question mark next to Gregory's name. He claimed to have no idea why Ludmila had screeched at him, but I kept an open mind. As for Keiko and Leslie, I could come up with no reason to suspect either of them. Leslie had not been at the Literacy Council, and Keiko had left while plenty of people were there. Ludmila could not have been murdered while the students were still there; she was much too voluble to go down with a whimper. Someone had lingered.

A waitress came by and refilled my glass. When I glanced up to thank her, I spotted a familiar face. Leslie was seated in a booth. Her companion, a man with dark hair and an olive complexion, was speaking emphatically and using his hands to stress his remarks. Neither appeared amiable. I wondered if he was her soon-to-be ex-husband, pleading his case for reconciliation. From Leslie's expression, he was doing a poor job of it. The man pulled out a dark brown cigarette, eliciting a glare from her.

Sadly, there was no way I could slither across the floor and into the booth behind them without being seen by them, as well as by the bartender, the waitress, and the patrons at the bar and in booths. If I left, I'd have to walk by their booth. Even the restroom would require covert action. I'd failed to bring a wig, theatrical makeup, or even sunglasses. Muttering under my breath, I looked down at the napkins as if one of them contained notes from a successful alchemist. I was beginning to regret the second glass of tea. When I glanced up a second time, hoping the odd couple had left, I saw Leslie was walking toward me, a tight smile on her face.

"Hi," I said inanely. "Would you like to join me?" I wadded up the napkins and pretended to wipe up a wet spot on the tabletop.

She sat down across from me. "I'm between classes, so I came over here for a sandwich. What about you?" She was trying not to sound accusatory, but her voice was tense.

"Keiko said that she didn't need me at the receptionist desk this afternoon. I left, but then I started feeling guilty and came back. I'm going to keep calling the names on the list until I've reached all of them. I came to get iced tea to go and ended up sitting here. It's so cool and quiet." I could see skepticism written all over her face. It seemed wise to change the subject. "I noticed someone sitting with you."

"One of my online students," Leslie said. "Omario is from Saudi Arabia, in the country with a conditional green card. He needed my advice."

"Oh, I thought it might be your husband, or ex-husband."

"I won't be seeing him again, trust me."

"Omario didn't look very happy about your advice," I murmured.

"Because I wouldn't give him any. I told him he needed to speak to a lawyer, but he was insistent. I know a little about immigration law because I worked as a paralegal years ago. I also know that I could find myself in a lawsuit if I gave him the wrong advice. I referred him to a Web site with a list of lawyers who specialize in these things." She looked at her watch. "I need to go, Claire. I have a three o'clock class."

She slid out of the booth and hurried out the door. Seconds later she walked past the window, looking very purposeful, so I was surprised when she stopped next to a black car and bent down to converse with the driver. Because of the angle, I was unable to see the driver's face. After less than a minute, she straightened up. I drew back, but not before we made eye contact. She gave me a little wave before heading across the road. The car drove away.

For a moment, my curiosity was greater than my need to locate the restroom. I toyed with the theory that Omario was a hit man whom she'd hired to kill Ludmila, but even I couldn't buy it. It made more sense that Omario was her lover, the cause of the divorce, and they'd arranged for a secret rendezvous to discuss legal complications. My story would not impress Peter, who would point out that Leslie's private life had nothing to do with his investigation. It failed to impress me. As I wound through the tables I went so far as to consider the possibility that Leslie had told me the truth. Maybe not the whole truth and nothing but the truth, but close enough.

I decided to forget about the muddle and go home. Caron was probably sulking on the sofa, devouring whatever she could find in the cabinets, refrigerator, and freezer. I wasn't confident I could wrest her out of her self-imposed misery, but I could try. It was likely that Peter would make it home for dinner, since he'd had a couple of days to interview every last person who had ever set foot in the Literacy Council building. There were steaks in the freezer and salad in the refrigerator. I stopped at my pet bakery and bought an apple pie, his favorite. After a nice dinner, we could have pie and wine on the terrace, and perhaps talk about the investigation. If that ploy failed, I had other ways to lull him into a complacent mood.

When I pulled away from the bakery, I noticed a black car doing the same. I drove slowly, but the car kept far enough away for me to see it clearly. There'd been too much talk about paranoia over the last two days, I scolded myself. Some little old lady had gone to the bakery to pick up tartlets for her book club meeting, and she was driving home as fast as she dared. I turned onto the shady street where Miss Parchester lived. I glanced in the rearview mirror. The black car had turned, too, but stopped in front of one of the houses. Now I knew where my hypothetical little old lady lived.

On a whim, I parked in front of Miss Parchester's house and went to the porch. I rang the bell. I heard a yowl, accompanied by footsteps on the staircase. Miss Parchester seemed a little breathless as she opened the door. "Claire, what a delightful surprise. Do come in. You're just in time for tea."

It was always time for tea at Miss Parchester's house. I stepped over a cat, scooted another aside to share the sofa, and said, "Please don't bother. I just wanted to ask you about something."

"You are never a bother. I'll be right back." The cats watched me from various perches. The very large cat was still at the top of the stairs, waiting for an opportunity to attack. I tried to stare him down, but I blinked first. He stalked out of sight, having determined I was an unworthy adversary.

Miss Parchester returned with a tea tray. I declined her offer of a cookie dusted with mold and waited until she'd poured the tea.

I accepted the cup and saucer. "I've been puzzled about something, and I hope you can help me. It's about Miao."

"Miao? I don't see how I can help you."

"Her roommate, Luo Shiwen, told me that Miao made airline reservations on the telephone Monday night. Her English is pretty basic. I don't understand how she could have done that without help."

Miss Parchester shook her head. "It is puzzling. The ESL students have a particularly difficult time on the telephone because they have no facial clues. I myself have a dreadful time when I'm required to choose options and push numbers. The last time I had to deal with my insurance company, I became so confused that I had to have a small glass of sherry before I made a second attempt. Despite what they said, my call was not important to them. If it had been, someone would have come on the line."

"How do you think Miao handled it?"

She took a sip of tea while she thought. "Like all of you young people, she was adept with a computer. She could have booked her ticket online."

I wished I'd thought of that. "You may be right, Miss Parchester."

"Have the police found out who murdered poor Ludmila?"

"My husband goes to extremes to keep me uninformed," I admitted, "but I would have heard something. You're aware the Literacy Council has reopened?"

"Oh, yes. I'm excited about seeing Mudada on Friday. Have I told you about him? He's a lovely man from Zimbabwe."

"You mentioned him the last time I was here." I had no desire for another lyrical essay about the great, gray-green, greasy Limpopo River. "I need to go home and prepare dinner for my husband. I've hardly seen him since Tuesday morning. Thank you for solving a minor mystery for me."

My perfect house was twenty minutes away from the center of Farberville. The city limits sign was within sight as I drove under the arched entrance to Hollow Valley. The wholesale nursery had been a thriving business only a month earlier; now the greenhouses were empty and its owners preoccupied with legal problems. I was preparing to turn into the driveway when a flash of light in the side mirror caught my eye. I looked back at the gate. A black car had stopped under the arch. I twisted around and took a hard look at it. Tinted windows blocked my view of its occupant. I hadn't seen Omario get in the car, but it seemed logical that he had and then waited for Leslie to leave the sports bar. Or it was merely a customer who didn't know the Hollow Valley Nursery was no longer in business. Or a lost soul who was turning around after having missed his turnoff. The city coffers were not sufficient to provide adequate signage. Speed limit signs were pockmarked. A highway sign hung upside down by its lone screw. A mile back, a developer had named the streets into his subdivision after his children. Those signs rarely lasted a week.

The car backed onto the highway and drove toward town. Feeling relieved, I continued to the house and parked. Caron's car was gone. Either she and Inez had mended their friendship or she had fled to Annabelle's house to engage in mean-spirited gossip. I left my purse on the island in the kitchen and went out to the terrace to call Peter.

"Any chance you'll be home for dinner?" I asked when he answered. "No French cuisine, I promise. Steaks, baked potatoes, salad, and apple pie."

"Shall I interpret this as a bribe?"

"If this is what it takes to have dinner with my husband, then it most certainly is a bribe. Why don't you pick up a bottle of wine on your way home?"

We engaged in a bit of silly talk about the efficacy of bribes and then hung up. I went inside and removed three steaks from the freezer, although I was hoping that Caron might call to say she was going out for pizza. I prepped the salad, tidied up the kitchen, and took a book out to the terrace. I tried to engross myself in the plot, but I couldn't stop my mind from leaping from one conversation to another. To characterize someone as a suspect, I needed motive and opportunity. Bartek regretted bringing his *babcia* over from Poland, a motive of sorts. Having intentionally arrived late to pick her up, he might have thought he'd find her waiting alone in front of a dark building. A locked building, I amended. It would be unlocked if Toby were there to clean, but the opportunity was less than perfect with a witness underfoot.

Gregory might have had a better opportunity, if there had been a slice of time when everyone but Ludmila had left and Toby hadn't arrived. I couldn't picture him convincing her to accompany him to the copy room, or physically dragging her there. His motive was harder to discern than Bartek's. Gregory might have been angry, or even enraged, by her verbal abuse, but he'd dealt with it for months.

I closed my book and gazed at the meadow for inspiration. Butterflies flitted among the wildflowers, and grasshoppers whirred. A hawk circled in hope a small rodent might make an imprudent foray. Something moved in the apple orchard. I put my hand above my eyes and tried to get a better look. Deer often grazed in the meadow and decimated the flower beds on the far side of the pool. Caron claimed to have seen a bear from her balcony. I stood up and went across the terrace to get a better look. My mouth turned dry as I realized my bear was wearing a dark jacket and sunglasses.

I went inside and locked the French doors. I called Peter but was sent to voice mail. I licked my lips as I called Jorgeson, who was more obliging than my husband.

"Good afternoon, Ms. Malloy. The deputy chief is conferring with the chief chief. Do you have a message for him?"

"Someone is watching the house." I realized I was whispering and raised my voice. "I caught a glimpse of a man in the apple orchard."

"Don't you still have some neighbors out there?"

"Only one, and *she's* out of town. She asked me to keep an eye on her house, and I've been doing so a couple of times a week. She won't be back for another three weeks."

"A hiker, maybe, or someone who read about the unfortunate business and came out to gawk? The road isn't posted to keep out trespassers."

I was getting annoyed. "I wish I could tell you that I'd been napping and was confused when I saw him — but I wasn't. I think I was followed earlier." I glanced at the French doors. I was visible and nicely framed. "If it's not a bother, would you please send a squad car immediately? Otherwise, I'm going to hang up and call nine-one-one." I may have sounded a tad hysterical.

"We'll have a car there as soon as possible," Jorgeson said, apparently taking me seriously. "In the meantime, make sure all the doors and windows are locked and stay out of sight. Does the deputy chief keep a gun at home?"

"Absolutely not, and if he did, I wouldn't touch it. The last thing I need to do is shoot myself in the foot." I ended the call and made sure the front door was locked. I peeked out the window in the master suite, but all I saw was birds, butterflies, grasshoppers, and apple trees. I began to wonder if I'd been mistaken. Black cars were not uncommon. Luanne drove one, and so did my old English professor. One of the men in my life before I met Peter drove a black Mercedes, but he'd moved to the East Coast years ago.

It would take the squad car at least fifteen minutes, presuming the officers turned on the siren and flashing lights. I wasn't confident they would, since I hadn't claimed to see a weapon. If he had a weapon. If he wasn't a delusion born of paranoia. I went upstairs and looked out of the window in one of the guest rooms. No bears, no hired killer. I sank down on the bed and forced myself to calm down. The idea of a hit man was absurd. I had no idea who'd murdered Ludmila. Well, I had some far-fetched theories, but I myself didn't take any of them seriously. The only thing that might be fraught with significance was Leslie's meeting with her Saudi student at the sports bar. I tried to recall his face. Reasonably handsome, in his thirties, no scars or tattoos, no dagger between his teeth, no camel in the parking lot.

My cell phone jangled. I'd left it in the kitchen, and I did my best not to trip as I hurried downstairs. It went silent before I grabbed it. Caron had given me innumerable lessons on how to retrieve calls. I tried to remember her instructions, but my hand was shaking so badly that I couldn't hit the right buttons. I sat down on a stool, took a couple of deep breaths, and looked at the spiteful device. After a few errors, I located the call, which had come as a text, source unknown. It read, "Stop meddling or you will pay the price."

If the text originated from out of state, it posed no urgent problem. If it originated from the apple orchard, it was high time to make a dramatic departure. I snatched my purse and ran out the front door. Seconds before I grabbed the car door, I saw the very flat tire. I circled the car. All four tires were rubbery puddles. My sprint back inside should have earned me a trophy. I locked and bolted the front door. I heard no sounds to suggest someone was in the house. Somewhere in the woods, crows battled over a savory tidbit. I froze as I heard a sound overhead before I realized that the local squirrels were engaged in the daily pecan bowling tournament on the roof.

I locked myself in the master bathroom. It seemed excessive to crawl into the bathtub, so I sat down at the dressing table and called Jorgeson.

"Should be there in a few minutes, Ms. Malloy. There was an accident on Thurber Street that snarled traffic." He had the audacity to sound unconcerned.

I updated him in a few terse sentences, interspersed with gulps. I realized I'd moved to a narrow space between the table and the side of the shower. When he demanded to know where I was, I could barely get out the words.

His voice was gruff. "Stay there and don't open the door until the police identify themselves."

"It's not like I'm going for a stroll," I muttered. I leaned against the wall, keeping the cell phone to my ear. One of the houseplants above the bathtub needed to be watered. The pearl gray towels matched the walls and tile work. A touch of cranberry might add interest, as might sage green. A champagne cork had hidden itself in a corner. I smiled as I remembered the romantic interlude that began with champagne and candlelight. And there could be someone in my house.

Jorgeson's voice startled me. "You still there, Ms. Malloy?"

"Yes, I'm still here. Where's Peter?"

"On his way."

"On his way here — or on his way to your office?"

The cell phone slipped out of my hands when I heard a shot.

10

I managed to pick up my cell phone. "I heard a shot," I said evenly. "I am not happy with the situation. If you have useful —"

"My men are outside, Ms. Malloy," said Jorgeson. "They have a device to unlock the front door. Just stay there, okay? I'll call back."

I calmed down enough to begin breathing, although I preferred that Jorgeson's men be inside rather than outside. I tried to concentrate on the cranberry-versus-sage accent color in the bathroom. After an interminable wait, I heard voices. I dislodged myself and crept to the door to listen. My cell jangled.

"It's okay, Ms. Malloy." Jorgeson's voice was mellifluous, warm, and welcome. "The officers have searched the house and found no one."

"They didn't search this bathroom. How do I know they searched the entire house?"

"Please unlock the door, Ms. Malloy. Show them where you thought you saw someone, and they'll continue searching."

He had done his best to glide right by the key phrase, but I had enough adrenaline in my veins to leap over tall buildings in a single bound. "Thought I saw?" I asked, speaking slowly and carefully. "In the same way I thought my tires had been slashed? You doubt me?"

"Not for a second, Ms. Malloy. Will you please show the officers where you saw the man?"

I was still miffed. "Oh, all right. They aren't going to shoot me, are they?"

"They're waiting for you on the terrace."

I went into the bedroom and on into the kitchen, my phone to my ear. "What about the shot I heard?"

"The officers will explain, Ms. Malloy. Deputy Chief Rosen ought to be there in ten minutes." He ended the call.

I hurried out to the terrace, where two unfamiliar officers were scanning the landscape for errant bears and armed men. "Thank you for coming," I said. "I saw the man at the edge of the apple orchard."

"Did you see a weapon, ma'am?"

"No, but I heard a shot." I sensed my credibility was slightly below average. "It was very close to the house."

One of the officers made a face. "That was me. As soon as we got out of the car, I saw something moving behind those fir trees. I fired a warning shot."

The other laughed. "Scared the living daylights out of a groundhog. Those things can scoot when they're panicked. I can assure you, Ms. Malloy, the groundhog will not return anytime soon."

He and his partner trudged toward the orchard, their hands on the hilts of their holstered guns. I was watching them when I heard a car door slam. Seconds later Peter came out to the terrace and wrapped his arms around me. I could feel the adrenaline begin to ebb as I collapsed against him. Husbands have their uses. I let my head rest on his shoulder while I struggled to put my thoughts in order.

"Are you okay?" he demanded.

"Yes, but I could use a drink." I sat down on the end of a chaise longue and licked my dry lips. When he returned, I blurted out the whole story, beginning at the sports bar. I could have mentioned my previous encounter with Leslie, but in the name of marital harmony I decided it was unworthy of inclusion. It was risky, since I didn't know if Peter had heard about my brief involuntary visit to the PD.

"It sounds as though I need to have a talk with Leslie," Peter said.

I was surprised that he accepted my story without question. I wasn't sure I hadn't allowed myself to overreact to a random series of coincidences. Good guys wear white hats; bad guys drive black cars. "I can't be certain," I admitted. "I did see someone in the apple orchard, but it could have been a hiker. He didn't realize anyone still lived in Hollow Valley and was having an innocent look around at the historic sites. When he saw me, he backtracked and is on the far side of the mountain by now. The four flat tires made a suicide pact."

"Do you believe that?"

"No, I believe I was followed by someone in a black car. That doesn't mean you have to believe it, too."

For some reason, Peter appeared to be confused. He gazed at the orchard for a long moment, his darling face wrinkled with thought. "Do you want me to believe it?"

My dilemma was straightforward. If I said yes, then he would send a squad car to drag Leslie out of her class and to the PD. He would ask questions, and she would answer them. However, I'd never find out what she said. I would not be invited to sit in, and I would not be privy to the report. If I said no, then Peter would not be happy that I demanded a squad car and all available manpower to converge on my bucolic environs. "Maybe I should ask her. Just a casual question. That way, if she does know something, she won't be tipped off."

The man was reading my mind. "You can't have it both ways, Claire."

"Whatever you think."

The uniformed officers emerged from the orchard. Peter told one of them to check out all the residences and buildings in the valley and the other to stay on the front porch. He promised me that he'd send someone to deal with the tires and be home for dinner. I forbade myself from cowering inside with the doors locked. That lasted about a minute, and then I retreated on the pretense I needed to use the computer in my office. I was confident something would inspire me to charge into a Google expedition of sites and links, and I would surface with a perfectly reasonable solution that explained all the craziness of the last three days.

All that, and how to squeeze blood from a turnip.

I was reduced to playing solitaire online

when Caron called to say she was at Ashley's house and would be home by midnight. It was the perfect time to master the dining room. I pulled out a tablecloth, crystal wineglasses, and candles. I took my bodyguard a glass of iced tea, cut some roses from the trellis by the front porch, and arranged them in a cut-glass vase. When I realized I was perilously close to polishing the silverware, I sat down on a kitchen stool until the obsessive (and excessive) enthusiasm waned. I've never wished to compete with Martha Stewart. Although my taste is impeccable, I have not yet learned how to fold napkins into swans, and I would gnaw off my fingers before I looked it up on the Internet.

I was startled when the doorbell rang. As a precaution, I peeked out the front window and saw a tow truck. I opened the door. A polite young man in a filthy uniform told me that he and his buddy would put spare tires on my car, but I needed to stop by the garage as soon as possible for a more permanent solution.

Peter brought home a nice bottle of wine. I allowed him to grill the steaks while I dealt with the accessories. I avoided mentioning the investigation, instead catching him up on Caron's crisis du jour and the possibility of building a small greenhouse. It was a highly civilized meal, right down to the apple pie and coffee. We took brandy snifters out to the terrace. The sky was clear, the stars glittering.

"Did you talk to Leslie?" I asked casually, as though inquiring about the probability of rain over the weekend.

"She agreed to come to the police station for a chat."

I gave him a dazzling smile. "And . . . ?"

His internal struggle was visible on his face. "I'll give you a brief account, since I don't think it has significance. Leslie teaches ESL and citizenship classes online. Omario is her student and was in need of information to change his green card status. She referred him to a lawyer. After she left the bar, a man in a black car asked her for directions to the campus registrar's office. She saw Omario drive away in a white hatchback. She told us his last name. We ran a check, and the only car registered to him is a five-year-old Honda. He has no record or outstanding warrants."

"You believed her?"

"I don't have any reason not to believe her. One of the officers confirmed that she teaches courses online via some dinky college in Iowa." He held up his palms. "This does not mean that I don't believe you, dear wife. Someone followed you from either the bar or the Literacy Council. It wasn't this Omario, unless he kept a spare car behind the bar."

I was unable to come up with a counter-argument. "Sometimes a car is just a car."

Duty beckoned the following morning. Keiko came out of her office as soon as I opened the front door. "Claire, I want to thank you again for volunteering. It will not be so crazy this morning, I think."

I hesitated. Although her effusive gratitude was growing tiresome, her tone of voice was dispassionate. Her expression was flat, and her eyes exuded no twinkles. "Have all the students and tutors been contacted?" I asked.

"Yes." She went back into her office and closed the door.

Leslie was in the classroom, reading aloud a gripping story about a woman in a grocery store. A dozen students were in the lounge area with newspapers and notebooks — and cell phones. I found a newspaper and sat down behind my desk. I was reading about natural disasters across the planet when Yelena came out of the ladies' room.

"Claire!" she said. "How are you? This is

nice day, yes?"

I smiled. "I'm fine, thank you. It's a very nice day."

She sat on a corner of the desk. "We have plan for tomorrow. It is day for monthly potluck. You must come. Everybody makes food from home country to share. I bring *soleniye ogurscy* and *okroshka*. Salted cucumbers and cold soup. You will like very much. I invited Ludmila's grandson to come and share with us. He said yes. We will all act like we are sorry that Ludmila is dead. In Russia, everyone goes to funeral and weeps and wails, then gets very drunk with vodka afterward. It is good tradition. I went to funeral in this country. Nobody cries. They have faces like dead person in coffin. I will weep for Ludmila, but I cannot get drunk on vodka because I have to go to work. Is a pity."

"Oh," I said. I hadn't wailed over Carlton's coffin, nor had any of his numerous nubile friends. A professor in the English Department had insisted that everyone come to his house afterward. We stood around and made stiff conversation, but we also made frequent trips to the array of bottles on a kitchen counter. Eventually it turned into an exceedingly jovial gathering. "Am I supposed to bring something?"

"Traditional American dish." Yelena picked up a pen and began to doodle on my pad. "Ludmila's grandson did not have funeral for her. He said that her body was . . ." She grimaced. "I do not know word, but he will send her ashes back to Poland to be buried with family."

"She wasn't happy here."

"That is truth." She glanced over her shoulder, then bent down to whisper, "I hear Keiko and Leslie talk about you earlier. Leslie said you are making her nervous. Keiko said you are with police. Leslie looked not happy to hear this. Then they see me and go into office to keep talking. Do you think Leslie killed Ludmila?"

"No," I said emphatically. The last thing the FLC needed was a rumor fest, courtesy of me. "Neither do the investigators."

"So what did you do to Leslie to make her feel this way?"

Beyond breaking into her house and calling the cops on her? "Nothing. We're all upset about Ludmila's death, even Keiko. I am not with the police, just married to one. They're still sorting out who was here Monday night and what they might have seen. What time did you leave?"

"Not until almost eight. I wanted book from library to learn idioms, but I could not find it. Miao helped me look. Am I out on a limb when I say this? Am I burning my bridges?"

"Not at all, Yelena," I said, trying not to laugh.

She laughed loudly enough for both of us. "These idioms make no sense. One time my husband tells me to get my ducks in row. I tell him I have no ducks, so how can I get them in row? Why would I want to? Ducks are stupid, but very good stuffed with *antonovka* apples and roasted in oven."

"So Miao was here until almost eight? Ludmila was, too. Did she speak to anyone?"

"Maybe you are KGB, or what you call it in this country. Ludmila sits in chair, making ugly faces and grumbling. I offer to bring her tea, but she shakes her head so hard that I hope one of her warts falls off. Poor Gregory is trapped in his office. He opens the door just a crack, sees her, and closes door. He does this two or three times. Miao and I hide behind bookshelf and giggle. Soon it is time to close, so I drive home."

"Can you remember who was here when you left?" I took the pad away from her and picked up a pen, as ready as a stenographer to record the boss's words.

"Ludmila," Yelena said, "and Gregory, unless he climbed out office window. Keiko in her office with man, Miao looking at books. Zayha, Nasreen, and Salima left to walk to bus stop. Graciela was getting in car of Herminia. I heard them talk about going to bar on Thurber Street. Aladino was teasing them from his car." She rubbed her mouth as she thought. "I think girls from South Korea were in restroom. I am not sure."

"All the board members had already gone?"

"I don't know. I saw woman with blond hair go in Leslie's office with movie star man, and I did not see them again. This is giving me headache, all this thinking. I want to think about how I make *okroshka* tonight. I will have to go to grocery store on way home after work." She wafted away.

I looked at my list. It was peculiar that Sonya and Rick had felt the need for a private conversation in an empty office. Either I had been totally fooled by their animosity toward each other or they'd made up. Leslie was in the classroom. I abandoned my post and walked nonchalantly to her office. I had my hand on the doorknob when she tapped me on the shoulder. "Are you looking for me, Claire?"

I froze — and my brain as well. I looked

at the ceiling for inspiration. It was not the Sistine Chapel. "I wanted to borrow one of your teaching manuals so I'll be ready for tutor training in August. I didn't want to disturb you during your class."

She nodded. "Let me see what I can find for you. You're certainly more eager than most of our tutors. It's a mess in here."

I followed her into the room and glanced around. If this was a mess, my lovely library would qualify for a visit from FEMA. There were a couple of folders on her desk next to her cell phone, and a coffee cup. The bookshelf behind her desk was full but not overflowing onto the floor. Unlike Gregory, she did not utilize cardboard boxes for a filing system.

"I'm new to this, so I'd better start with the basics," I said.

"Please sit down for a minute. We need to talk." She went around her desk and settled into her upholstered office chair. I sat on a sofa that was too small for a romantic tryst unless Sonya and Rick were contortionists. "You seem to be determined that I have something to do with Ludmila's death, even though I wasn't here Monday night. What can I say or do to convince you otherwise? I was at home on my computer, grading tests. I did not leave the house." She gave me an exasperated look.

"No, I don't think you had anything to do with Ludmila's death. The only reason I . . . ah, entered your house was to make sure you were okay. For all I knew at that time, Monday night you could have been here briefly to pick up a folder and been seen by the perpetrator." Have I mentioned that I have an overactive imagination, along with a talent for improv? "As for the business yesterday, I was convinced that I was followed home by someone in a black car. I saw you speak to someone in a black car. When the police arrived, I mentioned it. That's all."

"I assume you know what I told them."

"My husband is Deputy Chief Rosen, and he's leading the investigation. Yes, he told me. It was just a pesky coincidence, and I apologize if it inconvenienced you." I wasn't sure why I was pleading my case, since I didn't much care what she thought of me.

She looked at me for a long moment. "If you were intending to snoop through my files, you would have discovered that you need the key."

I couldn't admit that I was more curious about Sonya and Rick's rendezvous. "Not at all," I said earnestly. "I wanted to see if the perp could have hidden in here until everyone except Ludmila was gone. Do you keep your office door locked?"

"No, I keep my filing cabinet locked. It contains personal information about my online and private students. There are times when I need their Social Security and green card numbers to help them expedite paperwork. I have copies of birth certificates and visas. As far as I know, no one is a felon."

"I understand why you're concerned about their privacy. I'd better get back to desk duty before Keiko misses me. I don't want to be fired on my third day."

Nothing of significance happened for the next ninety minutes. I finished the crossword puzzle, answered the phone without panicking, and greeted students as they came in. Shortly before eleven o'clock, Caron and Inez arrived. I was thankful they were talking to each other, since I lacked energy for perpetual teenaged angst. I waved them over. "I love your hair, Inez," I said.

"Thank you. My uncle Carson sends me twenty dollars every year for my birthday. I've been saving it for something special."

I glanced at Caron, who's never held on to a quarter for thirty seconds if there was a vending machine within sight. She looked exceedingly disgruntled. "Who are your students today?" I asked her.

"Just Yelena. I was supposed to have Lud-mila, but that's not going to happen. Have you figured out who did it?"

"The police are still investigating," I said. "Are you two aware of the potluck tomor-row? Apparently, it's a major deal."

Caron shrugged. "Yeah, we're going to go halves on a pizza. Are you going to make something disgusting?"

My darling daughter was not at her most charming. "Yes, dear," I said sweetly. "I'm bringing chicken-fried snails and water-melon pie. Oh, look, it's eleven. You'd bet-ter round up your students."

She and Yelena disappeared into one cubicle, Inez and Zayha, her Egyptian student, into another. I was curious to know what had transpired between the girls. It seemed to have resulted in a cease-fire, but not a peace treaty. No one had warned me about the lethal summer before the senior year.

Gregory arrived, looking chipper. He acknowledged my presence with a wave and went into Keiko's office. I resumed reading a magazine one of the students had left in the lounge. The entire issue was dedicated to exposing celebrity shenanigans. Since almost all of them were unfamiliar to me, I was not engrossed, which was for the best when Leslie's friend Omario came through the front door. I gulped, then managed a civil expression and said, "Good morning. May I help you?"

At close range, he was far from menacing. His face was pudgy and wrinkled, and his lips were soft. He did not look as though he could hike the distance required to reach the apple orchard from a safe parking space. "Is Leslie available?" he asked with only a trace of an accent.

"She's in her office. Would you like me to let her know you're here?"

"You are Claire Malloy?"

I presumed the question was rhetorical. "And you are Omario. I saw you with Leslie yesterday afternoon."

"I needed her advice about a complicated matter."

We looked at each other for an uncomfortable moment. If it was my time to produce a witty response, he might be disappointed. I pictured him dressed in a long white robe and a headdress with a black band. Even in such garb, he would not make a dashing sheik. He might prefer me in a burka. I looked away when Jiang banged open the front door and advanced on my desk.

"I want to talk to Keiko," he said loudly.

I blinked. "She's in her office with Gregory. She should be free shortly."

Omario blinked, too. "Perhaps we will meet again, Ms. Malloy." He nodded and went in the direction of Leslie's office.

Jiang did not move. "You know Miao?"

"Miss Parchester introduced us last week, and I've seen her several times. I was told she went back to China for her grandfather's funeral."

"I saw you go to her apartment yesterday. Why was that?"

I wasn't sure I didn't prefer Omario's company. Jiang had a distinct redolence that suggested he had yet to be swayed by TV commercials for deodorants. I scooted my chair back before my eyes began to water. "I wasn't looking for Miao. I went there to make sure that Luo was all right. She discovered Ludmila's body Tuesday morning."

"What did she say about Miao?"

"That Miao is in China," I said.

"She is not there!" His face mottled with anger. "I e-mailed her brother, who has not heard from her. He said his grandfather is well."

Although Omario was not a sheik in polyester garb, Jiang could have been a model for one of the terra-cotta warriors from the Qin Dynasty. I reminded myself that I wasn't even the messenger. "Do you have any idea where she is?"

"Gregory is all the time bothering her. He asked her for a date. *Yin chong!* He is old enough to be her father. Still he keeps asking her and she says no, but she is worried. She is afraid he will not let her come here to learn better English." He sucked in a breath. "Do you think he did something to hurt her?"

"I don't know," I said, bemused by this new information. "I don't think so. Men get turned down for dates all the time, but they survive. Did she say something about him Monday night?"

"No, not about him. We had an argument, and she was angry at me." His ferocity deflated, and he looked close to tears. "She is so beautiful, even when she is angry. I want us to get married now, not wait three more years for her to get degree. If we have a baby, we can stay in the United States and apply for citizenship. Miao says we must wait, that she cannot have a baby while she is writing her dissertation. We have had this argument many times. The college has a place where people take care of babies. Our parents will help us pay rent, and I can find a job at night."

"Maybe she was so angry at you that she doesn't want to see you for a while. She told everyone that she was leaving so that you wouldn't try to find her."

"Then where is she?" he asked sadly.

I had a pretty good idea where she was, assuming she wasn't allergic to cats, but it wasn't my place to tell him. She had the right not to be bullied by him — or by Gregory. "Miao is most likely staying with a friend for a few days. Give her some time to cool off."

"She is too hot?"

"Cool off from her anger, Jiang. Women are like that. She doesn't seem like the type to punch you in the nose, so she retreated. I'm sure she's fine."

"Then she will still go to her classes. I will watch her building on the campus, and when she comes, we can talk again. Thank you, Ms. Malloy."

"No," I said hastily, "that's exactly what you shouldn't do. If she catches you spying on her, she'll be really angry. You need to wait or you'll make matters worse. She may be back here on Monday."

He said something under his breath and went to the lounge. I kept an eye on him until he settled down to brood. My theory that Miao was at Miss Parchester's house seemed more than plausible. Wily Miss Parchester had only said that Miao told her she was returning to China. I looked at the phone. Would Miss Parchester admit her complicity if I bluntly asked the pertinent question? I envisioned a conversation in which she evaded every accusation with a vague murmur and an invitation to tea. I couldn't barge into her house like a thug. If I mentioned this to Peter, I would be told to run along and bake something for the potluck. Which was a whole 'nother problem. My version of macaroni and cheese came from a box. Neither Caron nor Peter would eat my meat loaf. I'd sworn off frying anything after I'd been dinged with a splatter of oil. I couldn't hide behind another dish of *coq au vin.* I made a mental note to tackle the *haute cuisine* of my native country when I had some free time.

Gregory emerged from Keiko's office and went straight to his own without giving me so much as a nod or a quick smile. I suspected Leslie had confided in Keiko, who'd confided in Gregory. I waited for the phone to ring so that Frances could tell me that I'd been booted off the board and was no longer welcome at the Literacy Council. I was now a pariah, a veritable redheaded stepchild. It was the time for decorum. I took the magazine back to the lounge, sat down at my desk, and began to straighten the paper clips.

Shortly before noon Keiko came out of her office. Ignoring me, she stuck a sign about the potluck on the bulletin board, consulted with a couple of students, and disappeared into the bookshelves. I tapped my finger on the desk. Her behavior was immature, as if we were back in junior high and I was the designated "mean girl."

When she finally emerged, I said, "Will you need me this afternoon?"

"No, it is not so busy in the afternoons. Thank you for your help. I will try hard to find another volunteer so you will not have to do this. You are a very busy person with many better things to do."

"Oh, no," I said, "I enjoy meeting the students. Such a diverse group from so many different cultures and backgrounds. Please don't worry about me."

She was not prepared for my parry. "We need someone permanent. I would never ask that much of you. There is one thing that would be helpful. Ludmila's bag and a bowl that she brought her dinner in are still in my office. The police do not want these things. Can you take them to her grandson?"

Throw me in that briar patch. I saw no

reason to tell her that Bartok was coming the next day for the potluck. I much preferred having a legitimate reason to call on him. "Of course, Keiko, I'll be happy to do that this afternoon. I'm sure he'll be grateful to have his *babcia*'s personal items."

A few minutes later Caron, Inez, and their students came out of the cubicles. I was still amazed by Inez's transformation, but I knew better than to comment on it in Caron's presence. "Would you two like to go out for lunch?" I asked.

"I have a session with Graciela," Inez said.

"Caron and I don't mind waiting for an hour."

She blushed. "I have plans for this afternoon, but thank you, Ms. Malloy."

"I don't," Caron said. "I don't have any plans for the next three days. Joel gets home on Sunday night. I might as well go out to lunch with my mother."

I bit back a tart response. "Don't let me twist your arm, dear. I'm sure you can find someone more suitable to fill the void for the next three days. There's not much to eat at home, but you can find something. There's some brie, and maybe apples. Plenty of ice cream in the freezer. I need to go by the Book Depot anyway."

"You can take me out for lunch," she said.

Inez waggled her fingers and went to the lounge to seek her prey. Caron waited while I collected my purse and the list I'd made of those in the building Monday night. I contemplated telling Keiko that I was leaving, but decided she would figure it out when the phone rang and I failed to intercept the call.

Once we were outside, I looked around for a black car. Nothing in the parking lot or across the street qualified as such. I forced myself to relax. "Where would you like to eat?" I asked Caron as we walked to my car.

She shot me a sly smile. "How about that place by the old mill?"

It was the most expensive restaurant in Farberville. The lunch entrees cost more than dinner entrees at less pretentious places. "We may need a reservation."

Her cell phone was whipped out of her purse, and her fingers darted across the tiny keypad. Within seconds, she said, "I made them for one o'clock. That means we have time to stop at the mall. I have absolutely nothing to wear when school starts. I'm going to be a senior, you know, and that means I have the responsibility to be a good role model for the pitiful freshmen girls. Got your credit card, Mother?"

I did, but it wasn't burning any holes in my wallet. "Yes, dear." As I drove toward the dreaded mall, I said, "What's with you and Inez? I sensed hostility."

"I am not hostile. I am very happy for her now that she doesn't look like a loaf of day-old bread. In the last three days, she's had three dates with different boys. It's like she's trying to prove something." My darling daughter snorted. "Tonight she has a date with Toby Whitbream."

11

"Inez has a date with Toby Whitbream?" I echoed. I would have added something pithy, but I was too astonished.

Caron sniffed. "It's not much of a date, if you ask me. They're going to Toby's little brother's baseball game. That's not my idea of a good time. Inez gripes every time she has to go to her own brother's games. She says the parents get all weird and scream at the coaches and the umpires. I'm sure this game won't be any different, even if she's sitting by the big-shot quarterback."

I found a parking space at the mall. "From what you've told me I didn't think she'd even spoken to him in the past. Now a date?"

"Inez is like the new girl in town. She's been wearing skimpy tank tops, and she bought a bikini that wouldn't cover up a squirrel. So she got contacts and highlights in her hair. So what?"

"Do I hear undertones of jealousy?"

She got out of the car. "I came to shop, not to mope."

She wasn't kidding. In less than forty-five minutes, she dragged me into every upscale store in the mall. My only assignment was to proffer my credit card and stash the receipts in case she changed her mind. We both carried bags back to my car and put them in the trunk. I was then told to drive to the restaurant, where I was allowed to pay for an elegant lunch comprising tall salads and artfully arranged bits of things. Even after dessert, which consisted of squiggles of mousse and a sculpted *tuile,* I was still hungry. Caron's car was at the Literacy Council. I parked there and waited until she put her booty in her trunk and drove away, then went inside. All was calm, all was bright. I knocked on Keiko's door. Once I was given permission to enter, I did so and told her I was there to gather up Ludmila's things.

Keiko grimly handed me a paper grocery bag that contained a notebook, a purse, and a plastic container. "Thank you very much for doing this, Ms. Marroy."

"What happened to 'Claire-san'?" I asked

with what I hoped was a warm, reassuring smile.

"I am so busy trying to get everyone organized that I forgot, Claire-san. Please excuse me. I am in a bad mood today. Kazu's tutor sent home a note yesterday that he was not respectful. My husband and I tried to talk to him, but he was rude to us as well. He will not be allowed to play video games for a week."

"I can sympathize," I said. "My daughter was grounded for a weekend after she convinced her friends that she was an alien and would beam them up if they didn't obey her. She was in second grade at the time. She spent her incarceration building a spaceship out of Popsicle sticks and aluminum foil."

Keiko giggled. "I am not the only parent with such problems."

I hoped that I had patched things up between us. "I'm still planning to come in tomorrow so that I can share in the potluck."

"It is always great fun. I am bringing sashimi made with tuna and mackerel. I hope you like it, Claire-san." She bowed deeply.

I imitated her bow. "I know I will, Keiko-san. If you don't need me to do anything else, I'll drop off the bag at Bartek's house."

We parted on amiable terms. I put the bag in the backseat and headed for the road behind the stadium. This casual monthly potluck had become a demonic cloud above my head. Everything I thought of was ethnic. Spaghetti and tacos violated the spirit. Hamburgers originated in Hamburg, Germany; frankfurters in Frankfurt. French fries were out, as was a Greek salad with olives and feta. My recently acquired culinary skills were useless. Traditional American food. As I drove up the hillside, I promised myself that I would never stoop to a tuna-fish-and-noodle casserole, no matter how desperate I was at midnight. Presuming I found out how to make one.

Bartek was home, dressed in shorts, a bright red T-shirt, and sandals. He'd been cultivating the celebrity-style stubble on his cheeks and chin. Rock music blared from unseen speakers, and there were enough flowers and potted plants to shame a nursery. As he escorted me inside, he said, "The chair of the department insisted that I take off the rest of the week. Of course he never met dear Babcia. I'm going to sneak in tomorrow to meet with my seminar students and invite them here to debate phonological analysis of class diversity — or to get drunk and party. Would you like something to drink? I have wine, beer, and a well-stocked liquor cabinet."

"It's early for me. How about iced tea?"

"Early? It's after three, and it's five o'clock somewhere. Please let me make you a cocktail, Claire. You've been so kind. I was sorry we didn't have a chance to continue our conversation the other day. Tradition demands condolence calls, but they are a nuisance. I have three green-bean casseroles in the refrigerator, and six trays of smoked meats and cheeses from that place on Thurber Street. My students will eat well during our seminar."

"Just tea," I said. I held out the paper bag. "These are your grandmother's things from the Literacy Council."

"Joy of joys. Let me get you a glass of tea, and we can have a lovely chat on the patio."

I sat down in a wicker chair while he went inside for beverages. I was relieved that neither of us had to pretend to be in mourning for Ludmila. I remembered that I'd promised Duke to let him know about a funeral. Since there hadn't been one, I had not failed my obligation. I decided to invite him to the potluck, since it was as close to a memorial service as Ludmila was going to get. No weeping or wailing or maudlin eulogies — just sushi and salted cucumbers and whatever. When Bartek returned, I said, "I understand you're coming to the Literacy Council tomorrow at noon."

He sat down and crossed his legs. "I had no idea how to respond when the Russian woman called me. It was easier to agree with her than to decipher what she was saying about Babcia. She assured me that Babcia was a valued member of their little community and would be missed. Yeah, the same way I miss hemorrhoids."

"The students consider the Literacy Council as a haven, and they are close." I looked down so he couldn't see my expression. I am adept at lying when it's necessary, but I lack expertise. "There's something I meant to ask you about Monday night. You said you were detained by colleagues and arrived after the council was closed. What time was that?"

"Do we really have to talk about this?"

"I'm just trying to get things straight in my mind. Was the building dark?"

"It was eight fifteen, maybe eight thirty. The lights were on, but the door was locked. I pounded on it until I accepted that nobody was there. I went home, expecting to be lectured half the night by Babcia."

"Did the police ask you why you were so late?"

Bartek smiled wryly. "Yeah, they wanted details, and I'm sure they checked my story. Some of us went to Thurber Street to have a drink. I lost track of the time. We linguists are a rowdy bunch."

"Were there any cars in the parking lot?"

"I don't know. It was dark, and I was too busy rehearsing my apology to pay much attention. Yeah, I think there was a car in the far corner. Don't ask me what color or size it was. It may have been a sleeping elephant."

It was likely to have been Toby's, who was scheduled to mope and mop (but not to shop). Why hadn't he responded when Bartek pounded on the door? Peter already knew, but he hadn't passed it along to his devoted wife. I promoted Toby to the top of my list. He wasn't an obvious candidate for the murder, however. He had no motive. If Ludmila was still there, she probably found a reason to squawk at him, but he would have blown her off with typical teenaged contempt. If she was still alive. I wouldn't be receiving the medical examiner's autopsy results until Farberville hosted the Olympics.

"Earth to Claire," Bartek said, interrupting my mental rambling. "Are you there? Your eyes are glazed, and you're beginning to drool. How about something more potent to drink?"

I definitely was not beginning to drool. "No, thank you. It's not five o'clock in my fantasy land. Can you think of anything else that happened while you were at the Literacy Council?"

"I didn't notice anyone lurking in the shadows or breaking a window, if that's what you mean. If you won't have a drink, how about a plate of green-bean casserole? A slice of lemon bundt cake? A ham and cheese sandwich?"

It crossed my mind that green-bean casserole was the quintessential American covered dish, but I had not yet lost all my dignity. I ignored the plea from my stomach. "My daughter and I went out to lunch earlier. Oh, I tracked down Ludmila's friend from the senior citizens center. His name is Duke Kovac. I thought I'd invite him to the potluck."

"The more the merrier. We can reminisce about my grandmother, beloved member of the Farberville Literacy Council international family. I must ask him how he avoided her slings and arrows of outrage."

I needed to think, so I put all thoughts of

lemon bundt cake aside and told him that I needed to go home. He followed me to the front door and gave me a hug. "It was lovely, Claire, and I look forward to the festivities tomorrow."

I wiggled free and escaped to my car. Bartek was behaving like a child who'd been set free in a carnival with a pocketful of money. When he came home, he could revel in the solitude. The only lectures he had to endure were his own. His motive was blaring more loudly than his music, but I couldn't see how he'd done the deed. The Literacy Council was locked, and Toby was in a back room with the vacuum cleaner. If Bartek had told me the truth, that is. I came up with a scenario. Ludmila was sitting inside the building, working herself into a vile snit. Toby had not yet arrived. She admitted Bartek and tore into him with the fury of Euryale, daughter of the Gorgons and blessed with the art of bellowing death screams. They'd ended up in the copy room. What happened there could have been an accident. Once he concealed the body, he went out the front door and made sure it was locked. Toby arrived later and had no reason to look in the room.

I braked for a squirrel as I embellished my scenario, adding dialogue and choreographing the dance that ended in the copy room. It was plausible. Bartek seemed pleasant enough, but he could have been building resentment for a year. Hell hath no fury like a repressed linguist with a harridan for a houseguest. She wasn't a paragon of health, but she could have survived another decade. I doubt any assisted living facility would take her.

It was premature to take this to Peter, since he was obsessed with evidence and other petty annoyances, and I didn't know what he knew. Since I was near the campus, I decided to find out what Drake Whitbream knew about his son's arrival at the Literacy Council Monday night. We were on the board of directors. Surely that made us comrades. I found a parking space designated for visitors and walked to the building that housed the business school. Only a few students were visible. I surmised that most of them preferred morning classes in summer school so they could loll about their apartment complexes in the afternoon. No one needed to study at the library; everything was on the Internet and only a click away. The business majors were nowhere to be seen outside the building. I went inside and gazed at an empty hallway that was poorly lit and smelled like ammonia. The office was on my right, but the door was locked. A sign announced that summer hours were in effect and the office closed at four o'clock. I checked my watch and realized I'd missed the mass exodus by five minutes.

Footsteps echoed on an unseen staircase, and a woman with a briefcase appeared midway down the hall. She started toward a door at the far end of the hall. "Hello," I called. She obligingly stopped and looked back at me, assessing the possibility that I was a deranged grad student. "Can you please tell me where Dean Whitbream's office is?"

"Second floor, next to the elevator." She hurried away in the opposite direction, unconvinced by my pleasant voice and air of civility.

The sign taped on the elevator made it clear that the only way to the second floor was via a staircase. Even as I went upstairs to ask Drake if his son might be a murderer, I couldn't stop thinking about the potluck. Guacamole was more fitting at a Cinco de Mayo festival in Guadalajara, when margaritas might be on the menu. Peanut butter and jelly crepes? I realized I had reached the second floor without considering how to approach Drake. It was likely that he had left for the day, but I knocked on his door and then went inside. "Drake? It's Claire Malloy."

The first room was his secretary's domain. After a moment, an inner door opened and Drake stuck out his head. "Ah, Claire. What are you doing here?"

His face was flushed, and his shirt was partially unbuttoned. I turned as red as he had. "Please forgive me if I'm interrupting you," I said. "I just dropped by to talk about this dreadful mess at the Literacy Council. Nothing important, really. Why don't I come by at another time when you're not . . . occupied."

"Please sit down. I'll be out in a minute. I would like to know what's going on with the investigation. Help yourself to bottled water in the minifridge." The door closed.

I did my best to pretend I couldn't hear the hushed exchange of words in his inner sanctum. I took a bottle of water as suggested and then sat down on a hard bench. The only magazines on the end table were of a financial sort. I ordered myself to forget about the blasted potluck and formulate a plan to squeeze out all the information Drake had about Toby's arrival at the FLC. I couldn't respond if I were asked about Caron's whereabouts on any given evening.

She and Inez were always off to the mall, their favorite pizza place, the bowling alley, a movie theater, or someone's house. They might hit two or three of these destinations. We'd agreed on a midnight curfew unless she called. I doubted Toby had a curfew.

Drake's shirt was buttoned when he joined me, closing the door behind him. "My secretary is on vacation." He sat down behind her desk. "Have the police located the party responsible for Ludmila's death? What a terrible thing for the Literacy Council. We're already scrabbling for donations. If people associate the council with violence, they'll give their money elsewhere."

"Have the police questioned you?"

"A few perfunctory questions about what I did after the meeting was adjourned. Did Deputy Chief Rosen question you, too?" He smiled, but he was visibly nervous.

"I told him what I'd seen. I had the impression all of the board members were in the building when I left. Weren't you in Keiko's office?"

"She had someone in there, so I waited to talk to her. I just wanted to know if Toby was doing a satisfactory job. His bedroom looks like a vandalized thrift shop in a war zone. His bathroom should be tested for bacterial diseases. Even his car is a disgrace. I told the housekeeper not to venture into his room, but my wife overruled me. I hate to imagine what his dorm room will look like."

"Did he clean on Monday night?" Having failed to formulate a clever approach, I went for the jugular.

"Yes, but he didn't get there until ten o'clock. He had car trouble."

That stopped me. The lights had been on when Bartek showed up at eight thirty. I needed to find out who was the last person to leave. Had he or she left the lights on for Ludmila? It was difficult to imagine that person leaving her to sit in the dark. "The police have talked to him, I suppose," I said. "Were the lights on when he finally arrived?"

Drake shrugged. "I didn't ask him, but surely the police did. Is that important?"

"Maybe. Do you remember who was hanging around when you left?"

"There were a lot of students, but I don't know any of their names. Gregory was in his office. I didn't see Rick, Austin, or Sonya. Willie went into the classroom where some volunteer was lecturing. Frances's car was parked next to mine, so she was still inside somewhere."

"You recognized her car?"

"It's a new black Lexus, and she always takes up two parking spaces so no one can park too closely. She's very particular about it. After the May meeting, we walked outside together and she had a fit because a bird had . . . left its mark on it."

That stopped me, but only for a few seconds. The idea of Frances following me from the bakery to my house was ludicrous. Elementary school principals do not slash tires. If she wanted to know where I lived — and I couldn't imagine why she would — all she had to do was look in the telephone directory. Except my new address wasn't there, I realized. I hadn't filled out a form at the Literacy Council or had reason to mention my new house. Peter did not allow his address to be listed anywhere. Even so, it made no sense for Frances to be driving around during school hours.

"Is Toby going to clean tonight?" I asked.

"Yes, but not until ten or so. He's going to his brother's baseball game." Drake stood up. "If that's all, Claire, I need to finish up some paperwork and get out of this mausoleum into the sunshine."

"Thanks for seeing me." I left the office and trudged downstairs, mentally replaying the conversation. Drake might have been repeating what Toby had told him, or he might have been watching Toby change a flat tire. This reminded me that I was supposed to go by the garage and have my tires replaced or balanced or whatever needed to be done to them. While I sat in the waiting room, I could resume fretting about the potluck.

Peter was already home when I finally pulled into the driveway at six o'clock. My new tires had behaved impeccably during Farberville's version of rush hour. I could smell lasagna baking in the oven. I greeted my husband in a leisurely, immodest fashion, then went into the master bathroom for a long, hot shower. When I stepped out, I discovered a glass of wine and a rose on the dressing table. He had his flaws, one of them being his reticence to share confidential information with me, but he had many admirable qualities. I changed into clean clothes, towel-dried my hair, and applied a modest touch of perfume before I joined him on the terrace.

"Have you heard from Caron?" I asked him.

"She came home a few minutes ago and is in her room pouting. Now what's making her utterly miserable?"

He'd given me an excellent opening. "Inez has a date with Toby Whitbream. You know, the quarterback on janitorial duty at the Literacy Council. Have you interviewed him?"

"Of course. He's got boyish charm, but he's not the brightest kid I've met. Why would Inez want to go on a date with him? The last book he read probably featured superheroes."

"Did he mention what time he got to the Literacy Council Monday night?"

"Isn't there some kind of potluck there tomorrow? Have you decided what to take?"

I gritted my teeth and willed myself not to go there. "Please tell me what Toby told you. Did he really get there at ten o'clock because he had car trouble? Were the lights on?"

Peter sighed. "Is there any chance I can change the subject?"

"I can't think of one." I leaned over and nuzzled his neck. "Just get it out and then we can talk about putting in a greenhouse."

"Toby said he was skateboarding on the campus with some friends and lost track of time. When he tried to start his car, the battery was dead. His friends were gone, so he had to wait until someone stopped and offered to help him. Whoever it was had jumper cables, but it took them a long time to get the cables attached and start his car. Toby was positive that it was dark by the time he made it to the Literacy Council. When he went inside and saw that it was ten o'clock, he was worried that his father might be pissed at him."

"Were the lights on?"

"He didn't say. Why is this so important, Claire? Are you withholding information?"

I told him what Bartek had said, then added, "It is important. Who closed the building?"

"Whistler, at eight o'clock or so. He had to shoo out the last few students. He went home and had a couple of stiff drinks. Before you ask, he claims he's never embezzled a dollar and has no idea why he's been accused, nor does he know why Ludmila was giving him grief. Have you heard anything about that?"

"Nobody seems to know. I can't see him pinching her butt or whispering indecent proposals in her ear. He was, by the way, chasing Miao, the Chinese student. Her boyfriend was angry about it."

He took a sip of wine. "I don't remember her. Was she at the Literacy Council Monday night? Wait . . . didn't she fly home the next day for a funeral or something?"

"That's her story. Can you check with the airlines?" I wasn't ready to throw Miao and Miss Parchester under the red and white campus bus quite yet. If I was correct, which I needed to determine first. Miss Parchester would come to the potluck. "Oh no," I wailed suddenly. "The blasted potluck! I put it out of my mind and forgot to stop by the store to look for inspiration. I'm going to feel like a fool tomorrow when I show up empty-handed. I'm on the board of directors, for pity's sake. I'm a supporter, not a moocher. Can I take the lasagna?"

"Go look in the refrigerator."

I took our empty glasses inside and set them on the counter. I held my breath as I opened the refrigerator door, then let out a whoop when I saw a large platter of deviled eggs, garnished with fresh parsley. They were total Americana. I forgot about wine as I dashed back out to the terrace and threw myself in Peter's lap. "My darling, adorable, fantastic husband!" I smothered him with kisses until he eased me away.

"Calm down," he said soothingly. "I'm flattered, but I didn't make them. Caron did. She said she didn't want you to rip out your hair and embarrass her in front of her friends. She bought the eggs herself."

I stayed where I was because it was a very

nice place to be. "I underestimate her. One day she has a junior high mentality, the next day she's an adult. Almost an adult, anyway. A year from now she'll be letting me buy new clothes for college and driving away in whatever extravagant car she can weasel out of you."

"She may have forgotten to mention one of those junior high moments," he said as he wiggled around to get more comfortable. I am slender, but not emaciated. "It seems that she and Inez drove by the Literacy Council on Monday night. They wanted to hide in the bushes and try to get a photo of Toby with a mop."

"They what! She told you, but not me!" I plunked down on the adjoining chaise. "Those little vipers! What did they see?"

"They saw Bartek pounding on the door. They decided to try another night. Before you charge upstairs, you might think about the two dozen deviled eggs in the refrigerator."

I sank back and stewed on this for a long while. All they'd done was drive by and omit to tell me. Their story confirmed Bartek's version. I decided not to convene a grand jury until I heard all the details. It could wait. I went inside and returned with wine. When a buzzer went off, Peter announced that it was time for dinner.

I called Caron, and we all sat at the island to eat. Peter was highly amused for some reason, but I didn't let it irritate me. We conversed about a greenhouse and perhaps a water lily pond with koi. Caron pointed out their life expectancy was limited due to the herons we'd seen by the stream. Peter said he was more willing to invest in gold-fish. Caron wondered aloud if they were good for sushi. I thanked her for the deviled eggs, and she smiled smugly.

She insisted on cleaning up after we finished. I wasn't sure if she knew she'd need lots of brownie points in the future, but I kept it to myself. Peter went into his office. I leaned my elbows on the granite surface and said, "Why don't you invite over some friends tomorrow afternoon to swim? There's no reason for you to hide in your room until Joel gets back."

"What's that supposed to mean?"

"I just want you to enjoy the summer. I wasn't thinking about a big crowd, just Ashley, Carrie, Edison, Inez, the Maxwell boy, Toby, and a few others. I'll spring for hot dogs and chips."

"You didn't give birth to any knuckle-heads, Mother. Do you want to interrogate Toby about Monday night? Sure, I'll text everybody, but he'll freak out when he sees that it's from me. He's never glanced at me in the halls between classes. We were in the same world history class, but he sat in the back corner and slept. I'd be surprised if he knew my name."

"Maybe it would be better to have Inez invite him."

"Yeah, right." She dropped the dish towel in the sink and returned to her room.

Now that I was no longer in a cold sweat about the potluck, I went into my library to make more lists. I realized that I was fixated on the issue of lights in the building. Caron and Inez has seen the lights when they drove by; more importantly, they'd seen Bartek at the door. It was unfortunate they'd hadn't pulled over to see what happened next. I needed to talk to Toby and to Gregory. I could corner one at the potluck and the other in my own backyard.

I took out the directory and found Duke Kovac's number. The phone was answered by a woman with a heavy Southern drawl. I asked to speak to Duke. After a moment of silence, she said, "Now just who is this?"

"Claire Malloy. It's about an old friend of his named Ludmila."

"That bitch?" Each word had at least two syllables. "Duke hasn't seen her in ages.

266

What's this about?"

I added her to my list of suspects, sight unseen. I repeated my request, then winced as she muffled the receiver and yelled his name.

He came on the line. "This is Duke." I explained who I was and told him about the potluck. His voice dropped to a whisper. "I dunno, but I guess I'll try to make it. Tillie wasn't real fond of Ludmila. Noon, right?"

I confirmed the time and hung up. I made a note to explore the cause of Tillie's antipathy, although Ludmila had not endeared herself to many people. Duke seemed to be the sole exception. He'd either liked her (for some peculiar reason) or had felt so sorry for her that he put up with her. I decided to put it all aside for the time being and was searching the bookshelves for a distraction when the phone rang. I waited to see if Peter might answer it in his office, but after five rings I conceded that he would not.

"Hello," I said. "This is Claire."

"Thank goodness. I wasn't sure this was the right number. Willie gave it to me, but she can be such an airhead. There's a rumor she got confused in her chambers and undressed before she put on her robe. There she was on the platform, buck-naked under-neath. That's our Willie."

I recognized Sonya's high-pitched chatter. "Can I help you, Sonya?"

"I heard there's going to be some kind of memorial service for Ludmila, and I thought all of us on the board ought to go. Do you know the details?"

"Yes, indeed." I felt a tremor of glee, since I was sure she didn't have two dozen deviled eggs in her refrigerator. I tried to keep my voice neutral as I told her about the upcoming potluck, emphasizing that Bartek would be there. "He had her body cremated, so this is the only time for us to offer our condolences. Do you think the other board members can make it?"

"I can, because I set my own hours. Frances is on vacation this week, so she can come. Willie takes two hours for lunch; she can skip her nap this one time. Austin and Rick will have to work it out with their employers. Drake can make arrangements, too. That's everybody, isn't it?"

"Yes. Please let everyone know it's a potluck. The students take great pride in bringing dishes from their native countries. It's up to us to provide good old-fashioned American dishes." It was almost nine o'clock, I noted happily.

"That's not a problem," Sonya said. "I'll pick up a chocolate cake in the morning. Frances made some dynamite baked beans for the picnic last summer. If Austin and Rick show up with lemonade, be careful. Thanks so much, Claire. I'll see you tomorrow."

An Anglo-Saxon expletive came to mind.

12

I carried the platter into the Literacy Council and left it in the back classroom. The air-conditioning was on, so I presumed most of us would not come down with salmonella. The tables already held a large number of mysterious dishes from the first wave of students. I stuck my head into Keiko's office to announce my arrival and took my position at the reception desk. It was growing tedious. I'd envisioned tutoring for a couple of hours a week. If I was lucky enough to have Yelena as a student, we would have hilarious sessions attempting to make sense out of idioms and other English-language anomalies. If I was burdened with Ludmila's evil twin sister, I would decline politely. Volunteerism has its limitations — unless you need it on your college application.

Leslie was teaching a class. Some of the tutors brought food and, at my suggestion, took it to the back classroom. Miss Parchester's African student entered empty-handed and disappeared into a cubicle. I forgave him, since it appeared that we would have enough food to feed all the pupils at Frances's school. Which reminded me of two pertinent tidbits about her: She drove a black car, and she was on vacation all week. The idea was still absurd, but I decided to have a conversation with her about her free time — and with Sonya or Rick about their private meeting in Leslie's office, and with Gregory about locking up the building on Monday night, and with Miss Parchester about her guest room. I wondered if I would have time to sample the food.

The phone rang. "Waterford. I need to speak to Leslie Barnes."

"She's teaching right now. Would you like to leave a message?"

"Tell her if she doesn't contact me, she'll be in worse trouble. She's got twenty-four hours."

He hung up before I could formulate a question. I was baffled. It would be interesting to see her reaction when I gave her the message, which I supposed had something to do with her divorce. Waterford might be a lawyer, or he might be a private detective. It reeked of nastiness or even blackmail. I

271

debated calling Peter, but he would point out patiently that Leslie was not a suspect in the investigation and her personal life was precisely that.

At ten o'clock, Leslie's students streamed out of the classroom and she headed for her office. I intercepted her and handed her the slip of paper. "He said to tell you that you'll be in trouble if you don't get in touch with him," I said evenly. "He was pretty gruff."

"I'm sure he was." Her tone was unconcerned, but she looked pale.

"Is there anything I can do to help?"

"No." She continued into her office and slammed the door.

I spent the next hour reading the newspaper and exchanging pleasantries with the students and tutors. I was no longer terrified of callers with limited English. Two potential students came in, one from Sweden and the second from Estonia. I gave them forms to fill out and alerted Keiko. A tutor called in to cancel a session; I duly wrote a note. After a quick visit to the ladies' room, I started a fresh pot of coffee and took out cups, spoons, and the customary accoutrements. The tables were crowded with foil-covered dishes and plastic containers. When Keiko had given her report at the board meeting, she had said there were about a hundred students and fifteen tutors. There would be ample food for all if they escaped from their day jobs.

I'd just sat down at my desk when Miss Parchester tottered in. "Good morning, Claire. How are you?"

"Fine, Miss Parchester. I'd like to have a word with you, if you don't mind. It's about Miao."

"Is Mudada here?"

I pointed at the row of cubicles. "I really would like to talk to you now. I'm sure you know why." I gave her a steely look.

"I know you would, dear, but I can't keep Mudada waiting." She took a package of cookies out of her bag and put it on my desk. "I finally found them on a high shelf in the cupboard. Will you please find a plate for them?" She tottered away.

"That went well," I said under my breath. If I couldn't catch her during the potluck, I knew where she lived. It might be tricky to catch any one of the people on my list, I thought glumly. Caron and Inez came in. The latter was carrying a pizza box, but they both were texting madly. I sent Inez to the back room and asked Caron if her e-vites were successful.

"Yeah," she said without looking up from her cell, "but the word got around, and you're going to need more than one package of hot dogs."

"What about Toby?"

"For some reason that defies me, he wants to come. Maybe he's got the hots for you, too."

"Please don't tell me he has 'the hots' for Inez. I don't want to shave her head, but I will if I have to."

Inez appeared from the bookshelves. "You're going to what?"

"Just a little joke," I said. "Your hair looks wonderful. How was your date with Toby Whitbream?"

She glowered at Caron before saying, "Fine, Ms. Malloy. It wasn't really a date. We went to his little brother's baseball game. The kid got a home run, and his team won. That was about it."

"What did you think about him?" I prodded.

"He's okay for a jock. I'd better find Aladino." She went into the lounge area.

Caron grimaced. "So now you're the Grand Inquisitor? I am So Embarrassed. Inez will never tell me anything now. If this gets out no one will."

"Isn't Nasreen waiting for you? You don't want to run over your hour and miss your chance to taste all the exotic food." Thus spoke Torquemada.

Gregory was the next to appear onstage. He wore a dark suit and muted tie appropriate for funerals (and court appearances). "Good morning, Claire. Does Keiko have everything under control?"

"She's not sobbing in her office, so she most likely does. These potlucks happen every month. Don't you attend them?"

"Not if I can help it. I have an aversion to raw fish, incendiary curry, and unidentifiable glop. I prefer to have the bland buffet with the Rotarians. At least I know what I'm eating." His smile was faintly condescending as he continued into his office.

"How about a glass of water from the great, gray-green, greasy Limpopo River?" I said to his closed door. I did not stick out my tongue at him, although the thought crossed my mind. I resumed answering the phone, sending offerings to the back classroom, sorting thumbtacks by color, and scribbling cryptic notes to myself in what I hoped was an indecipherable code.

It was indeed indecipherable, and I was trying to recall the code names I'd assigned to people when Yelena perched on my desk.

"Good morning, Claire. I must ask favor from you. I am going to make speech in front of everybody about Ludmila. I looked on Internet and found traditional things, but I do not understand. Am I supposed to talk about ashes and dust? Ludmila is now ashes but not dust. Dust is what I have under sofa. That seems like bad thing to say."

"Why don't you just say a few words about how much Ludmila will be missed at the Farberville Literacy Council. Say she was part of our family, and we're all sorry that she passed away."

"Passed away?"

"It's a euphemism for 'died.' The mention of death makes some people uncomfortable," I said.

Yelena picked up a pen and crossed out part of her script. "So I say she didn't die, she passed away. I tried very hard to think of nice things to say about her, but I couldn't think of any. Please help me, Claire. Her grandson will be hearing me."

"He didn't like her, either."

Yelena gazed over my shoulder for a moment. "Then I shall present Russian poetry about death. I will be dramatic and everyone will weep, even if they do not understand words. I have black coat in car. A basket of flowers would be good." She leaned down and hugged me, then went off in search of props.

Austin and Rick came in together and stopped at my desk. Austin wore trousers and a white shirt, but his bow tie was bright green. Rick was in standard banker garb. "Glad you two could make it," I said. Austin had a large paper sack in his arms. "We're not having frozen daiquiris or Long Island iced tea for lunch. The Muslim students are here, and they won't appreciate it."

"Hey, don't overestimate me," he said, laughing. "I brought my Crock-Pot, little beef cocktail wienies, and barbecue sauce. It won't offend anyone."

"What about the Hindus?" Rick asked. "They don't eat beef. That's why I brought all-American doughnuts, freshly made and nicely glazed."

Austin waggled his finger. "What about the diabetics? Have you no compassion for the insulin-disabled?"

I smiled, but a quick glance at my notes reminded me that Rick was on my list. "Austin, why don't you plug in your Crock-Pot in the back room. Rick, I'd like to talk to you for a minute."

Austin gave me a crisp salute and left. Rick looked as though he wished he could do the same. "Claire," he began, "I need to apologize about the other afternoon in the beer garden. I can't claim I was distraught over that woman's death, since I barely knew who she was. I was worried about other things. I am sorry if I embarrassed you."

"You didn't embarrass me. I spent many an afternoon in a beer garden when I was in grad school. That's not what I want to talk about. On Monday night after the board meeting, someone saw you and Sonya go into Leslie's office and close the door. Was there something you two needed to discuss?"

"It had nothing to do with the meeting."

"I had the impression that you didn't like her." I took a deep breath and searched for a tactful way to continue. "If there's something going on between you two, it's none of my business."

"Between us? She's not my type, I can assure you. She thinks I'm brash, and I think she's trash. Why else would she be shacking up with Gregory?"

"With Gregory?" I stared numbly at him. "Are you serious?"

"I wish I wasn't. This isn't the best place to talk about it. Shall we meet at Mucha Mocha after this requiem potluck, say about one thirty?"

"Yes, of course," I said, still reeling. Luck-

278

ily, the front door opened and Willie, Frances, Drake, and Sonya herself came inside, all laden with dishes or boxes, and continued toward the back room. Gregory was older than Sonya, but the age difference wasn't incongruous. They were both single. I'd failed to see any intimate glances between them. On the first day I'd gone to the Literacy Council to volunteer, she'd been displeased with him, almost snappish. If they were having an affair, I didn't want to entertain any visions of what occurred in the bedroom. They were consenting adults.

Before I could assimilate this new information into my grand overview, Bartek arrived. I was glad to see he was in his tweedish outfit rather than shorts and sandals. He came over and said, "What am I supposed to do? I'm sure as hell not going to give a eulogy. I know almost nothing about her life in Poland, but she must have made everybody miserable there, too."

"All you have to do is look solemn and shake people's hands. This is nothing more than a pretense on everyone's behalf. The students will acknowledge her death, the board members will offer condolences, and we'll be out of here in less than an hour. If you want a drink to brace yourself, try Gregory's office. Let me know if you need glasses and ice."

I pointed him in the right direction, and he took my advice. I felt like a perky funeral director when Frances came to my desk.

"Shouldn't Gregory be out here?" she asked me.

I held up my hands. "I'm just the unpaid subordinate. He's in his office. Bartek Grabowski is in there, too. Feel free to join them."

"Perhaps I should talk to Keiko. I doubt Gregory has any idea what's going on here. He rarely does. I'm beginning to regret that we hired him. There were other suitable candidates. I followed up on his references, but I had doubts." When I raised my eyebrows, she shrugged. "He was the director of a similar nonprofit in one of those little New England states like Connecticut or Rhode Island. The woman I spoke to was vague about the reason he left. I had the impression she wanted to say more."

"Why did he say he left?"

"He didn't like the winters. We'd listed the opening on a Web site, and he e-mailed a cover letter and his résumé. I verified that he'd done quite well raising money and getting grants. That's the basic job description. Keiko's the one who runs the program, deals with the students' problems, coordinates with the tutors, orders supplies, and unlocks the door every morning. She puts in a lot more hours than Gregory for half his salary. I promised her a raise this fall — if we can afford it. I do want to tell you how much we appreciate your involvement, Claire."

"Thank you, Frances. I seem to have stepped in at an awkward time."

"One could say that," she said. She beckoned to Drake, who was hovering. "I was telling Claire how lucky we are to have her on the board."

"Very lucky," he said in a flat voice. "How's your investigation going?"

Clearly I hadn't fooled him by my visit the previous day. "The police are still looking into it," I said. "So many people to interview, and some of them in their native tongue. They've never had to deal with such a polyglot group. Did you ever meet Ludmila?"

Frances shook her head. "No, but I heard her squawking after several of our board meetings. I avoided her."

"So did I," Drake said. "She was obnoxious. Gregory should have found a way to get rid of her." He stiffened. "That's not to imply that he did. I wish we could blame this unfortunate event on a burglar or a random psychopath. I don't suppose the detectives found signs that a window had been tampered with. There are more than a dozen computers and some expensive audiovisual equipment. It would have been a lucrative heist."

"You've been watching those TV cop shows, haven't you?" Austin said as he joined us. "I prefer *Sesame Street.*"

"I'm sure you do," Drake said.

Austin laughed. "You must be Oscar the Grouch. Rick and I are Bert and Ernie. What about you, Frances? Big Bird?"

"This is not the time for frivolity," she said coldly. "In case you've forgotten, this is a memorial gathering for one of our students."

"Well, tickle me, Elmo."

I will admit I snorted, but I managed not to smile.

Students came out of the classroom, and more came in from outside. Gregory and Bartek emerged, both looking mellow. Leslie looked far from mellow, but she greeted the board members and accompanied them toward the back classroom. The reception area and lounge were uninhabited — as was Leslie's office. Feeling remarkably guilty, I hurried inside it and closed the door. My note from Waterford had been crumpled and discarded on the floor. I resisted an impulse to pick it up and opened a folder on her desk. Like the ones I'd found at her home, it contained a résumé and a photograph of a man, this one with a beard. I flipped over the page to expose a photograph of an earnest young blond woman. A second folder contained the résumé of an Asian man and a sticky note with "Jennifer?" written on it. The next folder was for a slightly older woman who, according to her résumé, was a graduate student at the University of Arizona. Her name was not Jennifer.

I was beginning to worry that my absence might be noticed. I replaced the folders as best I could and left Leslie's office. I almost yelped when Yelena materialized and grabbed my arm.

"You must taste my *soleniye ogurscy,* Claire."

The back classroom was crowded, and people were balancing plates in the hall and seated at cubicles. The cacophony of voices was louder than a college bar on Saturday night. Caron and Inez were in a corner, eating pizza and texting. As Yelena deftly elbowed people aside, I saw Duke in the doorway. I accepted a plate with a bright green pickle and squirmed my way out of the throng.

283

"I'm glad you could make it," I said to Duke. "Have you met Ludmila's grandson, Bartek?"

"Once when he came to pick her up at the senior center. He was impatient with her. One should respect one's grandparents. Without them, one would not be born, right?"

"I cannot argue with that. Would you like a pickle?"

"I would always like a pickle, Claire Malloy. Have the police found out who killed Ludmila?" He bit into the pickle, which crunched in response.

"I don't think they've made much progress. Can you remember anything she might have said about someone having a dirty secret?"

"I've been trying to think back. She detested the director and called him *swistak*." He spelled it for me. "I looked it up in a Polish dictionary. It means 'whistler.'"

"That's his name," I said. "Did you look up any other words?"

"They are not fit for your delicate ears. When I asked her why she used such words when speaking of him, she muttered and I could not understand her. To be honest, I didn't want to know. I tried to get her to talk about the weather, the flower gardens, the farmers' market, the news, anything. She did like to talk about how Bartek was an important professor at Farber College. I encouraged her."

I sent him into the fray to fight for food. It was curious that Ludmila's most vituperative curse was merely Gregory's last name. I couldn't envision anyone cringing if I were to throw his last name at him. A twenty-watt bulb lit up above my head. I hurried back to my desk and wrote down the word before I muddled it. It suggested a new line of inquiry that I'd totally missed.

The sudden silence caught my attention, so I returned to the back room. Yelena stood on a chair, dressed in a long black raincoat. "Passing away of life must be honored," she announced in trembling voice. "I will now tell you sad story about passing away of beautiful peasant girl." She reverted to Russian and leapt into her narrative. Her voice rose and fell, and her arms flapped like the wings of a convulsive condor. At the height of her recitation, she became so agitated that she would have fallen off the chair if Austin hadn't steadied her. She shrieked a few more words, took a quick glance at Austin, and collapsed into his arms with a shuddery sigh.

We all clapped with varying degrees of enthusiasm. Yelena bowed, reveling in her ten seconds of fame. Since I was not the emcee, I stayed by the door and let Frances take the spotlight. While she droned on about the terrible loss and the importance of carrying on in the face of tragedy, I eyed the remaining food. The platters, plates, and casserole dishes contained only scraps and smears. Even Yelena's pickles had been devoured. Austin's Crock-Pot was soaking in the sink. Chocolate cake crumbs looked like well-fed ants. I'd given my pickle to Duke.

Keiko sidled up to me. "Did you like my sashimi, Claire-san?"

I sadly admitted I hadn't had a chance to eat anything. I shot a dirty look at Gregory, who was still grazing on a laden plate. I hoped someone had brought pickled pigs' eyes and fried newts to the party and he had gulped them down, despite his snooty remarks made earlier. Frances introduced Bartek. He thanked everyone for the lovely memorial, shook hands as he made his way to the door, and gave me a harried smile.

"Survival of the fittest," he said. "I hope I'll see you soon, Claire. I'd love to drink wine with you and discuss anything else but Babcia. Anything else." Before I could retreat, he gave me yet another hug that made me uncomfortable. "Come by later," he whispered in my ear.

I freed myself. "I have plans for the afternoon — and I also have a husband whom I adore. If I have any more questions, I'll call." I caught Austin's arm as he came out and let him escort me to my desk.

"You and Bartek got a thing?" He smirked, but I wasn't offended. If I were a cougar, I'd be pursuing him. His smile faded. "What's going on with the investigation? Are they getting close?"

"My husband won't tell me anything. I have a long list of unanswered questions, but I'm floundering."

"I hope you don't suspect Rick."

"Should I?" I countered. "I can come up with a possible narration in which he stayed in Leslie's office until he thought everyone had gone. He went into Gregory's office to resume prowling through the paperwork. Ludmila surprised him. They scuffled and she fell. If you'll wait a minute, I'll come up with a more elaborate story."

"Rick and I left together and went across the street to the bar. He's a decent dude, maybe a tiny bit obsessive, but he wouldn't harm anyone. You know what they say about bankers' blood."

"No, I don't."

"They don't have any."

Austin waited for me to laugh, but I was considering this new scenario. Austin would give Rick an alibi in any circumstances. "How long did you stay at the bar?" I asked him.

"Maybe a couple of hours. He was pissed about what happened at the meeting. I was home before midnight. Take care of yourself, Claire. Somebody out there is not a nice person."

"True." He left, and I sat down at my desk, more confused than ever. Ludmila had been in the middle of a spiderweb, which she built herself, but there were lines radiating in all directions. It was a very complex web. I was fine-tuning the analogy when Caron and Inez came over.

Inez failed to make eye contact. It was preferable to Caron's glare. "You do remember that you have to go to the store on your way home," she said. "Expect at least twenty people. I Cannot Believe you made me do this. What's Joel going to think when he gets home and hears I've been having wild parties?"

"Then don't have a wild party, dear." I saw Miss Parchester slip out the door, but it would be unseemly to tackle her in the park-

ing lot and drag her back inside. "I'll get enough food for forty, and we can freeze what we don't use."

"Yeah, right. C'mon, Inez. Bikinis are still on sale at the mall."

No one else felt the need to speak to me as they left. Gregory, Keiko, and Leslie went into their respective offices. Bartek winked at me, but I failed to notice. Duke waved. Students left in groups. It was a few minutes after one o'clock, so I packed up my notes and prepared to go meet Rick at Mucha Mocha. I didn't mind waiting as long as I found something to eat. I wished I'd had a chance to sample Caron's deviled eggs so I could gush with sincerity. I would never admit to Yelena that I hadn't savored every bite of her pickle.

I opened Keiko's door and told her I was leaving. She glanced up briefly, nodded, and returned her attention to her computer. Hunger prevented me from barging into Gregory's office to ask about Monday night I could come back after I'd talked to Rick although I was in a time crunch to sho and be home at four o'clock. I hadn't care for Caron's casual reference to wild partie Not under my watch, I vowed.

Mucha Mocha was calm. I took my lur to the patio and sadly ate a ham sandw

instead of homemade food from across the planet. I love incendiary curry, cocktail wienies, doughnuts, and whatever else had been brought. I assessed all the information I'd heard from Rick, Austin, and, most interestingly, from Duke Kovac. I glanced at a frizzy-haired man clicking on his laptop. Why not? Brazen was not my middle name, but I was not above a polite disruption.

I sat down next to the man. "Hello," I said. "I'm just so helpless when it comes to computers, and I'm hoping you can help me. I'll treat you to the pastry of your choice. Please?"

"Yeah, why not?"

I pulled out a paper. "I want to find out about a company with the word *swistak* as part of the name. It may be a European pharmaceutical company." I spelled the word and gave him my most guileless smile. "This is so kind of you."

"I was just browsing. Did you know there are two hundred and thirty-eight thousand breeding pairs of emperor penguins in Antarctica?"

"Fascinating," I breathed. I wanted to poke him, but I only had a few minutes before Rick arrived. "The pharmaceutical company . . . ?"

He abandoned his quest for penguin data

and started clicking. "Okay, look." He pointed at a line on the screen. "Bergmann-Swistak Pharmaceuticals, headquartered in Hamburg and makers of a long list of bizarre-sounding drugs."

I took out a ten-dollar bill and handed it to him. "Enjoy your pastry."

"I'm gluten-free, but I can use the money."

I thanked him and went back to my table. Gregory's father had been a co-owner of Bergmann-Swistak Pharmaceuticals. At some time in the past, Gregory or his father had Anglicized the family name. Ludmila might have seen a photo of father and son and made the leap.

My new best friend sat down across from me. "I did a little more research," he said. "Bergmann-Swistak went bankrupt ten years ago after a massive class-action suit. For decades they sold drugs that were diluted, mislabeled, and in some cases lethal. The government closed them down. It turned out the company's assets had vanished, as had the executives. The lawsuit hasn't been settled, and there are outstanding warrants." He left before I could dig out another tip.

That was excellent motivation to change one's name. Ludmila had treasured an old photograph of a small child, perhaps a dear friend's grandchild. If the child had died because of a tainted drug, I could understand why Ludmila was so enraged whenever she saw Gregory. If he'd realized why, he would have known how much of a threat she posed. Her English was inadequate to expose him, but he couldn't be sure a new Polish student might not wander through the door of the Literacy Council. Ludmila would have a confidante, quite possibly one who remembered the Bergmann-Swistak scandal as well. On Monday night Ludmila had been waiting for Bartek to pick her up, giving Gregory the perfect opportunity.

I was tweaking my hypothesis when Rick joined me. "That was quite a production," he said. "Who is that Russian woman, and what was she doing?"

"Her version of a eulogy. She was an actress in Moscow before she came here. Why don't you tell me about Sonya and Gregory?"

He stirred his coffee for a moment. "Since I joined the board, I've been sorting through receipts and bills in Gregory's office. It's been frustrating. If I find a manila envelope with credit card bills, it disappears the following evening. That means I have to dig through all the blasted boxes again."

"Why don't you take them with you?"

292

"He'd accuse me of tampering with them. He knows I don't have any hard evidence."

"You could call in the police department's forensic accountant, you know."

Rick held up his hands. "The publicity would kill us whether I'm right or wrong. Who's going to give us grant money if there's any hint of embezzlement? We have to offer proof that we're using the money according to their specifications. That's a significant part of Gregory's job. We also have to send him to conferences to enhance our standing in the ESL community. Regrettably, this gives him a chance to double-bill his expenses. I know damn well he's comped for some hotel rooms and meals, but his credit card charges say otherwise. He then writes checks to reimburse himself."

"What does this have to do with Sonya?"

"After the board meeting Thursday, I went into Gregory's office. I almost fell over when she marched in. When I told her that he was gone, she growled and went out to her car. On a whim, I followed her." He caught my frown. "Hey, I don't fancy myself to be a private eye. I'm merely curious — just like you. She drove to his house. I saw them embrace in the doorway."

"They're adults. As long as they aren't . . . behaving indecorously in his office when other people are around, I don't see why it's a big deal."

"I've already told you that I don't like Sonya. She's a manipulator of the worst sort. From what I've heard from my younger colleagues, she frequents the bars on Thurber Street and rarely leaves alone. That's her business. The problem is I have a guilty conscience. Don't bother to ask — I'm not going to elaborate under any circumstances. I took her into Leslie's office Monday night to tell her that Gregory is an evil man."

"Because he may be embezzling money from the Literacy Council?"

"No, because he's a murderer."

13

I stared at him with what must have been a somewhat unattractive scowl. "Rick, you can't make an accusation like that if you don't have evidence!"

"Well, I just did. In any case, all I did Monday night was try to warn Sonya about him. She flipped me off. Having done my duty, I absolved myself from any future responsibility for her welfare. I need to get back to work." He picked up his coffee mug and the torn packets. "I'll see you at the next board meeting. I hope you enjoy fireworks."

He left me sitting in a daze. I wanted to chase after him and demand to hear the reason for his accusation, but I had a feeling it wouldn't do any good. He didn't know about Bergmann-Swistak Pharmaceuticals or he would have told me.

I had a little bit of time before I needed to buy supplies for Caron's party. I wanted to talk to Miss Parchester, but she would insist on tea and chatter. It might take a long time before I could take control of the conversation. I decided to try to corner Gregory in his office. I had no qualms about going after him as bluntly as necessary. I gave myself a few minutes to prioritize my questions and then drove back to the Literacy Council. As I came around the corner, I saw an ambulance in the parking lot. This was not good.

I parked on the street and walked to the door, reminding myself to breathe. Keiko was waiting inside, her hand plastered to her mouth and her eyes wide. "Thank goodness you came back, Claire. A most terrible thing has occurred. Miss Willie has suffered a great illness."

"Is she . . . ?" I couldn't say the word.

"They are taking her to the hospital. I don't know how bad it is."

Gregory appeared. "Claire, good. Keiko, talk to the students before we have another riot. Tell them one of the board members is ill, that's all." He gestured at me. "She's in one of the small classrooms that we don't use in the summer. She's unconscious but breathing."

I followed him past the cubicles. Leslie was standing near the open doorway, her hands clasped tightly. Inside the paramedics were lifting Willie onto a gurney. She had an oxygen mask over her mouth and nose, and her complexion was almost gray. Her arm looked pathetically thin where the IV needle was taped. We all stepped back as the paramedics maneuvered the gurney through the doorway and down the hallway.

"What are we supposed to do?" I asked in a small voice.

Leslie shook her head. "I have no idea. Should we notify someone? Do we have her office number at the courthouse?"

"I have her home telephone number," Keiko said as she trotted up to us, "but I think she lives alone."

Gregory was rubbing his face so hard that he was liable to erase his features. "Keiko, get on the Internet and find her office number. I have Sonya's cell number. Maybe she can get hold of Frances."

"Shouldn't someone go to the hospital?" I inserted. "Did they take her purse?"

Gregory went into the room. "No, and they'll want her insurance information. In their world, that's all that matters."

Leslie cleared her throat. "I need to deal with fifty panicky students."

"I'll get on my computer and notify her staff," Keiko said. "She told me she was hearing a case this afternoon."

"And I," Gregory said, "must stay here in my position as executive director. I can expect the police to show up in the next ten minutes."

I couldn't bring myself to announce that I had to go buy hot dogs and buns for my daughter's pool party. "All right," I said, trying not to sound spiteful. "Before I go, would someone please tell me what happened? Who found her?"

"Yelena," Keiko said. "She was helping clean up after the potluck. She didn't know what to do with all the bags full of trash, so she decided to put them in an empty room. She said some of them were stinky."

I was glad I hadn't been there. Yelena might have still been panting with passion from her recitation, and her reaction would have redefined melodrama. "Did Willie have a heart attack?"

Gregory shrugged. "The paramedics ordered us out of the room, and I couldn't understand them from the doorway." He handed me a large, worn leather purse. "Hadn't you better be going?"

I stopped in Keiko's office and scribbled my cell number on a piece of paper. When I got to my car, I called Caron and explained the situation, then said, "I promise to reimburse you, and I'll get home as soon as

I can." I allowed her to gripe for a moment and then ended the call. Peter's cell went to voice mail, as usual. I called Jorgeson and told him about Willie. "There's nothing I can do at the hospital, but I have to stay until someone else takes over. Please let Peter know that at least twenty teenagers are coming to the house at four o'clock to swim. If he can't be there, tell him to send a couple of uniformed officers. I do not want my house destroyed."

I parked in the hospital lot and went into the emergency room. There were a dozen people sitting on plastic chairs while they waited to be seen. I went to the desk and inquired about Wilhelmina Constantine.

The weary middle-aged woman glanced up. "Do you have her insurance card?"

I dug through Willie's purse and took out a bulging wallet. After a lengthy search, I found her card. Rather than handing it over, I said, "I'd like an update on her condition."

"I don't have that information. I need her card so I can process her." She held out her hand.

I dangled it temptingly. "Someone has information about her condition. I'll just wait over there."

"Do I need to call security?"

I chuckled unpleasantly. "Go right ahead.

In the meantime, I'll rip this card into little bitty pieces and eat them one by one. Ms. Constantine is a federal judge. She won't be pleased when she hears about you. Could you loan me a pen, please? I want to write down your name."

The woman, who was red-faced by now, looked as though she was about to charge out from behind her desk to wrest the card from my hand. I was disappointed when she snapped, "I shall speak to my supervisor!"

I plopped down on the nearest chair and crossed my arms. I was not surprised when Jorgeson sat down beside me. "How's she doing?" he asked.

"I don't know, and that woman is fixated on Willie's insurance card. I'm holding it hostage until I get a medical update. If I were next of kin, I could storm down the hallway, but I really don't want to have to deal with security. Why don't you go flash your badge at that woman and find out about Willie's condition?" I gritted my teeth as my eyes welled with tears.

Jorgeson patted my knee and went to the desk. A conversation ensued, although I couldn't hear any of it. He beckoned to me, and we went through the doors to the ER treatment corridor. Behind beige curtains, Willie was surrounded by people in white coats. I held my breath, wishing there was something I could do. My cell phone buzzed. I backed away and took it out of my purse.

"Claire-san?" Keiko whispered.

"They can't hear you, so you can speak up. Did you contact Willie's office?"

"The man I spoke to was very upset and asked me many questions. I told him she was at the hospital. I think he will come soon. Do you know how she's doing?"

"No, but I'm here with Lieutenant Jorgeson, and we should know something in a few minutes. She's alive, and that's a good sign. Did the police come?"

"Your husband is in Gregory's office now."

I thanked her and ended the call. I moved to Jorgeson's side and said, "Have they said anything?"

"They ran some tests and don't think it was a heart attack. She's conscious but disoriented, and her blood pressure is dangerously low. They're going to move her upstairs and do a scan for a stroke. They're also rushing through a blood analysis. From what I overheard, she may have overdosed on a sedative."

"That's impossible. She looked fine when I saw her about noon. I didn't have a chance to talk to her, but she was with the other board members. Surely one of them would have noticed if she was woozy or more confused than usual." I sat down on a stool, shivering. "I didn't see her during or after the potluck, but it was crowded." I bent my head and entwined my fingers over my neck, trying to think in spite of the relentless PA system.

Jorgeson pulled me up and we moved out of the way as the team pushed Willie's bed through the curtains. "You need to go to the waiting room, Ms. Malloy. I'll be back as soon as I know something. Don't worry yourself sick."

If I'd intended to do so, I was in the right place. I took Willie's driver's license and insurance card to the huffy woman at the desk by the entrance. We exchanged hostile looks as she accepted the cards and bent down to start "processing" Willie. I sat down in a far corner of the waiting room.

A young man and woman, both of them looking harried, came in the emergency entrance and went to the desk. I watched with a modicum of amusement as they tried to get information from the vulture. She grudgingly pointed in my direction.

"I'm Claire Malloy," I said as they approached me. "I was at the Farberville Literacy Council when Willie was put in the

302

ambulance."

They babbled their names, but I didn't make an effort to further burden my exhausted brain. I told them only that Willie was conscious and had been taken for more tests. They asked all the right questions, but I had none of the right answers. They found chairs and began texting. After more than an hour, Jorgeson appeared. I wanted to hug him, but it would have been unseemly.

"She's doing better," he told the three of us. "It wasn't a heart attack or a stroke. She's resting now and cannot have visitors until tomorrow." He looked at the law clerks. "You need to notify her family. Please send that information to me as well. We'll want to talk to you and the entire office staff, but it can wait." He gave them his card and sent them out the door, then sat down next to me. "They pumped her stomach and administered charcoal and IV fluids. If she doesn't respond well, they'll hook her up to a dialysis machine to cleanse her blood." He ran his fingers through his gray crew cut. "This is bad, Ms. Malloy. From what you told me, she didn't gulp down those pills with her morning coffee."

"Somebody laced her beverage."

"That's what it looks like. The deputy chief's on his way to the PD. There's nothing more for you to do, so go home. You don't want those teenagers snooping in your bathroom."

"Are you implying they might stumble onto something embarrassing? I assure you, Jorgeson, I keep such things in a locked box under my bed."

He went back to the elevator. I walked out to my car, almost getting myself run over by an ambulance. I paused, noticing a black car several rows away. Sunlight on the windshield prevented me from ascertaining if the car was occupied. The hospital had an overload of patients — but I was running out of patience. I took several deep breaths and persuaded myself that the car belonged to one of the sneezy, wheezy souls in the emergency room rather than to a knife-wielding tire slasher. Refusing to look in the rearview mirror, I drove to the Literacy Council to report. I couldn't divulge what Jorgeson had told me, so I needed to devise a story. My mind unhelpfully shut down.

As soon as I entered, Keiko dashed up. "How is Miss Willie? What's wrong with her? Will she have to stay in the hospital?"

Gregory hurried out of his office. I spotted Leslie in the classroom. She told her class to continue without her and came out to join us. I held up my palms to protect myself from a further onslaught of questions.

"Willie will be fine." I struggled to recall Jorgeson's abbreviated version. "It wasn't a stroke or a heart attack. They're doing tests to see if she has a virus or infection. I have no idea when she'll be released. Two of her clerks came and were told the same thing. There isn't anything we can do."

"Send flowers," Gregory said to Keiko. "I need to inform Frances as soon as possible. Some variety of flu, right? Nothing like food poisoning. Think of the lawsuits . . ." He returned to his office.

"No one is my class is feeling ill," Leslie said. "I must get back and share the good news."

Keiko was already on the phone in her office, asking about the price of carnations.

I realized I was standing by myself in the doorway as if I'd taken up a new career holding the door for tenants and whistling for taxis. There was no reason to linger. As I drove home, I tried to think, but I was too exhausted. Gregory, Bartek, Sonya, Rick, Leslie, Drake, Frances, and the entire cast of Armenians, Iranians, Japanese, Russians, Koreans, Mexicans, and Panamanians would have to wait. It was five o'clock somewhere.

■ ■ ■ ■

It was five o'clock at my house as well. I was relieved to see a patrol car parked in the clutter of compacts and battered behemoths. I found a spot and went inside. The counters and island were covered with six-packs of sodas, bags of chips, packages of hot dogs and buns, open dip, spilled dip, dripping dip, plastic cups, and boxes of cookies. Whoops and laughter came from the pool area. I made myself a stiff drink in a coffee mug and went to the terrace. Peter had sent a pair of rookies to maintain law and order. He'd chosen poorly. The two young men had removed their weapons and unbuttoned their shirts and were entertaining several girls in bikinis. Caron was not among them. It took me a while to spot her at the far end of the deck on a towel next to Ashley and Carrie. Inez was in the shallow end of the pool, laughing and exchanging splashes with Toby.

I needed a break before I decided how to approach Toby. His position on my list of suspects had dropped dramatically since my conversation with Rick. I needed him to confirm some details, however. I sipped my drink as I watched the teenagers, who had been children only moments ago and were now rapidly approaching adulthood. It would take some of them longer than others.

The phone inside rang, propelling me out of the chaise. As I reached for the receiver, I noticed the red light blinking frenetically. "Hello," I said.

Peter's endearing voice said, "What the hell is going on at that place? Jorgeson told me that Judge Constantine was doped during the potluck and found in an unused classroom. She's not even remotely a person of interest in the murder investigation — or she wasn't until this happened. I spoke with her Tuesday, and she said she hadn't noticed anything unusual on Monday night. She had a vague idea who Ludmila was. All of them did because of Ludmila's outbursts."

The mention of her outbursts reminded me of the café. I told him what I'd learned about Bergmann-Swistak Pharmaceuticals and my well-drawn conclusion about Gregory. "The photograph Ludmila insisted on showing people must have been a victim of shoddy medication or vaccines. It made her crazy that she couldn't communicate with anyone. Gregory knew it was only a matter of time before she found someone in whom she could confide."

"Awkward for Whistler, but he wasn't the responsible party — his father was."

"Yes," I said, "but he mentioned that he'd worked there, and his father absconded with the company's filthy lucre. Interpol might want to chat with him."

"It has nothing to do with Judge Constantine."

This required a stretch. "Maybe she was learning Polish with CDs while she drove to work. Maybe she told Gregory that her old pal Lech Walesa was coming for a visit. Ask her, not me. She should be able to talk by tomorrow."

He was silent for a minute. "The idea of interviewing everyone who was at the potluck is enough to make me resign. I'll notify the chief and spend the summer building the greenhouse. You want a lily pond? You can have a lily pond, a gazebo, and an herb garden. Once Caron goes back to school, we'll go on a long cruise to an unknown destination. Evenings sitting in deck chairs, gazing at the stars. Strolls around the deck."

"You'd better start working on your shuffleboard skills. We'll fit right in with the other retirees. Nothing like an afternoon of bingo to keep those withering neurons firing slower and slower . . ."

"If I promise to murder one of the other

passengers?"

"Sorry, Sherlock, but this conversation needs to wait twenty years." I heard a screech from the backyard. "I need to go back and chaperone the kids. Your officers are too busy writing down phone numbers in their little black books. Let me know if you're ever coming home, darling."

I returned to my guard tower. No one was flailing in the water or fending off a member of the opposite gender. Someone had started charcoal in the grill. Several kids trooped past me to the kitchen for more sodas. I was caught so far off balance that I nearly spilled my drink when Toby sat down next to me.

"Hey, Mrs. Malloy, it sure is nice of you to let us swim." He gave me a winsome grin. "My parents won't put in a pool. They say it's too much work to keep up and would play hell with the insurance rates."

"They have a valid point. You have a younger brother, right? Any other siblings?" When he looked blank, I said, "Brothers and sisters."

"Just the two of us. My mother was hoping for a girl, but she got Koby. He's a little brat, but I kinda like him anyway. His Little League team has a good chance to win the local tournament and go to the regional."

It was not my desired topic of conversation. I let my smile fade. "That was an awful thing at the Literacy Council, wasn't it?"

"You mean that old woman getting killed? No kidding. The police crawled all over me about it Monday night, but I couldn't tell them anything. Nobody told me to clean that little room. I've never even looked in there."

"What time did you arrive?"

He blushed. "Late. I had car trouble. My battery dies about every two weeks. My dad told me to buy a more reliable car, but I'm not gonna waste my money. Whatever college I choose will have plenty of alumni to help me out. I figure two years of college ball and I can go pro. I'm thinking a Nissan GT-R. That baby can tear ass." He caught himself. "Sorry, Mrs. Malloy. I hope I didn't offend you."

"Not at all," I said mendaciously. I was offended that he'd lumped me in with his grandmother's cronies. "When you got to the Literacy Council, were the lights on?"

He frowned. "I don't remember. I was pissed that I was running late and would be stuck there till midnight. One of my friends got us invited to a frat party. I didn't want to miss anything."

"Think, Toby. You drove into the parking

lot and shut off your engine. You walked to the front door. I assume you have a key."

"Yeah, but I hardly ever use it. I try to get there just as the place closes so I can get my hours in. My dad drives by a couple of times a week to check on me. He was really pissed when I skipped out early last week. He threatened to make me wear one of those ankle monitors. I said if he did, he could track me while I drove to California."

"Monday night," I persisted. "You unlocked the door. Were the lights on, or did you stumble around in the dark until you found the switch?"

This time his frown looked as if I'd asked him to solve a quadratic equation. He looked down, his hands on his brow to shade his eyes. I wanted to shake him until he coughed up a simple yes or no. He finally raised his head. "They were on," he announced in a wondrous voice, as if he had indeed solved the equation. "Now I remember thinking Whistler must have left them on by mistake."

"Was anyone there?"

"I didn't see anybody, if that's what you mean. I guess the old lady's body was in the copy room. I must have gone by the door three or four times with the bucket of cleaning crap. That back classroom reeked of gin.

311

I thought it was a real hoot. My dad talks about the board of directors like they're Supreme Court justices. I have a collection of corks from the wastebasket. I figure sooner or later I'll find a bra hanging from the light fixture."

"Beverages have been served, but I can assure you the meetings are hardly festive."

"So do the police have any suspects?" he asked me abruptly.

"They're still investigating."

"And you're married to that Rosen guy who's in charge? Has he told you anything about their leads?"

It seemed that we'd switched sides of the interrogation table. I held up my hand. "He doesn't keep me informed. I know they are actively pursuing the culprit." Once again he looked blank, but I decided to let him work on it. "You arrived at ten. The door was locked, but the lights were on. Did you see a car in the parking lot?"

"If I tell you something, will you promise not to repeat it to the cops?" I nodded. "I smoked a little weed on my way there, like always. It's the only way I can stand to deal with that shit. I put in earbuds and listen to music while I vacuum and clean toilets and collect trash. That's why my memory's not so good. My dad will kill me if he finds out, and Coach will sideline me for the opening game. I gotta look good this year, Ms. Malloy. I don't want to sell used cars for the next forty years."

His confession did not surprise me, although I vowed to have a conversation with Inez as soon as I had a chance. She needed to date chess players, not jocks. "Okay, Toby, I'll do my best to keep your secret. It smells like the charcoal is ready. Why don't you help with the hot dogs?"

He leaned forward and gazed earnestly into my eyes. "I know I can trust you. I'm sorry if I rambled too much. I feel bad about that old lady, lying on the rug all night while she bled to death."

I shooed him away before he started blubbering. He'd played his role well, I had to admit. Mothers probably beamed with pride as he ushered their daughters down the sidewalk to his car. I would have a conversation with Inez's mother, too. I nearly yelped when Inez sat down next to me.

"Are you satisfied? You grilled him for ten minutes like he was applying for a job in your bookstore. Did you run a background check on him, too?" Her eyes, no longer hidden by smudged lenses, were flickering with anger.

Her transformation was more than skin-deep, I realized. It was high time, but not the most opportune time. "I was asking him about what he saw at the Literacy Council Monday night. The investigation is still open, and he's a potential witness."

"He looked like he was going to cry."

"He was talking about his career in the pros. He has to play well this season in order to get a scholarship, then off to the pros before he has to take any upper-level classes. He's worried, naturally. It's a lot of pressure."

The flicker disappeared. "Wouldn't it be absolutely hysterical if his best offer was from Stanford? He wouldn't stand a chance in remedial freshman English." She squeezed my hand. "Don't worry about me, Ms. Malloy. I know how to play the game, but this is the first time I've been invited to participate." She looked down for a moment. "The rules are more intricate than I'd supposed. It's all about achieving a goal, no matter the degree of significance. You wouldn't believe the level of postpubescent angst."

"I was there once," I said, "but I suspect it was simpler. No cell phones, perpetual texting, social media. We led lives of quieter desperation."

Inez smiled sadly.

314

The party progressed under my benign supervision. At eight o'clock, the guests began to gather up their towels and bags and straggle around the corner of the house to their cars. Two of Caron's friends stayed to help her clean up. I watched from the chaise longue, having lost the spirit of volunteerism.

Caron came to the door. "Did you listen to your messages, Mother?" She sounded concerned.

"I'll get to them later," I said. "It's been a long day. Do you want some money to go to the movie or hang out at the mall?"

"Sure." She hesitated for a moment. "One of the messages was from a guy with a heavy accent. I think he said that you should mind your own business. I guess he doesn't know you."

It was really too much. My head was crammed with fragmented bits of theories, hypotheses, facts, and lies. I couldn't remember what I had — and hadn't — told Peter or Jorgeson. Now the mysterious villain had decided to butt in with no regard for my sensitive nature. "If you're here when he calls back, tell him to stuff it."

"Are you okay?"

"I'm just tired. Run along and have a good time. Midnight, right?"

She hesitated. "If you want, I can wait until Peter gets here."

"See you later, dear." Once she'd gone inside, I dragged myself to my feet and looked in the direction of the apple orchard. No one was visible. I uttered an unladylike oath and went through the French doors. I clicked the dead bolt, surveyed the almost tidy kitchen, and lay down on the leather sofa. I was still there, sleeping fitfully, when Peter came home. He kissed me on the forehead.

What took place afterward has no bearing on the story.

14

I woke up the next morning when I heard Peter turn on the shower. I went into the kitchen. My darling husband had started coffee. I searched for bread or bagels and had hot dog buns under the broiler when he joined me, smelling divine. I told him so and then rescued the buns. We ended up at the small table on the terrace.

"Did you run down that German pharmaceutical company?" I asked.

"Somebody's working on it. If you're right, it does give Gregory a motive. Are those meadowlarks in the meadow?"

"One would think so." I wasn't going to let him distract me with an ornithological ploy, although I could have tossed out the number of breeding pairs of emperor penguins in Antarctica, which would have led to further irrelevant comments. "Would you please check on Willie?"

He took out his cell, looked at me, and

went inside. I drank my coffee quickly so the caffeine could kick in before he returned. Gregory not only had a motive, he had the opportunity. Everyone had left except Ludmila, and by eight thirty, she was dead. Toby arrived at ten. It meshed perfectly — or would have if all sorts of people hadn't muddied it up. Miao had gone underground and sent Luo to the Literacy Council on a transparently feeble pretext. An unknown man with an accent was threatening me as though I knew something of immense significance. Keiko had turned on me, however briefly, when I'd done nothing to annoy her. Leslie was in deep trouble with an ill-tempered man named Waterford and was playing matchmaker with her students. Or something, anyway.

Peter resumed his seat. "Judge Constantine required dialysis, but the prognosis is good. Jorgeson put an officer outside her door. No visitors allowed, not even her clerks — and especially not any board members. That includes you, Claire. I want you out of this now. I listened to the messages on the machine before you woke up. We're tracing the number, but it's likely to be a throwaway cell. Criminals watch cop shows on TV, just like everybody else." He moved his chair next to mine and put his hands on my cheeks so I would have to look at him. "He's a nutcase, and we know what he did to your tires. I don't want anything to happen to you."

"So I should stay in my house, which is isolated and surrounded by woods?" I may have shivered a wee bit. "And no, you are not going to assign some rookie to sit outside and play bodyguard. I'm not going to give in to anonymous phone messages. This nasty person is keeping his distance. If he gets too close, I'll handle it."

"Well said, but you could spend more time at the Book Depot. Have lunch with your friends, go to matinees, shop. Just stay away from the Farberville Literacy Council until this is resolved."

He had enough sense not to suggest I volunteer somewhere else. "I will stay away from the Literacy Council for the time being," I said solemnly. "Maybe I can look online and find a culinary school. I've always liked Greek food. In a week's time, we can be dining on *moussaka* and grilled feta sandwiches."

"All I'm asking is for you to promise to stay away from there. Call that weepy Asian girl and tell her that you're resigning as receptionist. You don't have to resign from the board, since the next meeting is several weeks away. Once we have the perp, you can tutor to your heart's content."

I felt myself melting as his molasses-colored eyes gazed into mine. I knew he needed to leave, or I would have lured him back into the bedroom to have his way with me. Rather than swooning, I obediently repeated my promise. After all, the Literacy Council was closed until Monday, and I didn't have a key.

As soon as he left, I found the creased brochure in my purse and called Frances. She wasn't home. I tried Sonya's number and was sent to voice mail. I was irritated with Rick for his failure to confide in me, but I called out of duty — and to no avail. Drake was not hovering over the phone for an update on Willie's condition, nor was Austin. I left messages for everyone, took a shower, dressed, and returned to the terrace. I could not keep myself from glaring at the apple orchard.

Caron sat at the table, texting. She paused long enough to say, "Did you tell Peter about that weird caller?"

"He's having the number traced, but it may not lead anywhere. We both need to be careful until the jerk's caught. Stay in a group and keep an eye out for swarthy types."

"That's racial profiling."

"I suppose it is, but you heard the accent. I still suspect a man I saw talking to Leslie earlier in the week. The police don't agree. They have been known to be wrong. You don't have to overreact every time you see a Middle Eastern man in the vicinity."

"I rarely accept rides from strange men with twitchy eyes — unless they want me to help them find their lost puppies." With a snort, she resumed texting.

"Use common sense, okay?" I spread out my notes and morosely tried to make sense of them. I'd taken excellent notes in college, but it seemed I'd lost the knack. The napkins were so flimsy that my pen had left rips and the ink had seeped into the fiber. I flipped over one of the paper notes. The potluck had been chaotic and packed with students, tutors, and the rest of us. Bartek and Duke were there, but they most likely didn't know who Willie was. I'd seen her with various board members. It was going to be a major task to find out with whom she spoke, what she ate and drank, and whether or not she'd been present for Yelena's presentation and Frances's speech. I needed to question all of the board members to patch together a scenario of Willie's movements. It was ten o'clock. There was one very popular destination in Farberville on Saturday mornings, and it was a not unreasonable place to look for at least some of them.

"What are your plans?" I asked Caron.

"Inez's uncle is going to take us out on his boat all day. I'll come back here to shower and change. After that, I don't know. By the way, I was kidding about accepting rides with strange men who'd lost their puppies. I never get in their vans unless they have candy, too."

"That's comforting to know." I took my notes inside and left them on my desk, found a canvas shopping bag in the utility room, and headed for the farmers' market held weekly on the square surrounding the old post office. After ten minutes, I finally got lucky and eased into a parking space in the municipal lot. I put on sunglasses and strolled along the busy sidewalk. The four sides of the square had been allotted to the vendors. Most of them had backed pickup trucks into their slots or set up tents. Fresh fruits and vegetables, crafts, and flowers covered all the available surfaces. The crowd was composed of seniors, families with children, yuppies, old hippies, and people dressed oddly. A guitarist sat on the steps, singing ballads. Since I was not in search of the perfect summer squash, I kept my eyes on the shoppers and the wanderers.

My brilliant idea dimmed after I'd circled the square twice. I encountered a few friends and loyal bookstore patrons and commented on the pleasant weather half a dozen times. I was unable to resist a display of eggplants and bought several, along with a bag of vine-ripened tomatoes (*ratatouille* came to mind). After another half hour, I was ready to give up when I caught a glimpse of a yellow bow tie. I wormed my way through a group fighting over asparagus and caught up with Austin.

"Good morning," I panted.

"The same to you, Claire. I'd like to introduce you to the second-loveliest woman on the planet, my close friend Deli-lah. You are, of course, the loveliest. Delilah, this is Claire. She's on the Literacy Council board."

Delilah was indeed a lovely young woman with flawless skin and large eyes. Her lips smiled, but her eyes did not. "Pleased to meet you."

"Delilah's a film major at the college," Austin added. "She's my summer intern. I'm doing my best to sour her on the advertising business."

"I'll just take a minute," I assured her,

flattered that she would consider me as a potential rival. "Austin, I need to tell you about Willie."

"Frances left a message on my machine late yesterday afternoon. How's Willie doing? Still in the hospital? It wasn't food poisoning, was it? I felt queasy this morning, and I'm still kinda shaky. Of course, that may be due to a couple of bottles of wine last night."

"Willie is recovering," I said. "The hospital is keeping her to run some more tests. I wanted to ask you if you talked to her during the potluck."

"Delilah, honey, why don't you see if you can find some decent tomatoes?" After she stomped away, he said, "Not really. I saw her loading a plate with mysterious stuff, but after that she was lost in the crowd. She's not very tall, you know."

"That's a problem. She's shorter than most of the Asian students. Did you see her afterward?"

"I didn't hang around. What's this about, Claire?"

I scrambled for a response. "Well, if she's allergic to shellfish or nuts and inadvertently ate something, she would have started to feel ill pretty quickly."

"Or gone into anaphylactic shock within

seconds, and died unless someone administered a shot of epinephrine. I didn't arrive in town on that turnip truck over there. I'm allergic to bee venom. I carry an EpiPen with me everywhere and make sure my companions know what to do."

"Someone may have slipped something in her food or drink."

Austin sat down on the edge of a flower bed. "Sheesh, what the hell is going on at the place? First the Polish woman, and now Willie. It's supposed to be a big happy family of international students, volunteers, and caring staff members — or that's what I thought when I joined the board."

"Why did you?"

"I used to tutor, but I don't have time anymore. I still want to help."

I sat down beside him. "Can you think why anyone would do this to Willie? She may be a terror in her courtroom, but she hasn't said much of anything at the meetings I attended." I frowned as I recalled a snippet. "What's going on between her and Sonya? Do they know each other outside of the Literacy Council?"

"Yeah, I know what you're talking about. Sonya would be slapped with a fine or tossed in a cell for contempt of court if she acted that way in another judge's courtroom. It's embarrassing for the rest of us. Willie just clenches her jaw and takes it. If Sonya pulled that crap with me, I wouldn't be nearly so meek."

"Could she and Sonya be related?"

"If they are, it's the best-kept secret in town. The press would have themselves a fine ol' time if they caught Judge Constantine's granddaughter carousing on Thurber Street."

Delilah appeared with a bulging bag. "I'm thirsty, Austin. Are you and the lady finished? If not, I'm going with my roommates for Bloody Marys."

"Why don't we find someplace for a leisurely brunch and all the Bloody Marys your sweet heart desires." He looked at me, concerned. "If I hear anything, I'll let you know. Please do the same." He took the bag from Delilah and slid his arm under hers. They disappeared into the crowd.

I remained seated while I pondered what he'd said. He'd been on the board longer than I, and had seen a lot more of Sonya's insolence aimed at Willie. The question was whether it had anything to do with the unpleasant events. Since I couldn't talk to Willie, I needed to track down Sonya. She hadn't struck me as a farmers' market kind of shopper. I did one more circle of the stalls and pickup trucks before walking back to my car. None of the people I wanted to talk to had the decency to be walking toward me or parking in a nearby space. I moved on to another name on my list.

There were a few elderly people walking their dogs in Miss Parchester's neighborhood. I parked in front of her house and prepared myself to sit through tea and genteel conversation until I could find a way to elicit some answers from her. She was a master of evasion. I could be mulish. It would be a delicate duel.

As before, it took her several minutes to open the front door. "Why, Claire, was I expecting you? I am so forgetful these days. I'm forever trying to remember where I left my car keys or why I'm standing in the middle of the kitchen with an umbrella in my hand. Will you have some tea? I would offer cookies, but I don't think I have any. Do you have time for me to bake muffins?"

"Just tea, thank you." I sat down in my usual spot. While I waited, I tried to count cats, but they were gliding behind the furniture and up and down the staircase. I gave up when I reached an implausibly high number and flipped through the same issue of *National Geographic*. Miss Parchester brought in the tray, filled our cups, and sat down. Our eyes locked for a brief moment. Clearly, the game was afoot.

"Did you enjoy the food at the potluck?" I inquired politely.

"I always do. Some of the young women are remarkable cooks. I don't know how they find all those curious ingredients. Perhaps they have ethnic grocery stores in hidden alleys. I must say your deviled eggs were very tasty. Caron told me you stayed up late to make them. I do hope you're not overtaxing yourself, Claire."

"Not at all, Miss Parchester. Caron and Inez are enjoying their tutoring sessions, although Caron admitted she's relieved not to have to deal with Ludmila anymore."

"Leslie should have assigned easier students for the girls," she said, neatly dodging my ploy. "There are any number of students who are thankful for the private instruction. Mudada is such a dear man. His mother sent a tin of *mapopo,* a candy made with papaya, and he insisted on sharing it with me. My very first student was a woman from Turkey. She's a U.S. citizen now and has a fine job as an officer manager. I think she lives in Cleveland — or is it Columbus? I don't know why Ohio has so many cities starting with the letter *C.*"

"Have you heard from Miao since she arrived in China?"

"Not a peep, but I didn't expect her to have time to send a postcard."

"She might not have made it home," I said. "She must have required quite a few connecting flights. If she missed one, she might still be sitting in an airport. Don't you agree, Miss Parchester?"

"If that were the case, I would feel dreadful for her. Poor little thing, stranded in one of those vast, impersonal airports with those blaring speakers. No, something tells me she's just fine. I can't claim a little birdie told me, since the birdie wouldn't last five seconds in this house."

"Miao didn't fly anywhere. The police checked with the airlines." That wasn't true, I admit, but I didn't want to sit in her living room all day. "She's upstairs, isn't she?"

Miss Parchester's small mouth opened in surprise. "She is? Oh, my goodness, I must be more impaired than I thought. I'd like to think I'd notice if someone was in my own house at this very moment."

"You offered her a haven Monday night. Have you forgotten that?"

"Why would you think such a thing? Miao is not upstairs. If you care to have a look, please do so. Don't think badly of me if you encounter a few small brown objects under the beds. Presumed Livingston, the Siamese, has a devious sense of humor. Go on, Claire, I insist."

I knew she wasn't bluffing. All I'd find upstairs would be the consequences of Presumed Livingston's so-called sense of humor. "Do you know where she is now?"

"Who?" Miss Parchester took a sip of tea.

"Miao. You warned her that I would show up here. Did she go out the back door and head for the apartment she shares with Luo Shiwen?"

"I do so admire your thoroughness, dear. I really have no idea where Miao is at this time. Perhaps you should contact her family in Tai Po."

"Her boyfriend already did. She's not there."

"How frightful if she were stranded in Cleveland. I went there once with Mama and Papa. We went on a train. I was six years old, and it was a great adventure. I recall running up and down the aisles while a porter chased after me. Papa gave him a very large tip when we got off the train in Cleveland."

I accepted defeat, thanked her for the tea, and walked out to my car. She'd wanted me to search her house for Miao. Not to humiliate me, since she was too good-natured for

330

that, but to strengthen her position. As we stood, she knew that I knew. I knew that she knew that I knew. So what? I tried to think of a place where she might have stashed Miao. I'd never seen Miao talking to anyone at the Literacy Council. If she was avoiding Jiang after their argument, she wouldn't have gone to him. Luo wasn't going to offer me the names of Miao's friends. Maybe a professor or her adviser.

Miao was in the math department. I thought about my Saturday afternoons in grad school. The English majors could be found at the beer garden, ridiculing popular fiction (without admitting they'd read it). The physics students spent their free time playing some sport involving discs. The engineers seized the campus green, testing solar robots and dropping insulated eggs from the bell tower. No one ever saw the math majors. They were as pale as chalk and rarely emerged from their subterranean classrooms.

It wouldn't hurt to try. I had no trouble finding a parking space on the deserted campus. The math department shared a building with the chemistry department. The doors were unlocked; the hall was vacant. I studied the wall placard listing the offices and their numbers. The math department had the second and third floors, so I walked upstairs. The main office was locked. I wandered down the dim tunnel. There weren't any lights showing beneath the doors of professors' offices. I continued to the third floor, which was as gloomy as the second floor. The faculty lounge room was unlocked, but the coffeepot was cold, and Miao was not camped out on the worn sofa. The usual inhabitants had either taken refuge in their home offices or had succumbed to lethal emanations from the chemistry department in the basement.

I'd started toward the stairwell when I saw a figure crouched at the far end of the hall, almost invisible in the shadows. My heart began to thump. There was no way to know if the skulker had followed me into the building or was already there. The stairwell was equidistant between us. I stood for a long moment while I considered my options. Apparently my skulker was as indecisive as I was.

We both started walking slowly toward the stairwell, our footsteps echoing. It was high noon (or thereabouts). The only thing I could draw was a scribble on the faded green wall. When we were forty feet apart, I recognized my adversary and let out an exasperated growl. "Jiang, what are you doing? Did you follow me?"

"I am worried about Miao. You are look-ing for her like me, so I follow you. I am a student and you are a detective. Like you, I thought she might be at the house of Miss Parchester. I watched through the window while you drank tea and talked."

"How long have you been following me?"

"Only since I told you Miao was not in Tai Po. You had a funny look on your face that made me suspicious. You are a busy woman, Ms. Malloy. All day long you go one place and then another. My car has used much gasoline."

"What color is your car?" I said this levelly, although I wanted to yell at him. The idea of being relentlessly followed made me shiver.

"Old black Chevy. I bought it for two hundred dollars when I came here to study."

"Did you follow me to my house?"

"I think maybe you let Miao stay there. She told me you were nice."

"Let's get out of here." I made sure Jiang was behind me as we went down the flights of stairs. I couldn't be sure I might not shove him in the back. Had he peeked in the window while I changed clothes? Could he have found a way to slip inside the house to search the second floor? My stomach was roiling and my hands were clenched. I'd been spied on because Miao had run away from a marriage proposal.

Once we were outside, I turned around to glare at him. "Did you slash my tires, you little weasel?"

"What is a 'weasel'?"

"Someone who spies on people. Did you slash my tires?"

Jiang looked puzzled. "Why would I do that? All I did was follow you, Ms. Malloy. Today you go to the market, Miss Parchester's house, and now this building. You could not drive to these places if your tires were not good."

"I'm talking about Wednesday when you followed me to my house. I saw you in the apple orchard, didn't I? Did that make you so angry that you took it out on my perfectly contented tires? That's vandalism. You could go to jail."

"I was not in the apple orchard; I was on the other side of the river. I have excellent binoculars, made in Japan. I parked in a dirt road and walked across a pasture to some trees."

"How did you know which house I live in?"

"I didn't. I was trying to determine which house when I saw you come outside and look around. I never went near your car. I do not own a knife. If I am attacked, I will use my martial arts to defend myself. I have black belts in tae kwon do and jujitsu. No one bothers me a second time."

How handy that my stalker could fill in as my bodyguard, I thought. He'd have to keep his role straight, though. I pictured him on the far side of the stream, hunkered down in the small grove of oak trees. "Did you see anyone in the apple orchard? A man in a brown coat, also watching the house?"

He shook his head impatiently. "Where can Miao be? She has no friends but Luo. Luo is a serious student. She does not go out with us or have a boyfriend. She swears she does not know where Miao was. Last night I made sure Miao was not hiding in their apartment."

"How did you accomplish that?" I shouldn't have asked, since I knew what the answer would be and I really didn't want to hear it. His attitude reminded me of Caron's: If you believe you have right on your side, you're empowered to flout the rules. That's what she'd told me after she and Inez stole frozen frogs from the high school biology department in order to give them a Viking funeral.

"I climbed up to the balcony so I could

see into both the living room and the bedroom. Miao was not there."

"You're damn lucky you didn't get caught — or shot. A black belt in jujitsu won't stop a bullet. We're very touchy about our privacy in this country. Spying on people is rude — and against the law in certain situations."

"Privacy is not so important in China. There are nine members of my family, and we have three rooms. We are fortunate. But I will go to jail to protect Miao, if I must. What if Whistler has locked her in his house? Can you make him let me search for her?" He struck a fierce pose. "I will throw him out the door and stomp him into the dirt like a worm!"

"Did I mention jail?"

"I don't care what happens to me if he has poor Miao in a dirty room with only a mattress to sleep on and no food! He is an evil man!"

"Is that why you put a dead bird in his wastebasket?"

Jiang ducked his head. "Only to warn him to leave Miao alone," he muttered.

"Some kind of ancient Chinese curse?"

"No, from a comic book. He is worse than the local authorities in my town, who think they can push us around because of their power! It was meant to warn him!" He dropped into a posture that was, I supposed, meant to look menacing.

I poked him in the chest. "Stop bellowing. I'm not in the mood to deal with campus security. Do you know the names of Miao's adviser or any Chinese professors in her department?"

He scratched his head and scowled. "She told me the name of her adviser, but I don't remember. The woman is not Chinese. Miao does not dislike her, but they are not friends. Miao is too shy to make friends, even with the Chinese students in the International Students Association. She is the only girl in her family. She has two older brothers who were rough with her. When she and I first went on dates, one of her brothers always came with us."

"What about Chinese professors?" I thought of an easy way to find out. "Go back inside and find the placard with all the office numbers. See if any of the names in the three departments sound Chinese." He dashed away. I sat down on a concrete bench, marginally optimistic that he would find such a name and that within the hour we would be having lunch with Miao and her host. Miao might be unhappy that I'd led Jiang to her. Young love was a pain in the butt.

337

"No one," Jiang said as he reappeared and sat down on the grass. "What now, detective lady?"

"First off, you are to stop following me. I don't like it. Got that?" He nodded. "If I see you, you're toast!" I noted his expression and said, "You'll be in big trouble with me. You won't like that, I assure you." I wanted to embellish my dictum with a threat, but bleaching his black belts was rather lame. I went for the jugular. "I'll say dreadful things about you to Miao. I'll tell how badly you frightened me and ranted about violence. She won't toss you a grain of rice when I get finished."

He didn't look all that terrified, but he got up and said, "I will not follow you, Mrs. Malloy, as long as you promise to tell me if you find Miao. I am so worried that I cannot eat, I cannot sleep, I cannot study."

"I will let you know that she is safe. It's up to her to decide if she wants you to know where she is. Also, stay out of Gregory's office. Do we have a deal?"

It took him a moment to realize that he was supposed to shake my outstretched hand. His grip was firm, very firm. He took out a notepad and wrote down a telephone number. "Please call me. I need to know that she is unharmed." He walked across the grass and around the corner of the building.

As I walked back to my car, I saw a black car in the far corner of a student parking lot. Jiang had gone in a different direction. There were three or four other cars in the lot. I stared at it, but my laser vision needed to be recharged. I got into my car and drove toward Thurber Street. It was time for lunch.

I parked behind the Book Depot and went in through the back door. Jacob's head swiveled when he spotted me, but he merely raised an eyebrow and turned the page of the book in front of him. I sat behind my desk and flicked a paper clip in the direction of the wastebasket. I felt strangely gratified when it dropped in the basket. I took another one out of a holder and tried again. This one went sailing to the left. The next one was worth two points. I was lining up my next shot when Jacob cleared his throat.

"We received a catalog from a small mystery press," he said. "I put it aside for you, since you like that sort of thing."

"You mean mindless, escapist fiction in which people do more than make significant small talk riddled with symbolism and relive their imaginary childhood in ghettos? I'll take the catalog with me and look at it later.

Would you please go to the front of the store and see if there are any black cars parked in the vicinity? I don't care about the make or model, as long as it's black."

"As you wish." He turned around and did as I'd requested. A minute later he came to the doorway. "There's a black van in the alley beside the furniture store. Two women, possibly mother and daughter, are watching men struggle with a long sofa. It's a hideous shade of mauve." His lips curled briefly to indicate he meant to be funny. "A black sedan is parked in front of the beer garden. Those are the only two, Ms. Malloy. Is that all?"

"Yes, Jacob, that's all." It seemed as if every third car in Farberville was black. I came up with a plan to force the driver out of his car, if indeed he was watching me. If it proved to be Jiang, I wouldn't take responsibility for what happened. I went out the front door, stopped under the portico to look in both directions, and began walking briskly up Thurber Street. I crossed the side street and continued at the same pace, despite the dire possibility of sweat in the near future. Halfway up the block, I cut into an alley that would take me behind several restaurants to a narrow street. The Dumpsters reeked of rotting meat and produce. I sucked in a breath when I saw a rat dart into one.

When I reached the end of the alley, I glanced back. A figure lurched behind the garbage bins, redefining the art of Dumpster diving. I felt charmingly nefarious as I walked up a narrow street lined with decrepit rental houses on one side and parking lots on the other. A gray-haired hippie lying in his front yard offered me a beer, but I declined. The music drifting out of open windows was from the 1960s and early '70s. The scent of marijuana smoke was in the air. I'd entered a time warp.

I made sure the figure dodging between cars in the parking lots kept up with me. I stopped to chat with a woman in a long skirt and bare feet, who was nursing her baby on the steps of her front porch. We agreed that it was a wonderful day for all creatures under the sun. When I was nearly to the corner, I abruptly turned and went through the back door of a restaurant. The kitchen staff ignored me as I hurried through them and found a booth in the back of the room. I picked up a menu and held it up to cover most of my face.

Showtime.

15

"Today's special is grilled tilapia with rice pilaf," a waitress said. "Comes with choice of soup or salad. Soup of the day is creamy mushroom."

I lowered the menu. The man who was following me was not in sight, but I expected him any moment. "A cup of the soup and iced tea," I said to appease the waitress. The restaurant was busy with the lunch crowd. I was lucky to have found an empty booth. I raised the menu to nose level and watched the front entrance. A trio of women came in together and found a table. Patrons were eating, talking, and texting at the same time. I was not impressed. Boys in frat T-shirts spotted friends; chairs were borrowed from other tables to accommodate them. Waiters and waitresses wound through the narrow paths with laden trays and weary smiles.

Maybe I'd made a mistake. The figure in the alley could have been planning to urinate when he saw me. The figure in the parking lots could have been shopping for a new car radio. Or he could have failed to see me come into the restaurant. My incredibly clever ploy wouldn't work with a dimwit. I was about to give up on him when I heard a commotion in the kitchen. Several seconds later an olive-skinned man came out of the small hall and stopped in the doorway. He was in his twenties, with a small mustache, black hair, and dressed in a brown sports jacket. Caron and Inez would be madly jealous of his long eyelashes.

I put down the menu and waved at him. "Over here. I saved you a seat."

He gave me a startled look. I waved again and repeated my invitation for him to join me. He was clearly unnerved. In other circumstances, I would have felt sorry for him. He glanced back at the kitchen and then at the front entrance. I waited to see which way he would bolt. Odds were equal. He'd encountered a problem in the kitchen, but the door that opened onto Thurber Street required artful navigation between the crowded tables and the stream of waiters. He finally gave up and came to the booth, his lips clamped together and his dark brown eyes too bright for my taste.

"Sit," I said, indicating the opposite side

of the booth. "You must be exhausted after all that dashing and ducking behind cars." I held out the menu. "Hungry?"

He stared in response. If he wanted to sit and pout, I would at least have a chance to eat lunch. When the waitress appeared, he shook his head with the ferocity of a tiger ripping flesh off his prey. She glanced at me as she backed away. He still had not spoken when she returned with my soup and tea.

"He want anything?" she asked me.

"It doesn't seem like it, but go ahead and bring him a glass of water. He looks as though he needs to cool off." I looked across the table at him. "Do you speak English? My Arabic is rusty, and I was never able to learn Farsi. I had trouble with calculus, too. You're probably quite proficient, since it's part of your heritage. Didn't the Arabic scholars develop the decimal system in medieval times?"

"I have no idea." He had a British accent, to my surprise. "I studied bacteriology at Oxford."

"Oh." It took a minute to process this. "Then why have you been following me for the last few days? Shouldn't you be hunting for wild berries that cure cancer or dissecting cows' brains?"

"Only on weekends. What makes you

think I'm following you, Claire?"

I did not care for the informal use of my name. "Mostly from watching you in my rearview mirror. Are you going to claim you always come into restaurants through their kitchens? That by some great cosmic coincidence, my car appears in front of yours no matter where you're going?"

He pursed his lips. "An acquaintance asked me to see what you've been up to, that's all."

"What about my tires? Was that a harmless prank?"

"You shouldn't make wild accusations without proof."

I wanted to dump the soup in his lap. "What's your name, and who's this acquaintance of yours?"

"My name is Rashad, and my acquaintance prefers to remain anonymous."

"Are you a hit man?"

He smirked. "No, I'm a graduate assistant. It's not nearly as lucrative."

The waitress was less leery as she put down the bill, but she didn't linger or ask me if I wanted a refill. I put my forearms on the table and leaned forward. "Okay, enough baloney. I want to know who this 'acquaintance' is and why he or she thinks I deserve all this attention. Does it concern the murder at the Literacy Council on Monday night? Abetting a felon is a felony. The two of you could end up in adjoining cells."

"All I know about the murder is what I read in the newspaper. The police haven't made any progress."

"They don't give hourly press conferences or post reports on the Internet. If this doesn't have anything to do with that, then what does it have to do with? Yes, I may be poking around to assist the police. That's all I've been doing. If there's some major international plot to launder billions of dollars or blow up buildings, I don't know anything about it. Got that?"

He took sunglasses out his pocket and put them on. "I'm so glad we had this little talk, Claire. I'll pass along your statement."

"Do that, and stop following me!" I was thoroughly exasperated. I gauged whether or not there was enough tea in the bottom of my glass to emphasize my point. There were people in the booth behind him. I didn't want to nail one of them with a stray ice cube.

"Keep your eyes on the rearview mirror." He put a twenty-dollar bill on the table. "Allow me to treat you to lunch." He made his way to the front door and turned in the direction of the Book Depot.

I dug out my cell phone and called the store. When Jacob answered, I said, "Go across the street and get the license plate number of that black car. Quickly, before its driver returns." Jacob sighed as he acquiesced. I ended the call and punched Peter's number. I failed to exhale until he answered. "What's up, Claire?"

"Not much, if you exclude the conversation I just had with a man who followed me from the Book Depot to a restaurant on Thurber Street." I recounted what I could of the encounter. "Now he's walking to his car parked by the beer garden. Brown jacket, black hair, average height, sensational eyelashes. Send a patrol car to pick him up."

"And arrest him for what?"

"I'm not a police officer. You're the one who should figure out what law he's broken. How about stalking me? That's a criminal offense."

"There's a difference between stalking and talking, or even tailing someone. He didn't threaten you. The only time he's approached you is when you invited him to sit down at your booth. You're welcome to present it to the DA. He leaves early on Friday afternoons, so you'd better call quickly."

"You don't care that this . . . this man . . .

this foreigner who could be working for some terrorist outfit, for all we know — you don't care that he's watching me? You won't even ask Homeland Security about him?" My voice was rising, but I couldn't control it. "Don't be surprised if you find me in a pool of blood on the kitchen floor! That's if you find my body at all! Maybe I'll be checked luggage on a flight to Pakistan! You know how much I hate camels!" I had pretty much everyone's attention by now. Their expressions ranged from amusement to alarm. My waitress held a fist to her mouth, and her eyes were filled with tears. I waved the twenty-dollar bill at her so she'd be distracted by the possibility of a big tip. My other hand held the cell against my ear while Peter sputtered and stuttered.

He finally calmed down. "Do you want me to send a patrol car to pick you up?"

"No, I want you to send a patrol car to pick up Rashad. Haven't you listened to anything I've been saying? He admitted that he's been following me. Oh, and Jiang admitted to the same thing, but he promised to stop. This man implied that he has no intention of stopping."

Peter was quiet for a moment. "All right, I'll send a car. If we can locate him, I'll have him brought in. Go back to the Book Depot

— take the sidewalk, not the alley — and drive straight here. I'll have our sketch artist waiting. Work with him until you're satisfied, and I'll have flyers printed for all of our patrol officers and campus security. We can bring him in for the slightest traffic violation, and I can assure you that he'll commit one."

"It's comforting to know we're that close to totalitarianism." I told him I'd see him within half an hour and left the twenty-dollar bill on the table. As I walked down Thurber Street, I struggled not to glance over my shoulder. I'd already embarrassed myself in the restaurant; I didn't want to look as if I'd just broken out of jail. The black car was no longer parked across the street. Scowling, I went into the Book Depot and headed for the tiny restroom. I washed my hands and face, but I still felt grimy. I desperately wanted to know who'd persuaded him to follow me.

I wadded up the paper towel and dropped it in the wastebasket, confident that Jacob would empty it within minutes of my departure. He ran a tight ship. My casual approach to paying bills, reading invoices, replacing files, and returning calls to publishers' reps must have kept him from sleeping well at night. His waking hours were haunted by the specter of me coming into the bookstore and undoing his meticulous system. I stopped in the doorway to the front room in order not to cause him distress.

"Did you get the license plate?"

He handed me a piece of notepaper with a neatly printed line of letters and numbers. "The driver appeared about ten minutes ago and drove away."

"Describe him."

"Average size, black hair, brown jacket."

Even though the police hadn't arrived in time to grab Rashad, I had his number — if only that of his license plate. "Thanks, Jacob. I'll see you later."

He twitched. "Later today?"

"Monday or Tuesday." I went out the back door and drove to the PD. If Rashad was behind me, he was keeping a discreet distance. Jorgeson came out of his office as soon as I was inside. He clasped my hands and said, "Ms. Malloy, I am deeply disturbed about this man."

I gave him the notepaper. "This is his license plate."

"Very nice. Please wait in my office while I go deal with this."

I replayed the conversation with Rashad until I could almost recite it backward, which was a neat trick but of no significance. Peter did not arrive to embrace me tightly and swear to defend my honor. Five minutes inched by. Jorgeson had forgotten to flip over the page on his wall calendar. The plant on his desk was in peril of losing its leaves. I was in peril of losing my mind. I was reducing to drumming my fingers on my knee when Jorgeson returned.

He shook his head sadly as he consulted a paper. "The young man may have lied to you, Ms. Malloy. According to the vehicle registration, his name is Hamdan bin Zayed Al Marktoum. We ran his name by the CIS. He's from Syria and has been in this country for about three years. He became a citizen last month. His record is pristine, not even a parking ticket. He currently lives in a condo out by the golf course. The DMV faxed over his driver's license. Is this the man?"

I squinted at the blurry image. "I think so."

"You still need to work with the sketch artist in the conference room. Would you like some coffee before you sit down with him?"

His solicitude was so fishy that I could smell it. I suspected that someone else in the department wanted to keep me occupied for several hours. "Maybe I'll pop in on Peter and let him know I'm here," I said.

"He's in a meeting with the chief to evaluate the situation. We don't want to call in Homeland Security if this Zayed fellow isn't involved with certain unsavory groups."

I mumbled something and let him escort me to the conference room. The sketch artist, a middle-aged man with a bald head, looked at me expectantly. I sank down in the nearest chair and closed my eyes. I'd overreacted in the restaurant and was now about to create an international incident. I imagined the residents of Farberville gathered around City Hall, angrily demanding to know about bomb threats and armed terrorists. The airport and the college campus would be closed. City Hall would be guarded by heavily armed soldiers. Barricades would go up for no apparent reason. Grocery stores would be emptied of bread, milk, batteries, and DVD rentals.

I gave the man a vague smile and left the room to find Peter. If ever there was a need for damage control, this was it. Officers who recognized me ducked into the closest rooms; those who didn't ignored me. When I saw the chief's office, I barged inside. The room was empty. Taken aback, I studied the chairs and small sofa as if Peter and the chief had concealed themselves under the mismatched throw pillows. I was so unhinged that I went around the chief's desk to make sure they weren't tucked in the kneehole. "You need to calm down," I said aloud, hoping I'd pay attention to my own voice. "You need to sit down and breathe until you come to your senses."

"I do?" Jorgeson said from the doorway.

"No, I do. Where did they go? I need to speak to them now. This whole thing is out of control. Rashad — I mean Hamdan — didn't wave a gun under my nose or show me bombs in his backpack. He didn't even have a backpack!"

Jorgeson put his hands on my shoulders. "I don't guess you need more caffeine right now, Ms. Malloy. How about a cup of herbal tea instead? Don't tell anyone, but I have an electric teapot in my office. Mrs. Jorgeson says it helps my digestion."

"I need to speak to them," I repeated mulishly.

"Well, that may be difficult just now. The chief left for a scheduled meeting with the mayor. Deputy Chief Rosen has gone to talk to the local FBI boys. Come with me, Ms. Malloy. I'll make some tea and we'll have a nice chat, just the two of us. I hear you want to put in a greenhouse. Mrs. Jorgeson has the very same idea, so I did some research about wood and metal frames." He took my wrist and gave a little tug. "We'll talk about lily ponds, too."

No white-coated attendants appeared with a straightjacket. I allowed myself to be led to his office and seated in a chair. I accepted a cup of tea. It tasted like rain-barrel water. An idea of sorts came to mind. "Is there a file on Omario, the man I saw with Leslie in the sports bar?"

"I feel confident there is, Ms. Malloy."

"Might I have a look at it?"

"Deputy Chief Rosen gave me explicit instructions not to show you any files or reports involving this case. He said you might be looking for a culinary school. There are only a couple in Farberville, but the college has a bachelor's degree in culinary arts. You might find some classes that appeal."

Jorgeson wasn't a stone wall; he was more of a chain-link fence. I smiled. "That's a good idea. I'll look online when I get home. Thank you for the tea and the suggestion. After I take some classes, we'll have you and Mrs. Jorgeson over for dinner. You can admire my knife skills."

"We'd like that, Ms. Malloy."

"One other little thing, if you don't mind.

It doesn't have anything to do with the investigation, I promise. Gregory Whistler's wife, Rosie, died in an accident two years ago. He was all choked up when he told me. I felt awful that I didn't know about it, even though there must have been something in the local newspaper. Could you have a quick look on your computer and tell me what happened?"

"Deputy Chief Rosen will not be happy with me."

"Then we won't tell him, will we? I just felt so helpless when Gregory started crying and I wasn't able to comfort him. I don't need to read the file."

Jorgeson gave me a wry look as he turned to his computer. After a minute, he said, "Her body was found in their bathtub, under the water. The medical examiner declared it an accident as a courtesy to her spouse. She'd taken a massive dose of her prescribed antidepressants and drunk a bottle of wine. The officers spoke to her psychiatrist, with Whistler's permission, and he acknowledged that she was depressed and potentially suicidal."

"There's no way Whistler could have . . . assisted her?"

Jorgeson continued reading the monitor. "No, he'd gone to a conference in Boston two days earlier. The woman's closest friends were interviewed, and they all said they were worried about her. She'd stopped going out with them and hadn't attended any parties or benefits. One of them said that she'd discussed her concern with Whistler, and that neither of them could figure out what to do." He pushed a key to send the file back to the netherworld. "There you have it, Ms. Malloy."

"Our little secret. If the sketch artist is still here, I'm ready to meet with him. If not, give me a box of crayons and I'll do my best."

I waited while Jorgeson picked up his phone and inquired if Mr. Rimski was available. He was. I returned to the conference room and sat down next to dear Mr. Rimski. I was surprised that he had a laptop rather than a piece of charcoal and a pad of paper. I spent the next hour doing my best and, with his painfully patient encouragement, was pleased with the result.

"You know," I said as I picked up my purse, "you could be a billionaire if you could apply your technique to real people. Men and women would be pounding on your door, demanding you make their ears smaller and their noses straighter."

356

"I'll look into it," he said in a gloomy voice.

I was delighted to be back in the sunshine. I had new leads, some of which might be productive. I leaned against my car and looked across the street. The only black car was so battered that it might have lost at a demolition derby. It was also unoccupied. I took out my cell phone and called Rick's number. Five rings and voice mail. My next call was to Frances North, who was gracious enough to answer.

"This is Claire. Have you heard from Willie?"

"I spoke to her sister, who came last night from Tulsa. Willie is doing better, although they have her on a respirator as a precaution. The doctor hasn't said when she'll be released. I sent flowers from the board." Her voice hardened. "Who did this to her? Do the police have any suspects?"

"Everyone who was at the potluck is a suspect. Did you talk to Willie?"

"Of course I talked to Willie," she said. "I made a point of speaking to everyone, including the students. I complimented Willie on her chicken salad, even though I know where she bought it. Did you try my macaroni salad? It's my grandmother's recipe."

"It was divine. I need to ask you something else, Frances. You held an executive meeting on Thursday, right?"

"Yes, at my house. Sonya, Willie, Drake and I discussed the budget crisis over coffee." She stressed the beverage. "Sonya continued to voice support for Gregory and made the point that we've had this problem for the last several years. Drake disagreed and said that Gregory needs to step down if he's incapable of organizing the accounts. Willie kept talking about the phone bills. I don't know what she thought we ought to do." She hesitated. "I thought Willie might have had a martini or two in her chambers before she came to the meeting."

"Oh," I said as if scandalized. "You may be right. Did you see her talking to anyone in particular at the potluck."

"Let me think," she said. After what felt like a very long time, she said, "I know she tried to speak to Gregory, but he was babysitting Ludmila's grandson. On my way to the ladies' room, I saw her give Sonya an envelope. It was none of my business. I returned to the classroom and made sure Rick and Austin weren't pulling another one of their childish stunts. If they went to my school, they'd spend more time on the bench outside my office than in class. They seem to think our board meetings are nothing but a joke!"

I agreed with them, but this was not the time to share. "And Willie? Did she sit next to anyone while she ate?"

"You must have noticed there weren't enough chairs. I saw her leave the room with Leslie and assumed they'd gone into her office to sit down. I found myself sharing a cubicle with a large black man who refused to look at me while he ate. I was most uncomfortable, but since I assumed he was a student, I attempted to converse. He's from one of those queer African countries."

"Zimbabwe," I said absently. "One of its borders is the great, gray-green, greasy Limpopo River."

"I beg your pardon?"

"Thanks for talking to me, Frances. Will you call a special board meeting?"

"Not even if you threatened to stick a screwdriver in my ear. Have a nice day."

I closed my cell phone. Leslie was next on my list. I didn't have her phone number, but I wouldn't have called if I did. I drove to her house, with or without Hamdan, and parked around the corner in the same spot. If Charles, the surly neighbor who'd called the cops on me, was lurking, all the better. I had a few unsavory words for him. A pale green Mercedes was parked in the driveway; I'd seen it in the parking lot of the Literacy Council. I walked up the porch steps and rang the bell. I was preparing to ring it again when the door opened.

Leslie frowned. "Come in, Claire, and have a seat. There's coffee in the kitchen. I'm online with a class for fifteen more minutes." She went down the hall to her office.

I sat down in the living room. Leslie did not leave magazines or newspapers on the table. She did, however, leave mail in a basket under it. I listened to the gentle clatter from her keyboard. She would be occupied for another ten minutes. I slid out the basket and picked up a letter. It was from a lawyer's office. A second, unopened letter was from the CIS office in Phoenix. Another half-dozen sealed envelopes were from individuals in Arizona, New Mexico, California, and Colorado; the names on the address labels in the corner suggested the correspondents were female. I dug deeper and found letters from Saudi Arabia, China, and Tajikistan. It appeared that Leslie was into pen pals. No wonder she always seemed hassled, I thought as I replaced the letters.

The clatter ceased. I smiled at her as she came into the living room. She was wearing jeans and a T-shirt, and her feet were bare. "I must look like a mess," she said as she noticed my gaze. "I don't even have on any makeup. It's such a relief to chill out on a Saturday afternoon. Would you like a beverage?"

"No, thank you. I apologize for dropping in without calling first, but I don't have your number."

"Let me get some coffee and I'll join you." She walked silently into the kitchen and returned with a cup. "What can I do for you?"

"Did you hear about Willie?"

"Keiko called me yesterday afternoon. I'm so relieved that Willie is going to be okay. I understand it wasn't a heart attack."

"Something she ate or drank. Frances told me that you and Willie retreated to your office to eat. Did you notice what was on her plate?"

Leslie's eyes widened. "You think it was food poisoning? Oh my gawd, there were so many people there, taking spoonfuls of every dish. Is anyone else ill? Does Gregory know about this? This may be a disaster. Even if we're not liable, we'll lose all our funding and have to close down."

"No one else has reported any ill effects, so I think we can rule out food poisoning."

"That's a relief. You want to know what Willie ate? I wasn't paying attention, and I wouldn't be able to identify any of the dishes. Is she allergic to something?"

"There's nothing in her medical records to suggest it." I said this as if I'd reviewed them and consulted her doctor.

She made a helpless gesture. "I'm afraid I can't help you, Claire. We talked about the students. She complained about her crowded docket. She was fine when we took our plates to the plastic trash bags in the classroom. I drifted off to ask Graciela what she thought about her new tutor. Assami wanted to talk about the homework assignment. After that, Yelena put a stop to conversation with her peculiar performance. After Frances spoke, I went back to my office to continue my discussion with Assami. I didn't see Willie."

"What time did you leave?"

"After I finished with Assami, maybe one fifteen, I put all the homework assignments from the previous day in my briefcase, stopped in Keiko's office to wish her a pleasant weekend, and came here. No, that's not right. I stopped at a convenience store to get gas. I was here before two." She paused to push her hair out of her eyes. "Are you accusing me of something, Claire? I dislike playing games."

"Not yet," I replied. "Let's talk about Hamdan."

"Who? I have no idea who that might be. I thought our talk the other day convinced you that I'm not involved in any of this. I didn't like Ludmila, but that's hardly a reason to harm her. I have no strong opinion about Willie. I rarely see her. I've heard the rumors about Gregory, but I really don't have time to wonder if they're true. I'm more concerned with supporting myself and helping my students."

It was an elegant response, particularly when produced so glibly. "Perhaps Hamdan is a friend of Omario's. You do know who he is — your online student with a crisis, remember? If you'll give me his address and phone number, I'll try to clear this up without bothering you again." I mentally crossed my fingers, since I intended to badger her until the whole situation was resolved.

Leslie seemed to need a few seconds to compose herself. "I gave that information to the police. Is that all? I need to do some work before my online class later this afternoon. It has thirty students."

"TESOL students? I would imagine a large percentage of them are young women getting degrees in education. With the certification, they can get jobs in literacy programs just like you did. So many students graduate with enormous loans these days. What a depressing way to start a career in a field not known for generous salaries."

"I suppose so, although I never ask. I have a certain curriculum to cover each semester and tests to administer." She stood up, trying to hide her anger.

"One more question." I was a devotee of the *Columbo* series. "Did you ever return Waterford's calls?"

"That is a private matter. I have a lot of work, so please leave. If you have any more questions, write them down and slip them under my office door."

I nodded at her and went out the door, which closed firmly behind me. Snoopy Charles was nowhere to be seen, but I could hear music from within his house. Since I suspected Leslie was watching me, I walked up the street and turned the corner. I did not, however, drive away. I knew the neighborhood well. I cut through a sorority house yard and, when I reached the alley, turned toward Leslie's street. I looked over my shoulder several times in case Hamdan was tailing me, but the alley remained vacant of anything more menacing than a yellow cat investigating the sorority's garbage cans. I ducked into the yard of a house across the street from Leslie's and made myself uncomfortable between two shaggy forsythias. I alternated my surveillance between her house and the alley. I didn't know what I expected to happen, but I hoped Leslie would have a visitor in the next few minutes. If I recognized the visitor, I could confirm my suspicions; if I didn't, I could write down the license plate and wheedle Jorgeson into running it for me.

I did not expect to see Charles come out of his house and stop in his front yard. He surveyed the unoccupied sidewalk and then sauntered down Leslie's driveway to the garage. He stopped again and looked around. I squeezed against the foundation of the house and held my breath. I was assessing my chances of getting back to my car before he caught up with me when he turned back and unlocked the garage door. I saw a bright flash before he closed the door behind him. I began to laugh as I realized what he was doing inside. I didn't know if Leslie was aware that her garage was housing marijuana plants and grow lights. I understood why Charles had been nervous when he saw me in the driveway. He'd made a serious mistake when he messed with me, I thought smugly as I continued my surveillance.

After ten minutes, Charles came out of the garage, locked the door, and went back to his house. I sat for another twenty minutes before I decided that Leslie had not panicked as I'd hoped she would. I crawled out between the bushes, brushed off my fanny, and took my previous path to my car. There was no sign of a black car.

I sat down on the curb and called Peter. I was greeted by voice mail. I left a message apologizing for my hysterical outburst at the restaurant and added that alerting Homeland Security was unnecessary. I promised to unruffle his feathers at a later time, but I didn't go into details that might cause him to blush in front of the FBI agents. I am a thoughtful wife.

It was time for another unannounced visit.

16

Gregory lived in a neighborhood adjoining a private golf course. All the streets had cutesy names like Bunker Hill and Tee Circle. I found his house in a cul-de-sac at the end of Sand Trap Way. The white-brick house was one story, and abutting the backyard was a fairway. I caught a glimpse of a golf cart careening down a narrow asphalt path. There were occasional shouts, some the traditional warning cry "fore," others expressing extreme displeasure with a shot.

I rang Gregory's doorbell. His double garage was closed, so I couldn't know if he was home or not, but I intended to camp on his doorstep. I was relieved when he opened the door and said, "Claire?"

"Indeed. I'd like to talk to you."

"Can this wait until Monday? This has been one helluva week, and I need a break. I don't want to think about the Literacy

Council for the next forty-eight hours. I'm sure you understand."

I nudged him aside and went into the foyer. "I do understand, Gregory. First Ludmila, and then Willie. She's going to be okay." I grimaced. "Willie, not Ludmila. Bartek claimed he was going to send her ashes to be buried in Poland, but they're more likely to be sprinkled in his flower beds. Ludmila's, not Willie's." I continued into a large living room with a wall of glass windows. A foursome of golfers were hunting for a lost ball at the edge of his yard, which was delineated by overgrown bushes and weed-filled flower beds. "Aren't you worried about your windows? I hope your homeowner's insurance covers breakage."

"Three or four times a year." His growl suggested he was not in the mood to be a gracious host.

"Let's sit out here, shall we?" I continued to the flagstone patio and made myself comfortable in a padded chair. The golfers gave up and moved on.

Gregory sat down. "What's so urgent that it can't wait until Monday?"

"This is a lovely patio, even if one has to be prepared to duck. It must be like a perpetual Easter egg hunt out here." He failed to acknowledge my witticism. "Since you don't want to chat, let's get serious. What happened Monday night after the class ended and the students started to leave?"

"I don't know. I was livid after Rick made those wild accusations. Rather than risk another encounter, I went to my office and stayed there. I worked on a grant proposal until almost everyone was gone. I should have waited longer. Ludmila was seated on the bench in front of the reception desk. She began to screech at me as usual. I admit I was in a foul mood. I shouted at her to shut up. She got in my face, and it took great willpower not to slap her." He held up his palms. "I didn't, of course. She was a pathetic, delusional old woman. It would have been like slapping my grandmother."

"Grandmother Swistak, you mean?" Having tossed the grenade in the air, I waited to see where it fell.

Gregory was unprepared to catch it before it landed in his lap. After a moment of reverberating silence, he managed to say, "I don't know what you're talking about. I need a drink if you intend to spout more gibberish. My grandmother's last name was Hawkins." He pushed aside the screen door with unnecessary vigor as he went inside. I heard ice going into a glass, then glass clinking. Were I a better person, I would have felt a pang of guilt.

He held a glass of whiskey when he returned and sat down. "Ludmila used to screech *swistak* at me. I assumed it was an insult of some kind. I can assure you it isn't any name I've ever heard of."

"Maybe the name Bergmann-Swistak will sound more familiar. It's the name of your father's pharmaceutical company that was based in Germany before the scandal forced its closure. Ring any bells?" I watched his face turn pale. "C'mon, Gregory, the police have contacted Interpol." Or they should have, I amended.

He looked as if he'd been hit in the forehead by a golf ball. He took a big gulp of whiskey and choked on it, his face darkening to an interesting shade of mauve. He finally recovered from a bout of coughing and gasping. I ascertained there was no dent in his forehead.

"All right, all right," he said in a raspy voice. "That was the name of my father's company, but my father didn't know that Bergmann was cutting production costs. He was shocked and horrified when the truth came out. He severed the partnership immediately."

"And fled with half the remaining assets."

370

"According to the auditors. My father and I were not close. I was a sales associate in the Baltic region, very much a junior executive, and I knew nothing about the truthfulness of the accusations and the lawsuits. When I was informed that the corporation had been shut down, I packed up and moved back to my mother's house. Before you ask, I have no knowledge about my father's whereabouts."

"You're in communication with him," I said. "You mentioned his current wife."

"He calls every once in a while, but I don't ask questions. I've put all that behind me."

"How did Ludmila make the connection? Whistler isn't a common name, but it's not outlandish."

"The marketing department used corporate photos. Ludmila must have seen the ads in Polish magazines and recognized me. I should have changed my name instead of simply Anglicizing it."

"Why didn't you try to talk to her about it?" I asked. "It would have saved you from her daily rants."

"Did you try to talk to her? How's your Polish?"

I conceded that point. "But you knew that somewhere down the road another Polish student would show up."

"All I could do was pray that the 'sins of the father' business in the Old Testament was out of vogue by now. I didn't do anything wrong. I certainly didn't commit any crimes."

"Ludmila still liked the Old Testament, I guess. Let's go back to Monday night. You and she yelled at each other. Then what?"

He opened his mouth, but we both heard a voice shout, "Fore! Watch out, dammit!"

A small white missile slammed into a tree and bounced across the backyard. If it had taken a different tangent, Gregory might have lost another window — or one of us might have gained a bruise or worse. A rotund golfer in plaid shorts and a hideous Hawaiian shirt came into the yard. "Ya see where it went?" he asked loudly.

"That way." Gregory pointed in the opposite direction of the ball's trajectory. "It went into the ditch. Be careful, pal. There's a big-ass copperhead that lives in there, a good six feet long and real unfriendly." The golfer headed for the fairway.

I toyed with the same option as I looked at the ditch. "A six-foot copperhead?"

Gregory relaxed enough to smile. "Well, maybe not that long, and maybe not in that particular ditch. I did find a king snake in the garage once. I climbed on top of my car and hollered until Rosie came out. She scooped up the snake, scolded it for trespassing, and set it free in the woods."

"I know about her so-called accident," I said softly.

He slumped down in the chair and groaned. "It's not a secret. I just don't see any reason to tell everyone I meet. It makes me sound like I was cold and indifferent, or too self-absorbed to notice her depression. That's not true. I insisted she see a psychiatrist who specialized in the field. I made sure she took her medication. I brought her flowers several times a week. I encouraged her to go out to lunch with her friends. I would never have left her alone if her best friend hadn't promised to take care of her." He broke off and covered his face with his hands.

I needed the best friend's name, and Jorgeson had already reached the limit of his willingness to risk Peter's wrath. I decided to wait for an opening. "Is she the one who found Rosie's body?"

"I was at a conference. She was sobbing when she called me, but I finally understood what she'd said. I canceled my presentation and caught the first flight back here. At my insistence, the police checked for any sign of a break-in and took fingerprints, but they didn't find any indication that an unknown person was in the house. The housekeeper was there the day before and had polished all the furniture and other surfaces. I'd given her friend a house key — and thank God I did. Otherwise . . ."

I noticed something odd. Gregory hadn't mention Rosie's name during his revelation about her depression and his efforts to help her. Furthermore, he hadn't mentioned her best friend's name. I overlooked the former and said, "What's the name of Rosie's friend?"

His head jerked up. "Why? She was too late. The coroner's report said my wife's body had been in the water for ten hours. I almost threw up when I had to identify it at the morgue. She was so beautiful. What I saw was swollen and white."

I wanted to shake his shoulders and say, "Who was? Your wife? You mean Rosie?" I stared at the golf course until I felt my muscles unwind. "I want the friend's name because I had a similar experience once and I thought it would be good for us to share." Sure, and I'd ridden an alligator to his house. A blue alligator in drag.

"That was two years ago, and I don't know if Lilac wants to relive it. Lilac Benjamin. I don't know her number, but her husband's a urologist at a local clinic. Are we finished, Claire? You've destroyed any hope I had of a peaceful weekend."

"I wish we were. You haven't told me precisely what happened Monday night after this exchange with Ludmila."

"I returned to my office, embarrassed by my lack of control. At eight fifteen or so I went back out. Ludmila and the last few students were gone. I made a quick tour, locked up, and left."

"Which students were there when you and Ludmila exchanged unpleasantries?" I asked.

Gregory drained his glass. "I don't know. I wasn't paying attention to the audience." He bit his lower lip and looked away. "The Korean girls were gathering their backpacks. An old Latino guy came out from a cubicle to gawk. The Chinese girl was looking at books, I think. It hardly matters, since all of them were gone."

"Are you positive you turned off the lights before you left?"

"Yes. The only time I leave them on is if I see Toby in the parking lot. He usually sits out there and smokes pot before he comes inside. The only car in the parking lot was mine. I was very careful to lock the door because I can never count on Toby. The

375

lights were off. It was dark inside. I don't know what happened after I left, and I'm not going to discuss it anymore. Please let me show you out."

I was perplexed. He had no reason to lie about a minor detail, unless he'd killed Ludmila and was too distraught to think clearly. His motive wasn't as strong as I'd believed it was. He didn't seem worried that his father might lose his ill-gotten gains and end up in the dock in Germany.

I allowed him to escort me to the front porch, but I wasn't quite finished. "I hear you're dating Sonya."

"And I hear a voice in my head begging you to leave. Good-bye, Claire." He had the audacity to close the door. I considered punching the doorbell but let my hand drop. I still had half of his weekend to spoil. I took out my cell phone. Rick was not answering. I drove around the winding streets while I thought. Peter wouldn't be home until seven, so I had an hour before I needed to stop at the grocery store and the dry cleaner's. Gregory would be testy if I returned to his house and asked him to look up Lilac Benjamin's address. I stopped at what was marked as a golf cart crossing. No golf carts obliged, but I sat there anyway.

The Book Depot closed at five on Saturdays. Jacob would be toting up receipts and straightening the shelves. I dialed the number and wasn't surprised when he answered briskly and succinctly. "Book Depot."

"Jacob, this is Claire. I need you to look up an address on the computer. Don't even think about telling me that you would prefer not to. Please find an address for Lilac Benjamin. Her husband's a doctor."

"Very well, Ms. Malloy." I could almost hear his priggish frown. He came back on the line a minute later. "The address is 1337 St. Andrew's Way. Do you need directions?"

I'd been on St. Andrew's Way a few minutes earlier. "No, but thank you, Jacob. Enjoy your day off."

"I will make every effort to do so, Ms. Malloy." He hung up.

I backed into a driveway and retraced my route, trying to picture Jacob playing touch football or lounging at the lake. He was more likely to get his giggles from reading the latest translation of *Beowulf* while feasting on carrots and celery. I turned onto the pertinent street and looked at the house numbers until I arrived at a large brick home with ivy-covered walls, a circular driveway, a triple garage, and an expensive custom front door. I parked in the driveway, since there was room for a tanker to pull around my car and into the garage. I'd been lucky thus far, with the exception of Rick, who was AWOL. I crossed my fingers as I rang the doorbell.

A perky teenaged girl with braces opened the door. Before I could get out a word, she said, "Wow, you're Claire Malloy! I've seen you on the news. Caron's two years ahead of me, so I don't really know her. We sat next to each other at an assembly last fall, but I was too intimidated to talk to her."

I felt as if I should apologize. "Is this the Benjamin household?"

"Yes! Have you come to investigate us? My dad keeps saying he's going to shoot the next golfer that tramples the tomato plants."

"Is your mother home?"

"You're investigating her? Wow."

"Not at all," I said firmly. "I'd just like to speak to her for a few minutes. Is she here?"

The girl's face fell. "No, they went to a golf tournament in Springfield. They should be back early tomorrow afternoon. If it's an emergency, I can call them and tell them they have to get back here." Her blue eyes glittered as brightly as her braces. "Is it an emergency?"

"Please tell her that I'll call her tomorrow afternoon." I left the woebegone child standing in the doorway and climbed into my car. It was time to throw myself back into the mundane world of deciding between beef and chicken. I rather liked the idea.

Wow.

I had a roast and potatoes in the oven when Peter came home. He didn't say a word as he went into our bedroom. He came out, dressed in shorts and a T-shirt, and poured himself a glass of wine. I remained at the counter, slicing tomatoes and cucumbers for a salad. Several minutes passed with only the sound of my knife on the cutting board. I gritted my teeth, unwilling to concede. When I finally glanced at him, he said, "Other than that, Mrs. Lincoln . . ."

"How was my day? I suppose you're referring to my mildly frantic call from the restaurant?"

"The PD received forty-one mildly frantic calls from local citizens who were convinced that al Qaeda has planted bombs all over town. A few imaginative citizens reported that City Hall was occupied by terrorists who were holding the mayor hostage. Someone wanted to know the evacuation procedure. Another claimed that the terrorists were kidnapping children, including her fifteen-year-old son who didn't come home for lunch."

I winced. "My voice was loud, but I was upset. It's stressful to be followed everywhere you go. Didn't your friends at Quantico teach you that?"

"They taught me not to intentionally confront a suspect unless I was prepared to detain him."

"Detain him with what — a soup spoon?"

Peter was struggling to stay calm, which was quite sweet of him. His face was a tiny bit red, and he was strangling the wineglass. It was expensive, part of a set of twelve. I caught myself trying to recall whether they were Waterford. I scooped the sliced vegetables into a bowl. "Aren't you going to tell me what the FBI is going to do?"

"Nothing. They have no one named Hamdan Zayed bin whatever in their files."

"Well, he wouldn't go around flaunting his membership card in al Qaeda. Not that I think he has one." I was going to tell Peter what I did think about Hamdan's associations, but he was glaring at me. It was time to change the subject before the situation escalated. "I went to the farmers' market this morning. It was packed. I bought some produce, but I couldn't fight my way to the flower stalls." I took a pair of kitchen shears out of a drawer. "Would you like to help me cut some? The beds can spare a few snapdragons and dahlias."

He took his wine out to the terrace. Interpreting that as a no, I went out the front door and cut enough flowers to make an arrangement for the dining room table. After I finished, I sat down on the porch swing. I wasn't worried about Peter. He would do his best to stay miffed, but eventually he'd get over it. In the past, I'd enraged him. This was trivial in comparison.

Caron's car came down the gravel driveway and parked next to mine. I was pleased to see that Inez was with her. They took towels and beach bags out of the front seat. I heard Inez say something about her sunglasses as she climbed back in the car. Caron sat down next to me. "I made it all day without being kidnapped, Mother. Aren't you proud of me?"

"Even more than when you won the armwrestling tournament in seventh grade. That was quite a feat of strategy and strength."

"I told Glenda I'd let her eat my lunch for a month if she threw the bout. Did you find out anything about the nasty man with the lost puppy? I may want to play in the park tomorrow."

"Yes, I had a little talk with him earlier.

He didn't have a dagger in his belt. This may be hard to hear, but he's not interested in you. However, you need to stick with a crowd, even at the mall. He doesn't have a puppy, so don't fall for that ploy."

"Sometimes I don't know when you're teasing. Is this serious? Can't Peter arrest him for harassing you? Stalking is illegal."

"He's not breaking any laws. The police have a sketch of him and will pick him up on a flimsy charge if they spot him. Peter will give him a rough time, and that may be the end of it."

Inez walked toward us, her cell phone at her ear and her eyes blinking frenetically. She turned off the phone and stared at us. "There's an al Qaeda squad in town. They've concealed bombs at the mall, the high school, the campus, and City Hall. The governor called up the National Guard, and now there are armed soldiers on every corner. A friend of Ashley's cousin's roommate saw them. No one is allowed on Thurber Street after dark, and we're all under a ten o'clock curfew."

"What?" Caron said in a stunned voice. "A ten o'clock curfew? They can't do that, can they? The First Amendment guarantees the right to assemble. It doesn't say until ten o'clock."

I intervened before both of them started howling. "The whole story is total nonsense being spread by misinformed people. No al Qaeda, no National Guard, no bombs, no nothing. This is a rumor on steroids, that's all. This friend of Ashley's cousin's roommate doesn't exist outside the fringe of credibility."

Caron looked at me. "Does this have anything to do with the man without the puppy?"

"It might." I flipped a dried leaf on my shirt and watched it spiral to the ground.

Inez was gaping at us as if we'd crossed the fringe. "What man without a puppy? Who?"

"Would you two like to stay for dinner?" I asked. "No *haute cuisine,* just roast beef, potatoes, and salad."

Caron clearly wanted to demand a better answer but said, "Sure, we might as well. Our friends are evacuating in caravans."

"You have fifteen minutes. I suggest you whip out your cells and start texting everyone you know to tell them this rumor is a hoax. Tell them Deputy Chief Rosen assured you that nothing out of the ordinary is going on in Farberville, nor will anything dire happen in the future."

Caron dug through her beach bag for her

cell. "Nothing out of the ordinary ever happens in Farberville."

The naiveté of teenagers, I thought as I went inside and peered at the meat thermometer in the roast. I took the heavy pan out of the oven and set it on the stove. In one of my cookbooks I'd seen a recipe for Yorkshire pudding.

I gave myself a painful pinch on the arm and began to dress the salad.

On Sunday morning we settled on the terrace with coffee, bagels, lox and cream cheese, a bowl of melon chunks, and the newspaper. I had the book section. Peter was commenting as he read the travel section. "What about Bermuda? Pink beaches and scooters. Hmm, zip lines in Costa Rico that shoot you through the rain forest like a bullet. That sounds fun."

"I prefer to stroll through the rain forest so I can see the parrots and orchids." I turned the page. "If this erotica fluff is such a big seller, then why can't I sell the last five copies?"

"I've also wanted to climb Mount Kilimanjaro. Did you know it's on the border between Tanzania and Kenya?"

"No, but I do now. Do you know where the Limpopo River is?"

"The what?"

"On the border of Zimbabwe. More coffee?"

"Yes, please. Shall I toast another bagel? We can share."

"Lovely, dear."

Caron came out to the terrace with a glass of orange juice, found the comics section, and lay down on a chaise longue. "Why do they keep running this Prince Valiant strip? It makes no sense whatsoever and it's so boring."

"It started seventy-five years ago," Peter murmured.

I glanced at him. "And you know that because . . . ?"

He hid behind the newspaper. "When I was a kid, I was a big fan of King Arthur and his knights. I had a plastic suit of armor and a sword. I can't remember how many dragons I slew and maidens I rescued."

Caron and I exchanged grins. Peter had not been my knight in shining armor. When we first met, I'd disliked him intensely. If he'd tried to sweep me off my feet, I would have clawed his face. That was no longer the case, although he'd shown no indication of sweeping anything.

"Any plans for the rest of the day?" I asked him.

385

"I'm on a tight schedule. Baseball game, golf tournament, and a DIY show about restoring antique motorcycles."

I looked at Caron. "What time does Joel get home?"

"They have to go to church and out to eat with his grandmother, who's a lifelong fan of cafeteria food. They should be home by five or six. Joel will escape as soon as he can. He's going to text me when they're on the road so I'll have time to get ready. Can I borrow your yellow skirt?"

"Yes, you may. It's in your closet, not mine. Why aren't you going to wear any of the clothes we bought the other day?"

"Those are for school, Mother. I wish you'd pay more attention." She and Prince Valiant went upstairs to give themselves pedicures.

Once we'd taken the dishes and cups to the kitchen and put things away, Peter went into the living room and turned on the TV. He arranged the pillows, set a glass of iced tea within reach, and sprawled the length of the sofa. Men are easily amused.

I went into my library and called Rick for the umpteenth time. I was so startled when he answered that I was speechless for a moment. I recovered and said, "This is Claire. We need to talk. I promise I won't ask you

to divulge your big secret, because I'm pretty sure I know what it is."

"Then we have nothing to talk about, do we?"

"We have many things to talk about, including what happened to Willie on Friday. I need your help."

"Austin said you have a theory but no evidence. This should be left to the police, Claire. They can run tests and interview her. I went by the hospital yesterday, but I wasn't allowed to enter her room. She looked good and thanked me for coming by."

"Will you be home if I come by in an hour?" I immediately wished I could retract the question. It needed to be a statement: "I will come and you'd better be there." All it lacked was an ominous "or else," but nothing remotely plausible came to mind. I was pleased when he suggested meeting at Mucha Mocha.

I needed to come up with an explanation for my departure, but by the time I'd showered and prepped, Peter was sound asleep. I turned down the volume, put his glass on a coaster, and tiptoed out the front door.

The Mucha Mocha parking lot had only a few open spaces. I went inside and continued to the patio. Rick sat at a table, texting. He'd already purchased coffee and a pastry. I sat down across from him. "Updating the president on an outburst of terrorism in Farberville?"

"I got dozens of texts and e-mails that made no sense. Idiotic rumors, mass hysteria, evacuate before we're all blown to pieces. I waited for one to claim that aliens had landed in the football field and were beaming up our best players." He put down his cell phone. "I was sending my grandmother a birthday card. Dancing polar bears with candles on their heads. Before you sniff disdainfully, I sent real flowers yesterday."

I produced a small smile to reward him for his thoughtfulness, then said, "I was curious about Gregory's wife and her so-called accident. Once I learned the truth, an odd idea crossed my mind. I may be wrong. The easiest way to find out is for you to tell me your cousin's name and where she lived. I'll get online and search the local newspaper for her obituary. If that doesn't work, my husband can speak to the police department there."

He stirred his coffee, staring at the swirls. "Okay, she didn't die in Oregon. Her name was Rosalind McBrindell until she married that bastard Gregory. She sent me wedding pictures. I wanted to puke. I sensed from her earlier letters that he was controlling and abusive — not physically, but emotionally. He insisted on knowing everywhere she went and with whom, even when they were dating. Rosie refused to see it that way, since her father had been the same way throughout her childhood. She thought it showed how much he loved her."

"So what happened after they were married?"

"He became worse. He manipulated her, eroded her self-confidence with insidious little jabs, made her feel incompetent. He was careful when other people were around, but he had sly ways to belittle her. 'Rosie, honey, you always get that wrong. That's why I love you.' She stopped going to parties. If she went out to lunch with women friends, he'd call her cell and demand to know if she was drinking too much. She was embarrassed to let anyone know what he said."

I felt a chill as I imagined myself in her miserable situation. "Why didn't she divorce him?"

"I asked her that, too. I offered to fly in and hold her hand through the entire ordeal. She said that she could take care of herself and didn't want me to get involved. She may have thought I might attack Gregory, which I would have. After that, she tried to write me cheerful letters. I didn't believe half of what she wrote, and she wasn't adept at lying. Then she killed herself." He picked up a napkin and blotted his eyes. "I didn't know until another cousin told me three months later. He was in Afghanistan, and his parents didn't want to burden him until he came home."

"Your parents must have heard."

"They rented a house on one of the Hebrides islands. Very remote, no Internet, no cell service. My mother had decided to write a mystery novel, and my father's into birds and photography. They sent me a letter when they finally found out about Rosie, but I'd been transferred to Hong Kong, so I never received it."

"You said you'd been in Hong Kong since you graduated from college."

"I may not have been truthful. I've lived in several countries over the last ten years. I was in Bolivia at the time. It didn't seem prudent to mention it."

I nodded. "Because Rosie might have said something about her cousin in Bolivia, and Gregory could make the connection."

"Everybody in the family calls me Paddy

390

or Pat. I decided to go by Rick and hope she hadn't mentioned my last name." He was calmer now, but far from relaxed. Each time the word "Gregory" was spoken, his jaw tightened. It was too bad he hadn't ignored Rosie's plea to stay away. Gregory might have landed in the emergency room, too mangled to produce his insurance card.

"So now you're here to make him suffer. You haven't made much headway that I can tell. If he's found guilty of embezzlement, he'll get off with making restitution, probation, and maybe a fine. There are too many billionaires competing for beds in the federal prisons."

"What can I say? I'm not into torture and murder. I might kidnap his cat and demand a million dollars, but he doesn't have one because of his allergies. Rosie found that out when she brought home a kitten. He threatened to dispose of it unless she gave it back immediately." He paused, on the edge of a smile. "I hadn't remembered that until now. Some of my friends have cats. A sprinkle of dander in his office and his car could lead to sneezing and asthma. Rosie mentioned once that they kept a key hidden under a flowerpot on the patio. If it's still there, Gregory won't sleep well at night." He leaned forward and took my hand.

"Thank you, Claire. I knew there was a reason I agreed to meet you. Austin will love this."

I was not inclined to scold him for such a juvenile prank, and almost offered to help. However, the wife of the deputy chief has to hold herself to certain standards. "All I can say is don't get caught. Let's go back to your scheme to have Gregory nailed for embezzlement. Any progress?"

"Some. Gregory was at a conference when . . . Rosie's accident occurred. He turned in an expense account voucher for four nights at the hotel, but he only stayed three nights. The conference had told him that they would pay all his expenses. He booked the flights himself and paid cash when he checked out of the hotel. The conference reimbursed him, as did we. That cost almost three thousand dollars. Gregory swears he has to fly first class so that he can work during the flights. He's pulled that stunt several times in the last four years, but it's difficult to find the receipts and expense accounts in the hodgepodge of boxes and stacks of paperwork."

"It may have something to do with the telephone bills. Willie tried to bring up the subject at the executive board meeting Thursday evening, but nobody would pay attention. Frances implied that she thought Willie was drunk."

"I paid attention to her at the potluck," Rick said slowly. "She was onto something, and I told her so. Maybe I should have ignored her, too. Look what happened."

17

"Okay," I said slowly, "but before you go any further, have you told me the truth, the whole truth, and no surprises."

Rick grinned. "Everything I've told you today is absolutely true. Now, if you want the whole truth, I have to tell you about the escort in Bolivia and the drug dealers in Manila. In fact, maybe we ought to start with the blond cheerleader my senior year of high school. She drove a blue Mustang convertible that matched her eyes, and —"

"I get the point. What did Willie say to you Friday about the phone bills?"

"She needed the books before Frances's meeting, so she went into Gregory's office while he was gone and rooted through the mess. She stumbled across the phone bills, and they seemed too high. She's been the treasurer since Moses came down from the mountain, and her memory's not as bad as she lets everyone believe." He stopped to chuckle. "She says it prevents people from asking her stupid questions. Anyway, she had a clerk get copies of the phone bills for the last ten years."

"They shot up when Gregory was hired four years ago?"

"Not until about a year later. The board of directors voted to put an extension in the second office, although the teacher is part-time. It was a onetime charge of a little more than a hundred dollars plus the phone itself. Mysteriously, the phone bill doubled the next month."

I rubbed my nicely shaped chin. "Did Gregory have an explanation?"

"No one knew about it. He wrote the checks every month and hid the amount under the supplies and incidentals, like the water-bottle charges, carpet-cleaning service, and another outdoor light for the parking lot. If anyone on the board had been sharp, he couldn't have gotten away with it for the last three years."

"Did Willie figure out why the bill is so high?"

"At the potluck, we were pinned in a corner and it was loud. What I gathered was there have been lots and lots of overseas calls. The long-distance plan doesn't cover those." His shoulders rose, and he made a face. "There shouldn't be any overseas calls. Keiko used the phone once to call her family in Japan, but she told Willie and tried to pay for the call. Willie told her not to worry about it. That's as far as we got before Willie realized the food was disappearing and jumped in line."

"There was no place to sit and eat in the classroom. Leslie invited her to her office, where, according to Leslie, they engaged in an inconsequential conversation about the students. That seems to be the last anyone saw of Willie."

"Someone doped her food or drink," Rick said. "Leslie?"

"I don't know, but I suspect she's involved in something that might have to do with the overseas calls."

"Please elaborate."

"I will, I promise," I said, "but I need proof. Besides, why should I tell you everything when I had to pry your story out of you?"

He popped the last bite of pastry into his mouth. "Perhaps we should have a look around her office."

"Are we going to break a window or go down the nonexistent chimney?"

"I have a key. How could I prowl around Gregory's office without one?"

I needed to stall while I made a decision. I'd promised Peter not to go to the Literacy Council, although I hadn't specified for how long. I hadn't been there since Friday afternoon, so I'd lasted forty-eight hours thus far. "How did you get it?" I asked, feigning interest. Peter wouldn't necessarily find out that I'd revised my promise to mean "not in the next forty-eight hours." Well, maybe forty-six hours, but I wasn't going to quibble over details.

"I asked Willie to let me make a copy of hers. She's had doubts about Gregory for a long while, but she didn't know what to do. Drake said he was too busy running his department. Frances abhors the scent of scandal; she'd rather bury her head in the sandbox. Sonya refused to listen, and Austin's not the most reliable guy in the county. She was pleased when I promised to investigate."

I could delay hedging my promise for a while, but we had to search Leslie's office before the next morning when she showed up to teach. I told him about Rosie's friend Lilac Benjamin and suggested we visit her first.

He didn't fall for it. "Yeah, I'd really like to talk to her, but the Literacy Council's five minutes from here. Leslie could be there now, shredding her files and erasing damning evidence on her computer. Is that what you're worried about, Claire? I assure you I can fend her off if she attacks us with a letter opener."

"No," I said, unwilling to explain. "We can't stay more than fifteen minutes, though. The police may be keeping an eye on it, and I don't want to be dragged off to jail."

"We're members of the board of directors, and I have the key. I think we're safe from doing hard time for breaking and entering."

"Yes, but we need to be quick. I'll leave my car here and ride with you." If a patrol car drove by, the officers might note Rick's license plate. If they came to the door, he could wave his key at them to his heart's content. I'd be in a dark corner, listening to my heart thud.

The parking lot was empty. I suggested to Rick that he park across the street, but he didn't bother to respond. The lights were off, and the interior was dim. Rick stuck his all-powerful key in the lock, and we went inside. I trailed after him as he went down the narrow space and tried to unlock the door of Leslie's office. His key wasn't all that powerful, it seemed. "I have access to

Gregory's office," he said, irritated. "This key is supposed to unlock all the doors."

"She may have had the lock rekeyed without telling anyone. Keiko's the only person who might need to get inside when Leslie's not here. The storage room is so small that Leslie keeps some of the boxes of workbooks and copy paper in a corner of her office."

This time he trailed me as I went into Keiko's unlocked office and sat behind her desk. Some of the drawers were neat; others had free-range paper clips, rubber bands, a large assortment of makeup, pads of sticky notes, and keys attached to white ID circles bound in aluminum. I sorted through them and found one marked LB. "This should be it," I said as I handed it to Rick. "Go try it." I remained seated, looking at the scraps of papers with scrawled notes, some written in Japanese letters. I closed the drawers and studied her desk. Unlike in her drawers, everything was neatly aligned and in its proper place. She had a large monthly calendar stained with coffee rings and what appeared to be mustard. She'd jotted down phone numbers, the dates of the board meeting and of the potluck, my name (ahem), and rather elegant doodles. Nothing appeared to be worth a second look. On little more than a whim, I lifted up one corner of the calendar and saw a folded note. I pulled it out, hoping it wasn't highly personal. It read, "Waterford keeps calling. Tell him I resigned and went to Canada." Although it was unsigned, I knew it was from Leslie.

I leaned back in the chair and closed my eyes. I was trying to come up with anything but the obvious when Rick came to the door. "What's wrong, Claire? I thought you wanted to be out of here as soon as possible. Are you going to join in the fun or take a nap?"

"I never pass up an opportunity to snoop with a handsome guy who lies to me so eloquently." I returned the note to its hiding place and rose with the grace of a cherry blossom.

"I didn't lie to you," Rick said as we went back to Leslie's office. "I lied to everybody. You just happened to be there — and frankly, my dear, I didn't know if I could trust you. Austin's the only one who's heard the whole story."

"Is that why you called him to rescue you at the beer garden?"

"At the time, I didn't trust you, but I'd figured out that you're one tough broad. I was afraid that if you tried to pin me down about my mythical cousin in Oregon, I might lose control and get emotional. I didn't trust myself, either." He gestured at Leslie's computer. "It's password protected, and there's no way I can break into her files."

I sat down to go through her drawers. The smaller ones had folders of worksheets, class rosters with notes in the margin, a map of the United States, and another folder filled with letters from grateful students. The bottom drawers, one on each side, were locked. "Damn it," I muttered.

Rick looked up from his squatting position in front of the bookcase. "What?"

"The large drawers are locked, and I didn't see any little keys in Keiko's office." I rechecked the unlocked drawers and felt underneath the middle one in case she'd taped it there. "We are not going to pry them open, and I don't have my burglary kit with me. Whatever she's hiding is going to stay hidden for now. Let's go."

"She has a whole lot of government booklets about immigration and citizenship. Is that significant?"

"It would be if you'd been able to discern her password so I could look at her e-mails and files."

For some reason, Rick took my remark as

an insult. "I don't know her. I don't know her birth date, her current and past telephone numbers, her Social Security number, her mother's maiden name, or her wedding anniversary. I don't suppose you have any hackers on call?"

I did, but I doubted Caron and Inez could ferret out the password without the same information. "I don't want to confront Leslie until we have enough evidence for a warrant. She might delete the files."

"You haven't told me what's in these files or why she's making overseas calls."

"Because I'm not sure," I admitted. "I have a very feeble theory, that's all. Let me think about it tonight. Do you have any friends in the CIS?"

"I have a friend in the regional passport office, who's been able to expedite visas for me. I've dealt with people at several American consulates. There's an American Chamber of Commerce in Hong Kong. Bunch of guys in ties that take us out to dinner and offer perks of a licentious nature. The ambassador throws holiday cocktail parties. But the CIS? I've never had anything to do with them."

"Then you have a homework assignment. See if you can find someone named Waterford who's employed by them. I don't know his first name or where he's located, but you might try Phoenix." I paused and shook my head. "Not that I know if he works for the CIS. It's one of the more feeble premises in my theory."

His look had a tinge of dubiousness. "I'll see if I can find out anything. Do you want to swing by the hospital?"

"After that, will you come up with something else to do to avoid meeting Rosie's friend? Have a snack in the hospital cafeteria? See if Sonya's car is parked at Gregory's house? Track down Austin and ask him to come play with us?"

"I know that whatever she says will upset me. We could take a bottle of wine with us as a gesture of hospitality."

"It's Sunday, and the liquor stores are closed. All right, we'll go by the hospital and say hello to Willie. If you don't want to meet Lilac, you can go home and watch some golf tournament on TV. There's a show about restoring antique motorcycles on later." A good wife listens to her husband, especially when she needs to sneak out of the house.

"The hospital and this Lilac woman," Rick said. "What kind of name is that?"

Uninformed about lilacs, I had little to say as we drove to the hospital. Because

403

Sunday afternoon was prime visiting time, we were lucky to find a parking place in the same area code. I felt a distasteful dribble of perspiration in the middle of my back as we trudged uphill to the main entrance. Rick stopped at a desk and ascertained Willie's room number. We rode the elevator with people holding flower arrangements, helium balloons with perky messages, and bags of contraband. The confined space reeked of pastrami.

When the elevator doors slid open, Rick took off confidently toward the ward. I wished we'd stopped in the gift shop for flowers, although Willie might have preferred a discreet flask. I spotted a uniformed officer seated in a chair in the corridor. I was quite pleased when I recognized him as one of the men Peter had sent to supervise Caron's party Friday afternoon. He stood up as we stopped.

"Sorry, no one's allowed to go into this room," he said.

I gave him a wounded smile. "You don't remember me? You attended a swimming party at my house a couple of days ago."

"I was on duty, ma'am." His voice was shaky, and his ears were turning red.

Rick glanced at me, then stepped into the doorway. "Willie, you're looking a lot better. Feeling better, too?"

The policeman opened his mouth, but I said in a low voice, "I haven't told Deputy Chief Rosen about your conduct with the nubile young creatures in bikinis — not yet. We're close friends of the patient, and I think she'll prefer not to have to shout across the room. Don't you agree?"

"I'll have to go in with you."

"No, you'll have to stay right here. If either of us pulls out an ax, you can spring into action." I gave Rick a light shove as I entered the room. "Hey, Willie, I'm so glad you're better."

"They're doing one final round of blood tests just to be sure. If everything's copacetic, I can go home in the morning. This place is gawdawful. The PA system barks all night. When my glucose bag needs to be replaced, the machine beeps like a giant cricket. I seem to be the only one who hears it." She turned her attention on Rick. "Enough about me. Did you find out anything of significance about . . . the anomaly?"

"I told Claire, so you can speak openly. I studied the bills yesterday, and something's fishy. I called the overseas numbers, but ninety percent of them were disconnected. I got voice mail with the rest. Will the Literacy

Council reimburse me when my telephone bill arrives?"

"Sure, drop the bill in Frances's lap. She'll love it." Willie studied me for a moment. "Well, Claire, do you think Rick and I are delusional, that we're persecuting poor Gregory?"

"Not at all. He's a crook."

"Do you think he murdered Ludmila?" she persisted in her sternest courtroom voice.

Had I been in the witness chair, I would have been too terrified to speak. I cleared my throat. "I don't know. It seems to be a matter of who turned on the lights and when." I would have elaborated, but a nurse came into the room.

"Out, both of you," she said in a tone devoid of any hint of loving, tender care. She looked capable of lunging at us with a syringe if we dared linger for another second.

The young officer pretended not to notice us as we came out and turned toward the elevator. When we were out of earshot, Rick said, "Who turned on the lights? Really?"

"Could you and Austin see the Literacy Council from your booth at the sports bar?"

"We sat at a table, and the window blinds were closed. Would you care to explain the importance of the lights?"

"I need to explain it to my husband first, but I have to find the right time. He's annoyed because he knows I'm once again meddling in affairs best left to the boys in blue. Not that he wears blue, mind you. He usually wears a suit and tie. He does have a lovely blue dress shirt that goes well with the tie I gave him on his birthday." By this time, we were half-way to Rick's car. I let my voice fade, but I was prepared to resume rambling if he asked me the same question.

I gave him directions to Lilac's house and then gazed out the window. He made a few innocuous comments about the weather and his bank's softball team. I responded politely. I was relieved to see an SUV parked in the driveway. A man was pulling golf bags out of the rear section, and a woman was carrying a suitcase toward the house. I told Rick to park and then hurriedly got out of the car and caught up with the woman before she reached the front door.

"Are you Lilac Benjamin?" I asked, panting a wee bit.

"You must be Claire Malloy. My daughter texted me yesterday after you left."

She was a pretty woman, dressed in shorts and a blouse. She wore a visor with the logo of a country club on her short blond hair.

Most importantly, she appeared to be a reasonable sort.

"I hope this doesn't distress you, but it's about Rosie Whistler." I gestured at Rick, who was fidgeting. "This is her cousin, Rick Lester. You may know him as Paddy."

Lilac stared at Rick. "You're Paddy? I didn't expect to ever meet you. I heard so much about you from Rosie. If she hadn't shown me your letters and postcards, I wouldn't have believed you were real. Can you really dance on the head of a pin?" She dropped the suitcase, barely missing her foot. "Wow, this is such an incredible surprise. You'd both better come inside. My knees are shaking, and I'm light-headed. Is it too early for a glass of wine?"

Rick pretended to frown as he looked at his watch. "About an hour early, but this is an auspicious occasion that merits breaking the rule. Please let me take your arm, Lilac. Where would you like us to sit?" They went into the house.

Dr. Benjamin stood beside the SUV, looking bewildered. I went over to him and explained who Rick was. "He's still grieving for Rosie," I added. "Talking about her with Lilac might give him closure." I despise the term "closure," which is akin to "foreclosure" and implies that the feeling of loss can be erased by slamming a door.

He thought for a moment. "Tell Lilac I'm going to the club to brag about winning our flight." He leaned the golf bags against the garage door, climbed into the SUV, and drove away. I'd seen pain in his eyes, and I suspected he'd cared about Rosie, too.

I went through the house. Lilac was sitting in a bamboo deck chair on her patio. Rick came out of the house with three glasses of white wine. Once we were settled, I let Rick start the conversation. I was the outsider; I'd never met Rosie. I paid minimal attention as they talked about her childhood antics with Rick, stories that he laughingly denied, stories that made him blush, her delight with a sweater he'd sent from Manila. When I heard Gregory's name, I stopped trying to invent a semitruthful version of how I'd spent the afternoon. Lilac said that she'd liked him initially but had grown to despise him. Rick had harsh things to say. Lilac seconded them. Finally Rick brought up the suicide.

Lilac's eyes grew wet, and her voice was unsteady. "I should have suspected something when Rosie didn't answer my phone calls. She had an appointment with her gynecologist that morning. We were going to have lunch at a new bistro, but she left a message saying she had a headache and needed to take a nap. She was getting migraines frequently. Gregory always dismissed them as hangovers." Her eyes flickered with anger. "Rosie rarely had more than a glass of wine at parties, and we always drank iced tea at lunch. She told me that Gregory blamed her when he found empty bottles. He drank so heavily at night that he didn't remember in the morning."

"When did you go over to her house?" I asked.

"Around ten o'clock that evening. I was so edgy that my husband insisted I go check on her." Now her voice was ragged, filled with pain, and she was trembling. "I wish I could forget what I saw, but the image is etched on my brain. I am so sorry, Rick. I should have gone over right after I heard the message, but I let myself get distracted by the petty tasks that fill my days. When I called at noon, and again late in the afternoon to invite her to dinner, I assumed she was asleep. I'm in therapy, but I still feel so awful . . ."

He stood up and pulled her to her feet. They hugged tightly. I kept wiping away tears forming in the corners of my eyes. They were mourning. I was seething with fury, but I willed myself not to say something that might add to their grief. I listened to birds and the cries of golfers beyond the tree line, forcing myself to breathe slowly. Rosie had brought joy to their lives; Gregory had brought misery to hers. He'd sapped her self-confidence until she was a beaten puppy.

I thought about what Lilac had said about Rosie having an appointment with her gynecologist. What she'd learned must have been devastating. The autopsy would have indicated a pregnancy. Lilac and Rick had talked about her love of children, and Gregory had told me that she was eager to have babies. Finding out that she was pregnant would not have driven her to suicide. Finding out that she never would be pregnant, however, might have been too much to bear. I kept my thoughts to myself.

Lilac finished her wine in a gulp. "I'm sorry, but I can't handle any more of this today. I haven't even said hello to my kids. Rick, you're welcome to come back anytime. Rosie used to write the funniest things on birthday and Christmas cards, and I'd like to share them with you." She stood up and attempted to sound normal and brisk, as befitting a suburban wife. "Another time, then. Claire, thank you for bringing Rick. My daughter is still awed. She'll throw a fit when she finds out you were here and I didn't invite her to join us. That's what she deserves for staying in her bedroom texting as if she's trying to set a record for nimble fingers. I don't understand why they don't just call each other and talk."

I commiserated as we went to the front door. I'd forgotten to tell Lilac about her husband's departure, but after I'd told her, she smiled sadly. "He was very fond of Rosie. He saw what Gregory was doing and tried to talk to him, the man-to-man thing. He would end up so frustrated that I'd have to sit on his lap to prevent him from going to their house. After I found Rosie . . . the way she was, I called him right after I called nine-one-one. He came over and held me until the paramedics arrived."

Rick and I were somber as we got in his car. "Poor woman," he said as he pulled onto the main road.

"At least she's in therapy, which is healthier than nursing an obsession to seek revenge."

"If that bastard steps in front of my car, it will take me so long to decide whether or not to brake that this issue will be moot. But I'm not out for real blood, I promise. All I want to do is make him miserable for the rest of his life. If he's not nailed for embezzlement or gets off easy, I'll find out where he goes. It's way too easy to join the board of a nonprofit. You might have noticed that."

"And make your life miserable at the same time? For pity's sake, Rick, you're young, handsome, and single — better known as eligible. You'll never have a relationship if you devote your life to moving wherever Gregory goes."

"Maybe." He pulled in next to my car in the Mucha Mocha parking lot. "What next, Claire? Should we buy black ski masks and break into Leslie's house at midnight?"

I suddenly recalled a tidbit of an earlier conversation. "Why did you mention Leslie's wedding anniversary when you were talking about her password?"

"Because married people tend to remember the date they were married," he said cautiously as he shrank back.

"She doesn't wear a wedding ring."

"She introduced me to her husband at the spring open house. What does this have to do with anything?"

"Dark complexion, British accent?" I willed him to nod.

He nodded. "He seemed like a nice guy. I was a little surprised by the difference in their ages, but it didn't matter to me. Do

413

you suspect him of something? Did he murder Ludmila?"

"No." I felt sorry that Rick was bewildered, but I needed time to think. "Just concentrate on this Waterford guy. Tomorrow I have to go by the Literacy Council to proffer my resignation as receptionist. I'll call you if I find out anything worth repeating." Ignoring his salvo of questions, I climbed out of his car and got into my own. Once he'd driven off (in a huff), I sat back and tweaked my hypothesis. It might not pass muster with Peter, who was touchy about proof, but it made sense.

Feeling much better, I drove home.

I was miffed when Peter, who was still on the sofa, waved lamely to me with his free hand. The other held the remote control. I paused long enough to deduce the golf tournament had not yet concluded, but the motorcycle restorers were already talking about the challenge of finding vintage parts. Due to a common male chromosome, Peter was watching both shows. Within reach now were a beer and a plate of pizza-dough crusts. I hadn't been missed.

There were a few slices of pizza in one of the boxes. I put a small slice on a plate and stuck it in the microwave, then took my meal out to the terrace so I wouldn't have to listen to men gushing about spectacular drives that involved fairways or chrome restoration.

I'd clearly made progress, but I wasn't sure how to find any decent evidence. Leslie, Omario, Hamdan, and possibly Keiko had their cabal, with Gregory's assistance. Peter would demand something concrete before he attempted to get warrants. Gregory was an embezzler and a horrid man. With luck, the feds would come after him when Rick showed them the ledgers and the telephone bills. I had a glimmer of an idea about Ludmila's death, but I also had too many alternative scenarios . . . and no evidence. I had a theory about Miao's reason for going underground. I needed to pressure Miss Parchester until she told me where to find Miao — and I needed to do so before Jiang did.

I began to patch together a tentative schedule for the following day. It began with convincing Peter that I had to go to the Literacy Council and allow Keiko a chance to find a replacement. He would protest, of course, but he would eventually give in. Miss Parchester was next on my list. If I failed to persuade her, then I'd head back to the math department. I hoped Hamdan had a full tank of gas.

I carried my plate to the kitchen and was struggling to fit the pizza box in the already packed recycling container when the phone rang. "I'll get it," I called to Peter. It was merely a gesture, since the golf announcer was speculating about the specter of sudden death if someone didn't sink a putt. Although my husband was not a golfer, he had a peculiar propensity for caring about who won the tournaments.

"Hello," I said.

"This is Rick. You were right about Waterford, and I came across some very interesting information."

18

Before I could say anything, the TV went off and Peter ambled into the kitchen. I gave him a warm smile and then asked Rick if he could meet me at eight o'clock the next morning for coffee. He suggested a restaurant near the Literacy Council. Thoroughly sick of Mucha Mocha, I assured him I'd be there and ended the call. Peter did his best to conceal his curiosity while he dumped the pizza remains in the trash.

"Rick Lester," I said. "He's on the Literacy Council board of directors. He wants to tell me something about the phone bills."

"Ah, the embezzlement investigator who works at some bank. Still on the case, Miss Marple? I thought you said something about stepping back until we persuade this Zayed character to leave town — of his own accord, of course."

I pondered this for a moment. "I haven't seen him since Friday when we had our tête-à-tête at the restaurant. For all I know, he has left town. He must have figured that you'd put an APB out on him."

"I didn't put an APB out on him because he hasn't broken any laws," Peter said mildly.

"What about slashing my tires?"

"Did he admit it?"

"Not exactly," I said, "but he implied it. You can at least question him."

"Hard to do if he's left town."

I turned around to face Peter. I knew he was teasing me, and he had no idea of the emotional upheavals I'd experienced lately. I could play his game; I was quite as adept at it as he was. My lips began to quiver. My knees followed suit. To his surprise, and mine as well, I threw my arms around his neck and began to cry. He held on to me with strength and tenderness. This made me feel worse. I didn't want to deceive him with glib omissions and evasions.

When I could trust my voice, I said, "I want to tell you about Gregory's wife."

In the morning, Rick was waiting at a table with two mugs of coffee and a small plate of biscotti. He waited until I'd drunk and dunked for a few minutes.

"I have to be at the bank in half an hour,"

he said, "so let's get started. Waterford, first name Troy, works for the CIS out of the Phoenix office. He's been there for a decade. I don't know how he can stand the incessant heat. The average high temperature in the summer is in the triple digits. Yeah, it's dry heat, but —"

"You have to be at the bank in half an hour. Do we have time to discuss the weather in Phoenix?" I am not a morning person, and the caffeine was only beginning to ease me into a genteel outlook on the world.

Rick seemed to find my grouchiness amusing. "Once I determined where he lives, I tracked down his number and called him. I was so nervous that I didn't know if I wanted him to answer or not, but he did. I explained who I was and where I lived. He immediately brought up Leslie's name. This led to the Farberville Literacy Council and her connection. Since you refused to tell me what this is about, I'm sure I sounded like an ignorant do-gooder. I tried to get information from him, but he was as bad as you. He did say that he'd been investigating her for the years she lived in Phoenix and Tucson. He also dropped something about her multiple marriages."

"I knew it." I said this calmly despite the

outburst of elation in my brain. "She told me that she was in the middle of divorcing the man you met. I should have asked her how many other divorces she'd survived. My estimate is three, but it depends on her age when she started her little fund-raising scheme."

"Her what? I thought the bride had to bring a dowry."

"Not if the bride has a commodity to sell. I did some research online last night. If a foreigner with a temporary green card marries a U.S. citizen, he or she can expedite the citizenship process. Instead of five years, it takes three. Of course, the couple has to put up a good pretense of a marriage based on love and that sort of thing. A wedding album, a double bed, visits to relatives, socializing with friends — all the typical behavior. If the CIS is suspicious, they do home visits and ask questions. However, the paperwork is squirming its way through the bureaucratic maze, and eventually the alien receives full citizenship. Once that's accomplished, it's time for a quiet, uncontested divorce."

"Is it legal?" he asked.

"No, but it's damn hard to prove. People get divorced as often as they blow out birthday candles. There's no law that you have to stay in one of these marriages for a particular length of time. Leslie must be a master at adopting her so-called husband's name, notifying Social Security, getting a new driver's license, and setting up a joint bank account. Hubby makes a hefty deposit, which she siphons off over the three years."

"There ought to be records somewhere." He leaned back and widened his eyes in mock fear. "No, I do not know a single person who ever worked in the Social Security Administration in Arizona, and I'm not calling them. If you have seven hours to wait on hold, please do so."

I overlooked his puny effort at sarcasm. "What's more, I believe Leslie's running a much more involved faux-marriage scam. She teaches online classes to college students in their twenties, mostly women. She can offer them a sum of money to marry one of her overseas clients, explaining what's required. The women don't have to have sex with their so-called husbands as long as his clothes share a closet with hers and his toothbrush is in the bathroom. The women get a head start on their college loans, and some man from" — I made a vague gesture with my hands — "somewhere gets his citizenship."

"And you came up with this theory because . . . ?"

"Because I slipped into her office just as the potluck started and found two folders with foreign men's résumés and the names and photos of American women. It's a twist on mail-order brides."

Rick frowned, clearly overwhelmed by my brilliant deduction. "Why keep folders at the Literacy Council? She could do this at home on her own computer."

"It gives her scheme a sense of authenticity if she's associated with a respectable nonprofit. For all I know, she assures her clients that it's part of our program, one of our goals. These men pay her a substantial fee on the side."

"Why not just wait five years?"

"One could, but it's not so easy to stay in the country on a work or student visa. Once you're laid off or you've completed your degree, you're in an ambiguous position. The three-year requirement is bad enough, but being married will stave off deportation. Think of a young Saudi entrepreneur who wants to start up a business here. He has plenty of money, but he doesn't want to wait while some other smarty-pants comes up with the same idea."

Rick was still trying to assimilate what I'd said. While he gazed blankly at the sky, I finished my coffee and looked at my watch. After a few minutes, I opted to interrupt his musings. "You need to run along, Rick."

"Have you told your husband about this?"

I sighed. "Not yet. Sure, Leslie has a strong motive to want to shut Willie up before she figures out about the phone bill, and she could have slipped the sedatives in Willie's coffee. There's not any evidence to get a warrant, though, even to search Leslie's desk for a pillbox. Judges disapprove of fishing expeditions."

"Not all of them," he said with a sly look.

"I thought about that. The problem is that the defense would have a strong argument to throw out anything the police discovered on the grounds the warrant was unmerited."

"You must watch a lot of TV."

"I read a lot of police procedurals. It's a quarter to nine. I'm heading for the Literacy Council. I'll let you know if Leslie withers under my relentless stare and blurts out the entire story." We walked out to our cars. "Keep in touch."

"I'll try to track down divorce filings in Phoenix." He caught my hand before I could open the car door. "What about Ludmila? Is there a remote chance she realized what Leslie was up to?"

"I can't think of how that could happen.

She certainly couldn't eavesdrop on a conversation, and I doubt she ever set foot in Leslie's office for a conference." I got in my car and looked up at him. "Try Waterford when you have time. He may be more forthcoming after you tell him what we've uncovered. Well, not exactly uncovered, but definitely uncoverable with his help."

"Is 'uncoverable' a word?"

"It is now." I maneuvered out of the parking lot and drove to the Literacy Council. Leslie was teaching a class. Students were hooked up with tutors or sitting in the lounge area. Yelena waved at me from the classroom, and I waved back before I went into Keiko's office.

"I'm turning in my resignation as of tomorrow," I began. "I'm really sorry if this causes a problem for you. You're welcome to try to wheedle my daughter into some desk duty since she's down to three students. She needs the volunteer hours."

Keiko did not smile, much less twinkle. "I won't have a problem finding a replacement. I hope you will come back in the fall as a tutor. It's much more rewarding than answering the phone and taking messages. Will you also resign from the board of directors?"

"I haven't decided." I paused to rally my

courage to ask her the question that had come to mind the previous afternoon. There was no way to be extremely tactful, but I took my best shot. "Do you know Leslie had the office door rekeyed?"

"Yes, of course." Her giggle was forced, bereft of merriment. I waited quietly while she struggled to concoct a rational explanation. I considered telling her not to bother, but doing so might have been construed as an affront to her creativity. "She told me one of her students went inside her office while she was in the classroom. He was just sitting there when she came in, but it made her nervous because she keeps her purse and laptop there."

"Why not just lock her door with the regular key?"

This was more of a poser, but I was in no rush to sit behind the reception desk. "Well," Keiko said at last, "maybe I shouldn't tell you this, Claire. Gregory and some of the board members have keys, too. Leslie is a very private woman. She said that she kept trying to watch her office even when she was teaching. Very hard to concentrate, yes?"

"Does Gregory know his key won't open her office?"

"You'll have to ask him. Ooh, I thought of

425

something I may not have told you about last Monday night. Sonya went into his office after she talked to Rick."

"No, you didn't tell me that. Was she still there when you left?"

"They were arguing, but I didn't hear what they said. I am not as good a detective as you are. If you will forgive me, I need to make calls."

I stopped in the doorway and looked back at her. "Leslie wasn't here that night. How did Rick and Sonya get into her office?"

"Leslie had the lock rekeyed on Wednesday." She picked up the receiver and began to punch buttons.

I poured myself a mug of coffee and sat down at Reception Central. "Please hold for the next available agent," I informed no one. "Your call is very important to us." I thought about Miss Parchester's complaint about the airlines. I flipped through the card holder and found her number. Before I could call, the students emerged from the classroom. Leslie failed to acknowledge me as she walked by the desk.

Yelena, in contrast, perched on the corner of it and said, "I did not see you after my dramatic scene. Was good, yes? Please tell me it made you cry. Everybody liked it, yes?"

"It was so fraught with emotion that I was overwhelmed," I said with a sad frown. "I was especially moved when you almost fell off the chair."

"That added drama, I think. Chair was hard to stand on. Lucky to be caught by handsome man with bow tie. I must thank him more when I see him." She went on to tell about past performances of "highest drama" until I finally told her I needed to make a phone call. After making me promise to come watch her Russian women's club perform at a retirement home, she wandered away.

Miss Parchester answered the phone with a chirpy hello. Rather than give her the opportunity to come up with an excuse, I told her that I would be at her house shortly after noon with lunch. I did not mention that it would be lunch for three, aware that if I did, I would have a left-over sandwich in my bag.

When Gregory arrived, I grabbed my coffee mug and followed him into his office like a bird dog. He seemed unsettled as I sat down and waited for him to do the same. "Is there something I can help you with, Claire?"

"You omitted a detail when you told me what you did the night Ludmila was murdered," I began in a deceptively affable voice. "I'm disappointed in you, frankly."

"Omitted a detail? I don't think I did. I admitted shouting at Ludmila, which was inappropriate and ill-tempered. I was ashamed of myself afterward. If she'd still been there when I was ready to leave, I would have apologized." He shrugged. "I would have tried to apologize. She and I did not . . . communicate well. I presume that doesn't surprise you."

I waggled my finger at him. "You didn't mention that Sonya was in your office at the time."

"Does it matter? She and I had a couple of words about the meeting and how to deal with Rick in the future."

"Then she hopped into her Barbie-mobile and took off for the bars on Thurber Street. Do you really believe I'm that gullible? C'mon, Gregory, you're a big boy now. I don't want to hear about the mushy stuff, if there was any. You and she had a loud argument. Was it a lovers' quarrel?" I paused, but he didn't seem to have anything to contribute. "Did she say she was going to Thurber Street? Oh my goodness, Gregory, that must have pissed you off."

He flapped his hands in denial. "No, it had to do with a personal matter that's none of your business. Yes, she came into my office to wait until everybody left. We may have raised our voices, and we were still a bit testy when we came out of my office. Everyone was gone. I turned off the lights after Sonya went outside. She suggested that we resolve our little problem at my house. That's all I care to say about this matter — except I turned off the lights."

"Did Sonya ride with you?"

"What earthly difference does that make? She rode with me, and I dropped her off here the next morning at seven. Will you please go away and stop harassing me? I've done nothing wrong."

I felt my hands curl into fists. "I talked to Lilac yesterday afternoon. She told me how you treated your wife. You didn't love her. All you wanted to do was crush her into mindless servitude. You succeeded, didn't you?"

"She had mental problems long before I met her. I did my best to help her, but obviously I failed. As for Lilac, did she offer you wine while you talked? I don't remember when I've seen her without a drink in hand. I'll bet she didn't tell you about her numerous affairs. Her husband's so dense that he doesn't have an inkling there's anything wrong with his marriage." He climbed off his high horse and walked around me to open his door. "I don't think we can use your services in the future, Claire. There's no room here for highly opinionated tutors with abrasive tongues. Our students are our first priority."

His most vulnerable spot was well within reach of my knee, which was tensed in gleeful anticipation. I took a deep breath and exhaled slowly. The temptation was so strong that I could taste it. Repressing one's feelings can be harmful to one's health. However, the wife of the deputy chief should never stoop to committing bodily assault. I smiled evilly as I envisioned the act, replete with his shock as he crumpled to the floor and began to howl. In my fantasy, the expression on his face was, well, priceless. I may have been snickering as I left.

His door remained closed the rest of the time I was there. I answered the phone, wrote down messages in flawless cursive, and waited. Caron and Inez came in together, found their students, and disappeared into cubicles. Leslie went from her office to the classroom and back on the hour, apparently unaware of my existence. I found her behavior discourteous, be it justified or not. She was hardly a proper role model for the students. Yelena related another story of her glory on the Moscow stage before rushing off to finish her homework. Nasreen, Caron's student from Iran, gave me a baggie with a gooey piece of pastry, whispering that she'd noticed I hadn't tasted it at the potluck. I thanked her warmly, gobbled it down, and licked honey off my fingers for the next ten minutes.

At noon I straightened the desktop and went to the doorway of Keiko's office. "Good luck finding my replacement."

"We will see you no more?" She sounded disturbingly optimistic.

"I think you'll see me fairly soon." I drove to a sandwich shop and ordered three different subs in case Miao was a vegetarian and Miss Parchester loathed green peppers, or vice versa. I didn't bother to watch for a black car as I drove across town. Miss Parchester came to the door almost immediately and shooed me in. We went into the kitchen, where she put on the teakettle and I found three plates and napkins. I heard a faint gasp. "Shall we eat at the table or in the living room?" I asked.

"I, uh, I think the table. Cats, as I'm sure you know, go simply crazy at a whiff of turkey. They'd crawl all over us in the living room. Oh dear, Claire, I'm not sure this is wise."

"Eating lunch? It may not be a wise thing, but it's very popular these days." I set the table and took the sandwiches out of the sack. Miss Parchester kept her back to me as she took out cups and saucers. I waited until she brought them to the table, her hands trembling so badly that they clinked. "We'll need three cups and saucers," I said cheerfully as I took one of each out of the cabinet. "These sandwiches are warm and toasty, but they won't be nearly as yummy later. I'll look for the salt and pepper shakers while you fetch Miao."

"This is not wise," she repeated. "It's a very delicate situation involving other people. I refuse to force anyone to do something against her wishes."

I was relieved that she hadn't denied Miao's presence upstairs. "She can't hide up there indefinitely, Miss Parchester. I understand you're protecting her out of affection, and I applaud that. However, Ludmila was murdered one week ago today, and Miao may have seen something. If you won't go upstairs, I will."

"Did I tell you that I adopted a kitten from the animal shelter? He's too shy to come out when visitors are here, the poor little thing. He hasn't told me his name yet, so I just call him kitty. Puddy thinks I ought to give him a name —"

"One of us is going upstairs in the next five seconds. Miao might be less alarmed if you tell her that I'm here. We have to do this. Jiang's been following me all over town, and he suspects she's here. She'd rather talk to me than him."

Miss Parchester sat down and put her palm on her chest. "I feel a little flutter. I'm at an age when . . ." She saw me shaking my head. "Why don't you put out water glasses, too? We can save the tea for dessert."

I held out my hand to help her up. I did as she'd asked while I listened to her footsteps on the staircase. Almost five minutes later, I heard her footsteps coming down. I braced myself to hear that Miao had escaped out the window or been eaten by cats. When they both came into the kitchen, I noticed that Miao was shoeless. She gave me a terrified glance as she slid into a chair and lowered her head.

Miss Parchester and I began to eat, but Miao didn't move. I had to remind myself I was forcing myself on her for her own good. Mine, too, but that wasn't the point. After I'd finished the sandwich, I leaned toward

Miao and softly said, "You have to tell me what happened, Miao. No one is angry at you. We're all very worried about you. You cannot stay here forever. It will not solve the problem."

"No problem," she whispered.

Miss Parchester started to intervene, but I waved her back. "Yes, Miao, you know there is a bad problem. You saw something at the Literacy Council, didn't you? Please tell me."

"I see nothing."

"You saw Gregory. He was there, and so was Ludmila."

"I not there. I go home on bus."

I turned to Miss Parchester. "Let's have some tea. This is going to take a very long time."

I was right. Miao maintained her pathetic pose and answered in the fewest words possible. It took half an hour before she admitted she had been there when Gregory and Ludmila had exploded in each other's faces. ("They angry.") Another ten minutes to admit she was frightened. ("I frightful.") My cheeks began to ache from smiling sympathetically, and my head to throb as I scrambled to find the most effective words. Miss Parchester's chin had dropped to her chest, and she was snoring in a ladylike fashion. I gestured for Miao to follow me into the living room, if only to stretch my muscles. My bladder called for an intermission, but I didn't trust Miao enough to leave her alone.

I noticed she was glancing at the kitchen doorway. "Miao, are you concerned about Miss Parchester?" She nodded. "Is it her health?" She shook her head. I sat back and thought. An unsavory idea came to mind. "Did someone say he would hurt her if you told anyone what you saw?"

"I saw nothing." Her voice was a fraction louder, and tears filled her eyes. "I saw nothing."

"So after whatever happened, you came here to protect her? That is a brave thing to do, Miao. The police can protect her, too."

"No can do that. Police go away. Miss Parchester is alone. I stay here."

It took an effort to interpret this as progress, but I was desperate, and I didn't want to order out for dinner. Or for breakfast. Her lack of English was not the problem; her reticence was. I felt as though I knew the reason. I took a drink of water and studied her face. The stereotypical characterization of "inscrutable" was merited in this case. As painful as this is to confess, I realized I was making a whopping big mistake. I was treating Miao as though she were a porcelain doll of limited intelligence. She was working on a graduate degree in mathematics, not a degree for dummies.

"Listen, Miao," I said in a quiet but forceful tone, "you are not a child. You are not helpless. I can help you, but you have to help yourself — and Miss Parchester. Did you tell her what you saw?"

"I tell nobody." She gave me a defiant look. "I no tell you."

"Yes, you will. Will you stay in this house for a week? A month? A year or more? The police do not forget about murders. What about your degree? Do you want your adviser to scratch you off his list?" I demonstrated on the cover of a magazine.

"I no tell you."

"Then answer this. You told me you were frightened. Is this because Gregory was yelling and shouting?" She nodded faintly. "Jiang said that Gregory has acted badly to you. Did you hide from him?"

Her lips twitched. "In lady room. Ludmila hide also. We make shush-shush." She put her finger to her lips and blew. "Shush-shush."

"How long did you stay there?"

She shrugged. "Long time. Ludmila . . .

frightful he make her go. Dark outside."

I wanted to hug her, but I was afraid it would startle her into eternal silence. "You and Ludmila hid in the ladies' room. Everyone else but Gregory was gone?"

"I not know. I no hear in lady room."

Now the million-dollar question. "What happened when you and Ludmila left the ladies' room?"

Her chin shot out. "I no tell you. I no tell anyone. Please to leave now."

"The police will protect you and Miss Parchester," I said with all the earnestness I could muster. "I promise you. My husband is a very important policeman. I will tell him to take very good care of you."

She stared at the wall, once again inscrutable. I stood up and went into the kitchen to shake Miss Parchester's shoulder. "You might be more comfortable on the sofa. Miao has terminated the conversation. For such a fragile girl, she can be awfully stubborn."

Miss Parchester's eyes remained closed as she said, "Papa would say she was worse than a mule on a blazing August afternoon."

I was increasingly confident that my theory was correct. Of course, I had only the reluctant testimony of a woman who would

437

keep her mouth shut until blood squirted out of boulders and snowflakes were identical. Even if Peter found a Chinese interpreter, Miao wouldn't cooperate. Whoever had threatened her into remaining mute had also threatened to harm Miss Parchester, and possibly Luo, Jiang, and herself. If he was arrested, he had nasty friends. She could never go to class or ride the bus to the Literacy Council. I wondered how long it had taken him to make her understand. I realized why Luo had gone to the Literacy Council the next morning: Miao wanted someone to find Ludmila, who might still be alive. I was so proud of my deductive prowess that I nearly backed into the black car parked behind mine. It was a shiny new model of some pricey line. Despite Peter's pleas to upgrade, I drove an ancient hatchback. I looked in the rearview window and saw Hamdan behind the wheel, smirking.

"I warned you," I said aloud. I put my car in reverse, pressed my foot on the gas pedal, and plowed into his hood with a satisfactory *thwack.* Glass clinked on the pavement. The broken headlight gave the police a legitimate excuse to pull him over. I put my hand out the window and fluttered my fingers in farewell, then drove home all by myself, enjoying every mile of it.

■ ■ ■ ■

Caron was swinging on the front porch when I arrived. I sat down beside her and said, "No lake this afternoon?"

"Joel's coming to pick me up in half an hour. We're going to the matinee at the mall and probably eat in the food court. My life once again has meaning."

"I don't know how you survived ten whole days of wretchedness and despair. Did you have fun last night?"

She turned to look at a hawk circling above. "Yes, we had fun."

My hand instinctively went to my mouth. I took several deep breaths while I frantically tried to recall everything I'd read about significant conversations with one's daughter. My mind was blank. My maternal veneer of wisdom shattered into tiny shards. "Does that . . . that mean that you and Joel . . . ?"

"No, Mother. His father took all these hilarious videos at the family reunion, babies pooping on their daddies' laps, a toddler who belly-flopped in a gelatin salad, stuff like that." She touched my shoulder for a brief second. "I'm nearly eighteen and am leaving for college in a year."

"I know," I said, feeling inept, "but I'll still worry about you — and Inez, too. She seems so ingenuous about . . ."

Caron snorted. "Maybe last week. She may have spent a lot of time on the sidelines, but I can assure you she was taking meticulous notes. She's got more dates lined up than the Julian calendar. None of them are with Toby, though. She says he's a troglodyte."

"Good for her." I glanced up at the hawk, which was still trolling for a succulent snack. All a dedicated predator needs is a momentary opportunity, I thought sadly.

My daughter was more grounded. "I saw you were gone when I finished my session with Yelena. I was going to let you take Inez and me out to lunch. Did Keiko fire you?"

"Peter asked me to resign, and I did. Do you know about the Chinese girl who disappeared last week after the murder?"

"Miao? I heard she went back to China. Did she kill Ludmila? I don't see how someone so petite could budge that Polish mountain. She sure couldn't drag the body into a corner with heavy equipment."

"She's at Miss Parchester's house, living with cats. Don't say a word about this to Jiang. He's desperate to find her, but he'll make matters worse if he does."

"He's a lot more than desperate," Caron said, giving the swing a push with her foot. "He kind of scares me when he starts jabbering about how he has to find her, which is all he's done the last two sessions. He even wanted me to call all the cheap motels in town to see if Miao was staying there. Like I'm going to spend all afternoon talking to motel clerks!"

"I don't blame you. Anyway, Miao did not kill Ludmila. I'm convinced she knows who did but is too terrified to tell anyone." I gave her a brief description of what Miao had admitted. "I think she and Ludmila were both afraid of Gregory that night. He'd bellowed at Ludmila and come close to slapping her. He's been hitting on Miao, making her nervous around him. Ludmila couldn't leave until Bartek arrived to pick her up, and Miao probably thought Gregory would follow her to the bus stop. Maybe Ludmila told her that Bartek would drive her home."

"Did they bond in adjoining bathroom stalls?"

"It's only speculation, dear. According to Gregory, no one was hanging around when he left. He wouldn't have looked inside the restrooms. He turned off the lights and went outside, where Sonya was waiting for him.

They went to his house for the night."

Caron's lip curled. "That is Utterly Gross. He's way too old for her. Inez will literally barf when she hears this."

She pulled out her cell phone, but I caught her hand. "Inez can barf later. I need your help. If Gregory turned off the lights, who turned them on before Bartek arrived?"

"Ludmila," she said promptly. "She saw that Gregory was gone, and she didn't want to sit in the dark. That doesn't explain why Miao stayed, though, unless you actually believe Ludmila tried to be nice to her. Inez and I didn't see any fireworks when we drove by, or hear angels singing."

"I'll give you that. If we accept that Ludmila turned the lights back on and sat down to wait for Bartek, why didn't she go unlock the front door when he started pounding on it?"

Caron shot a look of longing at her cell on top of her purse. "Joel should get here pretty soon. Maybe you should be telling this to Peter, not me."

"He might find it entertaining, but he's a stickler for evidence. All I have is Miao's exceedingly brief statement. There's no way to substantiate it." It was my turn to give the swing a push. The gentle motion did not soothe my feverish mind, which was whirring like a grasshopper in the yard. Peter was not fond of speculation unless it involved greenhouses and lily ponds. I gritted my teeth as I pictured his condescending smile and flicker of boredom. There had to be a way to wrap the perp in shiny paper and put a bow on his head. The perp who'd lied to me, that is.

The swing bounced as Caron stood up. "Joel's here," she said unnecessarily, since his car had come to a stop near the steps. "You're not going to do something crazy, are you, Mother? I need you to hang around long enough to help me pack for college." She bent down and gave me a hug. "I Mean It."

"I won't do anything too crazy."

19

The phone was ringing as I came into the kitchen. I picked up the receiver and sat down on a stool next to the island. "Hello," I said in a less than delighted tone.

"Did you watch the noon news on TV?" demanded Rick.

"I was having lunch with our key witness. What happened?" I primed myself for more bad news.

"Willie announced her retirement. After she left the hospital, she went home and called a press conference. She said she was two years beyond the minimum age and felt as though she needed to step down because of health concerns."

"Interesting, but not earth-shattering." I carried the receiver with me as I took a glass out of a cabinet and held it under the ice maker in the refrigerator door. The ice cubes clattered so loudly that I missed his response. "You'll have to repeat that. It's tea time."

"Oh, I'll wait, and I suggest you have something stronger than iced tea. You'd better sit down, too."

I was intrigued. I ignored his suggestion and filled my glass from the pitcher on the bottom shelf. "Okay, I'm ready. What did you say?"

"After Willie said she was retiring, she said that during her career she had done something unworthy of her position and she wanted to apologize to the public. Violating their trust in the judicial system and such. This is the kicker. She said that when she presided over the class-action lawsuit brought by employees of Sell-Mart, she'd taken a bribe to rule in favor of the corporation. The reporters went wild and started pelting her with questions and waving their microphones at her like batons. There was almost a riot. Willie just smiled and refused to comment further."

"Sheesh." I took a gulp of tea. "She's a federal judge, not some county justice of the peace. Sheesh."

"No kidding," Rick said. "You can watch it on the six o'clock news, but that's pretty much the gist of it. The federal prosecutors must be huddled in their offices, weeping and trying to remember what other cases she presided over. Every ruling she's made in the last twenty years is in jeopardy. They'll all have to be reviewed. Why would Willie sabotage herself? All she had to do was keep her mouth shut and cash her hefty retirement checks."

"You're partially to blame. Once you agreed to go after Gregory, she started feeling guilty. What she did was similar to embezzlement, only her victim was the judicial system. Damn, I feel bad for her."

Rick gurgled. "For her? You just accused me of forcing her into making the confession."

"Get over it," I said. "This does explain the way she allowed Sonya to treat her so rudely. Sonya works in the corporate office of Sell-Mart. She must have found out about the bribe and dangled it over Willie's head. Blackmail comes to mind."

His gurgles grew louder. I hoped somebody was nearby in case he collapsed and needed medical attention. He finally regained control of himself. "It makes sense, but ouch. I can't believe I moved to what was billed as a cheerful little community with kids on bicycles, concerts in the park, festivals, high school football games, and the whole fantasy. Do you realize how many crooked people we've uncovered in a week?

This makes my acquaintances in Manila look like a bunch of missionaries who happen to peddle something other than religion. When's the next flight to Hong Kong?"

"I'll have to look online. Have you heard from Waterford?"

"I'm going to call him when I get home. The time's an hour earlier, so he should be in his office."

I was thankful I no longer suspected him of Ludmila's murder. He'd been such a good little helper thus far. It was time to find out how far out on the branch he was willing to crawl. I asked him to call me after he'd spoken to Waterford. Now I had the rest of the afternoon to polish my plan, which was only partially crazy.

I was driven to dusting when Rick finally called. Sounding like a birthday boy, he said, "Waterford left a message on my landline. He flew out this afternoon to the CIS office in Fort Smith. He's calling a meeting for this evening because he's ready to come down on Leslie like a load of loose gravel. He wants to talk to us first thing in the morning so we can go over the details. After that, we can tag along when he storms the Literacy Council and waves a warrant under her nose."

447

I hadn't expected anything associated with the federal bureaucracy to move so swiftly. "Good work, Rick," I said, somewhat stunned.

"I guess so. I've been thinking — always a bad sign — that maybe what Leslie's doing isn't so terrible. I mean, no one gets hurt. It's a scam, but who's the victim? A grad student gets enough money to have her car repaired, and a man from wherever realizes his dream of becoming a citizen."

I'd had the same reservations. "For one thing, it undermines the whole process. There are thousands of people who want citizenship, and it's an excruciatingly lengthy ordeal of filing paperwork, waiting, filing more paperwork, and still waiting. Leslie's clients cut in line, and they do so through deception. As for the women, they know they're breaking the law. I'd hate to spend the next forty years of my life worrying some bureaucrat might decide to investigate me for fraud. It's a federal offense. Even if she escapes with a fine or probation, she's a felon for life. Would you want to explain that to your children?"

"Trying to put a positive spin on it, huh?"

"Somebody has to." I took out my thick sheaf of notes and found the pertinent one. After I'd described my plan to expose the perp, there was a noticeable silence on his end. I wished I could see his expression, which I assumed was high on the dumbfounded spectrum. "What's more," I said to add to his anxiety, "we may be able to pull it off this evening if Peter has to go to Fort Smith. And, most importantly, if Austin isn't working late. We can't do this without him."

"I'll call him," Rick said glumly. "He wouldn't miss this for all the pot in California."

I told him that I'd call him back after I heard from Peter. My stomach was seizing as I sank down on the sofa. I'd lost my mind, or what was left of it. All I'd wanted to do was tutor a deserving foreigner for two hours a week to prove to myself that I wasn't just a parasite, that I still had a trace of my youthful sense of altruism. I'd donated clothes to charity shops, helped organize food drives, and signed enough petitions to constitute a telephone directory for a small village. As Rick had said, a lot of people were going to tumble in the next few days. Gregory deserved to tumble off a cliff in the Himalayas. Leslie was a professional felon. I was saddened that Keiko might be involved.

I hadn't moved when the phone rang.

Groaning, I went into the kitchen. As I'd anticipated, it was my adorable husband. "I have to go to some damn meeting in Fort Smith," he said. "I'm leaving now, and I should be home by midnight."

"Meeting?"

"It seems that someone — and I have no idea who — tipped off an CIS agent in Phoenix about criminal activity right here in little ol' Farberville. The guy decided he has to brief us at the regional office instead of here. Why not make it inconvenient for everybody? Bureaucrats!"

"I'll leave the light on for you." I added some other remarks of a private nature, and we were both giggling when we hung up.

Rick, Austin, and I entered the Literacy Council at eight, having spent the previous hour plotting over coffee at Mucha Mocha. Keiko was already gone. Since Gregory might not be pleased to see me, I sent Austin to tell him that we were having a publicity committee meeting in the back classroom and might stay late. Gregory, it seemed, was not at all interested. The evening class came out of the room and began to leave. I ducked behind a bookshelf until Yelena went out the front door. Some of the cubicles were still occupied. Leslie, accompanied by

Aladino and Graciela, went into her office. I didn't care if she'd seen us.

We spread advertising layouts and stencils on the table. Austin loosened his bow tie and produced a bottle of wine from his briefcase. "Might as well enjoy ourselves," he said, grinning. "What will dear Frances do if she finds out about this? Put me in time-out?"

"She's going to find out about it," I said, my face grim. "You need to get busy, buddy. The council's about to close its hallowed doors for the night."

Rick took the corkscrew out of Austin's hand. "If all we wanted was a wine steward, I would have found somebody cheaper."

"I'm getting paid?"

I urged Austin to do his assigned task and stood outside the room to watch out for Gregory. Everything proceeded without delays. I heard Leslie say good night to the students as they all left. Two Latino men laughed on their way out. I crept to the end of the cubicles and ascertained that only Gregory remained in the building. Five minutes later he came to the doorway and told us that he was leaving. I reminded him not to turn off the lights. He grumbled unpleasantly and stalked down the pathway to the front door. I waited to see if he'd turn

451

off the lights in a snit, but I heard the door bang closed.

Austin and Rick were seated at the table, discussing a scandal involving the college baseball coach. I was too nervous to sit. I paced around the table until I heard a car door slam. "Go," I said in an urgent voice, "and do try to pay attention."

They took the bottle of wine into the room where Willie had been found and closed the door. I waited to make sure they left the light off, then sat down at the table and re-arranged the layouts as if I could actually make sense of them.

"Hey, Ms. Malloy," Toby said from the hallway, "what're you doing here by your-self?"

"A committee meeting. Austin and Rick were here earlier, but they abandoned me to go to a party." I did my best to sound pathetic. "I hate committee meetings, but at least I don't have to listen to other people repeat themselves half the night."

"Sounds like my history class. The teach-er's a big fan of the Civil War, so no matter what the subject is, he finds a way to start talking about it."

I smiled. "I may have had the same teacher, although he preferred the French Revolution. It's amazing how it seems to have affected every single thing that happened afterward." I pushed a paper. "I'd better get back to this."

"And I'd better get back to my mop." He gave me a salute and returned to the main part of the building.

I wished I'd accepted a glass of wine. I twisted my fingers into pretzels while pretending to be absorbed by the array of meaningless material. I gave him half an hour and then went to find him. "Toby, my daughter might call on the phone here. Please answer it and let me know. I won't be able to hear it in the copy room."

He tugged on a stray lock of hair as he stared at me. "What are you gonna do in the copy room? Oh, I get it — you're going to make copies." He found this mildly hilarious. I overlooked it because of his age.

"No, I'm not going to make any copies. Earlier I was talking to someone who told me there might be a clue to the identity of Ludmila's killer in the room. Something the police missed because they didn't know it was significant. I had to wait until Rick and Austin left because" — I'd forgotten to script this moment — "I don't want to tell anyone until I'm sure. Don't worry about it. Just come find me if Caron calls."

I went into the copy room. It was as

dismal as it had been a week ago, but even dirtier because surfaces had been dusted for fingerprints. I sneezed as I stepped over an empty box. The copy machine feigned innocence, but I wasn't fooled. I examined it as if it were a vault rumored to be filled with gold bullion. When I pushed a button, a green light began to blink. I pushed another button that aroused a red light and a series of beeps. The machine hummed as I found more buttons. I lifted the cover and discovered a workbook page that had been left by mistake. I balanced on a two-legged stool and read over it. It proved to be a less than scintillating story about a woman buying fruit in a market.

Fifteen minutes had passed, and I began to wonder if I'd made a miscalculation. Teenagers are hard to predict, since they rarely know themselves what they might do next. I was sneezing on a regular schedule, and my lungs were beginning to ache. I could recite the order in which the workbook woman purchased fruit. I didn't dare pull another book off the shelves, since I would be rewarded with a cloud of dust. I was almost ready to give up when Toby appeared in the doorway.

"Excuse me, Ms. Malloy, but maybe I can help. I could hear you sneezing from the other classroom. What are you looking for?"

"A DNA sample. Apparently whoever was in here with Ludmila had an itchy scalp." I tried not to react as his hand, which had been scratching behind his ear, dropped to his side. "All it takes is one single hair to confirm a match that's ninety-nine percent accurate. Isn't science amazing?"

"Guess you didn't find one, huh?"

"I've found several hairs." I held up a small plastic bag that conveniently happened to contain several hairs (from Peter's hairbrush). "I think I'll take these straight to the police lab before I lose them. Of course, the crime scene techs can always find more, now that they know what to look for."

He remained in the doorway, his arms crossed. His demeanor had changed as I spoke. His boyish grin was now a tight-lipped scowl. I was quite sure his body had swelled to block the entire doorway. "Nobody knows about these stupid hairs?"

"The police just hate it when civilians meddle in their investigations. If I went to them without evidence, they'd laugh me out of the PD." I dangled the bag. "They won't be laughing after I show this to them."

"That's not such a good idea, Ms. Malloy. A lot of people come in here all the time. I clean in here every couple of days. Those hairs don't mean anything. They could belong to anybody."

"Including you," I said, nodding, "although I thought I heard that you never clean in here. Didn't you tell the police you hadn't even opened the door?"

His eyes narrowed like those of an irritable snake. "So I got confused when they asked me all those questions. It's no big deal. I think you ought to toss that bag in the trash and forget about it, Ms. Malloy."

"I wish Miao could forget as easily, but she's having a hard time. I really felt sorry for her when I talked to her today."

"You talked to her? Gimme a break. She doesn't know enough English to talk to a dog. She minces around like she thinks she's on a runway, all flirty and coy." I could swear his body was still swelling, and in a matter of seconds, his head would bump the top of the door frame. I gulped back a snicker.

"Her English isn't as limited as you think," I lied smoothly. "She told me what happened. Maybe I misunderstood her. I can't be sure. I need to tell the police where she is so they can get her with a translator."

"Where is she?"

"I'll tell you after you've told me what

really happened in here. There's no reason why you should be in trouble if she lied to me — or, as I said, I misunderstood her."

He was watching the bag with a greedy expression. I had no clue what to do if he crowded into the room and snatched it out of my hand. I relaxed a tad when he said, "If I tell you, it stays in this room. You okay with that?"

"Absolutely. I give you my solemn promise I won't repeat it." I didn't add that keeping promises was not among my more admirable traits. "It was all her fault, wasn't it?"

Toby realized his hand had crept up to his head and hastily put it at his side. "Yeah, I got here maybe earlier than I said, and there she was, creeping around in the dark like a spy. She about fell over her own feet when I turned on the lights. All I was gonna do was tell her to beat it when she started whimpering and then took off scurrying like a little bunny rabbit. I thought it was so damn funny, so I decided to play her game. I finally caught her trying to hide in here. I thought I deserved a reward. I picked her up and set her on the copy machine. She was wailing, so I had to shake her until she got quiet. Then, just as I was unzipping my pants, in barges this ugly fat woman, and she's screaming at me in some crazy language. She came right at me with her claws, so I had to defend myself. It was a friggin' nightmare. The China doll's back to wailing and this monster is going for my eyes. Somehow the monster trips and crashes into the copy machine." He stopped, as if I should be satisfied with his description of the events.

"Why didn't you call nine-one-one? You couldn't know if she was dead."

Toby looked at me as if I'd pulled a worm out of my mouth. "And get busted for attempted rape? I may not be at the top of my class, but I'm not that stupid. I'm the starting quarterback this year."

"That may not happen." A soon as I'd said it, I knew I'd made a mistake. There was no way to rewind the tape and erase my comment. And now I was quite sure his head was touching the top of the door frame, and likely to splinter it.

He chewed on his lip until it began to bleed. I assessed my chances of darting between his legs. My backup team had yet to show their faces. I heard voices in the distance, apt to be patrons going into the sports bar. He finally looked at me. "I'm sorry about this, Ms. Malloy, but I'm going to ask you to give me that bag and tell me where Miao is. I can't let her go around telling lies, even if nobody can make out what she's saying."

"You're the only person who seems to have trouble understanding me. Take the bag. You can vacuum this room all night, but you'll still miss a stray hair. The crime scene investigators have very fancy equipment designed to find every last strand of DNA."

"If they know to look. The thing is, Ms. Malloy, you're not going to tell anyone about what I said tonight. If you do and I'm arrested, I'll get out on bail because my father's all straightlaced and a big deal at the college. I sure had a good time with Inez the other day, and I know she and your daughter go to the lake all the time. They just seem to go everywhere, don't they?"

A sour taste flooded my mouth. "Are you threatening to harm them if I don't co-operate? Is that what you're saying, Toby? Just go ahead and spit it out."

"Yeah, I guess that's what I mean. If you turn me in, your pretty daughter's gonna need braces and a new nose. Maybe skin grafts all over her face."

He had the audacity to sneer at me, which made my words all the sweeter. "Guess what, Toby, you're going to be a big star sooner than you think. See that little red light way up there in the corner? It's a video camera, and it's captured every vile thing you've said. You'd better go home and find your toothbrush, because you're going to be in a cell before midnight." I did not mention the shiny paper and bow on his head.

"What's gonna stop me from climbing up there and ripping it off the wall?"

This was the moment the Mounties were supposed to yank him out of the doorway and kick him senseless. I tried to peer around him. "I lied when I told you Austin and Rick abandoned me. They're here, and they've heard everything you said."

"Those two preppie boys? I'll stuff 'em in the Dumpster on my way out. Cleaning up is my job, and I don't want to get hassled for leaving garbage on the floor." He held up a fist, which I estimated to be the size of a medium cantaloupe. I had to admit Rick and Austin had more charm than brawn. This was a minor wrinkle we'd failed to anticipate. Peter was in Fort Smith, due to my deductive prowess. Jorgeson was in his comfy living room with his wife, munching popcorn or whatever they did. If Yelena had been there, she could have mesmerized him (or put him into a stupor) with a melodramatic presentation of a Russian opera.

It was my turn to laugh, scoff, or plead

with him. I was juggling the options when I heard Austin say, "You heard what Ms. Malloy said, boy. You run along and get that toothbrush ready to go."

He spun around. "You gonna make me, little man?"

"No," Austin said, "but my gun might persuade you to do as you're told. Otherwise, I'll shoot you in one of those fine, manly kneecaps. You won't be able to play quarterback on the prison team."

Toby glared at me over his shoulder before he hurried down the pathway. Seconds later, his car roared and squealed out of the parking lot. I sank down on the stool, which was a mistake. As Austin helped me to my feet, I said, "Is that a real gun?"

"I have no idea. I found it in the prop room at the TV station, so I assume it's fake. Should we find out?"

"No. Where's Rick?"

"On the phone to the fuzz. He slipped into Keiko's office as soon as Toby started blabbing. He went outside and got a description of Toby's car and the license number. You in the mood for a glass of wine now?"

I was.

Peter arrived home long after midnight and departed for his office at a ludicrous hour

461

without bothering to wake me. By the time he dragged in late in the evening, his face was bristly and his eyes were glazed. After he took a shower, shaved, and put on jeans and a sweatshirt, we decided to share a chaise longue, a bottle of wine, and a bag of oatmeal cookies. They weren't nearly as tasty as *profiteroles au chocolat.*

I waited for a few minutes before I said, "You are going to tell me what's happened, aren't you? I deserve something for resisting the urge to call you or Jorgeson all day." Approximately a zillion urges. I'd come perilously close to polishing the silver.

"I wouldn't have had time to take a call from an astronaut," Peter said with a snort. "Waterford felt the need to fill us in on every detail of his seven-year investigation of Leslie Barnes. It was his first assignment out of CIS boot camp, and he was determined to resolve it with a flurry of warrants, arrests, and indictments. A nice young man, if a trifle obsessive."

"I envisioned him as a fat old flea-bitten bear with a cigar stub in his mouth. I presume he's a happy camper now."

"Couldn't stop talking about his successful raid on Leslie and company. He acted as though he'd brought down an international conspiracy to destroy the CIS, the U.S., the

UN, mom, and apple pie. He even called in the heavy artillery — the IRS. We had warrants for her office at the FLC, as well as her computers, home, and car. You won't believe what we found in her garage."

"A make-shift greenhouse filled with marijuana plants?" I told him about my brief surveillance across the street from her house. "Leslie most likely had no idea about Charles's cottage industry. Too risky, since she already had a lucrative scheme. I was going to tell you about it when you weren't so busy."

The poor dear sighed. "I'm sure you were. She kept meticulous files going back ten years. Waterford has a list of well over a hundred names of her so-called clients. Most of the women who married under false pretenses will probably get away with a fine and penalties from the IRS. Their pseudo-husbands will face deportation. I'd say Waterford was pleased with himself after all those years on this case."

"He'd still be on it if we hadn't tipped him off."

"Maybe," he said without conviction. "The wheels of the bureaucracy may grind exceedingly slow, but they do grind. He had a helluva time tracking down Leslie because she changed her name and moved so often.

Three years as Mrs. Somebody, followed by a quiet divorce and on to becoming the new Mrs. Somebody Else, four times in twelve years. She has more bank accounts than J. P. Morgan Chase, as well as an offshore account. Her wealthier clients paid her more than a hundred grand. The underachievers paid about half that."

I had a minor epiphany. "That explains why Gregory was so alarmed when he realized Ludmilla had recognized him. He may not have any of the pharmaceutical company's stolen assets, but he's been raking in money under the table. If the Interpol investigators came sniffing, he'd be in deep trouble. He just didn't have the nerve to silence her."

Another sigh ensued. "He realized what Leslie was doing when he saw the telephone bills, and demanded a cut. The two of them are in custody and facing prison. The program director — the Japanese woman — has decided to cooperate with the investigation in exchange for leniency. Her cut of the proceeds was enough to persuade her to overlook all the suspicious activity, but not enough to buy much loyalty. She said to tell you that she was very sorry about being rude to you, but she was afraid you might be snooping."

"She said that?"

"Not in those exact words."

I opted to overlook his editorial interpretation. "Is Hamdan as eager to cooperate?"

"Not at all. He's in custody, too, courtesy of the CIS. We may not be able to charge him with the vandalism to your car, but he has other worries. He was babbling about vandalism to *his* car, but Waterford wasn't interested. Any comments?"

"My foot slipped," I said with impressive dignity, then opted to change the subject. "I hope the literacy council can survive after all this. The members of the board do care, despite all the squabbling. With Gregory gone, maybe Rick can get the finances straightened out well enough to satisfy future donors."

"You and he seemed awfully cozy the last few days." He'd heard the entire story from Jorgeson, who'd arrived with the Mounties and kept Rick, Austin, and me at the police department for several hours while he took our statements. At some point during my fourth or fifth mind-numbing reiteration, Jorgeson had been informed that Toby had been arrested at the high school football stadium. We'd toasted with tepid coffee.

I curled my arm around Peter's neck to tickle his earlobe. "Rick is a nice guy, but he lacks the charming ways of a slightly older man with a regal profile and some really good tricks in bed. Now that Gregory's facing prison, he may work through his bitterness and find a wife. That means we'll have to buy a wedding present and go to the wedding. I know you don't like these tuxedo events. It's odd, since the Rosens are high society on the East Coast. I'll bet you had a tuxedo that disguised your diaper bulge."

"It was very uncomfortable, but I had to live up to the family name." He refilled our glasses. "Okay, how did you know Toby was the culprit?"

"It was all about the lights inside the Literacy Council. If Gregory had killed Ludmila, the last thing he'd do is forget to turn off the lights. That would have been unusual and caused unwanted attention to his departure. So I assumed he turned off the lights shortly after eight o'clock. However, the lights were on at eight-thirty, when Bartek arrived to pick up Ludmila. I have backup from disinterested parties who happened to drive by."

"Caron?"

I took a sip of wine and continued. "So who turned on the lights between eight-ten and eight-thirty? It couldn't have been Ludmila, because she would have unlocked the door for Bartek. The reason she didn't was that she was already unconscious in the copy room. Miao had fled to Miss Parchester's house. Bartek doesn't have a key. The board members who do have keys lacked any reason to return after the meeting. I tried to assign a motive to Leslie but couldn't come up with one. That left Toby. He had a key, but no apparent motive. It wasn't challenging to link Miao's disappearance to the crime, especially since her roommate behaved so suspiciously. Toby simply lied about the time he arrived. I don't know how much Drake knew, or suspected. He just couldn't tolerate the idea of not reliving his heroics on the field through his son."

Peter harrumphed. "We didn't buy Toby's alibi, but we had to make an effort to confirm it. His parents socialize with the mayor and his wife. As the mayor pointed out to me in unsubtle terms, Toby was to be given the benefit of the doubt unless we uncovered evidence to the contrary. That, and Toby started dating the mayor's daughter."

"I guess that covers everything," I murmured as I gazed at the stars. I did, however, hold my breath while I waited to see if my trophy husband brought up a certain deli-

467

cate issue involving promises.

" 'The woods are lovely, dark, and deep, but I have promises to keep,' " he said quietly. I was not prepared for poetry, but I knew where this was going. " 'And miles to go before I sleep.' "

I flipped on top of him and buried my hands in his curly hair. "Damn straight, Sherlock. Don't count on getting any sleep soon."

ABOUT THE AUTHOR

Joan Hess is the author of both the Claire Malloy and the Maggody mystery series. She is a winner of the American Mystery Award, a member of Sisters in Crime, and a former president of the American Crime Writers League. A long-time resident of Fayetteville, Arkansas, she now lives in Austin, Texas.

The employees of Thorndike Press hope you have enjoyed this Large Print book. All our Thorndike, Wheeler, and Kennebec Large Print titles are designed for easy reading, and all our books are made to last. Other Thorndike Press Large Print books are available at your library, through selected bookstores, or directly from us.

For information about titles, please call:
(800) 223-1244

or visit our Web site at:
http://gale.cengage.com/thorndike

To share your comments, please write:
Publisher
Thorndike Press
10 Water St., Suite 310
Waterville, ME 04901